Praise for the *Hunger Games* Trilogy:

"I was so obsessed with this book . . .
The Hunger Games is amazing"
Stephenie Meyer

"A throbbingly tense thriller"
Emma Donoghue

"As close to a perfect adventure novel
as I've ever read"
Rick Riordan

"Terrifying and exhilarating"
Sunday Telegraph

"Constant suspense . . . I couldn't stop reading"
Stephen King

"Endlessly entertaining"
L.A. Times

"Brilliantly plotted and perfectly paced"
John Green, ***New York Times***

"One of the best written and most thought-provoking
books I've read for a long time"
Anthony Horowitz

"Rip-roaring, bare-knuckle adventure
of the best kind"
The Times

THE HUNGER GAMES

CATCHING FIRE

SUZANNE COLLINS

SCHOLASTIC

Scholastic Children's Books
An imprint of Scholastic Ltd
Euston House, 24 Eversholt Street
London, NW1 1DB, UK
Registered office: Westfield Road, Southam, Warwickshire, CV47 0RA

First published in the US by Scholastic Inc, 2009
First published in the UK by Scholastic Ltd, 2009
This edition published in the UK by Scholastic Ltd, 2011

ISBN 978 1407 13209 9

A CIP catalogue record for this book is available from the British Library.

Printed and bound by CPI Group (UK) Ltd, Croydon, CR0 4YY
Papers used by Scholastic Children's Books are made from wood grown in sustainable forests.

13 15 17 19 20 18 16 14

www.scholastic.co.uk/zone

FOR MY PARENTS,
JANE AND MICHAEL COLLINS,

AND MY PARENTS-IN-LAW,
DIXIE AND CHARLES PRYOR

PART I

THE SPARK

1

I clasp the flask between my hands even though the warmth from the tea has long since leached into the frozen air. My muscles are clenched tight against the cold. If a pack of wild dogs were to appear at this moment, the odds of scaling a tree before they attacked are not in my favour. I should get up, move around, and work the stiffness from my limbs. But instead I sit, as motionless as the rock beneath me, while the dawn begins to lighten the woods. I can't fight the sun. I can only watch helplessly as it drags me into a day that I've been dreading for months.

By noon they will all be at my new house in the Victor's Village. The reporters, the camera crews, even Effie Trinket, my old escort, will have made their way to District 12 from the Capitol. I wonder if Effie will still be wearing that silly pink wig, or if she'll be sporting some other unnatural colour especially for the Victory Tour. There will be others waiting, too. A staff to cater to my every need on the long train trip. A prep team to beautify me for public appearances. My stylist and friend, Cinna, who designed the gorgeous outfits that first made the audience take notice of me in the Hunger Games.

If it were up to me, I would try to forget the Hunger Games entirely. Never speak of them. Pretend they were nothing but a bad dream. But the Victory Tour makes that impossible. Strategically placed almost midway between the annual Games, it is the Capitol's way of keeping the horror fresh and immediate. Not only are we in the districts forced to remember the iron grip of the Capitol's power each year, we are forced to celebrate it. And this year, I am one of the stars of the show. I will have to travel from district to district, to stand before the cheering crowds who secretly loathe me, to look down into the faces of the families whose children I have killed. . .

The sun persists in rising, so I make myself stand. All my joints complain and my left leg has been asleep for so long that it takes several minutes of pacing to bring the feeling back into it. I've been in the woods three hours, but as I've made no real attempt at hunting, I have nothing to show for it. It doesn't matter for my mother and little sister, Prim, any more. They can afford to buy butcher meat in town, although none of us likes it any better than fresh game. But my best friend, Gale Hawthorne, and his family will be depending on today's haul and I can't let them down. I start the hour-and-a-half trek it will take to cover our snare line. Back when we were in school, we had time in the afternoons to check the line and hunt and gather and still get back to trade in town. But now that Gale has gone to work in the coal mines – and I have nothing to do all day – I've taken over the job.

By this time Gale will have clocked in at the mines, taken the stomach-churning elevator ride into the depths of the earth, and be pounding away at a coal seam. I know what it's like down there. Every year in school, as part of our training, my class had to tour the mines. When I was little, it was just unpleasant. The claustrophobic tunnels, foul air, suffocating darkness on all sides. But after my father and several other miners were killed in an explosion, I could barely force myself on to the elevator. The annual trip became an enormous source of anxiety. Twice I made myself so sick in anticipation of it that my mother kept me home because she thought I had contracted the flu.

I think of Gale, who is only really alive in the woods, with its fresh air and sunlight and clean, flowing water. I don't know how he stands it. Well . . . yes, I do. He stands it because it's the way to feed his mother and two younger brothers and sister. And here I am with buckets of money, far more than enough to feed both our families now, and he won't take a single coin. It's even hard for him to let me bring in meat, although he'd surely have kept my mother and Prim supplied if I'd been killed in the Games. I tell him he's doing me a favour, that it drives me nuts to sit around all day. Even so, I never drop off the game while he's at home. Which is easy since he works twelve hours a day.

The only time I really get to see Gale now is on Sundays, when we meet up in the woods to hunt together. It's still the best day of the week, but it's not like it used to be before, when we could tell each other anything. The Games have spoiled even that. I keep hoping that as time passes we'll regain the ease between us, but part of me knows it's futile. There's no going back.

I get a good haul from the traps – eight rabbits, two squirrels and a beaver that swam into a wire contraption Gale designed himself. He's something of a whiz with snares, rigging them to bent saplings so they pull the kill out of the reach of predators, balancing logs on delicate stick triggers, weaving inescapable baskets to capture fish. As I go along, carefully resetting each snare, I know I can never quite replicate his eye for balance, his instinct for where the prey will cross the path. It's more than experience. It's a natural gift. Like the way I can shoot at an animal in almost complete darkness and still take it down with one arrow.

By the time I make it back to the fence that surrounds District 12, the sun is well up. As always, I listen a moment, but there's no telltale hum of electrical current running through the chain link. There hardly ever is, even though the thing is supposed to be charged full-time. I wriggle through the opening at the bottom of the fence and come up in the Meadow, just a stone's throw from my home. My old home. We still get to keep it since officially it's the designated dwelling of my mother and sister. If I should drop dead right now, they would have to return to it. But at present, they're both happily installed in the new house in the Victor's Village, and I'm the only one who uses the squat little place where I was raised. To me, it's my real home.

I go there now to switch my clothes. Exchange my father's old leather jacket for a fine wool coat that always seems too tight in the shoulders. Leave my soft, worn hunting boots for a pair of expensive machine-made shoes that my mother thinks are more appropriate for someone of my status. I've already stowed my bow and arrows in a hollow log in the woods. Although time is ticking away, I allow myself a few minutes to sit in the kitchen. It has an abandoned quality with no fire on the hearth, no cloth on the table. I mourn my old life here. We barely scraped by, but I knew where I fitted in, I knew what my place was in the tightly interwoven fabric that was our life. I wish I could go back to it because, in retrospect, it seems so secure compared with now, when I am so rich and so famous and so hated by the authorities in the Capitol.

A wailing at the back door demands my attention. I open it to find Buttercup, Prim's scruffy old tomcat. He dislikes the new house almost as much as I do and always leaves it when my sister's at school. We've never been particularly fond of each other, but now we have this new bond. I let him in, feed him a chunk of beaver fat, and even rub him between the ears for a bit. "You're hideous, you know that, right?" I ask him. Buttercup nudges my hand for more petting, but we have to go. "Come on, you." I scoop him up with one hand, grab my game bag with the other, and haul them both out on to the street. The cat springs free and disappears under a bush.

The shoes pinch my toes as I crunch along the cinder street. Cutting down alleys and through backyards gets me to Gale's house in minutes. His mother, Hazelle, sees me through the window, where she's bent over the kitchen sink. She dries her hands on her apron and disappears to meet me at the door.

I like Hazelle. Respect her. The explosion that killed my father took out her husband as well, leaving her with three boys and a baby due any day. Less than a week after she gave birth, she was out hunting the streets for work. The mines weren't an option, what with a baby to look after, but she managed to get laundry from some of the merchants in town. At fourteen, Gale, the eldest of the kids, became the main supporter of the family. He was already signed up for tesserae, which entitled them to a meagre supply of grain and oil in exchange for his entering his name extra times in the drawing to become a tribute. On top of that, even back then, he was a skilled trapper. But it wasn't enough to keep a family of five without Hazelle working her fingers to the bone on that washboard. In winter her hands got so red and cracked, they bled at the slightest provocation. Still would if it wasn't for a salve my mother concocted. But they are determined, Hazelle and Gale, that the other boys, twelve-year-old Rory and ten-year-old Vick, and the baby, four-year-old Posy, will never have to sign up for tesserae.

Hazelle smiles when she sees the game. She takes

the beaver by the tail, feeling its weight. "He's going to make a nice stew." Unlike Gale, she has no problem with our hunting arrangement.

"Good pelt, too," I answer. It's comforting here with Hazelle. Weighing the merits of the game, just as we always have. She pours me a mug of herb tea, which I wrap my chilled fingers around gratefully. "You know, when I get back from the tour, I was thinking I might take Rory out with me sometimes. After school. Teach him to shoot."

Hazelle nods. "That'd be good. Gale means to, but he's only got his Sundays, and I think he likes saving those for you."

I can't stop the redness that floods my cheeks. It's stupid, of course. Hardly anybody knows me better than Hazelle. Knows the bond I share with Gale. I'm sure plenty of people assumed that we'd eventually get married even if I never gave it any thought. But that was before the Games. Before my fellow tribute, Peeta Mellark, announced he was madly in love with me. Our romance became a key strategy for our survival in the arena. Only it wasn't just a strategy for Peeta. I'm not sure what it was for me. But I know now it was nothing but painful for Gale. My chest tightens as I think about how, on the Victory Tour, Peeta and I will have to present ourselves as lovers again.

I gulp my tea even though it's too hot and push back from the table. "I better get going. Make myself presentable for the cameras."

Hazelle hugs me. "Enjoy the food."

"Absolutely," I say.

My next stop is the Hob, where I've traditionally done the bulk of my trading. Years ago it was a warehouse to store coal, but when it fell into disuse, it became a meeting place for illegal trades and then blossomed into a full-time black market. If it attracts a somewhat criminal element, then I belong here, I guess. Hunting in the woods surrounding District 12 violates at least a dozen laws and is punishable by death.

Although they never mention it, I owe the people who frequent the Hob. Gale told me that Greasy Sae, the old woman who serves up soup, started a collection to sponsor Peeta and me during the Games. It was supposed to be just a Hob thing, but a lot of other people heard about it and chipped in. I don't know exactly how much it was, and the price of any gift in the arena was exorbitant. But for all I know, it made the difference between my life and death.

It's still odd to drag open the front door with an empty game bag, with nothing to trade, and instead feel the heavy pocket of coins against my hip. I try to hit as many stalls as possible, spreading out my purchases of coffee, buns, eggs, yarn and oil. As an afterthought, I buy three bottles of white liquor from a one-armed woman named Ripper, a victim of a mine accident who was smart enough to find a way to stay alive.

The liquor isn't for my family. It's for Haymitch, who acted as mentor for Peeta and me in the Games. He's surly, violent and drunk most of the time. But he did his job – more than his job – because for the first time in history, two tributes were allowed to win. So no matter who Haymitch is, I owe him, too. And that's for always. I'm getting the white liquor because a few weeks ago he ran out and there was none for sale and he had a withdrawal, shaking and screaming at terrifying things only he could see. He scared Prim to death and, frankly, it wasn't much fun for me to see him like that, either. Ever since then I've been sort of stockpiling the stuff just in case there's a shortage again.

Cray, our Head Peacekeeper, frowns when he sees me with the bottles. He's an older man with a few strands of silver hair combed sideways above his bright red face. "That stuff's too strong for you, girl." He should know. Next to Haymitch, Cray drinks more than anyone I've ever met.

"Aw, my mother uses it in medicines," I say indifferently.

"Well, it'd kill just about anything," he says, and slaps down a coin for a bottle.

When I reach Greasy Sae's stall, I boost myself up to sit on the counter and order some soup, which looks to be some kind of gourd and bean mixture. A Peacekeeper named Darius comes up and buys a bowl while I'm eating. As law enforcers go, he's one of my favourites. Never really throwing his weight around, usually good for a joke. He's probably in his twenties, but he doesn't seem much older than I do. Something about his smile, his red hair that sticks out every which way, gives him a boyish quality.

"Aren't you supposed to be on a train?" he asks me.

"They're collecting me at noon," I answer.

"Shouldn't you look better?" he asks in a loud whisper. I can't help smiling at his teasing, in spite of my mood. "Maybe a ribbon in your hair or something?" He flicks my braid with his hand and I brush him away.

"Don't worry. By the time they get through with me I'll be unrecognizable," I say.

"Good," he says. "Let's show a little district pride for a change, Miss Everdeen. Hm?" He shakes his head at Greasy Sae in mock disapproval and walks off to join his friends.

"I'll want that bowl back," Greasy Sae calls after him, but since she's laughing, she doesn't sound particularly stern. "Gale going to see you off?" she asks me.

"No, he wasn't on the list," I say. "I saw him Sunday, though."

"Think he'd have made the list. Him being your cousin and all," she says wryly.

It's just one more part of the lie the Capitol has concocted. When Peeta and I made it into the final eight in the Hunger Games, they sent reporters to do personal stories about us. When they asked about my friends, everyone directed them to Gale. But it wouldn't do, what with the romance I was playing out in the arena, to have my best friend be Gale. He was too handsome, too male, and not the least bit willing to smile and play nice for the cameras. We do resemble each other, though, quite a bit. We have that Seam look. Dark straight hair, olive skin, grey eyes. So some genius made him my cousin. I didn't know about it until we were already home, on the platform at the train station, and my mother said, "Your cousins can hardly wait to see you!" Then I turned and saw Gale and Hazelle and all the kids waiting for me, so what could I do but go along?

Greasy Sae knows we're not related, but even some of the people who have known us for years seem to have forgotten.

"I just can't wait for the whole thing to be over," I whisper.

"I know," says Greasy Sae. "But you've got to go through it to get to the end of it. Better not be late."

A light snow starts to fall as I make my way to the Victor's Village. It's about a kilometre-long walk from the square in the centre of town, but it seems like another world entirely. It's a separate community built around a beautiful green, dotted with flowering bushes. There are twelve houses, each large enough to hold ten of the one I was raised in. Nine stand empty, as they always have. The three in use belong to Haymitch, Peeta and me.

The houses inhabited by my family and Peeta give off a warm glow of life. Lit windows, smoke from the chimneys, bunches of brightly coloured corn affixed to the front doors as decoration for the upcoming Harvest Festival. However, Haymitch's house, despite the care taken by the groundskeeper, exudes an air of abandonment and neglect. I brace myself at his front door, knowing it will be foul, then push inside.

My nose immediately wrinkles in disgust. Haymitch refuses to let anyone in to clean and does a poor job himself. Over the years the odours of liquor and vomit, boiled cabbage and burned meat, unwashed clothes and mouse droppings have intermingled into a stench that brings tears to my eyes. I wade through a litter of discarded wrappings, broken glass and bones to where I know I will find Haymitch. He sits at the kitchen table, his arms sprawled across the wood, his face in a puddle of liquor, snoring his head off.

I nudge his shoulder. "Get up!" I say loudly, because I've learned there's no subtle way to wake him. His snoring stops for a moment, questioningly, and then resumes. I push him harder. "Get up, Haymitch. It's tour day!" I force the window up, inhaling deep breaths of the clean air outside. My feet shift through the rubbish on the floor, and I unearth a tin coffee pot and fill it at the sink. The stove isn't completely out and I manage to coax the few live coals into a flame. I pour some ground coffee into the pot, enough to make sure the resulting brew will be good and strong, and set it on the stove to boil.

Haymitch is still dead to the world. Since nothing else has worked, I fill a basin with icy cold water, dump it on his head, and spring out of the way. A guttural animal sound comes from his throat. He jumps up, kicking his chair a metre behind him and wielding a knife. I forgot he always sleeps with one clutched in his hand. I should have prised it from his fingers, but I've had a lot on my mind. Spewing profanities, he slashes the air a few moments before coming to his senses. He wipes his face on his shirtsleeve and turns to the window sill where I perch, just in case I need to make a quick exit.

"What are you doing?" he sputters.

"You told me to wake you an hour before the cameras come," I say.

"What?" he says.

"Your idea," I insist.

He seems to remember. "Why am I all wet?"

"I couldn't shake you awake," I say. "Look, if you wanted to be babied, you should have asked Peeta."

"Asked me what?" Just the sound of his voice twists my stomach into a knot of unpleasant emotions like guilt, sadness and fear. And longing. I might as well admit there's some of that, too. Only it has too much competition to ever win out.

I watch as Peeta crosses to the table, the sunlight from the window picking up the glint of fresh snow in his blond hair. He looks strong and healthy, so different from the sick, starving boy I knew in the arena, and you can barely even notice his limp now. He sets a loaf of fresh-baked bread on the table and holds out his hand to Haymitch.

"Asked you to wake me without giving me pneumonia," says Haymitch, passing over his knife. He pulls off his filthy shirt, revealing an equally soiled undershirt, and rubs himself down with the dry part.

Peeta smiles and douses Haymitch's knife in white liquor from a bottle on the floor. He wipes the blade clean on his shirt tail and slices the bread. Peeta keeps all of us in fresh baked goods. I hunt. He bakes. Haymitch drinks. We have our own ways to stay busy, to keep thoughts of our time as contestants in the Hunger Games at bay. It's not until he's handed Haymitch the heel that he even looks at me for the first time. "Would you like a piece?"

"No, I ate at the Hob," I say. "But thank you." My voice doesn't sound like my own, it's so formal. Just as it's been every time I've spoken to Peeta since the cameras finished filming our happy homecoming and we returned to our real lives.

"You're welcome," he says back stiffly.

Haymitch tosses his shirt somewhere into the mess. "Brrr. You two have got a lot of warming up to do before showtime."

He's right, of course. The audience will be expecting the pair of lovebirds who won the Hunger Games. Not two people who can barely look each other in the eye. But all I say is, "Take a bath,

Haymitch." Then I swing out of the window, drop to the ground, and head across the green to my house.

The snow has begun to stick and I leave a trail of footprints behind me. At the front door, I pause to knock the wet stuff from my shoes before I go in. My mother's been working day and night to make everything perfect for the cameras, so it's no time to be tracking up her shiny floors. I've barely stepped inside when she's there, holding my arm as if to stop me.

"Don't worry, I'm taking them off here," I say, leaving my shoes on the mat.

My mother gives an odd, breathy laugh and removes the game bag loaded with supplies from my shoulder. "It's just snow. Did you have a nice walk?"

"Walk?" She knows I've been in the woods half the night. Then I see the man standing behind her in the kitchen doorway. One look at his tailored suit and surgically perfected features and I know he's from the Capitol. Something is wrong. "It was more like skating. It's really getting slippery out there."

"Someone's here to see you," says my mother. Her face is too pale and I can hear the anxiety she's trying to hide.

"I thought they weren't due until noon." I pretend not to notice her state. "Did Cinna come early to help me get ready?"

"No, Katniss, it's—" my mother begins.

"This way, please, Miss Everdeen," says the man. He gestures down the hallway. It's weird to be ushered around your own home, but I know better than to comment on it.

As I go, I give my mother a reassuring smile over my shoulder. "Probably more instructions for the tour." They've been sending me all kinds of stuff about my itinerary and what protocol will be observed in each district. But as I walk towards the door of the study, a door I have never even seen closed until this moment, I can feel my mind begin to race. *Who is here? What do they want? Why is my mother so pale?*

"Go right in," says the Capitol man, who has followed me down the hallway.

I twist the polished brass knob and step inside. My nose registers the conflicting scents of roses and blood. A small, white-haired man who seems vaguely familiar is reading a book. He holds up a finger as if to say, "Give me a moment." Then he turns and my heart skips a beat.

I'm staring into the snakelike eyes of President Snow.

2

In my mind, President Snow should be viewed in front of marble pillars hung with oversized flags. It's jarring to see him surrounded by the ordinary objects in the room. Like taking the lid off a pot and finding a fanged viper instead of stew.

What could he be doing here? My mind rushes back to the opening days of other Victory Tours. I remember seeing the winning tributes with their mentors and stylists. Even some high government officials have made appearances occasionally. But I have never seen President Snow. He attends celebrations in the Capitol. Period.

If he's made the journey all the way from his city, it can only mean one thing. I'm in serious trouble. And if I am, so is my family. A shiver goes through me when I think of the proximity of my mother and sister to this man who despises me. Will always despise me. Because I outsmarted his sadistic Hunger Games, made the Capitol look foolish, and consequently undermined his control.

All I was doing was trying to keep Peeta and myself alive. Any act of rebellion was purely coincidental. But when the Capitol decrees that only one tribute can live and you have the audacity to challenge it, I guess that's a rebellion in itself. My only defence was pretending that I was driven insane by a passionate love for Peeta. So we were both allowed to live. To be crowned victors. To go home and celebrate and wave goodbye to the cameras and be left alone. Until now.

Perhaps it is the newness of the house or the shock of seeing him or the mutual understanding that he could have me killed in a second that makes me feel like the intruder. As if this is his home and I'm the uninvited party. So I don't welcome him or offer him a chair. I don't say anything. In fact, I treat him as if he's a real snake, the venomous kind. I stand motionless, my eyes locked on him, considering plans of retreat.

"I think we'll make this whole situation a lot simpler by agreeing not to lie to each other," he says. "What do you think?"

I think my tongue has frozen and speech will be

impossible, so I surprise myself by answering back in a steady voice, "Yes, I think that would save time."

President Snow smiles and I notice his lips for the first time. I'm expecting snake lips, which is to say none. But his are overly full, the skin stretched too tight. I have to wonder if his mouth has been altered to make him more appealing. If so, it was a waste of time and money, because he's not appealing at all. "My advisors were concerned you would be difficult, but you're not planning on being difficult, are you?" he asks.

"No," I answer.

"That's what I told them. I said any girl who goes to such lengths to preserve her life isn't going to be interested in throwing it away with both hands. And then there's her family to think of. Her mother, her sister, and all those . . . cousins." By the way he lingers on the word "cousins", I can tell he knows that Gale and I don't share a family tree.

Well, it's all on the table now. Maybe that's better. I don't do well with ambiguous threats. I'd much rather know the score.

"Let's sit." President Snow takes a seat at the large desk of polished wood where Prim does her homework and my mother her budgets. Like our home, this is a place that he has no right, but ultimately every right, to occupy. I sit in front of the desk on one of the carved, straight-backed chairs. It's made for someone taller than I am, so only my toes rest on the ground.

"I have a problem, Miss Everdeen," says President Snow. "A problem that began the moment you pulled out those poisonous berries in the arena."

That was the moment when I guessed that if the Gamemakers had to choose between watching Peeta and me commit suicide – which would mean having no victor – and letting us both live, they would take the latter.

"If the Head Gamemaker, Seneca Crane, had had any brains, he'd have blown you to dust right then. But he had an unfortunate sentimental streak. So here you are. Can you guess where he is?" he asks.

I nod because, by the way he says it, it's clear that Seneca Crane has been executed. The smell of roses and blood has grown stronger now that only a desk separates us. There's a rose in President Snow's lapel, which at least suggests a source of the flower perfume, but it must be genetically enhanced, because no real rose reeks like that. As for the blood . . . I don't know.

"After that, there was nothing to do but let you play out your little scenario. And you were pretty good, too, with the love-crazed schoolgirl bit. The people in the Capitol were quite convinced.

Unfortunately, not everyone in the districts fell for your act," he says.

My face must register at least a flicker of bewilderment, because he addresses it.

"This, of course, you don't know. You have no access to information about the mood in other districts. In several of them, however, people viewed your little trick with the berries as an act of defiance, not an act of love. And if a girl from District Twelve of all places can defy the Capitol and walk away unharmed, what is to stop them from doing the same?" he says. "What is to prevent, say, an uprising?"

It takes a moment for his last sentence to sink in. Then the full weight of it hits me. "There have been uprisings?" I ask, both chilled and somewhat elated by the possibility.

"Not yet. But they'll follow if the course of things doesn't change. And uprisings have been known to lead to revolution." President Snow rubs a spot over his left eyebrow, the very spot where I myself get headaches. "Do you have any idea what that would mean? How many people would die? What conditions those left would have to face? Whatever problems anyone may have with the Capitol, believe me when I say that if it released its grip on the districts for even a short time, the entire system would collapse."

I'm taken aback by the directness and even the sincerity of this speech. As if his primary concern is the welfare of the citizens of Panem, when nothing could be further from the truth. I don't know how I dare to say the next words, but I do. "It must be very fragile, if a handful of berries can bring it down."

There's a long pause while he examines me. Then he simply says, "It is fragile, but not in the way that you suppose."

There's a knock at the door, and the Capitol man sticks his head in. "Her mother wants to know if you want tea."

"I would. I would like tea," says the president. The door opens wider, and there stands my mother, holding a tray with a china tea set she brought to the Seam when she married. "Set it here, please." He places his book on the corner of the desk and pats the centre.

My mother sets the tray on the desk. It holds a china teapot and cups, cream and sugar, and a plate of cookies. They are beautifully iced with softly coloured flowers. The frosting work can only be Peeta's.

"What a welcome sight. You know, it's funny how often people forget that presidents need to eat, too," President Snow says charmingly. Well, it seems to relax my mother a bit, anyway.

"Can I get you anything else? I can cook something more substantial if you're hungry," she offers.

"No, this could not be more perfect. Thank you," he says, clearly dismissing her. My mother nods, shoots me a glance, and goes. President Snow pours tea for both of us and fills his with cream and sugar, then takes a long time stirring. I sense he has had his say and is waiting for me to respond.

"I didn't mean to start any uprisings," I tell him.

"I believe you. It doesn't matter. Your stylist turned out to be prophetic in his wardrobe choice. Katniss Everdeen, the girl who was on fire, you have provided a spark that, left unattended, may grow to an inferno that destroys Panem," he says.

"Why don't you just kill me now?" I blurt out.

"Publicly?" he asks. "That would only add fuel to the flames."

"Arrange an accident, then," I say.

"Who would buy it?" he asks. "Not you, if you were watching."

"Then just tell me what you want me to do. I'll do it," I say.

"If only it were that simple." He picks up one of the flowered cookies and examines it. "Lovely. Your mother made these?"

"Peeta." And for the first time, I find I can't hold

his gaze. I reach for my tea but set it back down when I hear the cup rattling against the saucer. To cover I quickly take a cookie.

"Peeta. How *is* the love of your life?" he asks.

"Good," I say.

"At what point did he realize the exact degree of your indifference?" he asks, dipping his cookie in his tea.

"I'm not indifferent," I say.

"But perhaps not as taken with the young man as you would have the country believe," he says.

"Who says I'm not?" I say.

"I do," says the president. "And I wouldn't be here if I were the only person who had doubts. How's the handsome cousin?"

"I don't know . . . I don't. . ." My revulsion at this conversation, at discussing my feelings for two of the people I care most about with President Snow, chokes me off.

"Speak, Miss Everdeen. Him I can easily kill off if we don't come to a happy resolution," he says. "You aren't doing him a favour by disappearing into the woods with him each Sunday."

If he knows this, what else does he know? And how does he know it? Many people could tell him that Gale and I spend our Sundays hunting. Don't we show up at the end of each one loaded down with game? Haven't we for years? The real question is what he thinks goes on in the woods beyond District 12. Surely they haven't been tracking us in there. Or have they? Could we have been followed? That seems impossible. At least by a person. Cameras? That never crossed my mind until this moment. The woods have always been our place of safety, our place beyond the reach of the Capitol, where we're free to say what we feel, be who we are. At least before the Games. If we've been watched since, what have they seen? Two people hunting, saying treasonous things against the Capitol, yes. But not two people in love, which seems to be President Snow's implication. We are safe on that charge. Unless . . . unless. . .

It only happened once. It was fast and unexpected, but it did happen.

After Peeta and I got home from the Games, it was several weeks before I saw Gale alone. First there were the obligatory celebrations. A banquet for the victors that only the most high-ranking people were invited to. A holiday for the whole district with free food and entertainers brought in from the Capitol. Parcel Day, the first of twelve, in which food packages were delivered to every person in the district. That was my favourite. To see all those hungry kids in the Seam running around, waving cans of apple sauce, tins of meat, even sweets. Back home, too big to carry, would be bags of grain, cans of oil. To know that once a month for a year they would all receive another parcel. That was one of the few times I actually felt good about winning the Games.

So between the ceremonies and events and the reporters documenting my every move as I presided and thanked and kissed Peeta for the audience, I had no privacy at all. After a few weeks, things finally died down. The camera crews and reporters packed up and went home. Peeta and I assumed the cool relationship we've had ever since. My family settled into our house in the Victor's Village. The everyday life of District 12 – workers to the mines, kids to school – resumed its usual pace. I waited until I thought the coast was really clear, and then one Sunday, without telling anyone, I got up hours before dawn and took off for the woods.

The weather was still warm enough that I didn't need a jacket. I packed along a bag filled with special foods, cold chicken and cheese and bakery bread and oranges. Down at my old house, I put on my hunting boots. As usual, the fence was not charged and it was simple to slip into the woods and retrieve my bow and arrows. I went to our place, Gale's and mine, where we had shared breakfast the morning of the reaping that sent me into the Games.

I waited at least two hours. I'd begun to think that he'd given up on me in the weeks that had passed. Or that he no longer cared about me. Hated me even. And the idea of losing him for ever, my best friend, the only person I'd ever trusted with my secrets, was so painful I couldn't stand it. Not on top of everything else that had happened. I could feel my eyes tearing up and my throat starting to close the way it does when I get upset.

Then I looked up and there he was, three metres away, just watching me. Without even thinking, I jumped up and threw my arms around him, making some weird sound that combined laughing, choking and crying. He was holding me so tightly that I couldn't see his face, but it was a really long time before he let me go and then he didn't have much choice, because I'd got this unbelievably loud case of the hiccups and had to get a drink.

We did what we always did that day. Ate breakfast. Hunted and fished and gathered. Talked about people in town. But not about us, his new life in the mines, my time in the arena. Just about other things. By the time we were at the hole in the fence that's nearest the Hob, I think I really believed that things could be the same. That we could go on as we always had. I'd given all the game to Gale to trade since we had so much food now. I told him I'd skip the Hob, even though I was looking forward to going there, because my mother and sister didn't even know I'd gone hunting and they'd be wondering where I was. Then suddenly, as I was suggesting I take over the daily snare run, he took my face in his hands and kissed me.

I was completely unprepared. You would think that after all the hours I'd spent with Gale – watching him talk and laugh and frown – that I would know all there was to know about his lips. But I hadn't imagined how warm they would feel pressed against my own. Or how those hands, which could set the most intricate of snares, could as easily entrap me. I think I made some sort of noise in the back of my throat, and I vaguely remember my fingers, curled tightly closed, resting on his chest. Then he let go and said, "I had to do that. At least once." And he was gone.

Despite the fact that the sun was setting and my family would be worried, I sat by a tree next to the fence. I tried to decide how I felt about the kiss, if I had liked it or resented it, but all I really remembered was the pressure of Gale's lips and the scent of the oranges that still lingered on his skin. It was pointless comparing it with the many kisses I'd exchanged with Peeta. I still hadn't figured out if any of those counted. Finally I went home.

That week I managed the snares and dropped off the meat with Hazelle. But I didn't see Gale until Sunday. I had this whole speech worked out, about how I didn't want a boyfriend and never planned on marrying, but I didn't end up using it. Gale acted as if the kiss had never happened. Maybe he was waiting for me to say something. Or kiss him back. Instead I just pretended it had never happened, either. But it had. Gale had shattered some invisible barrier between us and, with it, any hope I had of resuming our old, uncomplicated friendship. Whatever I pretended, I could never look at his lips in quite the same way.

This all flashes through my head in an instant as President Snow's eyes bore into me on the heels of his threat to kill Gale. How stupid I've been to think the Capitol would just ignore me once I'd returned home! Maybe I didn't know about the potential uprisings. But I knew they were angry with me. Instead of acting with the extreme caution the situation called for, what have I done? From the president's point of view, I've ignored Peeta and flaunted my preference for Gale's company before the whole district. And by doing so made it clear I was, in fact, mocking the Capitol. Now I've endangered Gale and his family and my family and Peeta, too, by my carelessness.

"Please don't hurt Gale," I whisper. "He's just my friend. He's been my friend for years. That's all that's between us. Besides, everyone thinks we're cousins now."

"I'm only interested in how it affects your dynamic with Peeta, thereby affecting the mood in the districts," he says.

"It will be the same on the tour. I'll be in love with him just as I was," I say.

"Just as you are," corrects President Snow.

"Just as I am," I confirm.

"Only you'll have to do even better if the uprisings are to be averted," he says. "This tour will be your only chance to turn things around."

"I know. I will. I'll convince everyone in the districts that I wasn't defying the Capitol, that I was crazy with love," I say.

President Snow rises and dabs his puffy lips with a napkin. "Aim higher in case you fall short."

"What do you mean? How can I aim higher?" I ask.

"Convince *me*," he says. He drops the napkin and

retrieves his book. I don't watch him as he heads for the door, so I flinch when he whispers in my ear. "By the way, I know about the kiss." Then the door clicks shut behind him.

3

The smell of blood . . . it was on his breath.

What does he do? I think. *Drink it?* I imagine him sipping it from a teacup. Dipping a cookie into the stuff and pulling it out dripping red.

Outside the window, a car comes to life, soft and quiet like the purr of a cat, then fades away into the distance. It slips off as it arrived, unnoticed.

The room seems to be spinning in slow, lopsided circles, and I wonder if I might black out. I lean forward and clutch the desk with one hand. The other still holds Peeta's beautiful cookie. I think it had a tiger lily on it, but now it's been reduced to crumbs in my fist. I didn't even know I was crushing it, but I guess I had to hold on to something while my world veered out of control.

A visit from President Snow. Districts on the verge

of uprisings. A direct death threat to Gale, with others to follow. Everyone I love doomed. And who knows who else will pay for my actions? Unless I turn things around on this tour. Quiet the discontent and put the president's mind at rest. And how? By proving to the country beyond any shadow of a doubt that I love Peeta Mellark.

I can't do it, I think. *I'm not that good.* Peeta's the good one, the likable one. He can make people believe anything. I'm the one who shuts up and sits back and lets him do as much of the talking as possible. But it isn't Peeta who has to prove his devotion. It's me.

I hear my mother's light, quick tread in the hall. *She can't know*, I think. *Not about any of this.* I reach my hands over the tray and quickly brush the bits of cookie from my palm and fingers. I take a shaky sip of my tea.

"Is everything all right, Katniss?" she asks.

"It's fine. We never see it on television, but the president always visits the victors before the tour to wish them luck," I say brightly.

My mother's face floods with relief. "Oh. I thought there was some kind of trouble."

"No, not at all," I say. "The trouble will start when my prep team sees how I've let my eyebrows grow back in." My mother laughs, and I think about how there was no going back after I took over caring for the family when I was eleven. How I will always have to protect her.

"Why don't I start your bath?" she asks.

"Great," I say, and I can see how pleased she is by my response.

Since I've been home I've been trying hard to mend my relationship with my mother. Asking her to do things for me instead of brushing aside any offer of help, as I did for years out of anger. Letting her handle all the money I won. Returning her hugs instead of tolerating them. My time in the arena made me realize how I needed to stop punishing her for something she couldn't help, specifically the crushing depression she fell into after my father's death. Because sometimes things happen to people and they're not equipped to deal with them.

Like me, for instance. Right now.

Besides, there's one wonderful thing she did when I arrived back in the district. After our families and friends had greeted Peeta and me at the train station, there were a few questions allowed from reporters. Someone asked my mother what she thought of my new boyfriend, and she replied that, while Peeta was the very model of what a young man should be, I wasn't old enough to have any boyfriend at all. She followed this with a pointed look at Peeta. There was a lot of laughter and comments like "Somebody's in trouble" from the press, and Peeta dropped my hand and sidestepped away from me. That didn't last long – there was too much pressure to act otherwise – but it gave us an excuse to be a little more reserved than we'd been in the Capitol. And maybe it can help account for how little I've been seen in Peeta's company since the cameras left.

I go upstairs to the bathroom, where a steaming tub awaits. My mother has added a small bag of dried flowers that perfumes the air. None of us are used to the luxury of turning on a tap and having a limitless supply of hot water at our fingertips. We had only cold at our home in the Seam, and a bath meant boiling the rest over the fire. I undress and lower myself into the silky water – my mother has poured in some kind of oil as well – and try to get a grip on things.

The first question is who to tell, if anyone. Not my mother or Prim, obviously; they'd only become sick with worry. Not Gale. Even if I could get word to him. What would he do with the information, anyway? If he were alone, I might try to persuade him to run away. Certainly he could survive in the woods. But he's not alone and he'd never leave his family. Or me. When I get home I'll have to tell him something about why our Sundays are a thing of the past, but I can't think about that now. Only about my next move. Besides, Gale's already so angry and frustrated with the Capitol that I sometimes think he's going to arrange his own uprising. The last thing he needs is an incentive. No, I can't tell anyone I'm leaving behind in District 12.

There are still three people I might confide in, starting with Cinna, my stylist. But my guess is Cinna might already be at risk, and I don't want to pull him into any more trouble by closer association with me. Then there's Peeta, who will be my partner in this deception, but how do I begin that conversation? *Hey, Peeta, remember how I told you I was kind of faking being in love with you? Well, I really need you to forget about that now and act extra in love with me or the president might kill Gale.* I can't do it. Besides, Peeta will perform well whether he knows what's at stake or not. That leaves Haymitch. Drunken, cranky, confrontational Haymitch, who I just poured a basin of ice water on. As my mentor in the Games it was his duty to keep me alive. I only hope he's still up for the job.

I slide down into the water, letting it block out the sounds around me. I wish the tub would expand so I could go swimming, like I used to on hot summer Sundays in the woods with my father.

Those days were a special treat. We would leave early in the morning and hike further into the woods than usual to a small lake he'd found while hunting. I don't even remember learning to swim, I was so young when he taught me. I just remember diving, turning somersaults, and paddling around. The muddy bottom of the lake beneath my toes. The smell of blossoms and greenery. Floating on my back, as I am now, staring at the blue sky while the chatter of the woods was muted by the water. He'd bag the waterfowl that nested around the shore, I'd hunt for eggs in the grasses, and we'd both dig for katniss roots, the plant after which he named me, in the shallows. At night, when we got home, my mother would pretend not to recognize me because I was so clean. Then she'd cook up an amazing dinner of roasted duck and baked katniss tubers with gravy.

I never took Gale to the lake. I could have. It's time-consuming to get there, but the waterfowl are such easy pickings you can make up for lost hunting time. It's a place I've never really wanted to share with anyone, though, a place that belonged only to my father and me. Since the Games, when I've had little to occupy my days, I've gone there a couple of times. The swimming was still nice, but mostly the visits depressed me. Over the course of the last five years, the lake's remarkably unchanged and I'm almost unrecognizable.

Even underwater I can hear the sounds of commotion. Honking car horns, shouts of greeting, doors banging shut. It can only mean my entourage has arrived. I just have time to towel off and slip into a robe before my prep team bursts into the bathroom. There's no question of privacy. When it comes to my body, we have no secrets, these three people and me.

"Katniss, your eyebrows!" Venia shrieks right off, and even with the black cloud hanging over me, I have to stifle a laugh. Her aqua hair has been styled so it sticks out in sharp points all over her head, and the gold tattoos that used to be confined above her brows have curled around under her eyes, all contributing to the impression that I've literally shocked her.

Octavia comes up and pats Venia's back soothingly, her curvy body looking plumper than usual next to Venia's thin, angular one. "There, there. You can fix those in no time. But what am I going to do with these nails?" She grabs my hand and pins it flat between her two pea-green ones. No, her skin isn't exactly pea green now. It's more of a light evergreen. The shift in shade is no doubt an attempt to stay abreast of the capricious fashion trends of the Capitol. "Really,

Katniss, you could have left me something to work with!" she wails.

It's true. I've bitten my nails to stubs in the past couple of months. I thought about trying to break the habit but couldn't think of a good reason I should. "Sorry," I mutter. I hadn't really been spending much time worrying about how it might affect my prep team.

Flavius lifts a few strands of my wet, tangled hair. He gives his head a disapproving shake, causing his orange corkscrew curls to bounce around. "Has anyone touched this since you last saw us?" he asks sternly. "Remember, we specifically asked you to leave your hair alone."

"Yes!" I say, grateful that I can show I haven't totally taken them for granted. "I mean, no, no one's cut it. I did remember that." No, I didn't. It's more like the issue never came up. Since I've been home, all I've done is stick it in its usual old braid down my back.

This seems to mollify them, and they all kiss me, set me on a chair in my bedroom, and, as usual, start talking non-stop without bothering to notice if I'm listening. While Venia reinvents my eyebrows and Octavia gives me fake nails and Flavius massages goo into my hair, I hear all about the Capitol. What a hit the Games were, how dull things have been since, how no one can wait until Peeta and I visit again at the end of the Victory Tour. After that, it won't be long before the Capitol begins gearing up for the Quarter Quell.

"Isn't it thrilling?"

"Don't you feel so lucky?"

"In your very first year of being a victor, you get to be a mentor in a Quarter Quell!"

Their words overlap in a blur of excitement.

"Oh, yes," I say neutrally. It's the best I can do. In a normal year, being a mentor to the tributes is the stuff of nightmares. I can't walk by the school now without wondering what kid I'll have to coach. But to make things even worse, this is the year of the Seventy-fifth Hunger Games, and that means it's also a Quarter Quell. They occur every twenty-five years, marking the anniversary of the districts' defeat with over-the-top celebrations and, for extra fun, some miserable twist for the tributes. I've never been alive for one, of course. But in school I remember hearing that for the second Quarter Quell, the Capitol demanded that twice the number of tributes be provided for the arena. The teachers didn't go into much more detail, which is surprising, because that was the year District 12's very own Haymitch Abernathy won the crown.

"Haymitch better be preparing himself for a lot of attention!" squeals Octavia.

Haymitch has never mentioned his personal experience in the arena to me. I would never ask. And if I ever saw his Games televised in reruns, I must've been too young to remember it. But the Capitol won't let him forget it this year. In a way, it's a good thing Peeta and I will both be available as mentors during the Quell, because it's a sure bet that Haymitch will be wasted.

After they've exhausted the topic of the Quarter Quell, my prep team launches into a whole lot of stuff about their incomprehensibly silly lives. Who said what about someone I've never heard of and what sort of shoes they just bought and a long story from Octavia about what a mistake it was to have everyone wear feathers to her birthday party.

Soon my brows are stinging, my hair's smooth and silky, and my nails are ready to be painted. Apparently they've been given instructions to prepare only my hands and face, probably because everything else will be covered in the cold weather. Flavius badly wants to use his own trademark purple lipstick on me but resigns himself to a pink as they begin to colour my face and nails. I can see by the palette Cinna has assigned that we're going for girlish, not sexy. Good. I'll never convince anyone of anything if I'm trying to be provocative. Haymitch made that very clear when he was coaching me for my interview for the Games.

My mother comes in, somewhat shyly, and says that Cinna has asked her to show the preps how she did my hair the day of the reaping. They respond with enthusiasm and then watch, thoroughly engrossed, as she breaks down the process of the elaborate braided hairdo. In the mirror, I can see their earnest faces following her every move, their eagerness when it is their turn to try a step. In fact, all three are so readily respectful and nice to my mother that I feel bad about how I go around feeling so superior to them. Who knows who I would be or what I would talk about if I'd been raised in the Capitol? Maybe my biggest regret would be having feathered costumes at my birthday party, too.

When my hair is done, I find Cinna downstairs in the living room, and just the sight of him makes me feel more hopeful. He looks the same as always, simple clothes, short brown hair, just a hint of gold eyeliner. We embrace, and I can barely keep from spilling out the entire episode with President Snow. But no, I've decided to tell Haymitch first. He'll know best who to burden with it. It's so easy to talk to Cinna, though. Lately we've been speaking a lot on the telephone that came with the house. It's sort of a joke, because almost no one else we know owns one. There's Peeta, but obviously I don't call him. Haymitch tore his out of the wall years ago. My friend Madge, the mayor's daughter, has a telephone in her house, but if we want to talk, we do it in person. At first, the thing barely ever got used. Then Cinna started to call to work on my talent.

Every victor is supposed to have one. Your talent is the activity you take up since you don't have to work either in school or your district's industry. It can be anything, really, anything that they can interview you about. Peeta, it turns out, actually has a talent, which is painting. He's been frosting those cakes and cookies for years in his family's bakery. But now that he's rich, he can afford to smear real paint on canvases. I don't have a talent, unless you count hunting illegally, which they don't. Or maybe singing, which I wouldn't do for the Capitol in a million years. My mother tried to interest me in a variety of suitable alternatives from a list Effie Trinket sent her. Cooking, flower arranging, playing the flute. None of them took, although Prim had a knack for all three. Finally Cinna stepped in and offered to help me develop my passion for designing clothes, which really required development since it was non-existent. But I said yes because it meant getting to talk to Cinna, and he promised he'd do all the work.

Now he's arranging things around my living room: clothing, fabrics and sketchbooks with designs he's drawn. I pick up one of the sketchbooks and examine a dress I supposedly created. "You know, I think I show a lot of promise," I say.

"Get dressed, you worthless thing," he says, tossing a bundle of clothes at me.

I may have no interest in designing clothes but I do love the ones Cinna makes for me. Like these. Flowing black pants made of a thick, warm material. A comfortable white shirt. A sweater woven from green and blue and grey strands of kitten-soft wool. Laced leather boots that don't pinch my toes.

"Did I design my outfit?" I ask.

"No, you aspire to design your outfit and be like me, your fashion hero," says Cinna. He hands me a small stack of cards. "You'll read these off camera while they're filming the clothes. Try to sound like you care."

Just then, Effie Trinket arrives in a pumpkin-orange wig to remind everyone, "We're on a schedule!" She kisses me on both cheeks while waving in the camera crew, then orders me into position. Effie's the only reason we got anywhere on time in the Capitol, so I try to accommodate her. I start bobbing around like a puppet, holding up outfits and saying meaningless things like "Don't you love it?" The sound team records me reading from my cards in a chirpy voice so they can insert it later, then I'm tossed out of the room so they can film my/Cinna's designs in peace.

Prim got out early from school for the event. Now she stands in the kitchen, being interviewed by another crew. She looks lovely in a sky-blue frock that brings out her eyes, her blonde hair pulled back in a matching ribbon. She's leaning a bit forward on the toes of her shiny white boots like she's about to take flight, like—

Bam! It's like someone actually hits me in the chest. No one has, of course, but the pain is so real I take a step back. I squeeze my eyes shut and I don't see Prim – I see Rue, the twelve-year-old girl from District 11 who was my ally in the arena. She could fly, birdlike, from tree to tree, catching on to the slenderest branches. Rue, who I didn't save. Who I let die. I picture her lying on the ground with the spear still wedged in her stomach. . .

Who else will I fail to save from the Capitol's vengeance? Who else will be dead if I don't satisfy President Snow?

I realize Cinna's trying to put a coat on me, so I raise my arms. I feel fur, inside and out, encasing me. It's from no animal I've ever seen. "Ermine," he tells me as I stroke the white sleeve. Leather gloves. A bright red scarf. Something furry covers my ears. "You're bringing earmuffs back in style."

I hate earmuffs, I think. They make it hard to hear, and since I was blasted deaf in one ear in the arena, I dislike them even more. After I won, the Capitol repaired my ear, but I still find myself testing it.

My mother hurries up with something cupped in her hand. "For good luck," she says.

It's the pin Madge gave me before I left for the Games. A mockingjay flying in a circle of gold. I tried to give it to Rue but she wouldn't take it. She said the pin was the reason she'd decided to trust me. Cinna fixes it on the knot in the scarf.

Effie Trinket's nearby, clapping her hands. "Attention, everyone! We're about to do the first outdoor shot, where the victors greet each other at the beginning of their marvellous trip. All right, Katniss, big smile, you're very excited, right?" I don't exaggerate when I say she shoves me out of the door.

For a moment I can't quite see right because of the snow, which is now coming down in earnest. Then I make out Peeta coming through his front door. In my head I hear President Snow's directive, "*Convince* me." And I know I must.

My face breaks into a huge smile and I start walking in Peeta's direction. Then, as if I can't stand it another second, I start running. He catches me and spins me around and then he slips – he still isn't entirely in command of his artificial leg – and we fall into the snow, me on top of him, and that's where we have our first kiss in months. It's full of fur and snowflakes and lipstick, but underneath all that, I can feel the steadiness that Peeta brings to everything. And I know I'm not alone. As badly as I have hurt him, he won't expose me in front of the cameras. Won't condemn me with a half-hearted kiss. He's still looking out for me. Just as he did in the arena. Somehow the thought makes me want to cry. Instead I pull him to his feet, tuck my glove through the crook of his arm, and merrily pull him on our way.

The rest of the day is a blur of getting to the station, bidding everyone goodbye, the train pulling out, the old team – Peeta and me, Effie and Haymitch, Cinna and Portia, Peeta's stylist – dining on an indescribably delicious meal I don't remember. And then I'm swathed in pyjamas and a voluminous robe, sitting in my plush compartment, waiting for the others to go to sleep. I know Haymitch will be up for hours. He doesn't like to sleep when it's dark out.

When the train seems quiet, I put on my slippers

and pad down to his door. I have to knock several times before he answers, scowling, as if he's certain I've brought bad news.

"What do you want?" he says, nearly knocking me out with a cloud of wine fumes.

"I have to talk to you," I whisper.

"Now?" he says. I nod. "This better be good." He waits, but I feel certain every word we utter on a Capitol train is being recorded. "Well?" he barks.

The train starts to brake and for a second I think President Snow is watching me and doesn't approve of my confiding in Haymitch and has decided to go ahead and kill me now. But we're just stopping for fuel.

"The train's so stuffy," I say.

It's a harmless phrase, but I see Haymitch's eyes narrow in understanding. "I know what you need." He pushes past me and lurches down the hall to a door. When he wrestles it open, a blast of snow hits us. He trips out on to the ground.

A Capitol attendant rushes to help, but Haymitch waves her away good-naturedly as he staggers off. "Just want some fresh air. Only be a minute."

"Sorry. He's drunk," I say apologetically. "I'll get him." I hop down and stumble along the track behind him, soaking my slippers with snow, as he leads me beyond the end of the train so we will not be overheard. Then he turns on me.

"What?"

I tell him everything. About the president's visit, about Gale, about how we're all going to die if I fail.

His face sobers, grows older in the glow of the red tail lights. "Then you can't fail."

"If you could just help me get through this trip—" I begin.

"No, Katniss, it's not just this trip," he says.

"What do you mean?" I say.

"Even if you pull it off, they'll be back in another few months to take us all to the Games. You and Peeta, you'll be mentors now, every year from here on out. And every year they'll revisit the romance and broadcast the details of your private life, and you'll never, ever be able to do anything but live happily ever after with that boy."

The full impact of what he's saying hits me. I will never have a life with Gale, even if I want to. I will never be allowed to live alone. I will have to be for ever in love with Peeta. The Capitol will insist on it. I'll have a few years maybe, because I'm still only sixteen, to stay with my mother and Prim. And then . . . and then. . .

"Do you understand what I mean?" he presses me.

I nod. He means there's only one future, if I want to keep those I love alive and stay alive myself. I'll have to marry Peeta.

4

We slog back to the train in silence. In the hallway outside my door, Haymitch gives my shoulder a pat and says, “You could do a lot worse, you know.” He heads off to his compartment, taking the smell of wine with him.

In my room, I remove my sodden slippers, my wet robe and pyjamas. There are more in the drawers but I just crawl between the covers of my bed in my underclothes. I stare into the darkness, thinking about my conversation with Haymitch. Everything he said was true about the Capitol’s expectations, my future with Peeta, even his last comment. Of course I could do a lot worse than Peeta. That isn’t really the point, though, is it? One of the few freedoms we have in District 12 is the right to marry who we want or not marry at all. And now even that has been taken away from me. I wonder if President Snow will insist we have children. If we do, they'll have to face the reaping each year. And wouldn't it be something to see the child of not one but two victors chosen for the arena? Victors' children have been in the ring before. It always causes a lot of excitement and generates talk about how the odds are not in that family's favour. But it happens too frequently to just be about odds. Gale's convinced the Capitol does it on purpose, rigs the drawings to add extra drama. Given all the trouble I've caused, I've probably guaranteed any child of mine a spot in the Games.

I think of Haymitch, unmarried, no family, blotting out the world with drink. He could have had his choice of any woman in the district. And he chose solitude. Not solitude – that sounds too peaceful. More like solitary confinement. Was it because, having been in the arena, he knew it was better than risking the alternative? I had a taste of that alternative when they called Prim's name on reaping day and I watched her walk to the stage to her death. But as her sister I could take her place, an option forbidden to our mother.

My mind searches frantically for a way out. I can't let President Snow condemn me to this. Even if it means taking my own life. Before that, though, I'd try to run away. What would they do if I simply vanished? Disappeared into the woods and never came out? Could I even manage to take everyone I love with me, start a new life deep in the wild? Highly unlikely but not impossible.

I shake my head to clear it. This is not the time to be making wild escape plans. I must focus on the Victory Tour. Too many people's fates depend on my giving a good show.

Dawn comes before sleep does, and there's Effie rapping on my door. I pull on whatever clothes are at the top of the drawer and drag myself down to the dining car. I don't see what difference it makes when I get up, since this is a travel day, but then it turns out that yesterday's makeover was just to get me to the train station. Today I'll get the works from my prep team.

"Why? It's too cold for anything to show," I grumble.

"Not in District Eleven," says Effie.

District 11. Our first stop. I'd rather start in any other district, since this was Rue's home. But that's not how the Victory Tour works. Usually it kicks off in 12 and then goes in descending district order to 1, followed by the Capitol. The victor's district is skipped and saved for the very last. Since 12 puts on the least fabulous celebration – usually just a dinner for the tributes and a victory rally in the square, where nobody looks like they're having any fun – it's probably best to get us out of the way as soon as possible. This year, for the first time since Haymitch won, the final stop on the tour will be 12, and the Capitol will spring for the festivities.

I try to enjoy the food like Hazelle said. The kitchen staff clearly wants to please me. They've prepared my favourite, lamb stew with dried plums, among other delicacies. Orange juice and a pot of steaming hot chocolate wait at my place at the table. So I eat a lot, and the meal is beyond reproach, but I can't say I'm enjoying it. I'm also annoyed that no one but Effie and me has shown up.

"Where's everybody else?" I ask.

"Oh, who knows where Haymitch is," says Effie. I didn't really expect Haymitch, because he's probably just getting to bed. "Cinna was up late working on organizing your garment car. He must have over a hundred outfits for you. Your evening clothes are exquisite. And Peeta's team is probably still asleep."

"Doesn't he need prepping?" I ask.

"Not the way you do," Effie replies.

What does this mean? It means I get to spend the morning having the hair ripped off my body while

Peeta sleeps in. I hadn't thought about it much, but in the arena at least some of the boys got to keep their body hair whereas none of the girls did. I can remember Peeta's now, as I bathed him by the stream. Very blond in the sunlight, once the mud and blood had been washed away. Only his face remained completely smooth. Not one of the boys grew a beard, and many were old enough to. I wonder what they did to them.

If I feel ragged, my prep team seems in worse condition, knocking back coffee and sharing brightly coloured little pills. As far as I can tell, they never get up before noon unless there's some sort of national emergency, like my leg hair. I was so happy when it grew back in, too. As if it were a sign that things might be returning to normal. I run my fingers along the soft, curly down on my legs and give myself over to the team. None of them are up to their usual chatter, so I can hear every strand being yanked from its follicle. I have to soak in a tub full of a thick, unpleasant-smelling solution, while my face and hair are plastered with creams. Two more baths follow in other, less offensive, concoctions. I'm plucked and scoured and massaged and anointed until I'm raw.

Flavius tilts up my chin and sighs. "It's a shame Cinna said no alterations on you."

"Yes, we could really make you something special," says Octavia.

"When she's older," says Venia almost grimly. "Then he'll have to let us."

Do what? Blow my lips up like President Snow's? Tattoo my breasts? Dye my skin magenta and implant gems in it? Cut decorative patterns in my face? Give me curved talons? Or cat's whiskers? I saw all these things and more on the people in the Capitol. Do they really have no idea how freakish they look to the rest of us?

The thought of being left to my prep team's fashion whims only adds to the miseries competing for my attention – my abused body, my lack of sleep, my mandatory marriage, and the terror of being unable to satisfy President Snow's demands. By the time I reach lunch, where Effie, Cinna, Portia, Haymitch and Peeta have started without me, I'm too weighed down to talk. They're raving about the food and how well they sleep on trains. Everyone's all full of excitement about the tour. Well, everyone but Haymitch. He's nursing a hangover and picking at a muffin. I'm not really hungry, either, maybe because I loaded up on too much rich stuff this morning or maybe because I'm so unhappy. I play around with a bowl of broth, eating only a spoonful or two. I can't even look at Peeta – my designated future husband – although I know none of this is his fault.

People notice, try to bring me into the conversation, but I just brush them off. At some point, the train stops. Our server reports it will not just be for a fuel stop – some part has malfunctioned and must be replaced. It will require at least an hour. This sends Effie into a state. She pulls out her schedule and begins to work out how the delay will impact every event for the rest of our lives. Finally I just can't stand to listen to her any more.

"No one cares, Effie!" I snap. Everyone at the table stares at me, even Haymitch, who you'd think would be on my side in this matter since Effie drives him nuts. I'm immediately put on the defensive. "Well, no one does!" I say, and get up and leave the dining car.

The train suddenly seems stifling and I'm definitely queasy now. I find the exit door, force it open – triggering some sort of alarm, which I ignore – and jump to the ground, expecting to land in snow. But the air's warm and balmy against my skin. The trees still wear green leaves. How far south have we come in a day? I walk along the track, squinting against the bright sunlight, already regretting my words to Effie. She's hardly to blame for my current predicament. I should go back and apologize. My outburst was the height of bad manners, and manners matter deeply to her. But my feet continue on along the track, past the end of the train, leaving it behind. An hour's delay. I can walk at least twenty minutes in one direction and make it back with plenty of time to spare. Instead, after a couple of hundred metres, I sink to the ground and sit there, looking into the distance. If I had a bow and arrows, would I just keep going?

After a while I hear footsteps behind me. It'll be Haymitch, coming to chew me out. It's not like I don't deserve it, but I still don't want to hear it. "I'm not in the mood for a lecture," I warn the clump of weeds by my shoes.

"I'll try to keep it brief." Peeta takes a seat beside me.

"I thought you were Haymitch," I say.

"No, he's still working on that muffin." I watch as Peeta positions his artificial leg. "Bad day, huh?"

"It's nothing," I say.

He takes a deep breath. "Look, Katniss, I've been wanting to talk to you about the way I acted on the train. I mean, the last train. The one that brought us home. I knew you had something with Gale. I was jealous of him before I even officially met you. And it wasn't fair to hold you to anything that happened in the Games. I'm sorry."

His apology takes me by surprise. It's true that Peeta froze me out after I confessed that my love for him during the Games was something of an act. But I don't hold that against him. In the arena, I'd played that romance angle for all it was worth. There had been times when I didn't honestly know how I felt about him. I still don't, really.

"I'm sorry, too," I say. I'm not sure for what exactly. Maybe because there's a real chance I'm about to destroy him.

"There's nothing for you to be sorry about. You were just keeping us alive. But I don't want us to go on like this, ignoring each other in real life and falling into the snow every time there's a camera around. So I thought if I stopped being so, you know, wounded, we could take a shot at just being friends," he says.

All my friends are probably going to end up dead, but refusing Peeta wouldn't keep him safe. "OK," I say. His offer does make me feel better. Less duplicitous somehow. It would be nice if he'd come to me with this earlier, before I knew that President Snow had other plans and just being friends was not an option for us any more. But either way, I'm glad we're speaking again.

"So what's wrong?" he asks.

I can't tell him. I pick at the clump of weeds.

"Let's start with something more basic. Isn't it strange that I know you'd risk your life to save mine . . . but I don't know what your favourite colour is?" he says.

A smile creeps on to my lips. "Green. What's yours?"

"Orange," he says.

"Orange? Like Effie's hair?" I say.

"A bit more muted," he says. "More like . . . sunset."

Sunset. I can see it immediately, the rim of the descending sun, the sky streaked with soft shades of orange. Beautiful. I remember the tiger lily cookie and, now that Peeta is talking to me again, it's all I can do not to recount the whole story about President Snow. But I know Haymitch wouldn't want me to. I'd better stick to small talk.

"You know, everyone's always raving about your paintings. I feel bad I haven't seen them," I say.

"Well, I've got a whole train car full." He rises and offers me his hand. "Come on."

It's good to feel his fingers entwined with mine again, not for show but in actual friendship. We walk back to the train hand in hand. At the door, I remember. "I've got to apologize to Effie first."

"Don't be afraid to lay it on thick," Peeta tells me.

So when we go back to the dining car, where the others are still at lunch, I give Effie an apology that I think is overkill but in her mind probably just manages to compensate for my breach of etiquette. To her credit, Effie accepts graciously. She says it's clear I'm under a lot of pressure. And her comments about the necessity of *someone* attending to the schedule only last about five minutes. Really, I've got off easily.

When Effie finishes, Peeta leads me down a few cars to see his paintings. I don't know what I expected. Larger versions of the flower cookies, maybe. But this is something entirely different. Peeta has painted the Games.

Some you wouldn't get right away, if you hadn't been with him in the arena yourself. Water dripping through the cracks in our cave. The dry pond bed. A pair of hands, his own, digging for roots. Others any viewer would recognize. The golden horn called the Cornucopia. Clove arranging the knives inside her jacket. One of the mutts, unmistakably the blond, green-eyed one meant to be Glimmer, snarling as it makes its way towards us. And me. I am everywhere. High up in a tree. Beating a shirt against the stones in the stream. Lying unconscious in a pool of blood. And one I can't place – perhaps this is how I looked when his fever was high – emerging from a silver-grey mist that matches my eyes exactly.

"What do you think?" he asks.

"I hate them," I say. I can almost smell the blood, the dirt, the unnatural breath of the mutt. "All I do is go around trying to forget the arena and you've brought it back to life. How do you remember these things so exactly?"

"I see them every night," he says.

I know what he means. Nightmares – which I was no stranger to before the Games – now plague me whenever I sleep. But the old standby, the one of my father being blown to bits in the mines, is rare. Instead I relive versions of what happened in the arena. My worthless attempt to save Rue. Peeta bleeding to death. Glimmer's bloated body disintegrating in my hands. Cato's horrific end with the muttations. These are the most frequent visitors. "Me, too. Does it help? To paint them out?"

"I don't know. I think I'm a little less afraid of going to sleep at night, or I tell myself I am," he says. "But they haven't gone anywhere."

"Maybe they won't. Haymitch's haven't." Haymitch doesn't say so, but I'm sure this is why he doesn't like to sleep in the dark.

"No. But for me, it's better to wake up with a

paintbrush than a knife in my hand," he says. "So you really hate them?"

"Yes. But they're extraordinary. Really," I say. And they are. But I don't want to look at them any more. "Want to see my talent? Cinna did a great job on it."

Peeta laughs. "Later." The train lurches forward, and I can see the land moving past us through the window. "Come on, we're almost at District Eleven. Let's go take a look at it."

We go down to the last car on the train. There are chairs and sofas to sit on, but what's wonderful is that the back windows retract into the ceiling so you're riding outside, in the fresh air, and you can see a wide sweep of the landscape. Huge open fields with herds of dairy cattle grazing in them. So unlike our own heavily wooded home. We slow slightly and I think we might be coming in for another stop, when a fence rises up before us. Towering at least ten metres in the air and topped with wicked coils of barbed wire, it makes ours back in District 12 look childish. My eyes quickly inspect the base, which is lined with enormous metal plates. There would be no burrowing under those, no escaping to hunt. Then I see the watchtowers, placed evenly apart, manned with armed guards, so out of place among the fields of wild flowers around them.

“That’s something different,” says Peeta.

Rue did give me the impression that the rules in District 11 were more harshly enforced. But I never imagined something like this.

Now the crops begin, stretched out as far as the eye can see. Men, women and children wearing straw hats to keep off the sun straighten up, turn our way, take a moment to stretch their backs as they watch our train go by. I can see orchards in the distance, and I wonder if that’s where Rue would have worked, collecting the fruit from the slimmest branches at the tops of the trees. Small communities of shacks – by comparison the houses in the Seam are upscale – spring up here and there, but they’re all deserted. Every hand must be needed for the harvest.

On and on it goes. I can’t believe the size of District 11. “How many people do you think live here?” Peeta asks. I shake my head. In school they refer to it as a large district, that’s all. No actual figures on the population. But those kids we see on camera waiting for the reaping each year, they can’t be but a sampling of the ones who actually live here. What do they do? Have preliminary drawings? Pick the winners ahead of time and make sure they’re in the crowd? How exactly did Rue end up on that stage with nothing but the wind offering to take her place?

I begin to weary of the vastness, the endlessness of this place. When Effie comes to tell us to dress, I don't object. I go to my compartment and let the prep team do my hair and make-up. Cinna comes in with a pretty orange frock patterned with autumn leaves. I think how much Peeta will like the colour.

Effie gets Peeta and me together and goes through the day's programme one last time. In some districts the victors ride through the city while the residents cheer. But in 11 – maybe because there's not much of a city to begin with, things being so spread out, or maybe because they don't want to waste so many people while the harvest is on – the public appearance is confined to the square. It takes place before their Justice Building, a huge marble structure. Once, it must have been a thing of beauty, but time has taken its toll. Even on television you can see ivy overtaking the crumbling facade, the sag of the roof. The square itself is ringed with run-down storefronts, most of which are abandoned. Wherever the well-to-do live in District 11, it's not here.

Our entire public performance will be staged outside on what Effie refers to as the veranda, the tiled expanse between the front doors and the stairs that's shaded by a roof supported by columns. Peeta and I will be introduced, the mayor of 11 will read a speech in our honour, and we'll respond with a scripted thank-you provided by the Capitol. If a victor had any special allies among the dead tributes, it is considered good form to add a few personal comments as well. I should say something about Rue, and Thresh, too, really, but every time I tried to write it at home, I ended up with a blank paper staring me in the face. It's hard for me to talk about them without getting emotional. Fortunately, Peeta has a little something worked out, and with some slight alterations, it can count for both of us. At the end of the ceremony, we'll be presented with some sort of plaque, and then we can withdraw to the Justice Building, where a special dinner will be served.

As the train is pulling into the District 11 station, Cinna puts the finishing touches to my outfit, switching my orange hairband for one of metallic gold and securing the mockingjay pin I wore in the arena to my dress. There's no welcoming committee on the platform, just a squad of eight Peacekeepers who direct us into the back of an armoured truck. Effie sniffs as the door clanks closed behind us. "Really, you'd think we were all criminals," she says.

Not all of us, Effie. Just me, I think.

The truck lets us out at the back of the Justice Building. We're hurried inside. I can smell an excellent meal being prepared, but it doesn't block out the odours of mildew and rot. They've left us no time to look around. As we make a beeline for the front entrance, I can hear the anthem beginning outside in the square. Someone clips a microphone on me. Peeta takes my left hand. The mayor's introducing us as the massive doors open with a groan.

"Big smiles!" Effie says, and gives us a nudge. Our feet start moving forward.

This is it. This is where I have to convince everybody how in love I am with Peeta, I think. The solemn ceremony is pretty tightly mapped out, so I'm not sure how to do it. It's not a time for kissing, but maybe I can work one in.

There's loud applause, but none of the other responses we got in the Capitol, the cheers and whoops and whistles. We walk across the shaded veranda until the roof runs out and we're standing at the top of a big flight of marble stairs in the glaring sun. As my eyes adjust, I see the buildings on the square have been hung with banners that help cover up their neglected state. It's packed with people, but again, just a fraction of the number who live here.

As usual, a special platform has been constructed at the bottom of the stage for the families of the dead tributes. On Thresh's side, there's only an old woman with a hunched back and a tall, muscular girl I'm guessing is his sister. On Rue's. . . I'm not prepared for Rue's family. Her parents, whose faces are still fresh with sorrow. Her five younger siblings, who resemble her so closely. The slight builds, the luminous brown eyes. They form a flock of small dark birds.

The applause dies out and the mayor gives the speech in our honour. Two little girls come up with tremendous bouquets of flowers. Peeta does his part of the scripted reply and then I find my lips moving to conclude it. Fortunately my mother and Prim have drilled me so I can do it in my sleep.

Peeta had his personal comments written on a card, but he doesn't pull it out. Instead he speaks in his simple, winning style about Thresh and Rue making it to the final eight, about how they both kept me alive – thereby keeping him alive – and about how this is a debt we can never repay. And then he hesitates before adding something that wasn't written on the card. Maybe because he thought Effie might make him remove it. "It can in no way replace your losses, but as a token of our thanks we'd like for each of the tributes' families from District Eleven to receive one month of our winnings every year for the duration of our lives."

The crowd can't help but respond with gasps and

murmurs. There is no precedent for what Peeta has done. I don't even know if it's legal. He probably doesn't know, either, so he didn't ask in case it isn't. As for the families, they just stare at us in shock. Their lives were changed for ever when Thresh and Rue were lost, but this gift will change them again. A month of tribute winnings can easily provide for a family for a year. As long as we live, they will not hunger.

I look at Peeta and he gives me a sad smile. I hear Haymitch's voice. "*You could do a lot worse.*" At this moment, it's impossible to imagine how I could do any better. The gift . . . it is perfect. So when I rise up on tiptoe to kiss him, it doesn't seem forced at all.

The mayor steps forward and presents us each with a plaque that's so large I have to put down my bouquet to hold it. The ceremony's about to end when I notice one of Rue's sisters staring at me. She must be about nine and is almost an exact replica of Rue, down to the way she stands with her arms slightly extended. Despite the good news about the winnings, she's not happy. In fact, her look is reproachful. Is it because I didn't save Rue?

No. It's because I still haven't thanked her, I think.

A wave of shame rushes through me. The girl is right. How can I stand here, passive and mute, leaving all the words to Peeta? If she had won, Rue would never have let my death go unsung. I remember how I took care in the arena to cover her with flowers, to make sure her loss did not go unnoticed. But that gesture will mean nothing if I don't support it now.

"Wait!" I stumble forward, pressing the plaque to my chest. My allotted time for speaking has come and gone, but I must say something. I owe too much. And even if I had pledged all my winnings to the families, it would not excuse my silence today. "Wait, please." I don't know how to start, but once I do, the words rush from my lips as if they've been forming in the back of my mind for a long time.

"I want to give my thanks to the tributes of District Eleven," I say. I look at the pair of women on Thresh's side. "I only ever spoke to Thresh one time. Just long enough for him to spare my life. I didn't know him, but I always respected him. For his power. For his refusal to play the Games on anyone's terms but his own. The Careers wanted him to team up with them from the beginning, but he wouldn't do it. I respected him for that."

For the first time the old hunched woman – is she Thresh's grandmother? – raises her head and the trace of a smile plays on her lips.

The crowd has fallen silent now, so silent that I

wonder how they manage it. They must all be holding their breath.

I turn to Rue's family. "But I feel as if I did know Rue, and she'll always be with me. Everything beautiful brings her to mind. I see her in the yellow flowers that grow in the Meadow by my house. I see her in the mockingjays that sing in the trees. But most of all, I see her in my sister, Prim." My voice is undependable, but I am almost finished. "Thank you for your children." I raise my chin to address the crowd. "And thank you all for the bread."

I stand there, feeling broken and small, thousands of eyes trained on me. There's a long pause. Then, from somewhere in the crowd, someone whistles Rue's four-note mockingjay tune. The one that signalled the end of the workday in the orchards. The one that meant safety in the arena. By the end of the tune, I have found the whistler, a wizened old man in a faded red shirt and overalls. His eyes meet mine.

What happens next is not an accident. It is too well executed to be spontaneous, because it happens in complete unison. Every person in the crowd presses the three middle fingers of their left hand against their lips and extends them to me. It's our sign from District 12, the last goodbye I gave Rue in the arena.

If I hadn't spoken to President Snow, this gesture might move me to tears. But with his recent orders to calm the districts fresh in my ears, it fills me with dread. What will he think of this very public salute to the girl who defied the Capitol?

The full impact of what I've done hits me. It was not intentional – I only meant to express my thanks – but I have elicited something dangerous. An act of dissent from the people of District 11. This is exactly the kind of thing I am supposed to be defusing!

I try to think of something to say to undermine what has just happened, to negate it, but I can hear the slight burst of static indicating my microphone has been cut off and the mayor has taken over. Peeta and I acknowledge a final round of applause. He leads me back towards the doors, unaware that anything has gone wrong.

I feel funny and have to stop for a moment. Little bits of bright sunshine dance before my eyes. "Are you all right?" Peeta asks.

"Just dizzy. The sun was so bright," I say. I see his bouquet. "I forgot my flowers," I mumble.

"I'll get them," he says.

"I can," I answer.

We would be safe inside the Justice Building by now, if I hadn't stopped, if I hadn't left my flowers.

Instead, from the deep shade of the veranda, we see the whole thing.

A pair of Peacekeepers dragging the old man who whistled to the top of the steps. Forcing him to his knees before the crowd. And putting a bullet through his head.

5

The man has only just crumpled to the ground when a wall of white Peacekeeper uniforms blocks our view. Several of the soldiers have automatic weapons held lengthwise as they push us back towards the door.

"We're going!" says Peeta, shoving the Peacekeeper who's pressing on me. "We get it, all right? Come on, Katniss." His arm encircles me and guides me back into the Justice Building. The Peacekeepers follow a pace or two behind us. The moment we're inside, the doors slam shut and we hear the Peacekeepers' boots moving back towards the crowd.

Haymitch, Effie, Portia and Cinna wait under a static-filled screen that's mounted on the wall, their faces tight with anxiety.

"What happened?" Effie hurries over. "We lost the feed just after Katniss's beautiful speech, and then

Haymitch said he thought he heard a gun fire, and I said it was ridiculous, but who knows? There are lunatics everywhere!"

"Nothing happened, Effie. An old truck backfired," says Peeta evenly.

Two more shots. The door doesn't muffle their sound much. Who was that? Thresh's grandmother? One of Rue's little sisters?

"Both of you. With me," says Haymitch. Peeta and I follow him, leaving the others behind. The Peacekeepers who are stationed around the Justice Building take little interest in our movements now that we are safely inside. We ascend a magnificent curved marble staircase. At the top, there's a long hall with worn carpet on the floor. Double doors stand open, welcoming us into the first room we encounter. The ceiling must be six metres high. Designs of fruit and flowers are carved into the moulding and small, fat children with wings look down at us from every angle. Vases of blossoms give off a cloying scent that makes my eyes itch. Our evening clothes hang on racks against the wall. This room has been prepared for our use, but we're barely there long enough to drop off our gifts. Then Haymitch yanks the microphones from our chests, stuffs them beneath a sofa cushion, and waves us on.

As far as I know, Haymitch has only been here once, when he was on his Victory Tour decades ago. But he must have a remarkable memory or reliable instincts, because he leads us up through a maze of twisting staircases and increasingly narrow halls. At times he has to stop and force a door. By the protesting squeak of the hinges you can tell it's been a long time since it was opened. Eventually we climb a ladder to a trapdoor. When Haymitch pushes it aside, we find ourselves in the dome of the Justice Building. It's a huge place filled with broken furniture, piles of books and ledgers, and rusty weapons. The coat of dust blanketing everything is so thick it's clear it hasn't been disturbed for years. Light struggles to filter in through four grimy square windows set in the sides of the dome. Haymitch kicks the trapdoor shut and turns on us.

"What happened?" he asks.

Peeta relates all that occurred in the square. The whistle, the salute, our hesitation on the veranda, the murder of the old man. "What's going on, Haymitch?"

"It will be better coming from you," Haymitch says to me.

I don't agree. I think it will be a hundred times worse coming from me. But I tell Peeta everything as calmly as I can. About President Snow, the unrest in the districts. I don't even omit the kiss with Gale. I lay out how we are all in jeopardy, how the whole country is in jeopardy because of my trick with the berries. "I was supposed to fix things on this tour. Make everyone who had doubted believe I acted out of love. Calm things down. But obviously, all I've done today is get three people killed, and now everyone in the square will be punished." I feel so sick that I have to sit down on a sofa, despite the exposed springs and stuffing.

"Then I made things worse, too. By giving the money," says Peeta. Suddenly he strikes out at a lamp that sits precariously on a crate and knocks it across the room, where it shatters against the floor. "This has to stop. Right now. This – this – game you two play, where you tell each other secrets but keep them from me like I'm too inconsequential or stupid or weak to handle them."

"It's not like that, Peeta—" I begin.

"It's exactly like that!" he yells at me. "I have people I care about, too, Katniss! Family and friends back in District Twelve who will be just as dead as yours if we don't pull this thing off. So, after all we went through in the arena, don't I even rate the truth from you?"

"You're always so reliably good, Peeta," says

Haymitch. "So smart about how you present yourself before the cameras. I didn't want to disrupt that."

"Well, you overestimated me. Because I really screwed up today. What do you think is going to happen to Rue's and Thresh's families? Do you think they'll get their share of our winnings? Do you think I gave them a bright future? Because I think they'll be lucky if they survive the day!" Peeta sends something else flying, a statue. I've never seen him like this.

"He's right, Haymitch," I say. "We were wrong not to tell him. Even back in the Capitol."

"Even in the arena, you two had some sort of system worked out, didn't you?" asks Peeta. His voice is quieter now. "Something I wasn't part of."

"No. Not officially. I just could tell what Haymitch wanted me to do by what he sent, or didn't send," I say.

"Well, I never had that opportunity. Because he never sent me anything until you showed up," says Peeta.

I haven't thought much about this. How it must have looked from Peeta's perspective when I appeared in the arena having received burn medicine and bread when he, who was at death's door, had got nothing. Like Haymitch was keeping me alive at his expense.

"Look, boy—" Haymitch begins.

"Don't bother, Haymitch. I know you had to choose one of us. And I'd have wanted it to be her. But this is something different. People are dead out there. More will follow unless we're very good. We all know I'm better than Katniss in front of the cameras. No one needs to coach me on what to say. But I have to know what I'm walking into," says Peeta.

"From now on, you'll be fully informed," Haymitch promises.

"I better be," says Peeta. He doesn't even bother to look at me before he leaves.

The dust he disrupted billows up and looks for new places to land. My hair, my eyes, my shiny gold pin.

"Did you choose me, Haymitch?" I ask.

"Yeah," he says.

"Why? You like him better," I say.

"That's true. But remember, until they changed the rules, I could only hope to get one of you out of there alive," he says. "I thought since he was determined to protect you, well, between the three of us, we might be able to bring you home."

"Oh" is all I can think to say.

"You'll see, the choices you'll have to make. If we survive this," says Haymitch. "You'll learn."

Well, I've learned one thing today. This place is not a larger version of District 12. Our fence is unguarded and rarely charged. Our Peacekeepers are unwelcome but less brutal. Our hardships evoke more fatigue than fury. Here in 11, they suffer more acutely and feel more desperation. President Snow is right. A spark could be enough to set them ablaze.

Everything is happening too fast for me to process it. The warning, the shootings, the recognition that I may have set something of great consequence in motion. The whole thing is so improbable. And it would be one thing if I had planned to stir things up, but given the circumstances . . . how on earth did I cause so much trouble?

"Come on. We've got a dinner to attend," says Haymitch.

I stand in the shower as long as they let me before I have to come out to be readied. The prep team seems oblivious to the events of the day. They're all excited about the dinner. In the districts they're important enough to attend, whereas back in the Capitol they almost never score invitations to prestigious parties. While they try to predict what dishes will be served, I keep seeing the old man's head being blown off. I don't even pay attention to what anyone is doing to me until I'm about to leave and I see myself in the mirror. A pale pink strapless dress brushes my shoes. My hair is pinned back from my face and falling down my back in a shower of ringlets.

Cinna comes up behind me and arranges a shimmering silver wrap around my shoulders. He catches my eye in the mirror. "Like it?"

"It's beautiful. As always," I say.

"Let's see how it looks with a smile," he says gently. It's his reminder that in a minute, there will be cameras again. I manage to raise the corners of my lips. "There we go."

When we all assemble to go down to the dinner, I can see Effie is out of sorts. Surely, Haymitch hasn't told her about what happened in the square. I wouldn't be surprised if Cinna and Portia know, but there seems to be an unspoken agreement to leave Effie out of the bad-news loop. It doesn't take long to hear about the problem, though.

Effie runs through the evening's schedule, then tosses it aside. "And then, thank goodness, we can all get on that train and get out of here," she says.

"Is something wrong, Effie?" asks Cinna.

"I don't like the way we've been treated. Being stuffed into trucks and barred from the platform. And then, about an hour ago, I decided to look around the Justice Building. I'm something of an expert in architectural design, you know," she says.

"Oh, yes, I've heard that," says Portia before the pause gets too long.

"So, I was just having a peek around because district ruins are going to be all the rage this year, when two Peacemakers showed up and ordered me back to our quarters. One of them actually poked me with her gun!" says Effie.

I can't help thinking this is the direct result of Haymitch, Peeta and me disappearing earlier in the day. It's a little reassuring, actually, to think that Haymitch might have been right. That no one would have been monitoring the dusty dome where we talked. Although I bet they are now.

Effie looks so distressed that I spontaneously give her a hug. "That's awful, Effie. Maybe we shouldn't go to the dinner at all. At least until they've apologized." I know she'll never agree to this, but she brightens considerably at the suggestion, at the validation of her complaint.

"No, I'll manage. It's part of my job to weather the ups and downs. And we can't let you two miss your dinner," she says. "But thank you for the offer, Katniss."

Effie arranges us in formation for our entrance. First the prep teams, then her, the stylists, Haymitch. Peeta and I, of course, bring up the rear.

Somewhere below, musicians begin to play. As the first wave of our little procession begins down the steps, Peeta and I join hands.

"Haymitch says I was wrong to yell at you. You were only operating under his instructions," says Peeta. "And it isn't as if I haven't kept things from you in the past."

I remember the shock of hearing Peeta confess his love for me in front of all of Panem. Haymitch had known about that and not told me. "I think I broke a few things myself after that interview."

"Just an urn," he says.

"And your hands. There's no point to it any more, though, is there? Not being straight with each other?" I say.

"No point," says Peeta. We stand at the top of the stairs, giving Haymitch a fifteen-step lead as Effie directed. "Was that really the only time you kissed Gale?"

I'm so startled I answer. "Yes." With all that has happened today, has that question actually been preying on him?

"That's fifteen. Let's do it," he says.

A light hits us, and I put on the most dazzling smile I can.

We descend the steps and are sucked into what

becomes an indistinguishable round of dinners, ceremonies and train rides. Each day it's the same. Wake up. Get dressed. Ride through cheering crowds. Listen to a speech in our honour. Give a thank-you speech in return, but only the one the Capitol gave us, never any personal additions now. Sometimes a brief tour: a glimpse of the sea in one district, towering forests in another, ugly factories, fields of wheat, stinking refineries. Dress in evening clothes. Attend dinner. Train.

During ceremonies, we are solemn and respectful but always linked together, by our hands, our arms. At dinners, we are borderline delirious in our love for each other. We kiss, we dance, we get caught trying to sneak away to be alone. On the train, we are quietly miserable as we try to assess what effect we might be having.

Even without our personal speeches to trigger dissent – needless to say, the ones we gave in District 11 were edited out before the event was broadcast – you can feel something in the air, the rolling boil of a pot about to run over. Not everywhere. Some crowds have the weary-cattle feel that I know District 12 usually projects at the victors' ceremonies. But in others – particularly 8, 4 and 3 – there is genuine elation in the faces of the people at the sight of us, and under the elation, fury. When they chant my name, it is more of a cry for vengeance than a cheer. When the Peacekeepers move in to quiet an unruly crowd, it presses back instead of retreating. And I know that there's nothing I could ever do to change this. No show of love, however believable, will turn this tide. If my holding out those berries was an act of temporary insanity, then these people will embrace insanity, too.

Cinna begins to take in my clothes around the waist. The prep team frets over the circles under my eyes. Effie starts giving me pills to sleep, but they don't work. Not well enough. I drift off only to be roused by nightmares that have increased in number and intensity. Peeta, who spends much of the night roaming the train, hears me screaming as I struggle to break out of the haze of drugs that merely prolong the horrible dreams. He manages to wake me and calm me down. Then he climbs into bed to hold me until I fall back to sleep. After that, I refuse the pills. But every night I let him into my bed. We manage the darkness as we did in the arena, wrapped in each other's arms, guarding against dangers that can descend at any moment. Nothing else happens, but our arrangement quickly becomes a subject of gossip on the train.

When Effie brings it up to me, I think, *Good.*

Maybe it will get back to President Snow. I tell her we'll make an effort to be more discreet, but we don't.

The back-to-back appearances in 2 and 1 are their own special kind of awful. Cato and Clove, the tributes from District 2, might have both made it home if Peeta and I hadn't. I personally killed the girl, Glimmer, and the boy from District 1. As I try to avoid looking at his family, I learn that his name was Marvel. How did I never know that? I suppose that before the Games I didn't pay attention, and afterwards I didn't want to know.

By the time we reach the Capitol, we are desperate. We make endless appearances to adoring crowds. There is no danger of an uprising here among the privileged, among those whose names are never placed in the reaping balls, whose children never die for the supposed crimes committed generations ago. We don't need to convince anybody in the Capitol of our love but hold to the slim hope that we can still reach some of those we failed to convince in the districts. Whatever we do seems too little, too late.

Back in our old quarters in the Training Centre, I'm the one who suggests the public marriage proposal. Peeta agrees to do it but then disappears to his room for a long time. Haymitch tells me to leave him alone.

"I thought he wanted it, anyway," I say.

"Not like this," Haymitch says. "He wanted it to be real."

I go back to my room and lie under the covers, trying not to think of Gale and thinking of nothing else.

That night, on the stage before the Training Centre, we bubble our way through a list of questions. Caesar Flickerman, in his twinkling midnight-blue suit, his hair, eyelids and lips still dyed powder blue, flawlessly guides us through the interview. When he asks us about the future, Peeta gets down on one knee, pours out his heart, and begs me to marry him. I, of course, accept. Caesar is beside himself, the Capitol audience is hysterical, shots of crowds around Panem show a country besotted with happiness.

President Snow himself makes a surprise visit to congratulate us. He clasps Peeta's hand and gives him an approving slap on the shoulder. He embraces me, enfolding me in the smell of blood and roses, and plants a puffy kiss on my cheek. When he pulls back, his fingers digging into my arms, his face smiling into mine, I dare to raise my eyebrows. They ask what my lips can't. *Did I do it? Was it enough? Was giving everything over to you, keeping up the game, promising to marry Peeta enough?*

In answer, he gives an almost imperceptible shake of his head.

6

In that one slight motion, I see the end of hope, the beginning of the destruction of everything I hold dear in the world. I can't guess what form my punishment will take, how wide the net will be cast, but when it is finished, there will most likely be nothing left. So you would think that at this moment, I would be in utter despair. Here's what's strange. The main thing I feel is a sense of relief. That I can give up this game. That the question of whether I can succeed in this venture has been answered, even if that answer is a resounding no. That if desperate times call for desperate measures, then I am free to act as desperately as I wish.

Only not here, not quite yet. It's essential to get back to District 12, because the main part of any plan will include my mother and sister, Gale and his family. And Peeta, if I can get him to come with us. I add

Haymitch to the list. These are the people I must take with me when I escape into the wild. How I will convince them, where we will go in the dead of winter, what it will take to evade capture are unanswered questions. But at least now I know what I must do.

So instead of crumpling to the ground and weeping, I find myself standing up straighter and with more confidence than I have in weeks. My smile, while somewhat insane, is not forced. And when President Snow silences the audience and says, "What do you think about us throwing them a wedding right here in the Capitol?" I pull off girl-almost-catatonic-with-joy without a hitch.

Caesar Flickerman asks if the president has a date in mind.

"Oh, before we set a date, we better clear it with Katniss's mother," says the president. The audience gives a big laugh and the president puts his arm around me. "Maybe if the whole country puts its mind to it, we can get you married before you're thirty."

"You'll probably have to pass a new law," I say with a giggle.

"If that's what it takes," says the president with conspiratorial good humour.

Oh, the fun we two have together.

The party, held in the banquet room of President Snow's mansion, has no equal. The twelve-metre ceiling has been transformed into the night sky, and the stars look exactly as they do at home. I suppose they look the same from the Capitol, but who would know? There's always too much light from the city to see the stars here. About halfway between the floor and the ceiling, musicians float on what look like fluffy white clouds, but I can't see what holds them aloft. Traditional dining tables have been replaced by innumerable stuffed sofas and chairs, some surrounding fireplaces, others beside fragrant flower gardens or ponds filled with exotic fish, so that people can eat and drink and do whatever they please in the utmost comfort. There's a large tiled area in the centre of the room that serves as everything from a dance floor, to a stage for the performers who come and go, to another spot to mingle with the flamboyantly dressed guests.

But the real star of the evening is the food. Tables laden with delicacies line the walls. Everything you can think of, and things you have never dreamed of, lie in wait. Whole roasted cows and pigs and goats still turning on spits. Huge platters of fowl stuffed with savoury fruits and nuts. Ocean creatures drizzled in sauces or begging to be dipped in spicy concoctions.

Countless cheeses, breads, vegetables, sweets, waterfalls of wine and streams of spirits that flicker with flames.

My appetite has returned with my desire to fight back. After weeks of feeling too worried to eat, I'm famished.

"I want to taste everything in the room," I tell Peeta.

I can see him trying to read my expression, to figure out my transformation. Since he doesn't know that President Snow thinks I have failed, he can only assume that I think we have succeeded. Perhaps even that I have some genuine happiness at our engagement. His eyes reflect his puzzlement but only briefly, because we're on camera. "Then you'd better pace yourself," he says.

"OK, no more than one bite of each dish," I say. My resolve is almost immediately broken at the first table, which has twenty or so soups, when I encounter a creamy pumpkin brew sprinkled with slivered nuts and tiny black seeds. "I could just eat this all night!" I exclaim. But I don't. I weaken again at a clear green broth that I can only describe as tasting like spring time, and again when I try a frothy pink soup dotted with raspberries.

Faces appear, names are exchanged, pictures taken, kisses brushed on cheeks. Apparently my mockingjay pin has spawned a new fashion sensation, because several people come up to show me their accessories. My bird has been replicated on belt buckles, embroidered into silk lapels, even tattooed in intimate places. Everyone wants to wear the winner's token. I can only imagine how nuts that makes President Snow. But what can he do? The Games were such a hit here, where the berries were only a symbol of a desperate girl trying to save her lover.

Peeta and I make no effort to find company but are constantly sought out. We are what no one wants to miss at the party. I act delighted, but I have zero interest in these Capitol people. They are only distractions from the food.

Every table presents new temptations, and even on my restricted one-taste-per-dish regimen, I begin filling up quickly. I pick up a small roasted bird, bite into it, and my tongue floods with orange sauce. Delicious. But I make Peeta eat the remainder because I want to keep tasting things, and the idea of throwing away food, as I see so many people doing so casually, is abhorrent to me. After about ten tables I'm stuffed, and we've only sampled a small number of the dishes available.

Just then my prep team descends on us. They're nearly incoherent between the alcohol they've consumed and their ecstasy at being at such a grand affair.

"Why aren't you eating?" asks Octavia.

"I have been, but I can't hold another bite," I say. They all laugh as if that's the silliest thing they've ever heard.

"No one lets that stop them!" says Flavius. They lead us over to a table that holds tiny stemmed wine glasses filled with clear liquid. "Drink this!"

Peeta picks one up to take a sip and they lose it.

"Not here!" shrieks Octavia.

"You have to do it in there," says Venia, pointing to doors that lead to the toilets. "Or you'll get it all over the floor!"

Peeta looks at the glass again and puts it together. "You mean this will make me puke?"

My prep team laughs hysterically. "Of course, so you can keep eating," says Octavia. "I've been in there twice already. Everyone does it, or else how would you have any fun at a feast?"

I'm speechless, staring at the pretty little glasses and all they imply. Peeta sets his back on the table with such precision you'd think it might detonate. "Come on, Katniss, let's dance."

Music filters down from the clouds as he leads me away from the team, the table, and out on to the floor.

We know only a few dances at home, the kind that go with fiddle and flute music and require a good deal of space. But Effie has shown us some that are popular in the Capitol. The music's slow and dreamlike, so Peeta pulls me into his arms and we move in a circle with practically no steps at all. You could do this dance on a pie plate. We're quiet for a while. Then Peeta speaks in a strained voice.

"You go along, thinking you can deal with it, thinking maybe they're not so bad, and then you—" He cuts himself off.

All I can think of is the emaciated bodies of the children on our kitchen table as my mother prescribes what the parents can't give. More food. Now that we're rich, she'll send some home with them. But often in the old days, there was nothing to give and the child was past saving, anyway. And here in the Capitol they're vomiting for the pleasure of filling their bellies again and again. Not from some illness of body or mind, not from spoiled food. It's what everyone does at a party. Expected. Part of the fun.

One day when I dropped by to give Hazelle the game, Vick was home sick with a bad cough. Being part of Gale's family, the kid has to eat better than ninety per cent of the rest of District 12. But he still spent about fifteen minutes talking about how they'd opened a can of corn syrup from Parcel Day and each had a spoonful on bread and were going to maybe have more later in the week. How Hazelle had said he could have a bit in a cup of tea to soothe his cough, but he wouldn't feel right unless the others had some, too. If it's like that at Gale's, what's it like in the other houses?

"Peeta, they bring us here to fight to the death for their entertainment," I say. "Really, this is nothing by comparison."

"I know. I know that. It's just sometimes I can't stand it any more. To the point where . . . I'm not sure what I'll do." He pauses, then whispers, "Maybe we were wrong, Katniss."

"About what?" I ask.

"About trying to subdue things in the districts," he says.

My head turns swiftly from side to side, but no one seems to have heard. The camera crew got sidetracked at a table of shellfish, and the couples dancing around us are either too drunk or too self-involved to notice.

"Sorry," he says. He should be. This is no place to be voicing such thoughts.

"Save it for home," I tell him.

Just then Portia appears with a large man who looks vaguely familiar. She introduces him as Plutarch

Heavensbee, the new Head Gamemaker. Plutarch asks Peeta if he can steal me for a dance. Peeta's recovered his camera face and good-naturedly passes me over, warning the man not to get too attached.

I don't want to dance with Plutarch Heavensbee. I don't want to feel his hands, one resting against mine, one on my hip. I'm not used to being touched, except by Peeta or my family, and I rank Gamemakers somewhere below maggots in terms of creatures I want in contact with my skin. But he seems to sense this and holds me almost at arm's length as we turn on the floor.

We chit-chat about the party, about the entertainment, about the food, and then he makes a joke about avoiding punch since training. I don't get it, and then I realize he's the man who tripped backwards into the punchbowl when I shot an arrow at the Gamemakers during the training session. Well, not really. I was shooting an apple out of their roast pig's mouth. But I made them jump.

"Oh, you're the one who—" I laugh, remembering him splashing back into the punchbowl.

"Yes. And you'll be pleased to know I've never recovered," says Plutarch.

I want to point out that twenty-two dead tributes will never recover from the Games he helped create, either. But I only say, "Good. So, you're the Head Gamemaker this year? That must be a big honour."

"Between you and me, there weren't many takers for the job," he says. "So much responsibility as to how the Games turn out."

Yeah, the last guy's dead, I think. He must know about Seneca Crane, but he doesn't look the least bit concerned. "Are you planning the Quarter Quell Games already?" I say.

"Oh, yes. Well, they've been in the works for years, of course. Arenas aren't built in a day. But the, shall we say, flavour of the Games is being determined now. Believe it or not, I've got a strategy meeting tonight," he says.

Plutarch steps back and pulls out a gold watch on a chain from a vest pocket. He flips open the lid, sees the time, and frowns. "I'll have to be going soon." He turns the watch so I can see the face. "It starts at midnight."

"That seems late for—" I say, but then something distracts me. Plutarch has run his thumb across the crystal face of the watch and for just a moment an image appears, glowing as if lit by candlelight. It's another mockingjay. Exactly like the pin on my dress. Only this one disappears. He snaps the watch closed.

"That's very pretty," I say.

"Oh, it's more than pretty. It's one of a kind," he says. "If anyone asks about me, say I've gone home to bed. The meetings are supposed to be kept secret. But I thought it'd be safe to tell you."

"Yes. Your secret's safe with me," I say.

As we shake hands, he gives a small bow, a common gesture here in the Capitol. "Well, I'll see you next summer at the Games, Katniss. Best wishes on your engagement, and good luck with your mother."

"I'll need it," I say.

Plutarch disappears and I wander through the crowd, looking for Peeta, as strangers congratulate me. On my engagement, on my victory at the Games, on my choice of lipstick. I respond, but really I'm thinking about Plutarch showing off his pretty, one-of-a-kind watch to me. There was something strange about it. Almost clandestine. But why? Maybe he thinks someone else will steal his idea of putting a disappearing mockingjay on a watch face. Yes, he probably paid a fortune for it and now he can't show it to anyone because he's afraid someone will make a cheap, knock-off version. Only in the Capitol.

I find Peeta admiring a table of elaborately decorated cakes. Bakers have come in from the kitchen especially to talk frosting with him, and you can see them tripping over one another to answer his questions. At his request, they assemble an assortment of little cakes for him to take back to District 12, where he can examine their work in quiet.

"Effie said we have to be on the train at one. I wonder what time it is," he says, glancing around.

"Almost midnight," I reply. I pluck a chocolate flower from a cake with my fingers and nibble on it, so beyond worrying about manners.

"Time to say thank you and farewell!" trills Effie at my elbow. It's one of those moments when I just love her compulsive punctuality. We collect Cinna and Portia, and she escorts us around to say goodbye to important people, then herds us to the door.

"Shouldn't we thank President Snow?" asks Peeta. "It's his house."

"Oh, he's not a big one for parties. Too busy," says Effie. "I've already arranged for the necessary notes and gifts to be sent to him tomorrow. There you are!" Effie gives a little wave to two Capitol attendants who have an inebriated Haymitch propped up between them.

We travel through the streets of the Capitol in a car with darkened windows. Behind us, another car brings the prep teams. The throngs of people celebrating are so thick it's slow going. But Effie has this all down to a science, and at exactly one o'clock we are back on the train and it's pulling out of the station.

Haymitch is deposited in his room. Cinna orders tea and we all take seats around the table while Effie rattles her schedule papers and reminds us we're still on tour. "There's the Harvest Festival in District Twelve to think about. So I suggest we drink our tea and head straight to bed." No one argues.

When I open my eyes, it's early afternoon. My head rests on Peeta's arm. I don't remember him coming in last night. I turn, being careful not to disturb him, but he's already awake.

"No nightmares," he says.

"What?" I ask.

"You didn't have any nightmares last night," he says.

He's right. For the first time in ages I've slept through the night. "I had a dream, though," I say, thinking back. "I was following a mockingjay through the woods. For a long time. It was Rue, really. I mean, when it sang, it had her voice."

"Where did she take you?" he says, brushing my hair off my forehead.

"I don't know. We never arrived," I say. "But I felt happy."

"Well, you slept like you were happy," he says.

"Peeta, how come I never know when you're having a nightmare?" I say.

"I don't know. I don't think I cry out or thrash around or anything. I just come to, paralysed with terror," he says.

"You should wake me," I say, thinking about how I can interrupt his sleep two or three times on a bad night. About how long it can take to calm me down.

"It's not necessary. My nightmares are usually about losing you," he says. "I'm OK once I realize you're here."

Ugh. Peeta makes comments like this in such an offhand way, and it's like being hit in the gut. He's only answering my question honestly. He's not pressing me to reply in kind, to make any declaration of love. But I still feel awful, as if I've been using him in some terrible way. Have I? I don't know. I only know that for the first time, I feel immoral about him being here in my bed. Which is ironic since we're officially engaged now.

"Be worse when we're home and I'm sleeping alone again," he says.

That's right, we're almost home.

The agenda for District 12 includes a dinner at Mayor Undersee's house tonight and a victory rally in the square during the Harvest Festival tomorrow. We always celebrate the Harvest Festival on the final day of the Victory Tour, but usually it means a meal at home or with a few friends if you can afford it. This year it will be a public affair, and since the Capitol will be throwing it, everyone in the whole district will have full bellies.

Most of our prepping will take place at the mayor's house, since we're back to being covered in furs for outdoor appearances. We're only at the train station briefly, to smile and wave as we pile into our car. We don't even get to see our families until the dinner tonight.

I'm glad it will be at the mayor's house instead of at the Justice Building, where the memorial for my father was held, where they took me after the reaping for those wrenching goodbyes to my family. The Justice Building is too full of sadness.

But I like Mayor Undersee's house, especially now that his daughter, Madge, and I are friends. We always were, in a way. It became official when she came to say goodbye to me before I left for the Games. When she gave me the mockingjay pin for luck. After I got home, we started spending time together. It turns out Madge has plenty of empty hours to fill, too. It was a little awkward at first because we didn't know what to do. Other girls our age, I've heard them talking about boys, or other girls, or clothes. Madge and I aren't gossipy and clothes bore me to tears. But after a few false starts, I realized she was dying to go into the woods, so I've taken her a couple of times and showed her how to shoot. She's trying to teach me the piano, but mostly I like to listen to her play. Sometimes we eat at each other's houses. Madge likes mine better. Her parents seem nice but I don't think she sees a whole lot of them. Her father has District 12 to run and her mother gets fierce headaches that force her to stay in bed for days.

"Maybe you should take her to the Capitol," I said during one of them. We weren't playing the piano that day, because even two floors away the sound caused her mother pain. "They can fix her up, I bet."

"Yes. But you don't go to the Capitol unless they invite you," said Madge unhappily. Even the mayor's privileges are limited.

When we reach the mayor's house, I only have time to give Madge a quick hug before Effie hustles me off to the third floor to get ready. After I'm prepped and dressed in a full-length silver gown, I've still got an hour to kill before the dinner, so I slip off to find her.

Madge's bedroom is on the second floor along with several guest rooms and her father's study. I stick my head in the study to say hello to the mayor but it's empty. The television's droning on, and I stop to watch shots of Peeta and me at the Capitol party last night. Dancing, eating, kissing. This will be playing in every household in Panem right now. The audience must be sick to death of the star-crossed lovers from District 12. I know I am.

I'm leaving the room when a beeping noise catches my attention. I turn back to see the screen of the television go black. Then the words "UPDATE ON DISTRICT 8" start flashing. Instinctively I know this is not for my eyes but something intended only for the mayor. I should go. Quickly. Instead I find myself stepping closer to the television.

An announcer I've never seen before appears. It's a woman with greying hair and a hoarse, authoritative voice. She warns that conditions are worsening and a Level 3 alert has been called. Additional forces are being sent into District 8, and all textile production has ceased.

They cut away from the woman to the main square in District 8. I recognize it because I was there only last week. There are still banners with my face waving from the rooftops. Below them, there's a mob scene. The square's packed with screaming people, their faces hidden with rags and home-made masks, throwing bricks. Buildings burn. Peacekeepers shoot into the crowd, killing at random.

I've never seen anything like it, but I can only be witnessing one thing. This is what President Snow calls an uprising.

7

A leather bag filled with food and a flask of hot tea. A pair of fur-lined gloves that Cinna left behind. Three twigs, broken from the naked trees, lying in the snow, pointing in the direction I will travel. This is what I leave for Gale at our usual meeting place on the first Sunday after the Harvest Festival.

I have continued on through the cold, misty woods, breaking a path that will be unfamiliar to Gale but is simple for my feet to find. It leads to the lake. I no longer trust that our regular rendezvous spot offers privacy, and I'll need that and more to spill my guts to Gale today. But will he even come? If he doesn't, I'll have no choice but to risk going to his house in the dead of night. There are things he has to know . . . things I need him to help me figure out. . .

Once the implications of what I was seeing on Mayor Undersee's television hit me, I made for the door and started down the hall. Just in time, too, because the mayor came up the steps moments later. I gave him a wave.

"Looking for Madge?" he said in a friendly tone.

"Yes. I want to show her my dress," I said.

"Well, you know where to find her." Just then, another round of beeping came from his study. His face turned grave. "Excuse me," he said. He went into his study and closed the door tightly.

I waited in the hall until I had composed myself. Reminded myself I must act naturally. Then I found Madge in her room, sitting at her dressing table, brushing out her wavy blonde hair before a mirror. She was in the same pretty white dress she'd worn on reaping day. She saw my reflection behind her and smiled. "Look at you. Like you came right off the streets of the Capitol."

I stepped in closer. My fingers touched the mockingjay. "Even my pin now. Mockingjays are all the rage in the Capitol, thanks to you. Are you sure you don't want it back?" I asked.

"Don't be silly, it was a gift," said Madge. She tied back her hair in a festive gold ribbon.

"Where did you get it, anyway?" I asked.

"It was my aunt's," she said. "But I think it's been in the family a long time."

"It's a funny choice, a mockingjay," I said. "I mean, because of what happened in the rebellion. With the jabberjays backfiring on the Capitol and all."

The jabberjays were muttations, genetically enhanced male birds created by the Capitol as weapons to spy on rebels in the districts. They could remember and repeat long passages of human speech, so they were sent into rebel areas to capture our words and return them to the Capitol. The rebels caught on and turned them against the Capitol by sending them home loaded with lies. When this was discovered, the jabberjays were left to die. In a few years, they became extinct in the wild, but not before they had mated with female mockingbirds, creating an entirely new species.

"But mockingjays were never a weapon," said Madge. "They're just songbirds. Right?"

"Yeah, I guess so," I said. But it's not true. A mockingbird is just a songbird. A mockingjay is a creature the Capitol never intended to exist. They hadn't counted on the highly controlled jabberjay having the brains to adapt to the wild, to pass on its genetic code, to thrive in a new form. They hadn't anticipated its will to live.

Now, as I trudge through the snow, I see the mockingjays hopping about on branches as they pick up on other birds' melodies, replicate them, and then transform them into something new. As always, they remind me of Rue. I think of the dream I had the last night on the train, where I followed her in mockingjay form. I wish I could have stayed asleep just a bit longer and found out where she was trying to take me.

It's a hike to the lake, no question. If he decides to follow me at all, Gale's going to be put out by this excessive use of energy that could be better spent in hunting. He was conspicuously absent from the dinner at the mayor's house, although the rest of his family came. Hazelle said he was home sick, which was an obvious lie. I couldn't find him at the Harvest Festival, either. Vick told me he was out hunting. That was probably true.

After a couple of hours, I reach an old house near the edge of the lake. Maybe "house" is too big a word for it. It's only one room, about four metres square. My father thought that a long time ago there were a lot of buildings – you can still see some of the foundations – and people came to them to play and fish in the lake. This house outlasted the others because it's made of concrete. Floor, roof, ceiling. Only one of four glass windows remains, wavy and yellowed by time. There's no plumbing and no electricity, but the fireplace still works and there's a woodpile in the corner that my father and I collected years ago. I start a small fire, counting on the mist to obscure any telltale smoke. While the fire catches, I sweep out the snow that has accumulated under the empty windows, using a twig broom my father made me when I was about eight and I played house here. Then I sit on the tiny concrete hearth, thawing out by the fire and waiting for Gale.

It's a surprisingly short time before he appears. A bow slung over his shoulder, a dead wild turkey he must have encountered along the way hanging from his belt. He stands in the doorway as if considering whether or not to enter. He holds the unopened leather bag of food, the flask, Cinna's gloves. Gifts he will not accept because of his anger at me. I know exactly how he feels. Didn't I do the same thing to my mother?

I look in his eyes. His temper can't quite mask the hurt, the sense of betrayal he feels at my engagement to Peeta. This will be my last chance, this meeting today, to not lose Gale for ever. I could take hours trying to explain, and even then have him refuse me. Instead I go straight to the heart of my defence.

"President Snow personally threatened to have you killed," I say.

Gale raises his eyebrows slightly, but there's no real show of fear or astonishment. "Anyone else?"

"Well, he didn't actually give me a copy of the list. But it's a good guess it includes both our families," I say.

It's enough to bring him to the fire. He crouches before the hearth and warms himself. "Unless what?"

"Unless nothing, now," I say. Obviously this requires more of an explanation, but I have no idea where to start, so I just sit there staring gloomily into the fire.

After about a minute of this, Gale breaks the silence. "Well, thanks for the heads-up."

I turn to him, ready to snap, but I catch the glint in his eye. I hate myself for smiling. This is not a funny moment, but I guess it's a lot to drop on someone. We're all going to be obliterated no matter what. "I do have a plan, you know."

"Yeah, I bet it's a stunner," he says. He tosses the gloves on my lap. "Here. I don't want your fiancé's old gloves."

"He's not my fiancé. That's just part of the act. And these aren't his gloves. They were Cinna's," I say.

"Give them back, then," he says. He pulls on the gloves, flexes his fingers, and nods in approval. "At least I'll die in comfort."

"That's optimistic. Of course, you don't know what's happened," I say.

"Let's have it," he says.

I decide to begin with the night Peeta and I were crowned victors of the Hunger Games, and Haymitch warned me of the Capitol's fury. I tell him about the uneasiness that dogged me even once I was back home, President Snow's visit to my house, the murders in District 11, the tension in the crowds, the last-ditch effort of the engagement, the president's indication that it hadn't been enough, my certainty that I'll have to pay.

Gale never interrupts. While I talk, he tucks the gloves in his pocket and occupies himself with turning the food in the leather bag into a meal for us. Toasting bread and cheese, coring apples, placing chestnuts in the fire to roast. I watch his hands, his beautiful, capable fingers. Scarred, as mine were before the Capitol erased all marks from my skin, but strong and deft. Hands that have the power to mine coal but the precision to set a delicate snare. Hands I trust.

I pause to take a drink of tea from the flask before I tell him about my homecoming.

"Well, you really made a mess of things," he says.

"I'm not even done," I tell him.

"I've heard enough for the moment. Let's skip ahead to this plan of yours," he says.

I take a deep breath. "We run away."

"What?" he asks. This has actually caught him off guard.

"We take to the woods and make a run for it," I say. His face is impossible to read. Will he laugh at me, dismiss this as foolishness? I rise in agitation, preparing for an argument. "You said yourself you thought that we could do it! That morning of the reaping. You said—"

He steps in and I feel myself lifted off the ground. The room spins, and I have to lock my arms around Gale's neck to brace myself. He's laughing, happy.

"Hey!" I protest, but I'm laughing, too.

Gale sets me down but doesn't release his hold on me. "OK, let's run away," he says.

"Really? You don't think I'm mad? You'll go with me?" Some of the crushing weight begins to lift as it transfers to Gale's shoulders.

"I *do* think you're mad and I'll *still* go with you," he says. He means it. Not only means it but welcomes it. "We can do it. I know we can. Let's get out of here and never come back!"

"You're sure?" I say. "Because it's going to be hard, with the kids and all. I don't want to get five miles into the woods and have you—"

"I'm sure. I'm completely, entirely, one hundred per cent sure." He tilts his forehead down to rest against mine and pulls me closer. His skin, his whole being, radiates heat from being so near the fire, and I close my eyes, soaking in his warmth. I breathe in the smell of snow-dampened leather and smoke and apples, the smell of all those wintry days we shared before the Games. I don't try to move away. Why should I, anyway? His voice drops to a whisper. "I love you."

That's why.

I never see these things coming. They happen too fast. One second you're proposing an escape plan and the next . . . you're expected to deal with something like this. I come up with what must be the worst possible response. "I know."

It sounds terrible. Like I assume he couldn't help loving me but that I don't feel anything in return. Gale starts to draw away, but I grab hold of him. "I know! And you . . . you know what you are to me." It's not enough. He breaks my grip. "Gale, I can't think about anyone that way now. All I can think about, every day, every waking minute since they drew Prim's name at the reaping, is how afraid I am. And there doesn't seem to be room for anything else. If we could get somewhere safe, maybe I could be different. I don't know."

I can see him swallowing his disappointment. "So, we'll go. We'll find out." He turns back to the fire, where the chestnuts are beginning to burn. He flips them out on to the hearth. "My mother's going to take some convincing."

I guess he's still going, anyway. But the happiness has fled, leaving an all-too-familiar strain in its place. "Mine, too. I'll just have to make her see reason. Take her for a long walk. Make sure she understands we won't survive the alternative."

"She'll understand. I watched a lot of the Games with her and Prim. She won't say no to you," says Gale.

"I hope not." The temperature in the house seems to have dropped twenty degrees in a matter of seconds. "Haymitch will be the real challenge."

"Haymitch?" Gale abandons the chestnuts. "You're not asking him to come with us?"

"I have to, Gale. I can't leave him and Peeta because they'd—" His scowl cuts me off. "What?"

"I'm sorry. I didn't realize how large our party was," he snaps at me.

"They'd torture them to death, trying to find out where I was," I say.

"What about Peeta's family? They'll never come. In fact, they probably couldn't wait to inform on us.

Which I'm sure he's smart enough to realize. What if he decides to stay?" he asks.

I try to sound indifferent, but my voice cracks. "Then he stays."

"You'd leave him behind?" Gale asks.

"To save Prim and my mother, yes," I answer. "I mean, no! I'll get him to come."

"And me, would you leave me?" Gale's expression is rock hard now. "Just if, for instance, I can't convince my mother to drag three young kids into the wilderness in winter."

"Hazelle won't refuse. She'll see sense," I say.

"Suppose she doesn't, Katniss. What then?" he demands.

"Then you have to force her, Gale. Do you think I'm making this stuff up?" My voice is rising in anger as well.

"No. I don't know. Maybe the president's just manipulating you. I mean, he's throwing your wedding. You saw how the Capitol crowd reacted. I don't think he can afford to kill you. Or Peeta. How's he going to get out of that one?" says Gale.

"Well, with an uprising in District Eight, I doubt he's spending much time choosing my wedding cake!" I shout.

The instant the words are out of my mouth I want

to reclaim them. Their effect on Gale is immediate – the flush on his cheeks, the brightness of his grey eyes. "There's an uprising in Eight?" he says in a hushed voice.

I try to backpedal. To defuse him, as I tried to defuse the districts. "I don't know if it's really an uprising. There's unrest. People in the streets—" I say.

Gale grabs my shoulders. "What did you see?"

"Nothing! In person. I just heard something." As usual, it's too little, too late. I give up and tell him. "I saw something on the mayor's television. I wasn't supposed to. There was a crowd, and fires, and the Peacekeepers were gunning people down but they were fighting back. . ." I bite my lip and struggle to continue describing the scene. Instead I say aloud the words that have been eating me up inside. "And it's my fault, Gale. Because of what I did in the arena. If I had just killed myself with those berries, none of this would've happened. Peeta could have come home and lived, and everyone else would have been safe, too."

"Safe to do what?" he says in a gentler tone. "Starve? Work like slaves? Send their kids to the reaping? You haven't hurt people – you've given them an opportunity. They just have to be brave enough to take it. There's already been talk in the mines. People who want to fight. Don't you see? It's happening! It's finally happening! If there's an uprising in District Eight, why not here? Why not everywhere? This could be it, the thing we've been—"

"Stop it! You don't know what you're saying. The Peacekeepers outside of Twelve, they're not like Darius, or even Cray! The lives of district people – they mean less than nothing to them!" I say.

"That's why we have to join the fight!" he answers harshly.

"No! We have to leave here before they kill us and a lot of other people, too!" I'm yelling again, but I can't understand why he's doing this. Why doesn't he see what's so undeniable?

Gale pushes me roughly away from him. "You leave, then. I'd never go in a million years."

"You were happy enough to go before. I don't see how an uprising in District Eight does anything but make it more important that we leave. You're just mad about—" No, I can't throw Peeta in his face. "What about your family?"

"What about the other families, Katniss? The ones who can't run away? Don't you see? It can't be about just saving *us* any more. Not if the rebellion's begun!" Gale shakes his head, not hiding his disgust with me. "You could do so much." He throws Cinna's gloves at my feet. "I changed my mind. I don't want anything they made in the Capitol." And he's gone.

I look down at the gloves. Anything they made in the Capitol? Was that directed at me? Does he think I am now just another product of the Capitol and therefore something untouchable? The unfairness of it all fills me with rage. But it's mixed up with fear over what kind of crazy thing he might do next.

I sink down next to the fire, desperate for comfort, to work out my next move. I calm myself by thinking that rebellions don't happen in a day. Gale can't talk to the miners until tomorrow. If I can get to Hazelle before then, she might straighten him out. But I can't go now. If he's there, he'll lock me out. Maybe tonight, after everyone else is asleep. . . Hazelle often works late into the night finishing up laundry. I could go then, tap at the window, tell her the situation so she'll keep Gale from doing anything foolish.

My conversation with President Snow in the study comes back to me.

"*My advisors were concerned you would be difficult, but you're not planning on being difficult at all, are you?*"

"*No.*"

"*That's what I told them. I said any girl who goes to such lengths to preserve her life isn't going to be interested in throwing it away with both hands.*"

I think of how hard Hazelle has worked to keep that family alive. Surely she'll be on my side in this matter. Or won't she?

It must be getting on towards noon now and the days are so short. No point in being in the woods after dark if you don't have to. I stamp out the remains of my little fire, clear up the scraps of food, and tuck Cinna's gloves in my belt. I guess I'll hang on to them for a while. In case Gale has a change of heart. I think of the look on his face when he flung them to the ground. How repelled he was by them, by me. . .

I trudge through the woods and reach my old house while there's still light. My conversation with Gale was an obvious setback, but I'm still determined to carry on with my plan to escape District 12. I decide to find Peeta next. In a strange way, since he's seen some of what I've seen on the tour, he may be an easier sell than Gale was. I run into him as he's leaving the Victor's Village.

"Been hunting?" he asks. You can see he doesn't think it's a good idea.

"Not really. Going to town?" I ask.

"Yes. I'm supposed to eat dinner with my family," he says.

"Well, I can at least walk you in." The road from

the Victor's Village to the square gets little use. It's a safe enough place to talk. But I can't seem to get the words out. Proposing it to Gale was such a disaster. I gnaw on my chapped lips. The square gets closer with every step. I may not have an opportunity again soon. I take a deep breath and let the words rush out. "Peeta, if I asked you to run away from the district with me, would you?"

Peeta takes my arm, bringing me to a stop. He doesn't need to check my face to see if I'm serious. "Depends on why you're asking."

"President Snow wasn't convinced by me. There's an uprising in District Eight. We have to get out," I say.

"By 'we' do you mean just you and me? No. Who else would be going?" he asks.

"My family. Yours, if they want to come. Haymitch, maybe," I say.

"What about Gale?" he says.

"I don't know. He might have other plans," I say.

Peeta shakes his head and gives me a rueful smile. "I bet he does. Sure, Katniss, I'll go."

I feel a slight twinge of hope. "You will?"

"Yeah. But I don't think for a minute you will," he says.

I jerk my arm away. "Then you don't know me. Be

ready. It could be any time." I take off walking and he follows a pace or two behind.

"Katniss," Peeta says. I don't slow down. If he thinks it's a bad idea, I don't want to know, because it's the only one I have. "Katniss, hold up." I kick a dirty, frozen chunk of snow off the path and let him catch up. The coal dust makes everything look especially ugly. "I really will go, if you want me to. I just think we better talk it through with Haymitch. Make sure we won't be making things worse for everyone." He raises his head. "What's that?"

I lift my chin. I've been so consumed with my own worries, I haven't noticed the strange noise coming from the square. A whistling, the sound of an impact, the intake of breath from a crowd.

"Come on," Peeta says, his face suddenly hard. I don't know why. I can't place the sound, even guess at the situation. But it means something bad to him.

When we reach the square, it's clear something's happening, but the crowd's too thick to see. Peeta steps up on a crate against the wall of the sweetshop and offers me a hand while he scans the square. I'm halfway up when he suddenly blocks my way. "Get down. Get out of here!" He's whispering, but his voice is harsh with insistence.

"What?" I say, trying to force my way back up.

"Go home, Katniss! I'll be there in a minute, I swear!" he says.

Whatever it is, it's terrible. I yank away from his hand and begin to push my way through the crowd. People see me, recognize my face, and then look panicked. Hands shove me back. Voices hiss.

"Get out of here, girl."

"Only make it worse."

"What do you want to do? Get him killed?"

But at this point, my heart is beating so fast and fierce I hardly hear them. I only know that whatever waits in the middle of the square is meant for me. When I finally break through to the cleared space, I see I am right. And Peeta was right. And those voices were right, too.

Gale's wrists are bound to a wooden post. The wild turkey he shot earlier hangs above him, the nail driven through its neck. His jacket's been cast aside on the ground, his shirt torn away. He slumps unconscious on his knees, held up only by the ropes at his wrists. What used to be his back is a raw, bloody slab of meat.

Standing behind him is a man I've never seen, but I recognize his uniform. It's the one designated for our Head Peacekeeper. This isn't old Cray, though.

This is a tall, muscular man with sharp creases in his trousers.

The pieces of the picture do not quite come together until I see his arm raise the whip.

8

"No!" I cry, and spring forward. It's too late to stop the arm from descending, and I instinctively know I won't have the power to block it. Instead I throw myself directly between the whip and Gale. I've flung out my arms to protect as much of his broken body as possible, so there's nothing to deflect the lash. I take the full force of it across the left side of my face.

The pain is blinding and instantaneous. Jagged flashes of light cross my vision and I fall to my knees. One hand cups my cheek while the other keeps me from tipping over. I can already feel the welt rising up, the swelling closing my eye. The stones beneath me are wet with Gale's blood, the air heavy with its scent. "Stop it! You'll kill him!" I shriek.

I get a glimpse of my assailant's face. Hard, with deep lines, a cruel mouth. Grey hair shaved almost to non-existence, eyes so black they seem all pupils, a long, straight nose reddened by the freezing air. The powerful arm lifts again, his sights set on me. My hand flies to my shoulder, hungry for an arrow, but, of course, my weapons are stashed in the woods. I grit my teeth in anticipation of the next lash.

"Hold it!" a voice barks. Haymitch appears and trips over a Peacekeeper lying on the ground. It's Darius. A huge purple lump pushes through the red hair on his forehead. He's knocked out but still breathing. What happened? Did he try to come to Gale's aid before I got here?

Haymitch ignores him and pulls me to my feet roughly. "Oh, excellent." His hand locks under my chin, lifting it. "She's got a photo shoot next week modelling wedding dresses. What am I supposed to tell her stylist?"

I see a flicker of recognition in the eyes of the man with the whip. Bundled against the cold, my face free of make-up, my braid tucked carelessly under my coat, it wouldn't be easy to identify me as the victor of the last Hunger Games. Especially with half my face swelling up. But Haymitch has been showing up on television for years, and he'd be difficult to forget.

The man rests the whip on his hip. "She interrupted the punishment of a confessed criminal."

Everything about this man, his commanding voice, his odd accent, warns of an unknown and dangerous threat. Where has he come from? District 11? Three? From the Capitol itself?

"I don't care if she blew up the blasted Justice Building! Look at her cheek! Think that will be camera ready in a week?" Haymitch snarls.

The man's voice is still cold, but I can detect a slight edge of doubt. "That's not my problem."

"No? Well, it's about to be, my friend. The first call I make when I get home is to the Capitol," says Haymitch. "Find out who authorized you to mess up my victor's pretty little face!"

"He was poaching. What business is it of hers, anyway?" says the man.

"He's her cousin." Peeta's got my other arm now, but gently. "And she's my fiancée. So if you want to get to him, expect to go through both of us."

Maybe we're it. The only three people in the district who could make a stand like this. Although it's sure to be temporary. There will be repercussions. But at the moment, all I care about is keeping Gale alive. The new Head Peacekeeper glances over at his back-up squad. With relief, I see they're familiar faces, old friends from the Hob. You can tell by their expressions that they're not enjoying the show.

One, a woman named Purnia who eats regularly at Greasy Sae's, steps forward stiffly. "I believe, for a first offence, the required number of lashes has been dispensed, sir. Unless your sentence is death, which we would carry out by firing squad."

"Is that the standard protocol here?" asks the Head Peacekeeper.

"Yes, sir," Purnia says, and several others nod in agreement. I'm sure none of them actually know because, in the Hob, the standard protocol for someone showing up with a wild turkey is for everybody to bid on the drumsticks.

"Very well. Get your cousin out of here, then, girl. And if he comes to, remind him that the next time he poaches off the Capitol's land, I'll assemble that firing squad personally." The Head Peacekeeper wipes his hand along the length of the whip, splattering us with blood. Then he coils it into quick, neat loops and walks off.

Most of the other Peacekeepers fall in an awkward formation behind him. A small group stays behind and hoists Darius's body up by the arms and legs. I catch Purnia's eye and mouth the word "Thanks" before she goes. She doesn't respond, but I'm sure she understood.

"Gale." I turn, my hands fumbling at the knots

binding his wrists. Someone passes forward a knife and Peeta cuts the ropes. Gale collapses to the ground.

"Better get him to your mother," says Haymitch.

There's no stretcher, but the old woman at the clothing stall sells us the board that serves as her countertop. "Just don't tell where you got it," she says, packing up the rest of her goods quickly. Most of the square has emptied, fear getting the better of compassion. But after what just happened, I can't blame anyone.

By the time we've laid Gale face down on the board, there's only a handful of people left to carry him. Haymitch, Peeta and a couple of miners who work on the same crew as Gale lift him up.

Leevy, a girl who lives a few houses down from mine in the Seam, takes my arm. My mother kept her little brother alive last year when he caught the measles. "Need help getting back?" Her grey eyes are scared but determined.

"No, but can you get Hazelle? Send her over?" I ask.

"Yeah," says Leevy, turning on her heel.

"Leevy!" I say. "Don't let her bring the kids."

"No. I'll stay with them myself," she says.

"Thanks." I grab Gale's jacket and hurry after the others.

"Get some snow on that," Haymitch orders over his shoulder. I scoop up a handful of snow and press it against my cheek, numbing a bit of the pain. My left eye's tearing heavily now, and in the dimming light it's all I can do to follow the boots in front of me.

As we walk I hear Bristel and Thom, Gale's crewmates, piece together the story of what happened. Gale must've gone to Cray's house, as he's done a hundred times, knowing Cray always pays well for a wild turkey. Instead he found the new Head Peacekeeper, a man they heard someone call Romulus Thread. No one knows what happened to Cray. He was buying white liquor in the Hob just this morning, apparently still in command of the district, but now he's nowhere to be found. Thread put Gale under immediate arrest and, of course, since he was standing there holding a dead turkey, there was little Gale could say in his own defence. Word of his predicament spread quickly. He was brought to the square, forced to plead guilty to his crime, and sentenced to a whipping to be carried out immediately. By the time I showed up, he'd been lashed at least forty times. He passed out around thirty.

"Lucky he only had the turkey on him," says Bristel. "If he'd had his usual haul, would've been much worse."

"He told Thread he found it wandering around the Seam. Said it got over the fence and he'd stabbed it with a stick. Still a crime. But if they'd known he'd been in the woods with weapons, they'd have killed him for sure," says Thom.

"What about Darius?" Peeta asks.

"After about twenty lashes, he stepped in, saying that was enough. Only he didn't do it smart and official, like Purnia did. He grabbed Thread's arm and Thread hit him in the head with the butt of the whip. Nothing good waiting for him," says Bristel.

"Doesn't sound like much good for any of us," says Haymitch.

Snow begins, thick and wet, making visibility even more difficult. I stumble up the walk to my house behind the others, using my ears more than my eyes to guide me. A golden light colours the snow as the door opens. My mother, who was no doubt waiting for me after a long day of unexplained absence, takes in the scene.

"New Head," Haymitch says, and she gives him a curt nod as if no other explanation is needed.

I'm filled with awe, as I always am, as I watch her transform from a woman who calls me to kill a spider to a woman immune to fear. When a sick or dying person is brought to her . . . this is the only time I think my mother knows who she is. In moments, the long kitchen table has been cleared, a sterile white cloth spread across it, and Gale hoisted on to it. My mother pours water from a kettle into a basin while ordering Prim to pull a series of her remedies from the medicine cabinet. Dried herbs and tinctures and store-bought bottles. I watch her hands, the long, tapered fingers crumbling this, adding drops of that, into the basin. Soaking a cloth in the hot liquid as she gives Prim instructions to prepare a second brew.

My mother glances my way. "Did it cut your eye?"

"No, it's just swelled shut," I say.

"Get more snow on it," she instructs. But I am clearly not a priority.

"Can you save him?" I ask my mother. She says nothing as she wrings out the cloth and holds it in the air to cool somewhat.

"Don't worry," says Haymitch. "Used to be a lot of whipping before Cray. She's the one we took them to."

I can't remember a time before Cray, a time when there was a Head Peacekeeper who used the whip freely. But my mother must have been around my age and still working at the apothecary shop with her parents. Even back then, she must have had healer's hands.

Ever so gently, she begins to clean the mutilated flesh on Gale's back. I feel sick to my stomach, useless, the remaining snow dripping from my glove into a puddle on the floor. Peeta puts me in a chair and holds a cloth filled with fresh snow to my cheek.

Haymitch tells Bristel and Thom to get home, and I see him press coins into their hands before they leave. "Don't know what will happen with your crew," he says. They nod and accept the money.

Hazelle arrives, breathless and flushed, fresh snow in her hair. Wordlessly, she sits on a stool next to the table, takes Gale's hand, and holds it against her lips. My mother doesn't acknowledge even her. She's gone into that special zone that includes only herself and the patient and occasionally Prim. The rest of us can wait.

Even in her expert hands, it takes a long time to clean the wounds, arrange what shredded skin can be saved, apply a salve and a light bandage. As the blood clears, I can see where every stroke of the lash landed and feel it resonate in the single cut on my face. I multiply my own pain once, twice, forty times and can only hope that Gale remains unconscious. Of course, that's too much to ask for. As the final bandages are being placed, a moan escapes his lips. Hazelle strokes his hair and whispers something while my mother and Prim go through their meagre store of painkillers, the kind usually accessible only to doctors. They are hard to come by, expensive and always in demand. My mother has to save the strongest for the worst pain, but what is the worst pain? To me, it's always the pain that is present. If I were in charge, those painkillers would be gone in a day because I have so little ability to watch suffering. My mother tries to save them for those who are actually in the process of dying, to ease them out of the world.

Since Gale is regaining consciousness, they decide on a herbal concoction he can take by mouth. "That won't be enough," I say. They stare at me. "That won't be enough, I know how it feels. That will barely knock out a headache."

"We'll combine it with sleep syrup, Katniss, and he'll manage it. The herbs are more for the inflammation—" my mother begins calmly.

"Just give him the medicine!" I scream at her. "Give it to him! Who are you, anyway, to decide how much pain he can stand!"

Gale begins stirring at my voice, trying to reach me. The movement causes fresh blood to stain his bandages and an agonized sound to come from his mouth.

"Take her out," says my mother. Haymitch and Peeta literally carry me from the room while I shout obscenities at her. They pin me down on a bed in one of the extra bedrooms until I stop fighting.

While I lie there, sobbing, tears trying to squeeze out of the slit of my eye, I hear Peeta whisper to Haymitch about President Snow, about the uprising in District 8. "She wants us all to run," he says, but if Haymitch has an opinion on this, he doesn't offer it.

After a while, my mother comes in and treats my face. Then she holds my hand, stroking my arm, while Haymitch fills her in on what happened with Gale.

"So it's starting again?" she says. "Like before?"

"By the looks of it," he answers. "Who'd have thought we'd ever be sorry to see old Cray go?"

Cray would have been disliked anyway because of the uniform he wore, but it was his habit of luring starving young women into his bed for money that made him an object of loathing in the district. In really bad times, the hungriest would gather at his door at nightfall, vying for the chance to earn a few coins to feed their families by selling their bodies. Had I been older when my father died, I might have been among them. Instead I learned to hunt.

I don't know exactly what my mother means by things starting again, but I'm too angry and hurting to ask. It's registered, though, the idea of worse times returning, because when the doorbell rings, I shoot straight out of bed. Who could it be at this hour of the night? There's only one answer. Peacekeepers.

"They can't have him," I say.

"Might be you they're after," Haymitch reminds me.

"Or you," I say.

"Not my house," Haymitch points out. "But I'll get the door."

"No, I'll get it," says my mother quietly.

We all go, though, following her down the hallway to the insistent ring of the bell. When she opens it, there's not a squad of Peacekeepers but a single, snow-caked figure. Madge. She holds out a small, damp cardboard box to me.

"Use these for your friend," she says. I take off the lid of the box, revealing half a dozen vials of clear liquid. "They're my mother's. She said I could take them. Use them, please." She runs back into the storm before we can stop her.

"Crazy girl," Haymitch mutters as we follow my mother into the kitchen.

Whatever my mother had given Gale, I was right, it isn't enough. His teeth are gritted and his flesh shines with sweat. My mother fills a syringe with the clear liquid from one of the vials and shoots it into his arm. Almost immediately, his face begins to relax.

"What is that stuff?" asks Peeta.

"It's from the Capitol. It's called morphling," my mother answers.

"I didn't even know Madge knew Gale," says Peeta.

"We used to sell her strawberries," I say almost angrily. What am I angry about, though? Not that she has brought the medicine, surely.

"She must have quite a taste for them," says Haymitch.

That's what nettles me. It's the implication that there's something going on between Gale and Madge. And I don't like it.

"She's my friend" is all I say.

Now that Gale has drifted away on the painkiller, everyone seems to deflate. Prim makes us each eat some stew and bread. A room is offered to Hazelle, but she has to go home to the other kids. Haymitch and Peeta are both willing to stay, but my mother sends them home to bed as well. She knows it's pointless to try this with me and leaves me to tend Gale while she and Prim rest.

Alone in the kitchen with Gale, I sit on Hazelle's stool, holding his hand. After a while, my fingers find his face. I touch parts of him I have never had cause to touch before. His heavy, dark eyebrows, the curve of his cheek, the line of his nose, the hollow at the base of his neck. I trace the outline of stubble on his jaw and finally work my way to his lips. Soft and full, slightly chapped. His breath warms my chilled skin.

Does everyone look younger asleep? Because right now he could be the boy I ran into in the woods years ago, the one who accused me of stealing from his traps. What a pair we were – fatherless, frightened, but fiercely committed, too, to keeping our families alive. Desperate, yet no longer alone after that day, because we'd found each other. I think of a hundred moments in the woods, lazy afternoons fishing, the day I taught him to swim, that time I twisted my knee and he carried me home. Mutually counting on each other, watching each other's backs, forcing each other to be brave.

For the first time, I reverse our positions in my head. I imagine watching Gale volunteering to save Rory in the reaping, having him torn from my life, becoming some strange girl's lover to stay alive, and then coming home with her. Living next to her. Promising to marry her.

The hatred I feel for him, for the phantom girl, for everything, is so real and immediate that it chokes me. Gale is mine. I am his. Anything else is unthinkable.

Why did it take him being whipped within an inch of his life to see it?

Because I'm selfish. I'm a coward. I'm the kind of girl who, when she might actually be of use, would run to stay alive and leave those who couldn't follow to suffer and die. This is the girl Gale met in the woods today.

No wonder I won the Games. No decent person ever does.

You saved Peeta, I think weakly.

But now I question even that. I knew good and well that my life back in District 12 would be unlivable if I let that boy die.

I rest my head forward on the edge of the table, overcome with loathing for myself. Wishing I had died in the arena. Wishing Seneca Crane had blown me to bits the way President Snow said he should have when I held out the berries.

The berries. I realize the answer to who I am lies in that handful of poisonous fruit. If I held them out to save Peeta because I knew I would be shunned if I came back without him, then I am despicable. If I held them out because I loved him, I am still self-centred, although forgivable. But if I held them out to defy the Capitol, I am someone of worth. The trouble is, I don't know exactly what was going on inside me at that moment.

Could it be the people in the districts are right? That it was an act of rebellion, even if it was an unconscious one? Because, deep down, I must know it isn't enough to keep myself, or my family, or my friends alive by running away. Even if I could. It wouldn't fix anything. It wouldn't stop people from being hurt the way Gale was today.

Life in District 12 isn't really so different from life in the arena. At some point, you have to stop running and turn around and face whoever wants you dead. The hard thing is finding the courage to do it. Well, it's not hard for Gale. He was born a rebel. I'm the one making an escape plan.

"I'm so sorry," I whisper. I lean forward and kiss him.

His eyelashes flutter and he looks at me through a haze of opiates. "Hey, Catnip."

"Hey, Gale," I say.

"Thought you'd be gone by now," he says.

My choices are simple. I can die like quarry in the woods or I can die here beside Gale. "I'm not going anywhere. I'm going to stay right here and cause all kinds of trouble."

"Me, too," Gale says. He just manages a smile before the drugs pull him back under.

9

Someone gives my shoulder a shake and I sit up. I've fallen asleep with my face on the table. The white cloth has left creases on my good cheek. The other, the one that took the lash from Thread, throbs painfully. Gale's dead to the world, but his fingers are locked around mine. I smell fresh bread and turn my stiff neck to find Peeta looking down at me with such a sad expression. I get the sense that he's been watching us a while.

"Go on up to bed, Katniss. I'll look after him now," he says.

"Peeta. About what I said yesterday, about running—" I begin.

"I know," he says. "There's nothing to explain."

I see the loaves of bread on the counter in the pale, snowy morning light. The blue shadows under his eyes. I wonder if he slept at all. Couldn't have been long. I think of his agreeing to go with me yesterday, his stepping up beside me to protect Gale, his willingness to throw his lot in with mine entirely when I give him so little in return. No matter what I do, I'm hurting someone. "Peeta—"

"Just go to bed, OK?" he says.

I feel my way up the stairs, crawl under the covers, and fall asleep at once. At some point, Clove, the girl from District 2, enters my dreams. She chases me, pins me to the ground, and pulls out a knife to cut my face. It digs deeply into my cheek, opening a wide gash. Then Clove begins to transform, her face elongating into a snout, dark fur sprouting from her skin, her fingernails growing into long claws, but her eyes remaining unchanged. She becomes the muttation form of herself, the wolflike creation of the Capitol that terrorized us the last night in the arena. Tossing back her head, she lets out a long, eerie howl that is picked up by other mutts nearby. Clove begins to lap the blood flowing from my wound, each lick sending a new wave of pain through my face. I give a strangled cry and wake with a start, sweating and shivering at once. Cradling my damaged cheek in my hand, I remind myself that it was not Clove but Thread who gave me this wound. I wish that Peeta were here to hold me, until I remember I'm not supposed to wish that any more. I have chosen Gale and the rebellion, and a future with Peeta is the Capitol's design, not mine.

The swelling around my eye has gone down and I can open it a bit. I push aside the curtains and see the snowstorm has strengthened to a full-out blizzard. There's nothing but whiteness and the howling wind that sounds remarkably like the muttations.

I welcome the blizzard, with its ferocious winds and deep, drifting snow. This may be enough to keep the real wolves, also known as the Peacekeepers, from my door. A few days to think. To work out a plan. With Gale and Peeta and Haymitch all at hand. This blizzard is a gift.

Before I go down to face this new life, though, I take some time making myself acknowledge what it will mean. Less than a day ago, I was prepared to head into the wilderness with my loved ones in midwinter, with the very real possibility of the Capitol pursuing us. A precarious venture at best. But now I am committing to something even more risky. Fighting the Capitol assures their swift retaliation. I must accept that at any moment I can be arrested. There will be a knock on the door, like the one last night, a band of Peacekeepers to haul me away. There might be torture.

Mutilation. A bullet through my skull in the town square, if I'm fortunate enough to go that quickly. The Capitol has no end of creative ways to kill people. I imagine these things and I'm terrified, but let's face it: they've been lurking in the back of my brain anyway. I've been a tribute in the Games. Been threatened by the president. Taken a lash across my face. I'm already a target.

Now comes the harder part. I have to face the fact that my family and friends might share this fate. Prim. I need only to think of Prim and all my resolve disintegrates. It's my job to protect her. I pull the blanket up over my head, and my breathing is so rapid I use up all the oxygen and begin to choke for air. I can't let the Capitol hurt Prim.

And then it hits me. They already have. They have killed her father in those wretched mines. They have sat by as she almost starved to death. They have chosen her as a tribute, then made her watch her sister fight to the death in the Games. She has been hurt far worse than I had at the age of twelve. And even that pales in comparison with Rue's life.

I shove off the blanket and suck in the cold air that seeps through the windowpanes.

Prim . . . Rue . . . aren't they the very reason I have to try to fight? Because what has been done to them is so wrong, so beyond justification, so evil that there is no choice? Because no one has the right to treat them as they have been treated?

Yes. This is the thing to remember when fear threatens to swallow me up. What I am about to do, whatever any of us are forced to endure, it is for them. It's too late to help Rue, but maybe not too late for those five little faces that looked up at me from the square in District 11. Not too late for Rory and Vick and Posy. Not too late for Prim.

Gale is right. If people have the courage, this could be an opportunity. He's also right that, since I have set it in motion, I could do so much. Although I have no idea what exactly that should be. But deciding not to run away is a crucial first step.

I take a shower, and this morning my brain is not assembling lists of supplies for the wild, but trying to figure out how they organized that uprising in District 8. So many, so clearly acting in defiance of the Capitol. Was it even planned, or something that simply erupted out of years of hatred and resentment? How could we do that here? Would the people of District 12 join in or lock their doors? Yesterday the square emptied so quickly after Gale's whipping. But isn't that because we all feel so impotent and have no idea what to do? We need someone to direct us and reassure us this is possible. And I don't think I'm that person. I may have been a catalyst for rebellion, but a leader should be someone with conviction, and I'm barely a convert myself. Someone with unflinching courage, and I'm still working hard at even finding mine. Someone with clear and persuasive words, and I'm so easily tongue-tied.

Words. I think of words and I think of Peeta. How people embrace everything he says. He could move a crowd to action, I bet, if he chose to. Would find the things to say. But I'm sure the idea has never crossed his mind.

Downstairs, I find my mother and Prim tending to a subdued Gale. The medicine must be wearing off, by the look on his face. I brace myself for another fight but try to keep my voice calm. "Can't you give him another shot?"

"I will, if it's needed. We thought we'd try the snow coat first," says my mother. She has removed his bandages. You can practically see the heat radiating off his back. She lays a clean cloth across his angry flesh and nods to Prim.

Prim comes over, stirring what appears to be a large bowl of snow. But it's tinted a light green and gives off a sweet, clean scent. Snow coat. She carefully begins to ladle the stuff on to the cloth. I can almost hear the sizzle of Gale's tormented skin meeting the snow mixture. His eyes flutter open, perplexed, and then he lets out a sound of relief.

"It's lucky we have snow," says my mother.

I think of what it must be like to recover from a whipping in midsummer, with the searing heat and the tepid water from the tap. "What did you do in warm months?" I ask.

A crease appears between my mother's eyebrows as she frowns. "Tried to keep the flies away."

My stomach turns at the thought. She fills a handkerchief with the snow-coat mixture and I hold it to the weal on my cheek. Instantly the pain withdraws. It's the coldness of the snow, yes, but whatever mix of herbal juices my mother has added numbs as well. "Oh. That's wonderful. Why didn't you put this on him last night?"

"I needed the wound to set first," she says.

I don't know what that means exactly, but as long as it works, who am I to question her? She knows what she's doing, my mother. I feel a pang of remorse about yesterday, the awful things I yelled at her as Peeta and Haymitch dragged me from the kitchen. "I'm sorry. About screaming at you yesterday."

"I've heard worse," she says. "You've seen how people are, when someone they love is in pain."

Someone they love. The words numb my tongue as if it's been packed in snow coat. Of course I love Gale. But what kind of love does she mean? What do *I* mean when I say I love Gale? I don't know. I did kiss him last night, in a moment when my emotions were running so high. But I'm sure he doesn't remember it. Does he? I hope not. If he does, everything will just get more complicated and I really can't think about kissing when I've got a rebellion to incite. I give my head a little shake to clear it. "Where's Peeta?" I say.

"He went home when we heard you stirring. Didn't want to leave his house unattended during the storm," says my mother.

"Did he get back all right?" I ask. In a blizzard, you can get lost in a matter of metres and wander off course into oblivion.

"Why don't you give him a call and check?" she says.

I go into the study, a room I've pretty much avoided since my meeting with President Snow, and dial Peeta's number. After a few rings he answers.

"Hey. I just wanted to make sure you got home," I say.

"Katniss, I live three houses away from you," he says.

"I know, but with the weather and all," I say.

"Well, I'm fine. Thank you for checking." There's a long pause. "How's Gale?"

"All right. My mother and Prim are giving him snow coat now," I say.

"And your face?" he asks.

"I've got some, too," I say. "Have you seen Haymitch today?"

"I checked in on him. Dead drunk. But I built up his fire and left him some bread," he says.

"I wanted to talk to – to both of you." I don't dare add more, here on my phone, which is surely tapped.

"Probably have to wait until after the weather calms down," he says. "Nothing much will happen before that, anyway."

"No, nothing much," I agree.

It takes two days for the storm to blow itself out, leaving us with drifts higher than my head. Another day before the path is cleared from the Victor's Village to the square. During this time I help tend to Gale, apply snow coat to my cheek, try to remember everything I can about the uprising in District 8, in case it will help us. The swelling in my face goes down, leaving me with an itchy, healing wound and a very black eye. But still, the first chance I get, I call Peeta to see if he wants to go into town with me.

We rouse Haymitch and drag him along with us.

He complains, but not as much as usual. We all know we need to discuss what happened and it can't be anywhere as dangerous as our homes in the Victor's Village. In fact, we wait until the village is well behind us to even speak. I spend the time studying the three-metre walls of snow piled up on either side of the narrow path that has been cleared, wondering if they will collapse in on us.

Finally Haymitch breaks the silence. "So we're all heading off into the great unknown, are we?" he asks me.

"No," I say. "Not any more."

"Worked through the flaws in that plan, did you, sweetheart?" he asks. "Any new ideas?"

"I want to start an uprising," I say.

Haymitch just laughs. It's not even a mean laugh, which is more troubling. It shows he can't even take me seriously. "Well, I want a drink. You let me know how that works out for you, though," he says.

"Then what's your plan?" I spit back at him.

"My plan is to make sure everything is just perfect for your wedding," says Haymitch. "I called and rescheduled the photo shoot without giving too many details."

"You don't even have a phone," I say.

"Effie had that fixed," he says. "Do you know she

asked me if I'd like to give you away? I told her the sooner the better."

"Haymitch." I can hear the pleading creeping into my voice.

"Katniss." He mimics my tone. "It won't work."

We shut up as a team of men with shovels passes us, headed out to the Victor's Village. Maybe they can do something about those three-metre walls. And by the time they're out of earshot, the square is too close. We step into it and all come to a stop simultaneously.

Nothing much will happen during the blizzard. That's what Peeta and I had agreed. But we couldn't have been more wrong. The square has been transformed. A huge banner with the seal of Panem hangs off the roof of the Justice Building. Peacekeepers, in pristine white uniforms, march on the cleanly swept cobblestones. Along the rooftops, more of them occupy nests of machine guns. Most unnerving is a line of new constructions – an official whipping post, several stockades and a gallows – set up in the centre of the square.

"Thread's a quick worker," says Haymitch.

Some streets away from the square, I see a blaze flare up. None of us has to say it. That can only be the Hob going up in smoke. I think of Greasy Sae, Ripper, all my friends who make their living there.

"Haymitch, you don't think everyone was still in—" I can't finish the sentence.

"Nah, they're smarter than that. You'd be, too, if you'd been around longer," he says. "Well, I better go see how much rubbing alcohol the apothecary can spare."

He trudges off across the square and I look at Peeta. "What's he want that for?" Then I realize the answer. "We can't let him drink it. He'll kill himself, or at the very least go blind. I've got some white liquor put away at home."

"Me, too. Maybe that will hold him until Ripper finds a way to be back in business," says Peeta. "I need to check on my family."

"I have to go see Hazelle." I'm worried now. I thought she'd be on our doorstep the moment the snow was cleared. But there's been no sign of her.

"I'll go, too. Drop by the bakery on my way home," he says.

"Thanks." I'm suddenly very scared at what I might find.

The streets are almost deserted, which would not be so unusual at this time of day if people were at the mines, kids at school. But they're not. I see faces peeking at us out of doorways, through cracks in shutters.

An uprising, I think. *What an idiot I am.* There's an inherent flaw in the plan that both Gale and I were too blind to see. An uprising requires breaking the law, thwarting authority. We've done that our whole lives, or our families have. Poaching, trading on the black market, mocking the Capitol in the woods. But for most people in District 12, a trip to buy something at the Hob would be too risky. And I expect them to assemble in the square with bricks and torches? Even the sight of Peeta and me is enough to make people pull their children away from the windows and draw the curtains tightly.

We find Hazelle in her house, nursing a very sick Posy. I recognize the measles spots. "I couldn't leave her," she says. "I knew Gale'd be in the best possible hands."

"Of course," I say. "He's much better. My mother says he'll be back in the mines in a couple of weeks."

"May not be open until then, anyway," says Hazelle. "Word is they're closed until further notice." She gives a nervous glance at her empty washtub.

"You closed down, too?" I ask.

"Not officially," says Hazelle. "But everyone's afraid to use me now."

"Maybe it's the snow," says Peeta.

"No, Rory made a quick round this morning. Nothing to wash, apparently," she says.

Rory wraps his arms around Hazelle. "We'll be all right."

I take a handful of money from my pocket and lay it on the table. "My mother will send something for Posy."

When we're outside, I turn to Peeta. "You go on back. I want to walk by the Hob."

"I'll go with you," he says.

"No. I've dragged you into enough trouble," I tell him.

"And avoiding a stroll by the Hob . . . that's going to fix things for me?" He smiles and takes my hand. Together we wind through the streets of the Seam until we reach the burning building. They haven't even bothered to leave Peacekeepers around it. They know no one would try to save it.

The heat from the flames melts the surrounding snow and a black trickle runs across my shoes. "It's all that coal dust, from the old days," I say. It was in every crack and crevice. Ground into the floorboards. It's amazing the place didn't go up before. "I want to check on Greasy Sae."

"Not today, Katniss. I don't think we'd be helping anyone by dropping in on them," he says.

We go back to the square. I buy some cakes from Peeta's father while they exchange small talk about the weather. No one mentions the ugly tools of torture just metres from the front door. The last thing I notice as we leave the square is that I do not recognize even one of the Peacekeepers' faces.

As the days pass, things go from bad to worse. The mines stay shut for two weeks, and by that time half of District 12 is starving. The number of kids signing up for tesserae soars, but they often don't receive their grain. Food shortages begin, and even those with money come away from stores empty-handed. When the mines reopen, wages are cut, hours extended, miners sent into blatantly dangerous work sites. The eagerly awaited food promised for Parcel Day arrives spoiled and defiled by rodents. The installations in the square see plenty of action as people are dragged in and punished for offences so long overlooked we've forgotten they are illegal.

Gale goes home with no more talk of rebellion between us. But I can't help thinking that everything he sees will only strengthen his resolve to fight back. The hardships in the mines, the tortured bodies in the square, the hunger on the faces of his family. Rory has signed up for tesserae, something Gale can't even speak about, but it's still not enough with the inconsistent availability and the ever-increasing price of food.

The only bright spot is, I get Haymitch to hire Hazelle as a housekeeper, resulting in some extra money for her and greatly increasing Haymitch's standard of living. It's weird going into his house, finding it fresh and clean, food warming on the stove. He hardly notices because he's fighting a whole different battle. Peeta and I tried to ration what white liquor we had, but it's almost run out, and the last time I saw Ripper, she was in the stocks.

I feel like a pariah when I walk through the streets. Everyone avoids me in public now. But there's no shortage of company at home. A steady supply of ill and injured is deposited in our kitchen before my mother, who has long since stopped charging for her services. Her stocks of remedies are running so low, though, that soon all she'll have to treat the patients with is snow.

The woods, of course, are forbidden. Absolutely. No question. Even Gale doesn't challenge this now. But one morning, I do. And it isn't the house full of the sick and dying, the bleeding backs, the gaunt-faced children, the marching boots, or the omnipresent misery that drives me under the fence. It's the arrival of a crate of wedding dresses one night with a note from

Effie saying that President Snow approved these himself.

The wedding. Is he really planning to go through with it? What, in his twisted brain, will that achieve? Is it for the benefit of those in the Capitol? A wedding was promised, a wedding will be given. And then he'll kill us? As a lesson to the districts? I don't know. I can't make sense of it. I toss and turn in bed until I can't stand it any more. I have to get out of here. At least for a few hours.

My hands dig around in my wardrobe until I find the insulated winter gear Cinna made for me for recreational use on the Victory Tour. Waterproof boots, a snowsuit that covers me from head to toe, thermal gloves. I love my old hunting stuff, but the trek I have in mind today is more suited to this high-tech clothing. I tiptoe downstairs, load my game bag with food, and sneak out of the house. Slinking along side streets and back alleys, I make my way to the weak spot in the fence closest to Rooba the butcher's. Since many workers cross this way to get to the mines, the snow's pockmarked with footprints. Mine will not be noticed. With all his security upgrades, Thread has paid little attention to the fence, perhaps feeling harsh weather and wild animals are enough to keep everyone safely inside. Even so, once I'm under the chain link, I cover my tracks until the trees conceal them for me.

Dawn is just breaking as I retrieve a set of bow and arrows and begin to force a path through the drifted snow in the woods. I'm determined, for some reason, to get to the lake. Maybe to say goodbye to the place, to my father and the happy times we spent there, because I know I'll probably never return. Maybe just so I can draw a complete breath again. Part of me doesn't really care if they catch me, if I can see it one more time.

The trip takes twice as long as usual. Cinna's clothes hold in the heat all right, and I arrive soaked with sweat under the snowsuit while my face is numb with cold. The glare of the winter sun off the snow has played games with my vision, and I am so exhausted and wrapped up in my own hopeless thoughts that I don't notice the signs. The thin stream of smoke from the chimney, the indentations of recent footprints, the smell of steaming pine needles. I am literally a few metres from the door of the cement house when I pull up short. And that's not because of the smoke or the prints or the smell. That's because of the unmistakable click of a weapon behind me.

Second nature. Instinct. I turn, drawing back the arrow, although I know already that the odds are not in my favour. I see the white Peacekeeper uniform, the pointed chin, the light brown iris where my arrow will find a home. But the weapon is dropping to the ground and the unarmed woman is holding something out to me in her gloved hand.

"Stop!" she cries.

I waver, unable to process this turn in events. Perhaps they have orders to bring me in alive so they can torture me into incriminating every person I ever knew. *Yeah, good luck with that*, I think. My fingers have all but decided to release the arrow when I see the object in the glove. It's a small white circle of flat bread. More of a cracker, really. Grey and soggy around the edges. But an image is clearly stamped in the centre of it.

It's my mockingjay.

PART II

THE QUELL

10

It makes no sense. My bird baked into bread. Unlike the stylish renderings I saw in the Capitol, this is definitely not a fashion statement. "What is it? What does that mean?" I ask harshly, still prepared to kill.

"It means we're on your side," says a tremulous voice behind me.

I didn't see her when I came up. She must have been in the house. I don't take my eyes off my current target. Probably the newcomer is armed, but I'm betting she won't risk letting me hear the click that would mean my death was imminent, knowing I would instantly kill her companion. "Come around where I can see you," I order.

"She can't, she's—" begins the woman with the cracker.

"Come around!" I shout. There's a step and a

dragging sound. I can hear the effort the movement requires. Another woman, or maybe I should call her a girl since she looks about my age, limps into view. She's dressed in an ill-fitting Peacekeeper's uniform complete with the white fur cloak, but it's several sizes too large for her slight frame. She carries no visible weapon. Her hands are occupied with steadying a rough crutch made from a broken branch. The toe of her right boot can't clear the snow, hence the dragging.

I examine the girl's face, which is bright red from the cold. Her teeth are crooked and there's a strawberry birthmark over one of her chocolate-brown eyes. This is no Peacekeeper. No citizen of the Capitol, either.

"Who are you?" I ask warily but less belligerently.

"My name's Twill," says the woman. She's older. Maybe thirty-five or so. "And this is Bonnie. We've run away from District Eight."

District 8! Then they must know about the uprising!

"Where'd you get the uniforms?" I ask.

"I stole them from the factory," says Bonnie. "We make them there. Only I thought this one would be for . . . for someone else. That's why it fits so poorly."

"The gun came from a dead Peacekeeper," says Twill, following my eyes.

"That cracker in your hand. With the bird. What's that about?" I ask.

"Don't you know, Katniss?" Bonnie appears genuinely surprised.

They recognize me. Of course they recognize me. My face is uncovered and I'm standing here outside of District 12 pointing an arrow at them. Who else would I be? "I know it matches the pin I wore in the arena."

"She doesn't know," says Bonnie softly. "Maybe not about any of it."

Suddenly I feel the need to appear on top of things. "I know you had an uprising in Eight."

"Yes, that's why we had to get out," says Twill.

"Well, you're good and out now. What are you going to do?" I ask.

"We're headed for District Thirteen," Twill replies.

"Thirteen?" I say. "There's no Thirteen. It got blown off the map."

"Seventy-five years ago," says Twill.

Bonnie shifts on her crutch and winces.

"What's wrong with your leg?" I ask.

"I twisted my ankle. My boots are too big," says Bonnie.

I bite my lip. My instinct tells me they're telling the truth. And behind that truth is a whole lot of information I'd like to get. I step forward and retrieve

Twill's gun before lowering my bow, though. Then I hesitate a moment, thinking of another day in these woods, when Gale and I watched a hovercraft appear out of thin air and capture two escapees from the Capitol. The boy was speared and killed. The red-headed girl, I found out when I went to the Capitol, was mutilated and turned into a mute servant called an Avox. "Anyone after you?"

"We don't think so. We think they believe we were killed in a factory explosion," says Twill. "Only a fluke that we weren't."

"All right, let's go inside," I say, nodding at the cement house. I follow them in, carrying the gun.

Bonnie makes straight for the hearth and lowers herself on to a Peacekeeper's cloak that has been spread before it. She holds her hands to the feeble flame that burns on one end of a charred log. Her skin is so pale as to be translucent and I can see the fire glow through her flesh. Twill tries to arrange the cloak, which must have been her own, around the shivering girl.

A tin gallon can has been cut in half, the lip ragged and dangerous. It sits in the ashes, filled with a handful of pine needles steaming in water.

"Making tea?" I ask.

"We're not sure, really. I remember seeing someone do this with pine needles on the Hunger Games a few years back. At least, I think it was pine needles," says Twill with a frown.

I remember District 8, an ugly urban place stinking of industrial fumes, the people housed in run-down tenements. Barely a blade of grass in sight. No opportunity, ever, to learn the ways of nature. It's a miracle these two have made it this far.

"Out of food?" I ask.

Bonnie nods. "We took what we could, but food's been so scarce. That's been gone for a while." The quaver in her voice melts my remaining defences. She is just a malnourished, injured girl fleeing the Capitol.

"Well, then this is your lucky day," I say, dropping my game bag on the floor. People are starving all over the district and we still have more than enough. So I've been spreading things around a little. I have my own priorities: Gale's family, Greasy Sae, some of the other Hob traders who were shut down. My mother has other people, patients mostly, who she wants to help. This morning I purposely overstuffed my game bag with food, knowing my mother would see the depleted pantry and assume I was making my rounds to the hungry. I was actually buying time to go to the lake without her worrying. I intended to deliver the food this evening on my return, but now I can see that won't be happening.

From the bag I pull two fresh buns with a layer of cheese baked into the top. We always seem to have a supply of these since Peeta found out they were my favourite. I toss one to Twill but cross over and place the other on Bonnie's lap since her hand–eye coordination seems a little questionable at the moment and I don't want the thing ending up in the fire.

"Oh," says Bonnie. "Oh, is this all for me?"

Something inside me twists as I remember another voice. Rue. In the arena. When I gave her the leg of groosling. "*Oh, I've never had a whole leg to myself before.*" The disbelief of the chronically hungry.

"Yeah, eat up," I say. Bonnie holds the bun as if she can't quite believe it's real and then sinks her teeth into it again and again, unable to stop. "It's better if you chew it." She nods, trying to slow down, but I know how hard it is when you're that hollow. "I think your tea's done." I scoot the tin can from the ashes. Twill finds two tin cups in her pack and I dip out the tea, setting it on the floor to cool. They huddle together, eating, blowing on their tea, and taking tiny, scalding sips as I build up the fire. I wait until they are sucking the grease from their fingers to ask, "So, what's your story?" And they tell me.

Ever since the Hunger Games, the discontent in District 8 had been growing. It was always there, of course, to some degree. But what differed was that talk was no longer sufficient, and the idea of taking action went from a wish to a reality. The textile factories that service Panem are loud with machinery, and the din also allowed word to pass safely, a pair of lips close to an ear, words unnoticed, unchecked. Twill taught at school, Bonnie was one of her pupils, and when the final bell had rung, both of them spent a four-hour shift at the factory that specialized in the Peacekeeper uniforms. It took months for Bonnie, who worked in the chilly inspection dock, to secure the two uniforms, a boot here, a pair of pants there. They were intended for Twill and her husband because it was understood that, once the uprising began, it would be crucial to get word of it out beyond District 8 if it were to spread and be successful.

The day Peeta and I came through and made our Victory Tour appearance was actually a rehearsal of sorts. People in the crowd positioned themselves according to their teams, next to the buildings they would target when the rebellion broke out. That was the plan: to take over the centres of power in the city like the Justice Building, the Peacekeepers' Headquarters and the Communication Centre in the square. And at other locations in the district: the railroad, the granary, the power station and the armoury.

The night of my engagement, the night Peeta fell to his knees and proclaimed his undying love for me in front of the cameras in the Capitol, was the night the uprising began. It was an ideal cover. Our Victory Tour interview with Caesar Flickerman was mandatory viewing. It gave the people of District 8 a reason to be out on the streets after dark, gathering either in the square or in various community centres around the city to watch. Ordinarily such activity would have been too suspicious. Instead everyone was in place by the appointed hour, eight o'clock, when the masks went on and all hell broke loose.

Taken by surprise and overwhelmed by sheer numbers, the Peacekeepers were initially overcome by the crowds. The Communication Centre, the granary and the power station were all secured. As the Peacekeepers fell, weapons were appropriated for the rebels. There was hope that this had not been an act of madness, that in some way, if they could get the word out to other districts, an actual overthrow of the government in the Capitol might be possible.

But then the axe fell. Peacekeepers began to arrive by the thousands. Hovercraft bombed the rebel strongholds into ashes. In the utter chaos that followed, it was all people could do to make it back to their homes alive. It took less than forty-eight hours to subdue the city. Then, for a week, there was a lockdown. No food, no coal, everyone forbidden to leave their homes. The only time the television showed anything but static was when the suspected instigators were hanged in the square. Then one night, as the whole district was on the brink of starvation, came the order to return to business as usual.

That meant school for Twill and Bonnie. A street made impassable by the bombs caused them to be late for their factory shift, so they were still a hundred metres away when it exploded, killing everyone inside – including Twill's husband and Bonnie's entire family.

"Someone must have told the Capitol that the idea for the uprising had started there," Twill tells me faintly.

The two fled back to Twill's, where the Peacekeeper suits were still waiting. They scraped together what provisions they could, stealing freely from neighbours they now knew to be dead, and made it to the railway station. In a warehouse near the tracks, they changed into the Peacekeeper outfits and, disguised, were able to make it on to a boxcar full of fabric on a train headed to District 6. They fled the train at a fuel stop along the way and travelled on foot. Concealed by woods, but using the tracks for guidance, they made it to the outskirts of District 12 two days ago, where they were forced to stop when Bonnie twisted her ankle.

"I understand why you're running, but what do you expect to find in District Thirteen?" I ask.

Bonnie and Twill exchange a nervous glance. "We're not sure exactly," Twill says.

"It's nothing but rubble," I say. "We've all seen the footage."

"That's just it. They've been using the same footage for as long as anyone in District Eight can remember," says Twill.

"Really?" I try to think back, to call up the images of 13 I've seen on television.

"You know how they always show the Justice Building?" Twill continues. I nod. I've seen it a thousand times. "If you look very carefully, you'll see it. Up in the far right-hand corner."

"See what?" I ask.

Twill holds out her cracker with the bird again. "A mockingjay. Just a glimpse of it as it flies by. The same one every time."

"Back home, we think they keep reusing the old footage because the Capitol can't show what's really there now," says Bonnie.

I give a grunt of disbelief. "You're going to District

Thirteen based on that? A shot of a bird? You think you're going to find some new city with people strolling around in it? And that's just fine with the Capitol?"

"No," Twill says earnestly. "We think the people moved underground when everything on the surface was destroyed. We think they've managed to survive. And we think the Capitol leaves them alone because, before the Dark Days, District Thirteen's principal industry was nuclear development."

"They were graphite miners," I say. But then I hesitate, because that's information I got from the Capitol.

"They had a few small mines, yes. But not enough to justify a population of that size. That, I guess, is the only thing we know for sure," says Twill.

My heart's beating too quickly. What if they're right? Could it be true? Could there be somewhere to run besides the wilderness? Somewhere safe? If a community exists in District 13, would it be better to go there, where I might be able to accomplish something, instead of waiting here for my death? But then . . . if there are people in District 13, with powerful weapons. . .

"Why haven't they helped us?" I say angrily. "If it's true, why do they leave us to live like this? With the hunger and the killings and the Games?" And suddenly I hate this imaginary underground city of District 13 and those who sit by, watching us die. They're no better than the Capitol.

"We don't know," Bonnie whispers. "Right now, we're just holding on to the hope that they exist."

That snaps me to my senses. These are delusions. District 13 doesn't exist because the Capitol would never let it exist. They're probably mistaken about the footage. Mockingjays are about as rare as rocks. And about as tough. If they could survive the initial bombing of 13, they're probably doing better than ever now.

Bonnie has no home. Her family is dead. Returning to District 8 or assimilating into another district would be impossible. Of course the idea of an independent, thriving District 13 draws her. I can't bring myself to tell her she's chasing a dream as insubstantial as a wisp of smoke. Perhaps she and Twill can carve out a life somehow in the woods. I doubt it, but they're so pitiful I have to try to help.

First I give them all the food in my pack, grain and dried beans mostly, but there's enough to hold them for a while if they're careful. Then I take Twill out in the woods and try to explain the basics of hunting. She's got a weapon that if necessary can convert solar energy into deadly rays of power, so that could last indefinitely. When she manages to kill her first squirrel, the poor thing is mostly a charred mess because it took a direct hit to the body. But I show her how to skin and clean it. With some practice, she'll figure it out. I cut a new crutch for Bonnie. Back at the house, I peel off an extra layer of socks for the girl, telling her to stuff them in the toes of her boots to walk, then wear them on her feet at night. Finally I teach them how to build a proper fire.

They beg me for details of the situation in District 12 and I tell them about life under Thread. I can see they think this is important information that they'll be bringing to those who run District 13, and I play along so as not to destroy their hopes. But when the light signals late afternoon, I'm out of time to humour them.

"I have to go now," I say.

They pour out thanks and embrace me.

Tears spill from Bonnie's eyes. "I can't believe we actually got to meet you. You're practically all anyone's talked about since—"

"I know. I know. Since I pulled out those berries," I say tiredly.

I hardly notice the walk home even though a wet snow begins to fall. My mind is spinning with new information about the uprising in District 8 and the unlikely but tantalizing possibility of District 13.

Listening to Bonnie and Twill confirmed one thing: President Snow has been playing me for a fool. All the kisses and endearments in the world couldn't have derailed the momentum building up in District 8. Yes, my holding out the berries had been the spark, but I had no way to control the fire. He must have known that. So why visit my home, why order me to persuade the crowd of my love for Peeta? It was obviously a ploy to distract me and keep me from doing anything else inflammatory in the districts. And to entertain the people in the Capitol, of course. I suppose the wedding is just a necessary extension of that.

I'm nearing the fence when a mockingjay lights on a branch and trills at me. At the sight of it I realize I never got a full explanation of the bird on the cracker and what it signifies.

"*It means we're on your side.*" That's what Bonnie said. I have people on my side? What side? Am I unwittingly the face of the hoped-for rebellion? Has the mockingjay on my pin become a symbol of resistance? If so, my side's not doing too well. You only have to look at what happened in 8 to know that.

I stash my weapons in the hollow log nearest my old home in the Seam and head for the fence. I'm crouched on one knee, preparing to enter the Meadow, but I'm still so preoccupied with the day's events that it takes a sudden screech of an owl to bring me to my senses.

In the fading light, the chain links look as innocuous as usual. But what makes me jerk back my hand is the sound, like the buzz of a tree full of tracker-jacker nests, indicating the fence is alive with electricity.

11

My feet back up automatically and I blend into the trees. I cover my mouth with my glove to disperse the white of my breath in the icy air. Adrenaline courses through me, wiping all the concerns of the day from my mind as I focus on the immediate threat before me. What is going on? Has Thread turned on the fence as an additional security precaution? Or does he somehow know I've escaped his net today? Is he determined to strand me outside District 12 until he can apprehend and arrest me? Drag me to the square to be locked in the stockade or whipped or hanged?

Calm down, I order myself. It's not as if this is the first time I've been caught outside of the district by an electrified fence. It's happened a few times over the years, but Gale was always with me. The two of us would just pick a comfortable tree to hang out in until the power shut off, which it always did eventually. If I was running late, Prim even got in the habit of going to the Meadow to check if the fence was charged, to spare my mother worry.

But today my family would never imagine I'd be in the woods. I've even taken steps to mislead them. So if I don't show up, worry they will. And there's a part of me that's worried, too, because I'm not sure it's just a coincidence, the power coming on the very day I return to the woods. I thought no one saw me sneak under the fence, but who knows? There are always eyes for hire. Someone reported Gale kissing me in that very spot. Still, that was in daylight and before I was more careful about my behaviour. Could there be surveillance cameras? I've wondered about this before. Is this the way President Snow knows about the kiss? It was dark when I went under and my face was bundled in a scarf. But the list of suspects likely to be trespassing into the woods is probably very short.

My eyes peer through the trees, past the fence, into the Meadow. All I can see is the wet snow illuminated here and there by the light from the windows on the edge of the Seam. No Peacekeepers in sight, no signs I am being hunted. Whether Thread knows I left the district today or not, I realize my course of action must be the same: to get back inside the fence unseen and pretend I never left.

Any contact with the chain link or the coils of barbed wire that guard the top would mean instant electrocution. I don't think I can burrow under the fence without risking detection, and the ground's frozen hard, anyway. That leaves only one choice. Somehow I'm going to have to go over it.

I begin to skirt along the tree line, searching for a tree with a branch high and long enough to fit my needs. After about a kilometre, I come upon an old maple that might do. The trunk is too wide and icy to shinny up, though, and there are no low branches. I climb a neighbouring tree and leap precariously on to the maple, almost losing my hold on the slick bark. But I manage to get a grip and slowly inch my way out on a limb that hangs above the barbed wire.

As I look down, I remember why Gale and I always waited in the woods rather than try to tackle the fence. Being high enough to avoid getting fried means you've got to be at least six metres in the air. I guess my branch must be eight. That's a dangerously long drop, even for someone who's had years of practice in trees. But what choice do I have? I could look for another branch, but it's almost dark now. The falling snow will obscure any moonlight. Here, at least, I can see I've got a snowbank to cushion my landing. Even if I could find another, which is doubtful, who knows what I'd be jumping into? I throw my empty game bag around my neck and slowly lower myself until I'm hanging by my hands. For a moment, I gather my courage. Then I release my fingers.

There's the sensation of falling, then I hit the ground with a jolt that goes right up my spine. A second later, my rear end slams the ground. I lie in the snow, trying to assess the damage. Without standing, I can tell by the pain in my left heel and my tailbone that I'm injured. The only question is how badly. I'm hoping for bruises, but when I force myself on to my feet, I suspect I've broken something as well. I can walk, though, so I get moving, trying to hide my limp as best I can.

My mother and Prim can't know I was in the woods. I need to work up some sort of alibi, no matter how thin. Some of the shops in the square are still open, so I go in one and purchase white cloth for bandages. We're running low, anyway. In another, I buy a bag of sweets for Prim. I stick one of them in my mouth, feeling the peppermint melt on my tongue, and realize it's the first thing I've eaten all day. I meant to make a meal at the lake, but once I saw Twill and

Bonnie's condition, it seemed wrong to take a single mouthful from them.

By the time I reach my house, my left heel will bear no weight at all. I decide to tell my mother I was trying to mend a leak in the roof of our old house and slid off. As for the missing food, I'll just be vague about who I handed it out to. I drag myself in the door, all ready to collapse in front of the fire. But instead I get another shock.

Two Peacekeepers, a man and a woman, are standing in the doorway to our kitchen. The woman remains impassive, but I catch the flicker of surprise on the man's face. I am unanticipated. They know I was in the woods and should be trapped there now.

"Hello," I say in a neutral voice.

My mother appears behind them, but keeps her distance. "Here she is, just in time for dinner," she says a little too brightly. I'm very late for dinner.

I consider removing my boots as I normally would but doubt I can manage it without revealing my injuries. Instead I just pull off my wet hood and shake the snow from my hair. "Can I help you with something?" I ask the Peacekeepers.

"Head Peacekeeper Thread sent us with a message for you," says the woman.

"They've been waiting for hours," my mother adds.

They've been waiting for me to fail to return. To confirm I got electrocuted by the fence or trapped in the woods so they could take my family in for questioning.

"Must be an important message," I say.

"May we ask where you've been, Miss Everdeen?" the woman asks.

"Easier to ask where I *haven't* been," I say with a sound of exasperation. I cross into the kitchen, forcing myself to use my foot normally even though every step is excruciating. I pass between the Peacekeepers and make it to the table all right. I fling my bag down and turn to Prim, who's standing stiffly by the hearth. Haymitch and Peeta are there as well, sitting in a pair of matching rockers, playing a game of chess. Were they here by chance or "invited" by the Peacekeepers? Either way, I'm glad to see them.

"So where haven't you been?" says Haymitch in a bored voice.

"Well, I haven't been talking to the Goat Man about getting Prim's goat pregnant, because someone gave me completely inaccurate information as to where he lives," I say to Prim emphatically.

"No, I didn't," says Prim. "I told you exactly."

"You said he lives beside the west entrance to the mine," I say.

"The east entrance," Prim corrects me.

"You distinctly said the west, because then I said, 'Next to the slag heap?' and you said, 'Yeah,'" I say.

"The slag heap next to the *east* entrance," says Prim patiently.

"No. When did you say that?" I demand.

"Last night," Haymitch chimes in.

"It was definitely the east," adds Peeta. He looks at Haymitch and they laugh. I glare at Peeta and he tries to look contrite. "I'm sorry, but it's what I've been saying. You don't listen when people talk to you."

"Bet people told you he didn't live there today and you didn't listen again," says Haymitch.

"Shut up, Haymitch," I say, clearly indicating he's right.

Haymitch and Peeta crack up and Prim allows herself a smile.

"Fine. Somebody else can arrange to get the stupid goat knocked up," I say, which makes them laugh more. And I think, *This is why they've made it this far, Haymitch and Peeta. Nothing throws them.*

I look at the Peacekeepers. The man's smiling but the woman is unconvinced. "What's in the bag?" she asks sharply.

I know she's hoping for game or wild plants.

Something that clearly condemns me. I dump the contents on the table. "See for yourself."

"Oh, good," says my mother, examining the cloth. "We're running low on bandages."

Peeta comes to the table and opens the bag of sweets. "Ooh, peppermints," he says, popping one in his mouth.

"They're mine." I take a swipe for the bag. He tosses it to Haymitch, who stuffs a fistful of sweets in his mouth before passing the bag to a giggling Prim. "None of you deserves sweets!" I say.

"What, because we're right?" Peeta wraps his arms around me. I give a small yelp of pain as my tailbone objects. I try to turn it into a sound of indignation, but I can see in his eyes that he knows I'm hurt. "OK, Prim said west. I distinctly heard west. And we're all idiots. How's that?"

"Better," I say, and accept his kiss. Then I look at the Peacekeepers as if I'm suddenly remembering they're there. "You have a message for me?"

"From Head Peacekeeper Thread," says the woman. "He wanted you to know that the fence surrounding District Twelve will now have electricity twenty-four hours a day."

"Didn't it already?" I ask, a little too innocently.

"He thought you might be interested in passing

this information on to your cousin," says the woman.

"Thank you. I'll tell him. I'm sure we'll all sleep a little more soundly now that security has addressed that lapse." I'm pushing things, I know it, but the comment gives me a sense of satisfaction.

The woman's jaw tightens. None of this has gone as planned, but she has no further orders. She gives me a curt nod and leaves, the man trailing in her wake. When my mother has locked the door behind them, I slump against the table.

"What is it?" says Peeta, holding me steadily.

"Oh, I banged up my left foot. The heel. And my tailbone's had a bad day, too." He helps me over to one of the rockers and I lower myself on to the padded cushion.

My mother eases off my boots. "What happened?"

"I slipped and fell," I say. Four pairs of eyes look at me with disbelief. "On some ice." But we all know the house must be bugged and it's not safe to talk openly. Not here, not now.

Having stripped off my sock, my mother's fingers probe the bones in my left heel and I wince. "There might be a break," she says. She checks the other foot. "This one seems all right." She judges my tailbone to be badly bruised.

Prim's dispatched to get my pyjamas and robe. When I'm changed, my mother makes a snow pack for my left heel and props it up on a hassock. I eat three bowls of stew and half a loaf of bread while the others dine at the table. I stare at the fire, thinking of Bonnie and Twill, hoping that the heavy, wet snow has erased my tracks.

Prim comes and sits on the floor next to me, leaning her head against my knee. We suck on peppermints as I brush her soft blonde hair back behind her ear. "How was school?" I ask.

"All right. We learned about coal by-products," she says. We stare at the fire for a while. "Are you going to try on your wedding dresses?"

"Not tonight. Tomorrow probably," I say.

"Wait until I get home, OK?" she says.

"Sure." *If they don't arrest me first.*

My mother gives me a cup of chamomile tea with a dose of sleep syrup, and my eyelids begin to droop immediately. She wraps my bad foot, and Peeta volunteers to get me to bed. I start out by leaning on his shoulder, but I'm so wobbly he just scoops me up and carries me upstairs. He tucks me in and says goodnight but I catch his hand and hold him there. A side effect of the sleep syrup is that it makes people less inhibited, like white liquor, and I know I have to control my tongue. But I don't want him to go. In fact, I want him to climb in with me, to be there when the nightmares hit tonight. For some reason that I can't quite form, I know I'm not allowed to ask that.

"Don't go yet. Not until I fall asleep," I say.

Peeta sits on the side of the bed, warming my hand in both of his. "Almost thought you'd changed your mind today. When you were late for dinner."

I'm foggy but I can guess what he means. With the fence going on and me showing up late and the Peacekeepers waiting, he thought I'd made a run for it, maybe with Gale.

"No, I'd have told you," I say. I pull his hand up and lean my cheek against the back of it, taking in the faint scent of cinnamon and dill from the breads he must have baked today. I want to tell him about Twill and Bonnie and the uprising and the fantasy of District 13, but it's not safe to and I can feel myself slipping away, so I just get out one more sentence. "Stay with me."

As the tendrils of sleep syrup pull me down, I hear him whisper a word back, but I don't quite catch it.

My mother lets me sleep until noon, then rouses me to examine my heel. I'm ordered to a week of bed rest and I don't object because I feel so lousy. Not just my heel and my tailbone. My whole body aches with exhaustion. So I let my mother doctor me and feed me breakfast in bed and tuck another quilt around me. Then I just lie there, staring out of my window at the winter sky, pondering how on earth this will all turn out. I think a lot about Bonnie and Twill, and the pile of white wedding dresses downstairs, and if Thread will figure out how I got back in and arrest me. It's funny, because he could just arrest me anyway, based on past crimes, but maybe he has to have something really irrefutable to do it, now that I'm a victor. And I wonder if President Snow's in contact with Thread. I think it's unlikely he ever acknowledged that old Cray existed, but now that I'm such a nationwide problem, is he carefully instructing Thread what to do? Or is Thread acting on his own? At any rate, I'm sure they'd both agree on keeping me locked up here inside the district with that fence. Even if I could figure out some way to escape – maybe get a rope up to that maple-tree branch and climb out – there'd be no escaping with my family and friends now. I told Gale I would stay and fight, anyway.

For the next few days, I jump every time there's a knock on the door. No Peacekeepers show up to arrest me, though, so eventually I begin to relax. I'm further reassured when Peeta casually tells me the power is off in sections of the fence because crews are out securing the base of the chain link to the ground. Thread must believe I somehow got under the thing, even with that deadly current running through it. It's a break for the district, having the Peacekeepers busy doing something besides abusing people.

Peeta comes by every day to bring me cheese buns and begins to help me work on the family book. It's an old thing, made of parchment and leather. Some herbalist on my mother's side of the family started it ages ago. The book's composed of page after page of ink drawings of plants with descriptions of their medical uses. My father added a section on edible plants that was my guidebook to keeping us alive after his death. For a long time, I've wanted to record my own knowledge in it. Things I learned from experience or from Gale, and then the information I picked up when I was training for the Games. I didn't because I'm no artist and it's so crucial that the pictures are drawn in exact detail. That's where Peeta comes in. Some of the plants he knows already, others we have dried samples of, and others I have to describe. He makes sketches on scrap paper until I'm satisfied they're right, then I let him draw them in the book. After that, I carefully print all I know about the plant.

It's quiet, absorbing work that helps take my mind

off my troubles. I like to watch his hands as he works, making a blank page bloom with strokes of ink, adding touches of colour to our previously black and yellowish book. His face takes on a special look when he concentrates. His usual easy expression is replaced by something more intense and removed that suggests an entire world locked away inside him. I've seen flashes of this before: in the arena, or when he speaks to a crowd, or that time he shoved the Peacekeepers' guns away from me in District 11. I don't know quite what to make of it. I also become a little fixated on his eyelashes, which ordinarily you don't notice much because they're so blond. But up close, in the sunlight slanting in from the window, they're a light golden colour and so long I don't see how they keep from getting all tangled up when he blinks.

One afternoon Peeta stops shading a blossom and looks up so suddenly that I start, as though I were caught spying on him, which in a strange way maybe I was. But he only says, "You know, I think this is the first time we've ever done anything normal together."

"Yeah," I agree. Our whole relationship has been tainted by the Games. Normal was never a part of it. "Nice for a change."

Each afternoon he carries me downstairs for a change of scenery and I unnerve everyone by turning on the television. Usually we only watch when it's mandatory, because the mixture of propaganda and displays of the Capitol's power – including clips from seventy-four years of Hunger Games – is so odious. But now I'm looking for something special. The mockingjay that Bonnie and Twill are basing all their hopes on. I know it's probably foolishness, but if it is, I want to rule it out. And erase the idea of a thriving District 13 from my mind for good.

My first sighting is in a news story referencing the Dark Days. I see the smouldering remains of the Justice Building in District 13 and just catch the black-and-white underside of a mockingjay's wing as it flies across the upper right-hand corner. That doesn't prove anything, really. It's just an old shot that goes with an old tale.

However, several days later, something else grabs my attention. The main newscaster is reading a piece about a shortage of graphite affecting the manufacturing of items in District 3. They cut to what is supposed to be live footage of a female reporter, encased in a protective suit, standing in front of the ruins of the Justice Building in 13. Through her mask, she reports that unfortunately a study has just today determined that the mines of District 13 are still too toxic to approach. End of story. But just before they cut back to the main newscaster, I see the unmistakable flash of that same mockingjay's wing.

The reporter has simply been incorporated into the old footage. She's not in District 13 at all. Which begs the question, *What is?*

12

Staying quietly in bed is harder after that. I want to be doing something, finding out more about District 13 or helping in the cause to bring down the Capitol. Instead I sit around stuffing myself with cheese buns and watching Peeta sketch. Haymitch stops by occasionally to bring me news from town, which is always bad. More people being punished or dropping from starvation.

Winter has begun to withdraw by the time my foot is deemed usable. My mother gives me exercises to do and lets me walk on my own a bit. I go to sleep one night, determined to go into town the next morning, but I awake to find Venia, Octavia and Flavius grinning down at me.

"Surprise!" they squeal. "We're here early!"

After I took that lash in the face, Haymitch got

their visit pushed back several months so I could heal up. I wasn't expecting them for another three weeks. But I try to act delighted that my bridal photo shoot is here at last. My mother hung up all the dresses, so they're ready to go, but to be honest, I haven't even tried one on.

After the usual histrionics about the deteriorated state of my beauty, they get right down to business. Their biggest concern is my face, although I think my mother did a pretty remarkable job healing it. There's just a pale pink strip across my cheekbone. The whipping's not common knowledge, so I tell them I slipped on the ice and cut it. And then I realize that's my same excuse for hurting my foot, which is going to make walking in high heels a problem. But Flavius, Octavia and Venia aren't the suspicious types, so I'm safe there.

Since I only have to look hairless for a few hours instead of several weeks, I get to be shaved instead of waxed. I still have to soak in a tub of something, but it isn't vile, and we're on to my hair and make-up before I know it. The team, as usual, is full of news, which I usually do my best to tune out. But then Octavia makes a comment that catches my attention. It's a passing remark, really, about how she couldn't get prawns for a party, but it tugs at me.

"Why couldn't you get prawns? Are they out of season?" I ask.

"Oh, Katniss, we haven't been able to get any seafood for weeks!" says Octavia. "You know, because the weather's been so bad in District Four."

My mind starts buzzing. No seafood. For weeks. From District 4. The barely concealed rage in the crowd during the Victory Tour. And suddenly I am absolutely sure that District 4 has revolted.

I begin to question them casually about what other hardships this winter has brought them. They are not used to want, so any little disruption in supply makes an impact on them. By the time I'm ready to be dressed, their complaints about the difficulty of getting different products – from crabmeat to music chips to ribbons – has given me a sense of which districts might actually be rebelling. Seafood from District 4. Electronic gadgets from District 3. And, of course, fabrics from District 8. The thought of such widespread rebellion has me quivering with fear and excitement.

I want to ask them more, but Cinna appears to give me a hug and check my make-up. His attention goes right to the scar on my cheek. Somehow I don't think he believes the slipping-on-the-ice story, but he doesn't question it. He simply adjusts the powder on my face, and what little you can see of the lash mark vanishes.

Downstairs, the living room has been cleared and lit for the photo shoot. Effie's having a fine time ordering everybody around, keeping us all on schedule. It's probably a good thing, because there are six gowns and each one requires its own headpiece, shoes, jewellery, hair, make-up, setting and lighting. Creamy lace and pink roses and ringlets. Ivory satin and gold tattoos and greenery. A sheath of diamonds and jewelled veil and moonlight. Heavy white silk and sleeves that fall from my wrist to the floor, and pearls. The moment one shot has been approved, we move right into preparing for the next. I feel like dough, being kneaded and reshaped again and again. My mother manages to feed me bits of food and sips of tea while they work on me, but by the time the shoot is over, I'm starving and exhausted. I'm hoping to spend some time with Cinna now, but Effie whisks everybody out of the door and I have to make do with the promise of a phone call.

Evening has fallen and my foot hurts from all the crazy shoes, so I abandon any thoughts of going into town. Instead I go upstairs and wash away the layers of make-up and conditioners and dyes and then go down to dry my hair by the fire. Prim, who came home from school in time to see the last two dresses, chatters on about them with my mother. They both seem overly happy about the photo shoot. When I fall into bed, I realize it's because they think it means I'm safe. That the Capitol has overlooked my interference with the whipping since no one is going to go to such trouble and expense for someone they plan on killing, anyway. Right.

In my nightmare, I'm dressed in the silk bridal gown, but it's torn and muddy. The long sleeves keep getting caught on thorns and branches as I run through the woods. The pack of muttation tributes draws closer and closer until it overcomes me with hot breath and dripping fangs and I scream myself awake.

It's too close to dawn to bother trying to get back to sleep. Besides, today I really have to get out and talk to someone. Gale will be unreachable in the mines. But I need Haymitch or Peeta or somebody to share the burden of all that has happened to me since I went to the lake. Fleeing outlaws, electrified fences, an independent District 13, shortages in the Capitol. Everything.

I eat breakfast with my mother and Prim and head out in search of a confidant. The air's warm with hopeful hints of spring in it. Spring would be a good time for an uprising, I think. Everyone feels less vulnerable once winter passes. Peeta's not home. I guess he's already gone into town. I'm surprised to see

Haymitch moving around his kitchen so early, though. I walk into his house without knocking. I can hear Hazelle upstairs, sweeping the floors of the now-spotless house. Haymitch isn't flat-out drunk, but he doesn't look too steady, either. I guess the rumours about Ripper being back in business are true. I'm thinking maybe I better let him just go to bed, when he suggests a walk to town.

Haymitch and I can speak in a kind of shorthand now. In a few minutes I've updated him and he's told me about rumours of uprisings in Districts 7 and 11 as well. If my hunches are right, this would mean almost half the districts have at least attempted to rebel.

"Do you still think it won't work here?" I ask.

"Not yet. Those other districts, they're much larger. Even if half the people cower in their homes, the rebels stand a chance. Here in Twelve, it's got to be all of us or nothing," he says.

I hadn't thought of that. How we lack strength of numbers. "But maybe at some point?" I insist.

"Maybe. But we're small, we're weak, and we don't develop nuclear weapons," says Haymitch with a touch of sarcasm. He didn't get too excited over my District 13 story.

"What do you think they'll do, Haymitch? To the districts that are rebelling?" I ask.

"Well, you've heard what they did in Eight. You've seen what they did here, and that was without provocation," says Haymitch. "If things really do get out of hand, I think they'd have no problem killing off another district, same as they did Thirteen. Make an example of it, you know?"

"So you think Thirteen was really destroyed? I mean, Bonnie and Twill were right about the footage of the mockingjay," I say.

"OK, but what does that prove? Nothing, really. There are plenty of reasons they could be using old footage. Probably it looks more impressive. And it's a lot simpler, isn't it? To just press a few buttons in the editing room than to fly all the way out there and film it?" he says. "The idea that Thirteen has somehow rebounded *and* the Capitol is ignoring it? That sounds like the kind of rumour desperate people cling to."

"I know. I was just hoping," I say.

"Exactly. Because you're desperate," says Haymitch.

I don't argue because, of course, he's right.

Prim comes home from school bubbling over with excitement. The teachers announced there was mandatory programming tonight. "I think it's going to be your photo shoot!"

"It can't be, Prim. They only did the pictures yesterday," I tell her.

"Well, that's what somebody heard," she says.

I'm hoping she's wrong. I haven't had time to prepare Gale for any of this. Since the whipping, I only see him when he comes to the house for my mother to check how he's healing. He's often scheduled seven days a week in the mine. In the few minutes of privacy we've had, with me walking him back to town, I gather that the rumblings of an uprising in 12 have been subdued by Thread's crackdown. He knows I'm not going to run. But he must also know that if we don't revolt in 12, I'm destined to be Peeta's bride. Seeing me lounging around in gorgeous gowns on his television . . . what can he do with that?

When we gather around the television at seven-thirty, I discover that Prim is right. Sure enough, there's Caesar Flickerman, speaking before a standing-room-only crowd in front of the Training Centre, talking to an appreciative crowd about my upcoming nuptials. He introduces Cinna, who became an overnight star with his costumes for me in the Games, and after a minute of good-natured chit-chat, we're directed to turn our attention to a giant screen.

I see now how they could photograph me yesterday and present the special tonight. Initially, Cinna designed two dozen wedding gowns. Since then, there's been the process of narrowing down the designs, creating the dresses, and choosing the accessories. Apparently, in the Capitol, there were opportunities to vote for your favourites at each stage. This is all culminating with shots of me in the final six dresses, which I'm sure took no time at all to insert in the show. Each shot is met with a huge reaction from the crowd. People screaming and cheering for their favourites, booing the ones they don't like. Having voted, and probably bet on the winner, people are very invested in my wedding gown. It's bizarre to watch when I think how I never even bothered to try one on before the cameras arrived. Caesar announces that interested parties must cast their final vote by noon on the following day.

"Let's get Katniss Everdeen to her wedding in style!" he hollers to the crowd. I'm about to shut off the television, but then Caesar is telling us to stay tuned for the other big event of the evening. "That's right, this year will be the seventy-fifth anniversary of the Hunger Games, and that means it's time for our third Quarter Quell!"

"What will they do?" asks Prim. "It isn't for months yet."

We turn to our mother, whose expression is solemn and distant, as if she's remembering something. "It must be the reading of the card."

The anthem plays, and my throat tightens with revulsion as President Snow takes the stage. He's followed by a young boy dressed in a white suit, holding a simple wooden box. The anthem ends, and President Snow begins to speak, to remind us all of the Dark Days from which the Hunger Games were born. When the laws for the Games were laid out, they dictated that every twenty-five years the anniversary would be marked by a Quarter Quell. It would call for a glorified version of the Games to make fresh the memory of those killed by the districts' rebellion.

These words could not be more pointed, since I suspect several districts are rebelling right now.

President Snow goes on to tell us what happened in the previous Quarter Quells. "On the twenty-fifth anniversary, as a reminder to the rebels that their children were dying because of their choice to initiate violence, every district was made to hold an election and vote on the tributes who would represent it."

I wonder how that would have felt. Picking the kids who had to go. It is worse, I think, to be turned over by your own neighbours than have your name drawn from the reaping ball.

"On the fiftieth anniversary," the president continues, "as a reminder that two rebels died for each

Capitol citizen, every district was required to send twice as many tributes."

I imagine facing a field of forty-seven instead of twenty-three. Worse odds, less hope, and ultimately more dead kids. That was the year Haymitch won. . .

"I had a friend who went that year," says my mother quietly. "Maysilee Donner. Her parents owned the sweetshop. They gave me her songbird afterwards. A canary."

Prim and I exchange a look. It's the first we've ever heard of Maysilee Donner. Maybe because my mother knew we would want to know how she died.

"And now we honour our third Quarter Quell," says the president. The little boy in white steps forward, holding out the box as he opens the lid. We can see the tidy, upright rows of yellowed envelopes. Whoever devised the Quarter Quell system had prepared for centuries of Hunger Games. The president removes an envelope clearly marked with a 75. He runs his finger under the flap and pulls out a small square of paper. Without hesitation, he reads, "On the seventy-fifth anniversary, as a reminder to the rebels that even the strongest among them cannot overcome the power of the Capitol, the male and female tributes will be reaped from their existing pool of victors."

My mother gives a faint shriek and Prim buries her

face in her hands, but I feel more like the people I see in the crowd on television. Slightly baffled. What does it mean? Existing pool of victors?

Then I get it, what it means. At least, for me. District 12 only has three existing victors to choose from. Two male. One female. . .

I am going back into the arena.

13

My body reacts before my mind does and I'm running out of the door, across the lawns of the Victor's Village, into the dark beyond. Moisture from the sodden ground soaks my socks and I'm aware of the sharp bite of the wind, but I don't stop. Where? Where to go? The woods, of course. I'm at the fence before the hum makes me remember how very trapped I am. I back away, panting, turn on my heel, and take off again.

The next thing I know I'm on my hands and knees in the cellar of one of the empty houses in the Victor's Village. Faint shafts of moonlight come in through the window wells above my head. I'm cold and wet and winded, but my escape attempt has done nothing to subdue the hysteria rising up inside me. It will drown me unless it's released. I ball up the front of my shirt, stuff it into my mouth, and begin to scream. How long this continues, I don't know. But when I stop, my voice is almost gone.

I curl up on my side and stare at the patches of moonlight on the cement floor. Back in the arena. Back in the place of nightmares. That's where I am going. I have to admit I didn't see it coming. I saw a multitude of other things. Being publicly humiliated, tortured and executed. Fleeing through the wilderness, pursued by Peacekeepers and hovercraft. Marriage to Peeta with our children forced into the arena. But never that I myself would have to be a player in the Games again. Why? Because there's no precedent for it. Victors are out of the reaping for life. That's the deal if you win. Until now.

There's some kind of sheeting, the kind they put down when they paint. I pull it over me like a blanket. In the distance, someone is calling my name. But at the moment, I excuse myself from thinking about even those I love most. I think only of me. And what lies ahead.

The sheeting's stiff but holds warmth. My muscles relax, my heart rate slows. I see the wooden box in the little boy's hands, President Snow drawing out the yellowed envelope. Is it possible that this was really the Quarter Quell written down seventy-five years ago? It seems unlikely. It's just too perfect an answer for the troubles that face the Capitol today. Getting rid of me and subduing the districts all in one neat little package.

I hear President Snow's voice in my head. "*On the seventy-fifth anniversary, as a reminder to the rebels that even the strongest among them cannot overcome the power of the Capitol, the male and female tributes will be reaped from their existing pool of victors.*"

Yes, victors are our strongest. They're the ones who survived the arena and slipped the noose of poverty that strangles the rest of us. They, or should I say we, are the very embodiment of hope where there is no hope. And now twenty-three of us will be killed to show how even that hope was an illusion.

I'm glad I won only last year. Otherwise I'd know all the other victors, not just because I see them on television but because they're guests at every Games. Even if they're not mentoring like Haymitch always has to, most return to the Capitol each year for the event. I think a lot of them are friends. Whereas the only friend I'll have to worry about killing will be either Peeta or Haymitch. *Peeta or Haymitch!*

I sit straight up, throwing off the sheeting. What just went through my mind? There's no situation in which I would ever kill Peeta or Haymitch. But one of them will be in the arena with me, and that's a fact.

They may have even decided between them who it will be. Whoever is picked first, the other will have the option of volunteering to take his place. I already know what will happen. Peeta will ask Haymitch to let him go into the arena with me no matter what. For my sake. To protect me.

I stumble around the cellar, looking for an exit. How did I even get into this place? I feel my way up the steps to the kitchen and see the glass window in the door has been shattered. Must be why my hand seems to be bleeding. I hurry back into the night and head straight to Haymitch's house. He's sitting alone at the kitchen table, a half-emptied bottle of white liquor in one fist, his knife in the other. Drunk as a skunk.

"Ah, there she is. All tuckered out. Finally did the maths, did you, sweetheart? Worked out you won't be going in alone? And now you're here to ask me . . . what?" he says.

I don't answer. The window's wide open and the wind cuts through me just as if I were outside.

"I'll admit, it was easier for the boy. He was here before I could snap the seal on a bottle. Begging me for another chance to go in. But what can you say?" He mimics my voice. "'Take his place, Haymitch, because all things being equal, I'd rather Peeta had a crack at the rest of his life than you'?"

I bite my lip because once he's said it, I'm afraid that's what I do want. For Peeta to live, even if it means Haymitch's death. No, I don't. He's dreadful, of course, but Haymitch is my family now. *What did I come for?* I think. *What could I possibly want here?*

"I came for a drink," I say.

Haymitch bursts out laughing and slams the bottle on the table before me. I run my sleeve across the top and take a couple of gulps before I come up choking. It takes a few minutes to compose myself, and even then my eyes and nose are still streaming. But inside me, the liquor feels like fire and I like it.

"Maybe it should be you," I say matter-of-factly as I pull up a chair. "You hate life, anyway."

"Very true," says Haymitch. "And since last time I tried to keep *you* alive . . . seems like I'm obligated to save the boy this time."

"That's another good point," I say, wiping my nose and tipping up the bottle again.

"Peeta's argument is that since I chose you, I now owe him. Anything he wants. And what he wants is the chance to go in again to protect you," says Haymitch.

I knew it. In this way, Peeta's not hard to predict. While I was wallowing around on the floor of that cellar, thinking only of myself, he was here, thinking only of me. Shame isn't a strong enough word for what I feel.

"You could live a hundred lifetimes and not deserve him, you know," Haymitch says.

"Yeah, yeah," I say brusquely. "No question, he's the superior one in this trio. So, what are you going to do?"

"I don't know." Haymitch sighs. "Go back in with you, maybe, if I can. If my name's drawn at the reaping, it won't matter. He'll just volunteer to take my place."

We sit for a while in silence. "It'd be bad for you in the arena, wouldn't it? Knowing all the others?" I ask.

"Oh, I think we can count on it being unbearable wherever I am." He nods at the bottle. "Can I have that back now?"

"No," I say, wrapping my arms around it. Haymitch pulls another bottle out from under the table and gives the top a twist. But I realize I am not just here for a drink. There's something else I want from Haymitch. "OK, I figured out what I'm asking," I say. "If it is Peeta and me in the Games, this time we try to keep *him* alive."

Something flickers across his bloodshot eyes. Pain.

"Like you said, it's going to be bad no matter how you slice it. And whatever Peeta wants, it's his turn to be saved. We both owe him that." My voice takes on a pleading tone. "Besides, the Capitol hates me so much, I'm as good as dead now. He still might have a chance. Please, Haymitch. Say you'll help me."

He frowns at his bottle, weighing my words. "All right," he says finally.

"Thanks," I say. I should go see Peeta now, but I don't want to. My head's spinning from the drink, and I'm so wiped out, who knows what he could get me to agree to? No, now I have to go home to face my mother and Prim.

As I stagger up the steps to my house, the front door opens and Gale pulls me into his arms. "I was wrong. We should have gone when you said," he whispers.

"No," I say. I'm having trouble focusing, and liquor keeps sloshing out of my bottle and down the back of Gale's jacket, but he doesn't seem to care.

"It's not too late," he says.

Over his shoulder, I see my mother and Prim clutching each other in the doorway. We run. They die. And now I've got Peeta to protect. End of discussion. "Yeah, it is." My knees give way and he's holding me up. As the alcohol overcomes my mind, I hear the glass bottle shatter on the floor. This seems appropriate since I have obviously lost my grip on everything.

When I wake up, I barely get to the toilet before the white liquor makes its reappearance. It burns just as much coming up as it did going down, and tastes twice as bad. I'm trembling and sweaty when I finish vomiting, but at least most of the stuff is out of my system. Enough made it into my bloodstream, though, to result in a pounding headache, parched mouth and boiling stomach.

I turn on the shower and stand under the warm rain for a minute before I realize I'm still in my underclothes. My mother must have just stripped off my filthy outer ones and tucked me in bed. I throw the wet undergarments into the sink and pour shampoo on my head. My hands sting, and that's when I notice the stitches, small and even, across one palm and up the side of the other hand. Vaguely I remember breaking that glass window last night. I scrub myself from head to toe, only stopping to throw up again right in the shower. It's mostly just bile and goes down the drain with the sweet-smelling bubbles.

Finally clean, I pull on my robe and head back to bed, ignoring my dripping hair. I climb under the blankets, sure this is what it must feel like to be poisoned. The footsteps on the stairs renew my panic from last night. I'm not ready to see my mother and Prim. I have to pull myself together to be calm and reassuring, the way I was when we said our goodbyes the day of the last reaping. I have to be strong. I struggle into an upright position, push my wet hair off my throbbing temples, and brace myself for this meeting. They appear in the doorway, holding tea and toast, their faces filled with concern. I open my mouth, planning to start off with some kind of joke, and burst into tears.

So much for being strong.

My mother sits on the side of the bed and Prim crawls right up next to me and they hold me, making quiet soothing sounds, until I am mostly cried out. Then Prim gets a towel and dries my hair, combing out the knots, while my mother coaxes tea and toast into me. They dress me in warm pyjamas and layer more blankets on me and I drift off again.

I can tell by the light it's late afternoon when I come round again. There's a glass of water on my bedside table and I gulp it down thirstily. My stomach and head still feel rocky, but much better than they did earlier. I rise, dress, and braid back my hair. Before I go down, I pause at the top of the stairs, feeling slightly embarrassed about the way I've handled the news of the Quarter Quell. My erratic flight, drinking with Haymitch, weeping.

Given the circumstances, I guess I deserve one day of indulgence. I'm glad the cameras weren't here for it, though.

Downstairs, my mother and Prim embrace me again, but they're not overly emotional. I know they're holding things in to make it easier on me. Looking at Prim's face, it's hard to imagine she's the same frail little girl I left behind on reaping day nine months ago. The combination of that ordeal and all that has followed – the cruelty in the district, the parade of sick and wounded that she often treats by herself now if my mother's hands are too full – these things have aged her by years. She's grown quite a bit, too; we're practically the same height now, but that isn't what makes her seem so much older.

My mother ladles out a mug of broth for me, and I ask for a second mug to take to Haymitch. Then I walk across the lawn to his house. He's only just waking up and accepts the mug without comment. We sit there, almost peacefully, sipping our broth and watching the sun set through his living-room window. I hear someone walking around upstairs and I assume it's Hazelle, but a few minutes later Peeta comes down and tosses a cardboard box of empty liquor bottles on the table with finality.

"There, it's done," he says.

It's taking all of Haymitch's resources to focus his eyes on the bottles, so I speak up. "What's done?"

"I've poured all the liquor down the drain," says Peeta.

This seems to jolt Haymitch out of his stupor, and he paws through the box in disbelief. "You what?"

"I tossed the lot," says Peeta.

"He'll just buy more," I say.

"No, he won't," says Peeta. "I tracked down Ripper this morning and told her I'd turn her in the second she sold to either of you. I paid her off, too, just for good measure, but I don't think she's eager to be back in the Peacekeepers' custody."

Haymitch takes a swipe with his knife but Peeta deflects it so easily it's pathetic. Anger rises up in me. "What business is it of yours what he does?"

"It's completely my business. However it falls out, two of us are going to be in the arena again with the other as mentor. We can't afford any drunkards on this team. Especially not you, Katniss," says Peeta to me.

"What?" I sputter indignantly. It would be more convincing if I weren't still so hungover. "Last night's the only time I've ever even been drunk."

"Yeah, and look at the shape you're in," says Peeta.

I don't know what I expected from my first meeting with Peeta after the announcement. A few hugs and kisses. A little comfort maybe. Not this. I turn to Haymitch. "Don't worry, I'll get you more liquor."

"Then I'll turn you both in. Let you sober up in the stocks," says Peeta.

"What's the point to this?" asks Haymitch.

"The point is that two of us are coming home from the Capitol. One mentor and one victor," says Peeta. "Effie's sending me recordings of all the living victors. We're going to watch their Games and learn everything we can about how they fight. We're going to put on weight and get strong. We're going to start acting like Careers. And one of us is going to be victor again whether you two like it or not!" He sweeps out of the room, slamming the front door.

Haymitch and I wince at the bang.

"I don't like self-righteous people," I say.

"What's to like?" says Haymitch, who begins sucking the dregs out of the empty bottles.

"You and me. That's who he plans on coming home," I say.

"Well, then the joke's on him," says Haymitch.

But after a few days, we agree to act like Careers, because this is the best way to get Peeta ready as well. Every night we watch the old recaps of the Games that the remaining victors won. I realize we never met any of them on the Victory Tour, which seems odd in retrospect. When I bring it up, Haymitch says the last thing President Snow would've wanted was to show Peeta and me – especially me – bonding with other victors in potentially rebellious districts. Victors have a special status, and if they appeared to be supporting my defiance of the Capitol, it would've been dangerous politically. Adjusting for age, I realize some of our opponents may be elderly, which is both sad and reassuring. Peeta takes copious notes, Haymitch volunteers information about the victors' personalities, and slowly we begin to know our competition.

Every morning we do exercises to strengthen our bodies. We run and lift things and stretch our muscles. Every afternoon we work on combat skills, throwing knives, fighting hand to hand; I even teach them to climb trees. Officially, tributes aren't supposed to train, but no one tries to stop us. Even in regular years, the tributes from Districts 1, 2 and 4 show up able to wield spears and swords. This is nothing by comparison.

After all the years of abuse, Haymitch's body resists improvement. He's still remarkably strong, but the shortest run winds him. And you'd think a guy who sleeps every night with a knife might actually be able to hit the side of a house with one, but his hands shake so badly it takes weeks for him to achieve even that.

Peeta and I excel under the new regimen, though. It gives me something to do. It gives us all something to do besides accept defeat. My mother puts us on a special diet to gain weight. Prim treats our sore muscles. Madge sneaks us her father's Capitol newspapers. Predictions on who will be victor of the victors show us among the favourites. Even Gale steps into the picture on Sundays, although he's got no love for Peeta or Haymitch, and teaches us all he knows about snares. It's weird for me, being in conversations with both Peeta and Gale, but they seem to have set aside whatever issues they have about me.

One night, as I'm walking Gale back into town, he even admits, "It'd be better if he were easier to hate."

"Tell me about it," I say. "If I could've just hated him in the arena, we all wouldn't be in this mess now. He'd be dead, and I'd be a happy little victor all by myself."

"And where would we be, Katniss?" asks Gale.

I pause, not knowing what to say. Where *would* I be with my pretend cousin who wouldn't be my cousin if it weren't for Peeta? Would he have still kissed me and would I have kissed him back had I been free to do so? Would I have let myself open up to him, lulled by the security of money and food and the illusion of safety being a victor could bring under different circumstances? But there would still always be the reaping looming over us, over our children. No matter what I wanted. . .

"Hunting. Like every Sunday," I say. I know he didn't mean the question literally, but this is as much as I can honestly give. Gale knows I chose him over Peeta when I didn't make a run for it. To me, there's no point in talking about things that might have been. Even if I had killed Peeta in the arena, I still wouldn't have wanted to marry anyone. I only got engaged to save people's lives, and that completely backfired.

I'm afraid, anyway, that any kind of emotional scene with Gale might cause him to do something drastic. Like start that uprising in the mines. And as Haymitch says, District 12 isn't ready for that. If anything, they're less ready than before the Quarter Quell announcement, because the following morning another hundred Peacekeepers arrived on the train.

Since I don't plan on making it back alive a second time, the sooner Gale lets me go, the better. I do plan on saying one or two things to him after the reaping, when we're allowed an hour for goodbyes. To let Gale know how essential he's been to me all these years. How much better my life has been for knowing him. For loving him, even if it's only in the limited way that I can manage.

But I never get the chance.

The day of the reaping's hot and sultry. The population of District 12 waits, sweating and silent, in the square with machine guns trained on them. I stand alone in a small roped-off area with Peeta and Haymitch in a similar pen to the right of me. The reaping takes only a minute. Effie, shining in a wig of metallic gold, lacks her usual verve. She has to claw around the girls' reaping ball for quite a while to snag the one piece of paper that everyone already knows has my name on it. Then she catches Haymitch's name. He barely has time to shoot me an unhappy look before Peeta has volunteered to take his place.

We are immediately marched into the Justice Building to find Head Peacekeeper Thread waiting for us. "New procedure," he says with a smile. We're ushered out of the back door, into a car, and taken to the train station. There are no cameras on the platform, no crowd to send us on our way. Haymitch and Effie appear, escorted by guards. Peacekeepers hurry us all on to the train and slam the door. The wheels begin to turn.

And I'm left staring out of the window, watching District 12 disappear, with all my goodbyes still hanging on my lips.

14

I remain at the window long after the woods have swallowed up the last glimpse of my home. This time I don't have even the slightest hope of return. Before my first Games, I promised Prim I would do everything I could to win, and now I've sworn to myself to do all I can to keep Peeta alive. I will never reverse this journey again.

I'd actually figured out what I wanted my last words to my loved ones to be. How best to close and lock the doors and leave them sad but safely behind. And now the Capitol has stolen that as well.

"We'll write letters, Katniss," says Peeta from behind me. "It will be better, anyway. Give them a piece of us to hold on to. Haymitch will deliver them for us if . . . they need to be delivered."

I nod and go straight to my room. I sit on the bed,

knowing I will never write those letters. They will be like the speech I tried to write to honour Rue and Thresh in District 11. Things seemed clear in my head and even when I talked before the crowd, but the words never came out of the pen right. Besides, they were meant to go with embraces and kisses and a stroke of Prim's hair, a caress of Gale's face, a squeeze of Madge's hand. They cannot be delivered with a wooden box containing my cold, stiff body.

Too heartsick to cry, all I want is to curl up on the bed and sleep until we arrive in the Capitol tomorrow morning. But I have a mission. No, it's more than a mission. It's my dying wish. *Keep Peeta alive.* And as unlikely as it seems that I can achieve it in the face of the Capitol's anger, it's important that I be at the top of my game. This won't happen if I'm mourning for everyone I love back home. *Let them go,* I tell myself. *Say goodbye and forget them.* I do my best, thinking of them one by one, releasing them like birds from the protective cages inside me, locking the doors against their return.

By the time Effie knocks on my door to call me to dinner, I'm empty. But the lightness isn't entirely unwelcome.

The meal's subdued. So subdued, in fact, that there are long periods of silence relieved only by the removal of old dishes and presentation of new ones. A cold soup of puréed vegetables. Fish cakes with creamy lime paste. Those little birds filled with orange sauce, with wild rice and watercress. Chocolate custard dotted with cherries.

Peeta and Effie make occasional attempts at conversation that quickly die out.

"I love your new hair, Effie," Peeta says.

"Thank you. I had it especially done to match Katniss's pin. I was thinking we might get you a golden ankle band and maybe find Haymitch a gold bracelet or something so we could all look like a team," says Effie.

Evidently, Effie doesn't know that my mockingjay pin is now a symbol used by the rebels. At least in District 8. In the Capitol, the mockingjay is still a fun reminder of an especially exciting Hunger Games. What else could it be? Real rebels don't put a secret symbol on something as durable as jewellery. They put it on a wafer of bread that can be eaten in a second if necessary.

"I think that's a great idea," says Peeta. "How about it, Haymitch?"

"Yeah, whatever," says Haymitch. He's not drinking but I can tell he'd like to be. Effie had them take her own wine away when she saw the effort he was making, but he's in a miserable state. If he were the tribute, he would have owed Peeta nothing and could be as drunk as he liked. Now it's going to take all he's got to keep Peeta alive in an arena full of his old friends, and he'll probably fail.

"Maybe we could get you a wig, too," I say in an attempt at lightness. He just shoots me a look that says to leave him alone, and we all eat our custard in silence.

"Shall we watch the recap of the reapings?" says Effie, dabbing at the corners of her mouth with a white linen napkin.

Peeta goes off to retrieve his notebook on the remaining living victors, and we gather in the compartment with the television to see who our competition will be in the arena. We are all in place as the anthem begins to play and the annual recap of the reaping ceremonies in the twelve districts begins.

In the history of the Games, there have been seventy-five victors. Fifty-nine are still alive. I recognize many of their faces, either from seeing them as tributes or mentors at previous Games or from our recent viewing of the victors' tapes. Some are so old or wasted by illness, drugs or drink that I can't place them. As one would expect, the pools of Career tributes from Districts 1, 2 and 4 are the largest. But every district has managed to scrape up at least one female and one male victor.

The reapings go by quickly. Peeta studiously puts stars by the names of the chosen tributes in his notebook. Haymitch watches, his face devoid of emotion, as friends of his step up to take the stage. Effie makes hushed, distressed comments like "Oh, not Cecelia" or "Well, Chaff never could stay out of a fight", and sighs frequently.

For my part, I try to make some mental record of the other tributes, but like last year, only a few really stick in my head. There's the classically beautiful brother and sister from District 1 who were victors in consecutive years when I was little. Brutus, a volunteer from District 2, who must be at least forty and apparently can't wait to get back in the arena. Finnick, the handsome bronze-haired guy from District 4 who was crowned ten years ago at the age of fourteen. A hysterical young woman with flowing brown hair is also called from 4, but she's quickly replaced by a volunteer, an eighty-year-old woman who needs a cane to walk to the stage. Then there's Johanna Mason, the only living female victor from 7, who won a few years back by pretending she was a weakling. The woman from 8 who Effie calls Cecelia, who looks about thirty, has to detach herself from the three kids who run up to cling to her. Chaff, a man from 11 who I know to be one of Haymitch's particular friends, is also in.

I'm called. Then Haymitch. And Peeta volunteers. One of the announcers actually gets teary because it seems the odds will never be in our favour, we star-crossed lovers of District 12. Then she pulls herself together to say she bets that "these will be the best Games ever!"

Haymitch leaves the compartment without a word, and Effie, after making a few unconnected comments about this tribute or that, bids us goodnight. I just sit there watching Peeta rip out the pages of the victors who were not picked.

"Why don't you get some sleep?" he says.

Because I can't handle the nightmares. Not without you, I think. They are sure to be dreadful tonight. But I can hardly ask Peeta to come sleep with me. We've barely touched since that night Gale was whipped. "What are you going to do?" I ask.

"Just review my notes a while. Get a clear picture of what we're up against. But I'll go over it with you in the morning. Go to bed, Katniss," he says.

So I go to bed and, sure enough, within a few hours I awake from a nightmare where that old woman from District 4 transforms into a large rodent and gnaws on my face. I know I was screaming, but no one comes. Not Peeta, not even one of the Capitol attendants. I pull on a robe to try to calm the gooseflesh crawling over my body. Staying in my compartment is impossible, so I decide to go find someone to make me tea or hot chocolate or anything. Maybe Haymitch is still up. Surely he isn't asleep.

I order warm milk, the most calming thing I can think of, from an attendant. Hearing voices from the television room, I go in and find Peeta. Beside him on the sofa is the box Effie sent of tapes of the old Hunger Games. I recognize the episode in which Brutus became victor.

Peeta rises and flips off the tape when he sees me. "Couldn't sleep?"

"Not for long," I say. I pull the robe more securely around me as I remember the old woman transforming into the rodent.

"Want to talk about it?" he asks. Sometimes that can help, but I just shake my head, feeling weak that people I haven't even fought yet already haunt me.

When Peeta holds out his arms, I walk straight into them. It's the first time since they announced the Quarter Quell that he's offered me any sort of affection. He's been more like a very demanding trainer, always pushing, always insisting Haymitch and I run faster, eat more, know our enemy better. Lover? Forget about that. He abandoned any pretence of even being my friend. I wrap my arms tightly around his neck before he can order me to do push-ups or something. Instead he pulls me in close and buries his face in my hair. Warmth radiates from the spot where his lips just touch my neck, slowly spreading through the rest of me. It feels so good, so impossibly good, that I know I will not be the first to let go.

And why should I? I have said goodbye to Gale. I'll never see him again, that's for certain. Nothing I do now can hurt him. He won't see it or he'll think I am acting for the cameras. That, at least, is one weight off my shoulders.

The arrival of the Capitol attendant with the warm milk is what breaks us apart. He sets a tray with a steaming ceramic jug and two mugs on a table. "I brought an extra cup," he says.

"Thanks," I say.

"And I added a touch of honey to the milk. For sweetness. And just a pinch of spice," he adds. He looks at us like he wants to say more, then gives his head a slight shake and backs out of the room.

"What's with him?" I say.

"I think he feels bad for us," says Peeta.

"Right," I say, pouring the milk.

"I mean it. I don't think the people in the Capitol are going to be all that happy about our going back in," says Peeta. "Or the other victors. They get attached to their champions."

"I'm guessing they'll get over it once the blood starts flowing," I say flatly. Really, if there's one thing I don't have time for, it's worrying about how the Quarter Quell will affect the mood in the Capitol. "So, you're watching all the tapes again?"

"Not really. Just sort of skipping around to see people's different fighting techniques," says Peeta.

"Who's next?" I ask.

"You pick," says Peeta, holding out the box.

The tapes are marked with the year of the Games and the name of the victor. I dig around and suddenly find one in my hand that we have not watched. The year of the Games is fifty. That would make it the second Quarter Quell. And the name of the victor is Haymitch Abernathy.

"We never watched this one," I say.

Peeta shakes his head. "No. I knew Haymitch didn't want to. The same way we didn't want to relive our own Games. And since we're all on the same team, I didn't think it mattered much."

"Is the person who won in twenty-five in here?" I ask.

"I don't think so. Whoever it was must be dead by now, and Effie only sent me victors we might have to face." Peeta weighs Haymitch's tape in his hand. "Why? You think we ought to watch it?"

"It's the only Quell we have. We might pick up something valuable about how they work," I say. But I feel weird. It seems like some major invasion of Haymitch's privacy. I don't know why it should, since the whole thing was public. But it does. I have to admit I'm also extremely curious. "We don't have to tell Haymitch we saw it."

"OK," Peeta agrees. He puts in the tape and I curl up next to him on the sofa with my milk, which is really delicious with the honey and spices, and lose myself in the Fiftieth Hunger Games. After the anthem, they show President Snow drawing the envelope for the second Quarter Quell. He looks younger but just as repellent. He reads from the square of paper in the same onerous voice he used for ours, informing Panem that in honour of the Quarter Quell, there will be twice the number of tributes. The editors smash cut right into the reapings, where name after name after name is called.

By the time we get to District 12, I'm completely overwhelmed by the sheer number of kids going to certain death. There's a woman, not Effie, calling the names in 12, but she still begins with “Ladies first!” She calls out the name of a girl who’s from the Seam, you can tell by the look of her, and then I hear the name “Maysilee Donner”.

“Oh!” I say. “She was my mother’s friend.” The camera finds her in the crowd, clinging to two other girls. All blonde. All definitely merchants’ kids.

“I think that’s your mother hugging her,” says Peeta quietly. And he’s right. As Maysilee Donner bravely disengages herself and heads for the stage, I catch a glimpse of my mother at my age, and no one has exaggerated her beauty. Holding her hand and weeping is another girl who looks just like Maysilee. But a lot like someone else I know, too.

“Madge,” I say.

“That’s her mother. She and Maysilee were twins or something,” Peeta says. “My dad mentioned it once.”

I think of Madge’s mother. Mayor Undersee’s wife. Who spends half her life in bed immobilized with terrible pain, shutting out the world. I think of how I never realized that she and my mother shared this connection. Of Madge showing up in that snowstorm to bring the painkiller for Gale. Of my mockingjay pin and how it means something completely different now that I know that its former owner was Madge’s aunt,

Maysilee Donner, a tribute who was murdered in the arena.

Haymitch's name is called last of all. It's more of a shock to see him than my mother. Young. Strong. Hard to admit, but he was something of a looker. His hair dark and curly, those grey Seam eyes bright and, even then, dangerous.

"Oh. Peeta, you don't think he killed Maysilee, do you?" I burst out. I don't know why, but I can't stand the thought.

"With forty-eight players? I'd say the odds are against it," says Peeta.

The chariot rides – in which the District 12 kids are dressed in awful coal miners' outfits – and the interviews flash by. There's little time to focus on anyone. But since Haymitch is going to be the victor, we get to see one full exchange between him and Caesar Flickerman, who looks exactly as he always does in his twinkling midnight-blue suit. Only his dark green hair, eyelids and lips are different.

"So, Haymitch, what do you think of the Games having one hundred per cent more competitors than usual?" asks Caesar.

Haymitch shrugs. "I don't see that it makes much difference. They'll still be one hundred per cent as stupid as usual, so I figure my odds will be roughly the same."

The audience bursts out laughing and Haymitch gives them a half-smile. Snarky. Arrogant. Indifferent.

"He didn't have to reach far for that, did he?" I say.

Now it's the morning the Games begin. We watch from the point of view of one of the tributes as she rises up through the tube from the Launch Room and into the arena. I can't help but give a slight gasp. Disbelief is reflected on the faces of the players. Even Haymitch's eyebrows lift in pleasure, although they almost immediately knit themselves back into a scowl.

It's the most breathtaking place imaginable. The golden Cornucopia sits in the middle of a green meadow with patches of gorgeous flowers. The sky is azure blue with puffy white clouds. Bright songbirds flutter overhead. By the way some of the tributes are sniffing, it must smell fantastic. An aerial shot shows that the meadow stretches for kilometres. Far in the distance, in one direction, there seems to be woods, in the other, a snowcapped mountain.

The beauty disorients many of the players, because when the gong sounds, most of them seem like they're trying to wake from a dream. Not Haymitch, though. He's at the Cornucopia, armed with weapons and a backpack of choice supplies. He heads for the woods before most of the others have stepped off their plates.

Eighteen tributes are killed in the bloodbath that first day. Others begin to die off and it becomes clear that almost everything in this pretty place – the luscious fruit dangling from the bushes, the water in the crystalline streams, even the scent of the flowers when inhaled too directly – is deadly poisonous. Only the rainwater and the food provided at the Cornucopia are safe to consume. There's also a large, well-stocked Career pack of ten tributes scouring the mountain area for victims.

Haymitch has his own troubles over in the woods, where the fluffy golden squirrels turn out to be carnivorous and attack in packs, and the butterfly stings bring agony if not death. But he persists in moving forward, always keeping the distant mountain at his back.

Maysilee Donner turns out to be pretty resourceful herself, for a girl who leaves the Cornucopia with only a small backpack. Inside she finds a bowl, some dried beef and a blowgun with two dozen darts. Making use of the readily available poisons, she soon turns the blowgun into a deadly weapon by dipping the darts in lethal substances and directing them into her opponents' flesh.

Four days in, the picturesque mountain erupts in a volcano that wipes out another dozen players, including all but five of the Career pack. With the mountain spewing liquid fire, and the meadow offering no means of concealment, the remaining thirteen tributes – including Haymitch and Maysilee – have no choice but to confine themselves to the woods.

Haymitch seems bent on continuing in the same direction, away from the now volcanic mountain, but a maze of tightly woven hedges forces him to circle back into the centre of the woods, where he encounters three of the Careers and pulls his knife. They may be much bigger and stronger, but Haymitch has remarkable speed and has killed two when the third disarms him. That Career is about to slit his throat when a dart drops him to the ground.

Maysilee Donner steps out of the woods. "We'd live longer with two of us."

"Guess you just proved that," says Haymitch, rubbing his neck. "Allies?" Maysilee nods. And there they are, instantly drawn into one of those pacts you'd be hard-pressed to break if you ever expect to go home and face your district.

Just like Peeta and me, they do better together. Get more rest, work out a system to salvage more rainwater, fight as a team, and share the food from the dead tributes' packs. But Haymitch is still determined to keep moving on.

"Why?" Maysilee keeps asking, and he ignores her until she refuses to move any further without an answer.

"Because it has to end somewhere, right?" says Haymitch. "The arena can't go on for ever."

"What do you expect to find?" Maysilee asks.

"I don't know. But maybe there's something we can use," he says.

When they finally do make it through that impossible hedge, using a blowtorch from one of the dead Careers' packs, they find themselves on flat, dry earth that leads to a cliff. Far below, you can see jagged rocks.

"That's all there is, Haymitch. Let's go back," says Maysilee.

"No, I'm staying here," he says.

"All right. There's only five of us left. May as well say goodbye now, anyway," she says. "I don't want it to come down to you and me."

"OK," he agrees. That's all. He doesn't offer to shake her hand or even look at her. And she walks away.

Haymitch skirts along the edge of the cliff as if trying to figure something out. His foot dislodges a pebble and it falls into the abyss, apparently gone for ever. But a minute later, as he sits to rest, the pebble shoots back up beside him. Haymitch stares at it, puzzled, and then his face takes on a strange intensity. He lobs a rock the size of his fist over the cliff and waits. When it flies back out and right into his hand, he starts laughing.

That's when we hear Maysilee begin to scream. The alliance is over and she broke it off, so no one could blame him for ignoring her. But Haymitch runs for her, anyway. He arrives only in time to watch the last of a flock of candy-pink birds, equipped with long, thin beaks, skewer her through the neck. He holds her hand while she dies, and all I can think of is Rue and how I was too late to save her, too.

Later that day, another tribute is killed in combat and a third gets eaten by a pack of those fluffy squirrels, leaving Haymitch and a girl from District 1 to vie for the crown. She's bigger than he is and just as fast, and when the inevitable fight comes, it's bloody and awful and both have received what could well be fatal wounds, when Haymitch is finally disarmed. He staggers through the beautiful woods, holding his intestines in, while she stumbles after him, carrying the axe that should deliver his death blow. Haymitch makes a beeline for his cliff and has just reached the edge when she throws the axe. He collapses on the ground and it flies into the abyss. Now weaponless as well, the girl just stands there, trying to staunch the flow of blood pouring from her empty eye socket. She's thinking perhaps that she can outlast Haymitch, who's starting to convulse on the ground. But what she doesn't know, and what he does, is that the axe will return. And when it flies back over the ledge, it buries itself in her head. The cannon sounds, her body is removed, and the trumpets blow to announce Haymitch's victory.

Peeta clicks off the tape and we sit there in silence for a while.

Finally Peeta says, "That force field at the bottom of the cliff, it was like the one on the roof of the Training Centre. The one that throws you back if you try to jump off and commit suicide. Haymitch found a way to turn it into a weapon."

"Not just against the other tributes, but the Capitol, too," I say. "You know they didn't expect that to happen. It wasn't meant to be part of the arena. They never planned on anyone using it as a weapon. It made them look stupid that he figured it out. I bet they had a good time trying to spin that one. Bet that's why I don't remember seeing it on television. It's almost as bad as us and the berries!"

I can't help laughing, really laughing, for the first time in months. Peeta just shakes his head like I've lost my mind – and maybe I have, a little.

"Almost, but not quite," says Haymitch from behind us. I whip around, afraid he's going to be angry over us watching his tape, but he just smirks and takes a swig from a bottle of wine. So much for sobriety. I guess I should be upset he's drinking again, but I'm preoccupied with another feeling.

I've spent all these weeks getting to know who my competitors are, without even thinking about who my teammates are. Now a new kind of confidence is lighting up inside of me, because I think I finally know who Haymitch is. And I'm beginning to know who I am. And surely, two people who have caused the Capitol so much trouble can think of a way to get Peeta home alive.

15

Having been through prep with Flavius, Venia and Octavia numerous times, it should just be an old routine to survive. But I haven't anticipated the emotional ordeal that awaits me. At some point during the prep, each of them bursts into tears at least twice, and Octavia pretty much keeps up a running whimper throughout the morning. It turns out they really have become attached to me, and the idea of my returning to the arena has undone them. Combine that with the fact that by losing me they'll be losing their ticket to all kinds of big social events, particularly my wedding, and the whole thing becomes unbearable. The idea of being strong for someone else having never entered their heads, I find myself in the position of having to console them. Since I'm the person going in to be slaughtered, this is somewhat annoying.

It's interesting, though, when I think of what Peeta said about the attendant on the train being unhappy about the victors having to fight again. About people in the Capitol not liking it. I still think all of that will be forgotten once the gong sounds, but it's something of a revelation that those in the Capitol feel anything at all about us. They certainly don't have a problem watching children being murdered every year. But maybe they know too much about the victors, especially the ones who've been celebrities for ages, to forget we're human beings. It's more like watching your own friends die. More like the Games are for those of us in the districts.

By the time Cinna shows up, I am irritable and exhausted from comforting the prep team, especially because their constant tears are reminding me of the ones undoubtedly being shed at home. Standing there in my thin robe with my stinging skin and heart, I know I can't bear even one more look of regret. So the moment he walks in the door I snap, "I swear if you cry, I'll kill you here and now."

Cinna just smiles. "Had a damp morning?"

"You could wring me out," I reply.

Cinna puts his arm around my shoulder and leads me into lunch. "Don't worry. I always channel my emotions into my work. That way I don't hurt anyone but myself."

"I can't go through that again," I warn him.

"I know. I'll talk to them," says Cinna.

Lunch makes me feel a bit better. Pheasant with a selection of jewel-coloured jellies, and tiny versions of real vegetables swimming in butter, and potatoes mashed with parsley. For dessert we dip chunks of fruit in a pot of melted chocolate, and Cinna has to order a second pot because I start just eating the stuff with a spoon.

"So, what are we wearing for the opening ceremonies?" I finally ask as I scrape the second pot clean. "Headlamps or fire?" I know the chariot ride will require Peeta and me to be dressed in something coal related.

"Something along that line," he says.

When it's time to get in costume for the opening ceremonies, my prep team shows up but Cinna sends them away, saying they've done such a spectacular job in the morning, there's nothing left to do. They go off to recover, thankfully leaving me in Cinna's hands. He puts up my hair first, in the braided style my mother introduced him to, then proceeds with my make-up. Last year he used little so that the audience would recognize me when I landed in the arena. But now my face is almost obscured by the dramatic highlights and dark shadows. High arching eyebrows, sharp cheekbones, smouldering eyes, deep purple lips. The costume looks deceptively simple at first, just a fitted black jumpsuit that covers me from the neck down. He places a half crown like the one I received as victor on my head, but it's made of a heavy black metal, not gold. Then he adjusts the light in the room to mimic twilight and presses a button just inside the fabric on my wrist. I look down, fascinated, as my ensemble slowly comes to life, first with a soft golden light but gradually transforming to the orange-red of burning coal. I look as if I have been coated in glowing embers – no, that I *am* a glowing ember straight from our fireplace. The colours rise and fall, shift and blend, in exactly the way the coals do.

"How did you do this?" I say in wonder.

"Portia and I spent a lot of hours watching fires," says Cinna. "Now look at yourself."

He turns me towards a mirror so that I can take in the entire effect. I do not see a girl, or even a woman, but some unearthly being who looks like she might make her home in the volcano that destroyed so many in Haymitch's Quell. The black crown, which now appears red-hot, casts strange shadows on my dramatically made-up face. Katniss, the girl on fire, has left behind her flickering flames and bejewelled gowns and soft candlelight frocks. She is as deadly as fire itself.

"I think . . . this is just what I needed to face the others," I say.

"Yes, I think your days of pink lipstick and ribbons are behind you," says Cinna. He touches the button on my wrist again, extinguishing my light. "Let's not run down your power pack. When you're on the chariot this time, no waving, no smiling. I just want you to look straight ahead, as if the entire audience is beneath your notice."

"Finally something I'll be good at," I say.

Cinna has a few more things to attend to, so I decide to head down to the ground floor of the Remake Centre, which houses the huge gathering place for the tributes and their chariots before the opening ceremonies. I'm hoping to find Peeta and Haymitch, but they haven't arrived yet. Unlike last year, when all the tributes were practically glued to their chariots, the scene is very social. The victors, both this year's tributes and their mentors, are standing around in small groups, talking. Of course, they all know one another and I don't know anyone, and I'm not really the sort of person to go around introducing myself. So I just stroke the neck of one of my horses and try not to be noticed.

It doesn't work.

The crunching hits my ear before I even know he's

beside me, and when I turn my head, Finnick Odair's famous sea-green eyes are only centimetres from mine. He pops a sugar cube in his mouth and leans against my horse.

"Hello, Katniss," he says, as if we've known each other for years, when in fact we've never met.

"Hello, Finnick," I say, just as casually, although I'm feeling uncomfortable at his closeness, especially since he's got so much bare skin exposed.

"Want a sugar cube?" he says, offering his hand, which is piled high. "They're supposed to be for the horses, but who cares? They've got years to eat sugar, whereas you and I . . . well, if we see something sweet, we better grab it quick."

Finnick Odair is something of a living legend in Panem. Since he won the Sixty-fifth Hunger Games when he was only fourteen, he's still one of the youngest victors. Being from District 4, he was a Career, so the odds were already in his favour, but what no trainer could claim to have given him was his extraordinary beauty. Tall, athletic, with golden skin and bronze-coloured hair and those incredible eyes. While other tributes that year were hard-pressed to get a handful of grain or some matches for a gift, Finnick never wanted for anything, not food or medicine or weapons. It took about a week for his competitors to realize that he was the one to kill, but it was too late. He was already a good fighter with the spears and knives he had found in the Cornucopia. When he received a silver parachute with a trident – which may be the most expensive gift I've ever seen given in the arena – it was all over. District 4's industry is fishing. He'd been on boats his whole life. The trident was a natural, deadly extension of his arm. He wove a net out of some kind of vine he found, used it to entangle his opponents so he could spear them with the trident, and within a matter of days the crown was his.

The citizens of the Capitol have been drooling over him ever since.

Because of his youth, they couldn't really touch him for the first year or two. But ever since he turned sixteen, he's spent his time at the Games being dogged by those desperately in love with him. No one retains his favour for long. He can go through four or five in his annual visit. Old or young, lovely or plain, rich or very rich, he'll keep them company and take their extravagant gifts, but he never stays, and once he's gone he never comes back.

I can't argue that Finnick isn't one of the most stunning, sensuous people on the planet. But I can honestly say he's never been attractive to me.

Maybe he's too pretty, or maybe he's too easy to get, or maybe it's really that he'd just be too easy to lose.

"No, thanks," I say to the sugar. "I'd love to borrow your outfit sometime, though."

He's draped in a golden net that's strategically knotted at his groin so that he can't technically be called naked, but he's about as close as you can get. I'm sure his stylist thinks the more of Finnick the audience sees, the better.

"You're absolutely terrifying me in that get-up. What happened to the pretty little-girl dresses?" he asks. He wets his lips just ever so slightly with his tongue. Probably this drives most people crazy. But for some reason all I can think of is old Cray, salivating over some poor, starving young woman.

"I outgrew them," I say.

Finnick takes the collar of my outfit and runs it between his fingers. "It's too bad about this Quell thing. You could have made out like a bandit in the Capitol. Jewels, money, anything you wanted."

"I don't like jewels, and I have more money than I need. What do you spend all yours on, anyway, Finnick?" I say.

"Oh, I haven't dealt in anything as common as money for years," says Finnick.

"Then how do they pay you for the pleasure of your company?" I ask.

"With secrets," he says softly. He tips his head in so his lips are almost in contact with mine. "What about you, girl on fire? Do you have any secrets worth my time?"

For some stupid reason, I blush, but I force myself to hold my ground. "No, I'm an open book," I whisper back. "Everybody seems to know my secrets before I know them myself."

He smiles. "Unfortunately, I think that's true." His eyes flicker off to the side. "Peeta is coming. Sorry you have to cancel your wedding. I know how devastating that must be for you." He tosses another sugar cube in his mouth and saunters off.

Peeta's beside me, dressed in an outfit identical to mine. "What did Finnick Odair want?" he asks.

I turn and put my lips close to Peeta's and drop my eyelids in imitation of Finnick. "He offered me sugar and wanted to know all my secrets," I say in my best seductive voice.

Peeta laughs. "Ugh. Not really."

"Really," I say. "I'll tell you more when my skin stops crawling."

"Do you think we'd have ended up like this if only one of us had won?" he asks, glancing around at the other victors. "Just another part of the freak show?"

"Sure. Especially you," I say.

"Oh. And why especially me?" he says with a smile.

"Because you have a weakness for beautiful things and I don't," I say with an air of superiority. "They would lure you into their Capitol ways and you'd be lost entirely."

"Having an eye for beauty isn't the same thing as a weakness," Peeta points out. "Except possibly when it comes to you." The music is beginning and I see the wide doors opening for the first chariot, hear the roar of the crowd. "Shall we?" He holds out a hand to help me into the chariot.

I climb up and pull him up after me. "Hold still," I say, and straighten his crown. "Have you seen your suit turned on? We're going to be fabulous again."

"Absolutely. But Portia says we're to be very above it all. No waving or anything," he says. "Where are they, anyway?"

"I don't know." I eye the procession of chariots. "Maybe we better go ahead and switch ourselves on." We do, and as we begin to glow, I can see people pointing at us and chattering, and I know that, once again, we'll be the talk of the opening ceremonies.

We're almost at the door. I crane my head around, but neither Portia nor Cinna, who were with us right up to the final second last year, are anywhere in sight. "Are we supposed to hold hands this year?" I ask.

"I guess they've left it up to us," says Peeta.

I look up into those blue eyes that no amount of dramatic make-up can make truly deadly and remember how, just a year ago, I was prepared to kill him. Convinced he was trying to kill me. Now everything is reversed. I'm determined to keep him alive, knowing the cost will be my own life, but the part of me that is not so brave as I could wish is glad that it's Peeta, not Haymitch, beside me. Our hands find each other without further discussion. Of course we will go into this as one.

The voice of the crowd rises into one universal scream as we roll into the fading evening light, but neither one of us reacts. I simply fix my eyes on a point far in the distance and pretend there is no audience, no hysteria. I can't help catching glimpses of us on the huge screens along the route, and we are not just beautiful, we are dark and powerful. No, more. We star-crossed lovers from District 12, who suffered so much and enjoyed so little the rewards of our victory, do not seek the fans' favour, grace them with our smiles, or catch their kisses. We are unforgiving.

And I love it. Getting to be myself at last.

As we curve around into the loop of the City Circle, I can see that a couple of the other stylists have tried to steal Cinna and Portia's idea of illuminating their tributes. The electric-light-studded outfits from District 3, where they make electronics, at least make sense. But what are the livestock keepers from District 10, who are dressed as cows, doing with flaming belts? Broiling themselves? Pathetic.

Peeta and I, on the other hand, are so mesmerizing with our ever-changing coal costumes that most of the other tributes are staring at us. We seem particularly riveting to the pair from District 6, who are known morphling addicts. Both bone thin, with sagging yellowish skin. They can't tear their overlarge eyes away, even when President Snow begins to speak from his balcony, welcoming us all to the Quell. The anthem plays, and as we make our final trip around the circle, am I wrong? Or do I see the president fixated on me as well?

Peeta and I wait until the doors of the Training Centre have closed behind us to relax. Cinna and Portia are there, pleased with our performance, and Haymitch has made an appearance this year as well, only he's not at our chariot, he's over with the tributes of District 11. I see him nod in our direction and then they follow him over to greet us.

I know Chaff by sight because I've spent years watching him pass a bottle back and forth with Haymitch on television. He's dark-skinned, about two metres tall, and one of his arms ends in a stump because he lost his hand in the Games he won thirty years ago. I'm sure they offered him some artificial replacement, like they did Peeta when they had to amputate his lower leg, but I guess he didn't take it.

The woman, Seeder, looks almost like she could be from the Seam, with her olive skin and straight black hair streaked with silver. Only her golden-brown eyes mark her as from another district. She must be around sixty, but she still looks strong, and there's no sign she's turned to liquor or morphling or any other chemical form of escape over the years. Before either of us says a word, she embraces me. I know somehow it must be because of Rue and Thresh. Before I can stop myself, I whisper, "The families?"

"They're alive," she says back softly before letting me go.

Chaff throws his good arm around me and gives me a big kiss right on the mouth. I jerk back, startled, while he and Haymitch guffaw.

That's about all the time we get before the Capitol

attendants are firmly directing us towards the elevators. I get the distinct feeling they're not comfortable with the camaraderie among the victors, who couldn't seem to care less. As I walk towards the elevators, my hand still linked with Peeta's, someone else rustles up to my side. The girl pulls off a headdress of leafy branches and tosses it behind her without bothering to look where it falls.

Johanna Mason. From District 7. Lumber and paper, thus the tree. She won by very convincingly portraying herself as weak and helpless so that she would be ignored. Then she demonstrated a wicked ability to murder. She ruffles up her spiky hair and rolls her wide-set brown eyes. "Isn't my costume awful? My stylist's the biggest idiot in the Capitol. Our tributes have been trees for forty years under her. Wish I'd got Cinna. You look fantastic."

Girl talk. That thing I've always been so bad at. Opinions on clothes, hair, make-up. So I lie. "Yeah, he's been helping me design my own clothing line. You should see what he can do with velvet." Velvet. The only fabric I could think of off the top of my head.

"I have. On your tour. That strapless number you wore in District Two? The deep blue one with the diamonds? So gorgeous I wanted to reach through the screen and tear it right off your back," says Johanna.

I bet you did, I think. *With a few centimetres of my flesh*.

While we wait for the elevators, Johanna unzips the rest of her tree, letting it drop to the floor, and then kicks it away in disgust. Except for her forest-green slippers, she doesn't have on a stitch of clothing. "That's better."

We end up on the same elevator with her, and she spends the whole ride to the seventh floor chatting to Peeta about his paintings while the light of his still-glowing costume reflects off her bare breasts. When she leaves, I ignore him, but I just know he's grinning. I toss aside his hand as the doors close behind Chaff and Seeder, leaving us alone, and he breaks out laughing.

"What?" I say, turning on him as we step out on our floor.

"It's you, Katniss. Can't you see?" he says.

"What's me?" I say.

"Why they're all acting like this. Finnick with his sugar cubes and Chaff kissing you and that whole thing with Johanna stripping down." He tries to take on a more serious tone, unsuccessfully. "They're playing with you because you're so . . . you know."

"No, I don't know," I say. And I really have no idea what he's talking about.

"It's like when you wouldn't look at me naked in the arena even though I was half dead. You're so . . . pure," he says finally.

"I am not!" I say. "I've been practically ripping your clothes off every time there's been a camera for the last year!"

"Yeah, but . . . I mean, for the Capitol, you're pure," he says, clearly trying to mollify me. "For me, you're perfect. They're just teasing you."

"No, they're laughing at me, and so are you!" I say.

"No." Peeta shakes his head, but he's still suppressing a smile. I'm seriously rethinking the question of who should get out of these Games alive when the other elevator opens.

Haymitch and Effie join us, looking pleased about something. Then Haymitch's face grows hard.

What did I do now? I almost say, but I see he's staring behind me at the entrance to the dining room.

Effie blinks in the same direction, then says brightly, "Looks like they've got you a matched set this year."

I turn around and find the red-headed Avox girl who tended to me last year until the Games began. I think how nice it is to have a friend here. I notice that the young man beside her, another Avox, also has red hair. That must be what Effie meant by a matched set.

Then a chill runs through me. Because I know him, too. Not from the Capitol but from years of having easy conversations in the Hob, joking over Greasy Sae's soup, and that last day watching him lie unconscious in the square while the life bled out of Gale.

Our new Avox is Darius.

16

Haymitch grips my wrist as if anticipating my next move, but I am as speechless as the Capitol's torturers have rendered Darius. Haymitch once told me they did something to Avoxes' tongues so they could never talk again. In my head I hear Darius's voice, playful and bright, ringing across the Hob to tease me. Not as my fellow victors make fun of me now, but because we genuinely liked each other. If Gale could see him. . .

I know any move I would make towards Darius, any act of recognition, would only result in punishment for him. So we just stare into each other's eyes. Darius, now a mute slave; me, now headed to death. What would we say, anyway? That we're sorry for the other's lot? That we ache for the other's pain? That we're glad we had the chance to know each other?

No, Darius shouldn't be glad he knew me. If I had been there to stop Thread, he wouldn't have stepped forward to save Gale. Wouldn't be an Avox. And more specifically, wouldn't be *my* Avox, because President Snow has so obviously had him placed here for my benefit.

I twist my wrist from Haymitch's grasp and head down to my old bedroom, locking the door behind me. I sit on the side of my bed, elbows on my knees, forehead on my fists, and watch my glowing suit in the darkness, imagining I am in my old home in District 12, huddled beside the fire. It slowly fades back to black as the power pack dies out.

When Effie eventually knocks on the door to summon me to dinner, I get up and take off my suit, fold it neatly, and set it on the table with my crown. In the bathroom, I wash the dark streaks of make-up from my face. I dress in a simple shirt and trousers and go down the hall to the dining room.

I'm not aware of much at dinner except that Darius and the red-headed Avox girl are our servers. Effie, Haymitch, Cinna, Portia and Peeta are all there, talking about the opening ceremonies, I suppose. But the only time I really feel present is when I purposely knock a dish of peas to the floor and, before anyone can stop me, crouch down to clean them up. Darius is right by me when I send the dish over, and we two are briefly side by side, obscured from view, as we scoop up the peas. For just one moment our hands meet. I can feel his skin, rough under the buttery sauce from the dish. In the tight, desperate clench of our fingers are all the words we will never be able to say. Then Effie's clucking at me from behind about how "that isn't your job, Katniss!" and he lets go.

When we go in to watch the recap of the opening ceremonies, I wedge myself in between Cinna and Haymitch on the sofa because I don't want to be next to Peeta. This awfulness with Darius belongs to me and Gale and maybe even Haymitch, but not to Peeta. He might've known Darius to nod hello, but Peeta wasn't Hob the way the rest of us were. Besides, I'm still angry with him for laughing at me along with the other victors, and the last thing I want is his sympathy and comfort. I haven't changed my mind about saving him in the arena, but I don't owe him more than that.

As I watch the procession to the City Circle, I think how it's bad enough that they dress us all up in costumes and parade us through the streets in chariots on a regular year. Kids in costumes are silly, but ageing victors, it turns out, are pitiful. A few who are on the younger side, like Johanna and Finnick, or whose bodies haven't fallen into disrepair, like Seeder and

Brutus, can still manage to maintain a little dignity. But the majority, who are in the clutches of drink or morphling or illness, look grotesque in their costumes, depicting cows and trees and loaves of bread. Last year we chattered away about each contestant, but tonight there's only the occasional comment. Small wonder the crowd goes wild when Peeta and I appear, looking so young and strong and beautiful in our brilliant costumes. The very image of what tributes should be.

As soon as it's over, I stand up and thank Cinna and Portia for their amazing work and head off to bed. Effie calls a reminder to meet early for breakfast to work out our training strategy, but even her voice sounds hollow. Poor Effie. She finally had a decent year in the Games with Peeta and me, and now it's all broken down into a mess that even she can't put a positive spin on. In Capitol terms, I'm guessing this counts as a true tragedy.

Soon after I go to bed, there's a quiet knock on my door, but I ignore it. I don't want Peeta tonight. Especially not with Darius around. It's almost as bad as if Gale were here. Gale. How am I supposed to let him go with Darius haunting the hallways?

Tongues figure prominently in my nightmares. First I watch frozen and helpless while gloved hands carry out the bloody dissection in Darius's mouth.

Then I'm at a party where everyone wears masks and someone with a flicking, wet tongue, who I suppose is Finnick, stalks me, but when he catches me and pulls off his mask, it's President Snow, and his puffy lips are dripping in bloody saliva. Finally I'm back in the arena, my own tongue as dry as sandpaper, while I try to reach a pool of water that recedes every time I'm about to touch it.

When I wake, I stumble to the bathroom and gulp water from the tap until I can hold no more. I strip off my sweaty clothes and fall back into bed, naked, and somehow find sleep again.

I delay going down to breakfast as long as possible the next morning because I really don't want to discuss our training strategy. What's to discuss? Every victor already knows what everybody else can do. Or used to be able to do, anyway. So Peeta and I will continue to act in love and that's that. Somehow I'm just not up to talking about it, especially with Darius standing mutely by. I take a long shower, dress slowly in the outfit Cinna has left for training, and order food from the menu in my room by speaking into a mouthpiece. In a minute, sausage, eggs, potatoes, bread, juice and hot chocolate appear. I eat my fill, trying to drag out the minutes until ten o'clock, when we have to go down to the Training Centre. By nine-thirty, Haymitch is pounding on my door, obviously fed up with me, ordering me to the dining room NOW! Still, I brush my teeth before meandering down the hall, effectively killing another five minutes.

The dining room's empty except for Peeta and Haymitch, whose face is flushed with drink and anger. On his wrist he wears a solid-gold bangle with a pattern of flames – this must be his concession to Effie's matching-token plan – that he twists unhappily. It's a very handsome bangle, really, but the movement makes it seem like something confining, a shackle, rather than a piece of jewellery. "You're late," he snarls at me.

"Sorry. I slept in after the mutilated-tongue nightmares kept me up half the night." I mean to sound hostile, but my voice catches at the end of the sentence.

Haymitch gives me a scowl, then relents. "All right, never mind. Today, in training, you've got two jobs. One, stay in love."

"Obviously," I say.

"And two, make some friends," says Haymitch.

"No," I say. "I don't trust any of them, I can't stand most of them, and I'd rather operate with just the two of us."

"That's what I said at first, but—" Peeta begins.

"But it won't be enough," Haymitch insists. "You're going to need more allies this time around."

"Why?" I ask.

"Because you're at a distinct disadvantage. Your competitors have known each other for years. So who do you think they're going to target first?" he says.

"Us. And nothing we're going to do is going to override any old friendship," I say. "So why bother?"

"Because you can fight. You're popular with the crowd. That could still make you desirable allies. But only if you let the others know you're willing to team up with them," says Haymitch.

"You mean you want us in the Career pack this year?" I ask, unable to hide my distaste. Traditionally the tributes from Districts 1, 2 and 4 join forces, possibly taking in a few other exceptional fighters, and hunt down the weaker competitors.

"That's been our strategy, hasn't it? To train like Careers?" counters Haymitch. "And who makes up the Career pack is generally agreed upon before the Games begin. Peeta barely got in with them last year."

I think of the loathing I felt when I discovered Peeta was with the Careers during the last Games. "So we're to try to get in with Finnick and Brutus – is that what you're saying?"

"Not necessarily. Everyone's a victor. Make your

own pack if you'd rather. Choose who you like. I'd suggest Chaff and Seeder. Although Finnick's not to be ignored," says Haymitch. "Find someone to team up with who might be of some use to you. Remember, you're not in a ring full of trembling children any more. These people are all experienced killers, no matter what shape they appear to be in."

Maybe he's right. Only who could I trust? Seeder maybe. But do I really want to make a pact with her, only to possibly have to kill her later? No. Still, I made a pact with Rue under the same circumstances. I tell Haymitch I'll try, even though I think I'll be pretty bad at the whole thing.

Effie shows up a bit early to take us down because last year, even though we were on time, we were the last two tributes to show up. But Haymitch tells her he doesn't want her taking us down to the gym. None of the other victors will be showing up with a babysitter, and being the youngest, it's even more important we look self-reliant. So she has to satisfy herself with taking us to the elevator, fussing over our hair, and pushing the button for us.

It's such a short ride that there's no real time for conversation, but when Peeta takes my hand, I don't pull it away. I may have ignored him last night in private, but in training we must appear as an inseparable team.

Effie needn't have worried about us being the last to arrive. Only Brutus and the woman from District 2, Enobaria, are present. Enobaria looks to be about thirty and all I can remember about her is that, in hand-to-hand combat, she killed one tribute by ripping open his throat with her teeth. She became so famous for this act that, after she was a victor, she had her teeth cosmetically altered so each one ends in a sharp point like a fang and is inlaid with gold. She has no shortage of admirers in the Capitol.

By ten o'clock, only about half of the tributes have shown up. Atala, the woman who runs training, begins her spiel right on time, unfazed by the poor attendance. Maybe she expected it. I'm sort of relieved, because that means there are a dozen people I don't have to pretend to make friends with. Atala runs through the list of stations, which include both combat and survival skills, and releases us to train.

I tell Peeta I think we'd do best to split up, thus covering more territory. When he goes off to chuck spears with Brutus and Chaff, I head over to the knot-tying station. Hardly anyone ever bothers to visit it. I like the trainer and he remembers me fondly, maybe because I spent time with him last year. He's pleased when I show him I can still set the trap that leaves an enemy dangling by a leg from a tree. Clearly he took note of my snares in the arena last year and now sees me as an advanced pupil, so I ask him to review every kind of knot that might come in handy and a few that I'll probably never use. I'd be content to spend the morning alone with him, but after about an hour and a half, someone puts his arms around me from behind, his fingers easily finishing the complicated knot I've been sweating over. Of course it's Finnick, who seems to have spent his childhood doing nothing but wielding tridents and manipulating ropes into fancy knots for nets, I guess. I watch for a minute while he picks up a length of rope, makes a noose, and then pretends to hang himself for my amusement.

Rolling my eyes, I head over to another vacant station where tributes can learn to build fires. I already make excellent fires, but I'm still pretty dependent on matches for starting them. So the trainer has me work with flint, steel and some charred cloth. This is much harder than it looks, and even working as intently as I can, it takes me about an hour to get a fire going. I look up with a triumphant smile only to find I have company.

The two tributes from District 3 are beside me, struggling to start a decent fire with matches. I think about leaving, but I really want to try using the flint again, and if I have to report back to Haymitch that I tried to make friends, these two might be a bearable choice. Both are small in stature with ashen skin and black hair. The woman, Wiress, is probably around my mother's age and speaks in a quiet, intelligent voice. But right away I notice she has a habit of dropping off her words in mid-sentence, as if she's forgotten you're there. Beetee, the man, is older and somewhat fidgety. He wears glasses but spends a lot of time looking under them. They're a little strange, but I'm pretty sure neither of them is going to try to make me uncomfortable by stripping naked. And they're from District 3. Maybe they can even confirm my suspicions of an uprising there.

I glance around the Training Centre. Peeta is at the center of a ribald circle of knife throwers. The morphlings from District 6 are in the camouflage station, painting each other's faces with bright pink swirls. The male tribute from District 5 is vomiting wine on the sword-fighting floor. Finnick and the old woman from his district are using the archery station. Johanna Mason is naked again and oiling her skin down for a wrestling lesson. I decide to stay put.

Wiress and Beetee make decent company. They seem friendly enough but don't pry. We talk about our talents; they tell me they both invent things, which makes my supposed interest in fashion seem pretty weak. Wiress brings up some sort of stitching device she's working on.

"It senses the density of the fabric and selects the strength," she says, and then becomes absorbed in a bit of dry straw before she can go on.

"The strength of the thread," Beetee finishes explaining. "Automatically. It rules out human error." Then he talks about his recent success creating a musical chip that's tiny enough to be concealed in a flake of glitter but can hold hours of songs. I remember Octavia talking about this during the wedding shoot, and I see a possible chance to allude to the uprising.

"Oh, yeah. My prep team was all upset a few months ago, I think, because they couldn't get hold of that," I say casually. "I guess a lot of orders from District Three were getting backed up."

Beetee examines me under his glasses. "Yes. Did you have any similar back-ups in coal production this year?" he asks.

"No. Well, we lost a couple of weeks when they brought in a new Head Peacekeeper and his crew, but nothing major," I say. "To production, I mean. Two weeks sitting around your house doing nothing just means two weeks of being hungry for most people."

I think they understand what I'm trying to say.

That we've had no uprising. "Oh. That's a shame," says Wiress in a slightly disappointed voice. "I found your district very. . ." She trails off, distracted by something in her head.

"Interesting," fills in Beetee. "We both did."

I feel bad, knowing that their district must have suffered much worse than ours. I feel I have to defend my people. "Well, there aren't very many of us in Twelve," I say. "Not that you'd know it nowadays by the size of the Peacekeeping force. But I guess we're interesting enough."

As we move over to the shelter station, Wiress stops and gazes up at the stands where the Gamemakers are roaming around, eating and drinking, sometimes taking notice of us. "Look," she says, giving her head a slight nod in their direction. I look up and see Plutarch Heavensbee in the magnificent purple robe with the fur-trimmed collar that designates him as Head Gamemaker. He's eating a turkey leg.

I don't see why this merits comment, but I say, "Yes, he's been promoted to Head Gamemaker this year."

"No, no. There by the corner of the table. You can just. . ." says Wiress.

Beetee squints under his glasses. "Just make it out."

I stare in that direction, perplexed. But then I see

it. A patch of space about fifteen centimetres square at the corner of the table seems almost to be vibrating. It's as if the air is rippling in tiny visible waves, distorting the sharp edges of the wood and a goblet of wine someone has set there.

"A force field. They've set one up between the Gamemakers and us. I wonder what brought that on," Beetee says.

"Me, probably," I confess. "Last year I shot an arrow at them during my private training session." Beetee and Wiress look at me curiously. "I was provoked. So, do all force fields have a spot like that?"

"Chink," says Wiress vaguely.

"In the armour, as it were," finishes Beetee. "Ideally it'd be invisible, wouldn't it?"

I want to ask them more, but lunch is announced. I look for Peeta, but he's hanging out with a group of about ten other victors, so I decide just to eat with District 3. Maybe I can get Seeder to join us.

When we make our way into the dining area, I see some of Peeta's gang have other ideas. They're dragging all the smaller tables to form one large table so that we all have to eat together. Now I don't know what to do. Even at school I used to avoid eating at a crowded table. Frankly, I'd probably have sat alone if Madge hadn't made a habit of joining me. I guess I'd have eaten with Gale except, being two grades apart, our lunch never fell at the same time.

I take a tray and start making my way around the food-laden carts that ring the room. Peeta catches up with me at the stew. "How's it going?"

"Good. Fine. I like the District Three victors," I say. "Wiress and Beetee."

"Really?" he asks. "They're something of a joke to the others."

"Why does that not surprise me?" I say. I think of how Peeta was always surrounded at school by a crowd of friends. It's amazing, really, that he ever took any notice of me except to think I was odd.

"Johanna's nicknamed them Nuts and Volts," he says. "I think she's Nuts and he's Volts."

"And so I'm stupid for thinking they might be useful. Because of something Johanna Mason said while she was oiling up her breasts for wrestling," I retort.

"Actually I think the nickname's been around for years. And I didn't mean that as an insult. I'm just sharing information," he says.

"Well, Wiress and Beetee are smart. They invent things. They could tell by sight that a force field had been put up between us and the Gamemakers. And if we have to have allies, I want them." I toss the ladle back in a pot of stew, splattering us both with the gravy.

"What are you so angry about?" Peeta asks, wiping the gravy from his shirtfront. "Because I teased you in the elevator? I'm sorry. I thought you would just laugh about it."

"Forget it," I say with a shake of my head. "It's a lot of things."

"Darius," he says.

"Darius. The Games. Haymitch making us team up with the others," I say.

"It can just be you and me, you know," he says.

"I know. But maybe Haymitch is right," I say. "Don't tell him I said so, but he usually is, where the Games are concerned."

"Well, you can have final say about our allies. But right now, I'm leaning towards Chaff and Seeder," says Peeta.

"I'm OK with Seeder, not Chaff," I say. "Not yet, anyway."

"Come on and eat with him. I promise, I won't let him kiss you again," says Peeta.

Chaff doesn't seem as bad at lunch. He's sober, and while he talks too loud and makes bad jokes a lot, most of them are at his own expense. I can see why he would be good for Haymitch, whose thoughts run so darkly. But I'm still not sure I'm ready to team up with him.

I try hard to be more sociable, not just with Chaff but with the group at large. After lunch I do the edible-insect station with the District 8 tributes – Cecelia, who's got three kids at home, and Woof, a really old guy who's hard of hearing and doesn't seem to know what's going on since he keeps trying to stuff poisonous bugs in his mouth. I wish I could mention meeting Twill and Bonnie in the woods, but I can't figure out how. Cashmere and Gloss, the sister and brother from District 1, invite me over and we make hammocks for a while. They're polite but cool, and I spend the whole time thinking about how I killed both the tributes from their district, Glimmer and Marvel, last year, and that they probably knew them and might even have been their mentors. Both my hammock and my attempt to connect with them are mediocre at best. I join Enobaria at sword training and exchange a few comments, but it's clear neither of us wants to team up. Finnick appears again when I'm picking up fishing tips, but mostly just to introduce me to Mags, the elderly woman who's also from District 4. Between her district accent and her garbled speech – possibly she's had a stroke – I can't make out more than one in four words. But I swear she can make a decent fishhook out of anything – a thorn, a wishbone, an earring. After a while I tune out the trainer and simply try to copy whatever Mags does. When I make a pretty good hook out of a bent nail and fasten it to some strands of my hair, she gives me a toothless smile and an unintelligible comment I think might be praise. Suddenly I remember how she volunteered to replace the young, hysterical woman in her district. It couldn't be because she thought she had any chance of winning. She did it to save the girl, just like I volunteered last year to save Prim. And I decide I want her on my team.

Great. Now I have to go back and tell Haymitch I want an eighty-year-old and Nuts and Volts for my allies. He'll love that.

So I give up trying to make friends and go over to the archery range for some sanity. It's wonderful there, getting to try out all the different bows and arrows. The trainer, Tax, seeing that the standing targets offer no challenge for me, begins to launch these silly fake birds high into the air for me to hit. At first it seems stupid, but it turns out to be kind of fun. Much more like hunting a moving creature. Since I'm hitting everything he throws up, he starts increasing the number of birds he sends airborne. I forget the rest of the gym and the victors and how miserable I am and lose myself in the shooting. When I manage to take down five birds in one round, I realize it's so quiet I can hear each one hit the floor. I turn and see the majority of the victors have stopped to watch me. Their faces show everything from envy to hatred to admiration.

After training, Peeta and I hang out, waiting for Haymitch and Effie to show up for dinner. When we're called to eat, Haymitch pounces on me immediately. "So at least half the victors have instructed their mentors to request you as an ally. I know it can't be your sunny personality."

"They saw her shoot," says Peeta with a smile. "Actually, I saw her shoot, for real, for the first time. I'm about to put in a formal request myself."

"You're that good?" Haymitch asks me. "So good that Brutus wants you?"

I shrug. "But I don't want Brutus. I want Mags and District Three."

"Of course you do." Haymitch sighs and orders a bottle of wine. "I'll tell everybody you're still making up your mind."

After my shooting exhibition, I still get teased some, but I no longer feel like I'm being mocked. In fact, I feel as if I've somehow been initiated into the victors' circle. During the next two days, I spend time with almost everybody headed for the arena. Even the morphlings, who, with Peeta's help, paint me into a field of yellow flowers. Even Finnick, who gives me an hour of trident lessons in exchange for an hour of archery instruction. And the more I come to know these people, the worse it is. Because, on the whole, I don't hate them. And some I like. And a lot of them are so damaged that my natural instinct would be to protect them. But all of them must die if I'm to save Peeta.

The final day of training ends with our private sessions. We each get fifteen minutes before the Gamemakers to amaze them with our skills, but I don't know what any of us might have to show them. There's a lot of kidding about it at lunch. What we might do. Sing, dance, strip, tell jokes. Mags, who I can understand a little better now, decides she's just going to take a nap. I don't know what I'm going to do. Shoot some arrows, I guess. Haymitch said to surprise them if we could, but I'm fresh out of ideas.

As the girl from 12, I'm scheduled to go last. The dining room gets quieter and quieter as the tributes file out to go and perform. It's easier to keep up the irreverent, invincible manner we've all adopted when there are more of us. As people disappear through the door, all I can think is that they have a matter of days to live.

Peeta and I are finally left alone. He reaches across the table to take my hands. "Decided what to do for the Gamemakers yet?"

I shake my head. "I can't really use them for target practice this year, with the force field up and all. Maybe make some fishhooks. What about you?"

"Not a clue. I keep wishing I could bake a cake or something," he says.

"Do some more camouflage," I suggest.

"If the morphlings have left me anything to work with," he says wryly. "They've been glued to that station since training started."

We sit in silence a while and then I blurt out the thing that's on both our minds. "How are we going to kill these people, Peeta?"

"I don't know." He leans his forehead down on our entwined hands.

"I don't want them as allies. Why did Haymitch want us to get to know them?" I say. "It'll make it so much harder than last time. Except for Rue maybe. But I guess I never really could've killed her, anyway. She was just too much like Prim."

Peeta looks up at me, his brow creased in thought.

"Her death was the most despicable, wasn't it?"

"None of them were very pretty," I say, thinking of Glimmer's and Cato's ends.

They call Peeta, so I wait by myself. Fifteen minutes pass. Then half an hour. It's close to forty minutes before I'm called.

When I go in, I smell the sharp odour of cleaning fluid and notice that one of the mats has been dragged to the centre of the room. The mood is very different from last year's, when the Gamemakers were half drunk and distractedly picking at titbits from the banquet table. They whisper among themselves, looking somewhat annoyed. What did Peeta do? Something to upset them?

I feel a pang of worry. That isn't good. I don't want Peeta singling himself out as a target for the Gamemakers' anger. That's part of my job. To draw fire away from Peeta. But how did he upset them? Because I'd love to do just that and more. To break through the smug veneer of those who use their brains to find amusing ways to kill us. To make them realize that while we're vulnerable to the Capitol's cruelties, they are as well.

Do you have any idea how much I hate you? I think. *You, who have given your talents to the Games?*

I try to catch Plutarch Heavensbee's eye, but he

seems to be intentionally ignoring me, as he has the entire training period. I remember how he sought me out for a dance, how pleased he was to show me the mockingjay on his watch. His friendly manner has no place here. How could it, when I'm a mere tribute and he's the Head Gamemaker? So powerful, so removed, so safe. . .

Suddenly I know just what I'm going to do. Something that will blow anything Peeta did right out of the water. I go over to the knot-tying station and get a length of rope. I start to manipulate it, but it's hard because I've never made this actual knot myself. I've only watched Finnick's clever fingers, and they moved so fast. After about ten minutes, I've come up with a respectable noose. I drag one of the target dummies out into the middle of the room and, using some chinning bars, hang it so it dangles by the neck. Tying its hands behind its back would be a nice touch, but I think I might be running out of time. I hurry over to the camouflage station, where some of the other tributes, undoubtedly the morphlings, have made a colossal mess. But I find a partial container of blood-red berry juice that will serve my needs. The flesh-coloured fabric of the dummy's skin makes a good, absorbent canvas. I carefully finger-paint the words on its body, concealing them from view. Then I step away quickly to watch the reaction on the Gamemakers' faces as they read the name on the dummy.

Seneca Crane.

17

The effect on the Gamemakers is immediate and satisfying. Several let out small shrieks. Others lose their grips on their wine glasses, which shatter musically against the ground. Two seem to be considering fainting. The look of shock is unanimous.

Now I have Plutarch Heavensbee's attention. He stares steadily at me as the juice from the peach he crushed in his hand runs through his fingers. Finally he clears his throat and says, "You may go now, Miss Everdeen."

I give a respectful nod and turn to go, but at the last moment I can't resist tossing the container of berry juice over my shoulder. I can hear the contents splatter against the dummy while a couple more wine glasses break. As the elevator doors close before me, I see no one has moved.

That surprised them, I think. It was rash and dangerous and no doubt I will pay for it ten times over. But for the moment, I feel something close to elation and I let myself savour it.

I want to find Haymitch immediately and tell him about my session, but no one's around. I guess they're getting ready for dinner and I decide to go take a shower myself, since my hands are stained from the juice. As I stand in the water, I begin to wonder about the wisdom of my latest trick. The question that should now always be my guide is "Will this help Peeta stay alive?" Indirectly, this might not. What happens in training is highly secretive, so there's no point in taking action against me when no one will know what my transgression was. In fact, last year I was rewarded for my brashness. This is a different sort of crime, though. If the Gamemakers are angry with me and decide to punish me in the arena, Peeta could get caught up in the attack as well. Maybe it was too impulsive. Still . . . I can't say I'm sorry I did it.

As we all gather for dinner, I notice Peeta's hands are faintly stained with a variety of colours, even though his hair is still damp from bathing. He must have done some form of camouflage after all. Once the soup is served, Haymitch gets right to the issue on everyone's mind. "All right, so how did your private sessions go?"

I exchange a look with Peeta. Somehow I'm not that eager to put what I did into words. In the calm of the dining room, it seems very extreme. "You first," I say to him. "It must have been really special. I had to wait for forty minutes to go in."

Peeta seems to be struck with the same reluctance I'm experiencing. "Well, I – I did the camouflage thing, like you suggested, Katniss." He hesitates. "Not exactly camouflage. I mean, I used the dyes."

"To do what?" asks Portia.

I think of how ruffled the Gamemakers were when I entered the gym for my session. The smell of cleaning fluids. The mat pulled over that spot in the centre of the gym. Was it to conceal something they were unable to wash away? "You painted something, didn't you? A picture."

"Did you see it?" Peeta asks.

"No. But they'd made a real point of covering it up," I say.

"Well, that would be standard. They can't let one tribute know what another did," says Effie, unconcerned. "What did you paint, Peeta?" She looks a little misty. "Was it a picture of Katniss?"

"Why would he paint a picture of me, Effie?" I ask, somehow annoyed.

"To show he's going to do everything he can to

defend you. That's what everyone in the Capitol's expecting, anyway. Didn't he volunteer to go in with you?" Effie says, as if it's the most obvious thing in the world.

"Actually, I painted a picture of Rue," Peeta says. "How she looked after Katniss had covered her in flowers."

There's a long pause at the table while everyone absorbs this. "And what exactly were you trying to accomplish?" Haymitch asks in a very measured voice.

"I'm not sure. I just wanted to hold them accountable, if only for a moment," says Peeta. "For killing that little girl."

"This is dreadful." Effie sounds like she's about to cry. "That sort of thinking . . . it's forbidden, Peeta. Absolutely. You'll only bring down more trouble on yourself and Katniss."

"I have to agree with Effie on this one," says Haymitch. Portia and Cinna remain silent, but their faces are very serious. Of course, they're right. But even though it worries me, I think what he did was amazing.

"I guess this is a bad time to mention I hung a dummy and painted Seneca Crane's name on it," I say. This has the desired effect. After a moment of disbelief, all the disapproval in the room hits me like a ton of bricks.

"You . . . hung . . . Seneca Crane?" says Cinna.

"Yes. I was showing off my new knot-tying skills, and he somehow ended up at the end of the noose," I say.

"Oh, Katniss," says Effie in a hushed voice. "How do you even know about that?"

"Is it a secret? President Snow didn't act like it was. In fact, he seemed eager for me to know," I say. Effie leaves the table with her napkin pressed to her face. "Now I've upset Effie. I should have lied and said I shot some arrows."

"You'd have thought we planned it," says Peeta, giving me just the hint of a smile.

"Didn't you?" asks Portia. Her fingers press her eyelids closed as if she's warding off a very bright light.

"No," I say, looking at Peeta with a new sense of appreciation. "Neither of us even knew what we were going to do before we went in."

"And, Haymitch?" says Peeta. "We decided we don't want any other allies in the arena."

"Good. Then I won't be responsible for you killing off any of my friends with your stupidity," he says.

"That's just what we were thinking," I tell him.

We finish the meal in silence, but when we rise to go into the sitting room, Cinna puts his arm around me and gives me a squeeze. "Come on and let's go get those training scores."

We gather around the television set and a red-eyed Effie rejoins us. The tributes' faces come up, district by district, and their scores flash under their pictures. One through twelve. Predictably high scores for Cashmere, Gloss, Brutus, Enobaria and Finnick. Low to medium for the rest.

"Have they ever given a zero?" I ask.

"No, but there's a first time for everything," Cinna answers.

And it turns out he's right. Because when Peeta and I each pull a twelve, we make Hunger Games history. No one feels like celebrating, though.

"Why did they do that?" I ask.

"So that the others will have no choice but to target you," says Haymitch flatly. "Go to bed. I can't stand to look at either one of you."

Peeta walks me down to my room in silence, but before he can say goodnight, I wrap my arms around him and rest my head against his chest. His hands slide up my back and his cheek leans against my hair. "I'm sorry if I made things worse," I say.

"No worse than I did. Why did you do it, anyway?" he says.

"I don't know. To show them that I'm more than just a piece in their Games?" I say.

He laughs a little, no doubt remembering the night before the Games last year. We were on the roof, neither of us able to sleep. Peeta had said something of the sort then, but I hadn't understood what he meant. Now I do.

"Me, too," he tells me. "And I'm not saying I'm not going to try. To get you home, I mean. But if I'm perfectly honest about it. . ."

"If you're perfectly honest about it, you think President Snow has probably given them direct orders to make sure we die in the arena anyway," I say.

"It's crossed my mind," says Peeta.

It's crossed my mind, too. Repeatedly. But while I know I'll never leave that arena alive, I'm still holding on to the hope that Peeta will. After all, he didn't pull out those berries, I did. No one has ever doubted that Peeta's defiance was motivated by love. So maybe President Snow will prefer keeping him alive, crushed and heartbroken, as a living warning to others.

"But even if that happens, everyone will know we've gone out fighting, right?" Peeta asks.

"Everyone will," I reply. And for the first time, I

distance myself from the personal tragedy that has consumed me since they announced the Quell. I remember the old man they shot in District 11, and Bonnie and Twill, and the rumoured uprisings. Yes, everyone in the districts will be watching me to see how I handle this death sentence, this final act of President Snow's dominance. They will be looking for some sign that their battles have not been in vain. If I can make it clear that I'm still defying the Capitol right up to the end, the Capitol will have killed me . . . but not my spirit. What better way to give hope to the rebels?

The beauty of this idea is that my decision to keep Peeta alive at the expense of my own life is itself an act of defiance. A refusal to play the Hunger Games by the Capitol's rules. My private agenda dovetails completely with my public one. And if I really could save Peeta . . . in terms of a revolution, this would be ideal. Because I will be more valuable dead. They can turn me into some kind of martyr for the cause and paint my face on banners, and it will do more to rally people than anything I could do if I was living. But Peeta would be more valuable alive, and tragic, because he will be able to turn his pain into words that will transform people.

Peeta would lose it if he knew I was thinking any

of this, so I only say, "So what should we do with our last few days?"

"I just want to spend every possible minute of the rest of my life with you," Peeta replies.

"Come on, then," I say, pulling him into my room.

It feels like such a luxury, sleeping with Peeta again. I didn't realize until now how starved I've been for human closeness. For the feel of him beside me in the darkness. I wish I hadn't wasted the last couple of nights shutting him out. I sink down into sleep, enveloped in his warmth, and when I open my eyes again, daylight's streaming through the windows.

"No nightmares," he says.

"No nightmares," I confirm. "You?"

"None. I'd forgotten what a real night's sleep feels like," he says.

We lie there for a while, in no rush to begin the day. Tomorrow night will be the televised interview, so today Effie and Haymitch should be coaching us. *More high heels and sarcastic comments*, I think. But then the red-headed Avox girl comes in with a note from Effie saying that, given our recent tour, both she and Haymitch have agreed we can handle ourselves adequately in public. The coaching sessions have been cancelled.

"Really?" says Peeta, taking the note from my hand and examining it. "Do you know what this means? We'll have the whole day to ourselves."

"It's too bad we can't go somewhere," I say wistfully.

"Who says we can't?" he asks.

The roof. We order a bunch of food, grab some blankets, and head up to the roof for a picnic. A daylong picnic in the flower garden that tinkles with wind chimes. We eat. We lie in the sun. I snap off hanging vines and use my newfound knowledge from training to practise knots and weave nets. Peeta sketches me. We make up a game with the force field that surrounds the roof – one of us throws an apple into it and the other person has to catch it.

No one bothers us. By late afternoon, I lie with my head on Peeta's lap, making a crown of flowers while he fiddles with my hair, claiming he's practising his knots. After a while, his hands go still. "What?" I ask.

"I wish I could freeze this moment, right here, right now, and live in it for ever," he says.

Usually this sort of comment, the kind that hints of his undying love for me, makes me feel guilty and awful. But I feel so warm and relaxed and beyond worrying about a future I'll never have, I just let the word slip out. "OK."

I can hear the smile in his voice. "Then you'll allow it?"

"I'll allow it," I say.

His fingers go back to my hair and I doze off, but he rouses me to see the sunset. It's a spectacular yellow and orange blaze behind the skyline of the Capitol. "I didn't think you'd want to miss it," he says.

"Thanks," I say. Because I can count on my fingers the number of sunsets I have left, and I don't want to miss any of them.

We don't go and join the others for dinner, and no one summons us.

"I'm glad. I'm tired of making everyone around me so miserable," says Peeta. "Everybody crying. Or Haymitch. . ." He doesn't need to go on.

We stay on the roof until bedtime and then quietly slip down to my room without encountering anyone.

The next morning, we're roused by my prep team. The sight of Peeta and me sleeping together is too much for Octavia, because she bursts into tears right away. "You remember what Cinna told us," Venia says fiercely. Octavia nods and goes out sobbing.

Peeta has to return to his room for prep, and I'm left alone with Venia and Flavius. The usual chatter has been suspended. In fact, there's little talk at all, other than to have me raise my chin or comment on a make-up technique. It's nearly lunch when I feel something dripping on my shoulder and turn to find Flavius, who's snipping away at my hair with silent tears running down his face. Venia gives him a look, and he gently sets the scissors on the table and leaves.

Then it's just Venia, whose skin is so pale her tattoos appear to be leaping off it. Almost rigid with determination, she does my hair and nails and make-up, fingers flying swiftly to compensate for her absent teammates. The whole time, she avoids my gaze. It's only when Cinna shows up to approve me and dismiss her that she takes my hands, looks me straight in the eye, and says, "We would all like you to know what a . . . privilege it has been to make you look your best." Then she hastens from the room.

My prep team. My foolish, shallow, affectionate pets, with their obsessions with feathers and parties, nearly break my heart with their goodbye. It's certain from Venia's last words that we all know I won't be returning. *Does the whole world know it?* I wonder. I look at Cinna. He knows, certainly. But as he promised, there's no danger of tears from him.

"So, what am I wearing tonight?" I ask, eyeing the garment bag that holds my dress.

"President Snow put in the dress order himself," says Cinna. He unzips the bag, revealing one of the wedding dresses I wore for the photo shoot. Heavy white silk with a low neckline and tight waist and sleeves that fall from my wrists to the floor. And pearls. Everywhere pearls. Stitched into the dress and in ropes at my throat and forming the crown for the veil. "Even though they announced the Quarter Quell the night of the photo shoot, people still voted for their favourite dress, and this was the winner. The president says you're to wear it tonight. Our objections were ignored."

I rub a bit of the silk between my fingers, trying to figure out President Snow's reasoning. I suppose since I was the greatest offender, my pain and loss and humiliation should be in the brightest spotlight. This, he thinks, will make that clear. It's so barbaric, the president turning my bridal gown into my shroud, that the blow strikes home, leaving me with a dull ache inside. "Well, it'd be a shame to waste such a pretty dress" is all I say.

Cinna helps me carefully into the gown. As it settles on my shoulders, they can't help giving a shrug of complaint. "Was it always this heavy?" I ask. I remember several of the dresses being dense, but this one feels like it weighs a ton.

"I had to make some slight alterations because of the lighting," says Cinna. I nod, but I can't see what that has to do with anything. He decks me out in the shoes and the pearl jewellery and the veil. Touches up my make-up. Has me walk.

"You're ravishing," he says. "Now, Katniss, because this bodice is so fitted, I don't want you raising your arms above your head. Well, not until you twirl, anyway."

"Will I be twirling again?" I ask, thinking of my dress last year.

"I'm sure Caesar will ask you. And if he doesn't, you suggest it yourself. Only not right away. Save it for your big finale," Cinna instructs me.

"You give me a signal so I know when," I say.

"All right. Any plans for your interview? I know Haymitch left you two to your own devices," he says.

"No, this year I'm just winging it. The funny thing is, I'm not nervous at all." And I'm not. However much President Snow may hate me, this Capitol audience is mine.

We meet up with Effie, Haymitch, Portia and Peeta at the elevator. Peeta's in an elegant tuxedo and white gloves. The sort of thing grooms wear to get married in, here in the Capitol.

Back home everything is so much simpler. A

woman usually rents a white dress that's been worn hundreds of times. The man wears something clean that's not mining clothes. They fill out some forms at the Justice Building and are assigned a house. Family and friends gather for a meal or bit of cake, if it can be afforded. Even if it can't, there's always a traditional song we sing as the new couple crosses the threshold of their home. And we have our own little ceremony, where they make their first fire, toast a bit of bread, and share it. Maybe it's old-fashioned, but no one really feels married in District 12 until after the toasting.

The other tributes have already gathered offstage and are talking softly, but when Peeta and I arrive, they fall silent. I realize everyone's staring daggers at my wedding dress. Are they jealous of its beauty? The power it might have to manipulate the crowd?

Finally Finnick says, "I can't believe Cinna put you in that thing."

"He didn't have any choice. President Snow made him," I say, somewhat defensively. I won't let anyone criticize Cinna.

Cashmere tosses her flowing blonde curls back and spits out, "Well, you look ridiculous!" She grabs her brother's hand and pulls him into place to lead our procession on to the stage. The other tributes begin to line up as well. I'm confused because, while they all are angry, some are giving us sympathetic pats on the shoulder, and Johanna Mason actually stops to straighten my pearl necklace.

"Make him pay for it, OK?" she says.

I nod, but I don't know what she means. Not until we're all sitting out onstage and Caesar Flickerman, hair and face highlighted in lavender this year, has done his opening spiel and the tributes begin their interviews. This is the first time I realize the depth of betrayal felt among the victors and the rage that accompanies it. But they are so smart, so wonderfully smart about how they play it, because it all comes back to reflect on the government and President Snow in particular. Not everyone. There are the old throwbacks, like Brutus and Enobaria, who are just here for another Games, and those too baffled or drugged or lost to join in on the attack. But there are enough victors who still have the wits and the nerve to come out fighting.

Cashmere starts the ball rolling with a speech about how she just can't stop crying when she thinks of how much the people in the Capitol must be suffering because they will lose us. Gloss recalls the kindness shown here to him and his sister. Beetee questions the legality of the Quell in his nervous, twitchy way, wondering if it's been fully examined by experts of late. Finnick recites a poem he wrote to his one true love in the Capitol, and about a hundred people faint because they're sure he means them. By the time Johanna Mason gets up, she's asking if something can't be done about the situation. Surely the creators of the Quarter Quell never anticipated such love forming between the victors and the Capitol. No one could be so cruel as to sever such a deep bond. Seeder quietly ruminates about how, back in District 11, everyone assumes President Snow is all-powerful. So if he's all-powerful, why doesn't he change the Quell? And Chaff, who comes right on her heels, insists the president could change the Quell if he wanted to, but he must not think it matters much to anyone.

By the time I'm introduced, the audience is an absolute wreck. People have been weeping and collapsing and even calling for change. The sight of me in my white silk bridal gown practically causes a riot. No more me, no more star-crossed lovers living happily ever after, no more wedding. I can see even Caesar's professionalism showing some cracks as he tries to quiet them so I can speak, but my three minutes are ticking quickly away.

Finally there's a lull and he gets out, "So, Katniss, obviously this is a very emotional night for everyone. Is there anything you'd like to say?"

My voice trembles as I speak. "Only that I'm so sorry you won't get to be at my wedding . . . but I'm glad you at least get to see me in my dress. Isn't it just . . . the most beautiful thing?" I don't have to look at Cinna for a signal. I know this is the right time. I begin to twirl slowly, raising the sleeves of my heavy gown above my head.

When I hear the screams of the crowd, I think it's because I must look stunning. Then I notice something is rising up around me. Smoke. From fire. Not the flickery stuff I wore last year in the chariot, but something much more real that devours my dress. I begin to panic as the smoke thickens. Charred bits of black silk swirl into the air, and pearls clatter to the stage. Somehow I'm afraid to stop because my flesh doesn't seem to be burning and I know Cinna must be behind whatever is happening. So I keep spinning and spinning. For a split second I'm gasping, completely engulfed in the strange flames. Then all at once, the fire is gone. I slowly come to a stop, wondering if I'm naked and why Cinna has arranged to burn away my wedding dress.

But I'm not naked. I'm in a dress of the exact design of my wedding dress, only it's the colour of coal and made of tiny feathers. Wonderingly, I lift my long, flowing sleeves into the air, and that's when I see myself on the television screen. Clothed in black except for the white patches on my sleeves. Or should I say my wings.

Because Cinna has turned me into a mockingjay.

18

I'm still smouldering a little, so it's with a tentative hand that Caesar reaches out to touch my headpiece. The white has burned away, leaving a smooth, fitted veil of black that drapes into the neckline of the dress in the back. "Feathers," says Caesar. "You're like a bird."

"A mockingjay, I think," I say, giving my wings a small flap. "It's the bird on the pin I wear as a token."

A shadow of recognition flickers across Caesar's face, and I can tell he knows that the mockingjay isn't just my token. That it's come to symbolize so much more. That what will be seen as a flashy costume change in the Capitol is resonating in an entirely different way throughout the districts. But he makes the best of it.

"Well, hats off to your stylist. I don't think anyone

can argue that that's not the most spectacular thing we've ever seen in an interview. Cinna, I think you better take a bow!" Caesar gestures for Cinna to rise. He does, and makes a small, gracious bow. And suddenly I am so afraid for him. What has he done? Something terribly dangerous. An act of rebellion in itself. And he's done it for me. I remember his words . . .

"*Don't worry. I always channel my emotions into my work. That way I don't hurt anyone but myself.*"

. . . and I'm afraid he has hurt himself beyond repair. The significance of my fiery transformation will not be lost on President Snow.

The audience, who's been stunned into silence, breaks into wild applause. I can barely hear the buzzer that indicates that my three minutes are up. Caesar thanks me and I go back to my seat, my dress now feeling lighter than air.

As I pass Peeta, who's headed for his interview, he doesn't meet my eyes. I take my seat carefully, but aside from the puffs of smoke here and there, I seem unharmed, so I turn my attention to him.

Caesar and Peeta have been a natural team since they first appeared together a year ago. Their easy give-and-take, comic timing, and ability to segue into heart-wrenching moments, like Peeta's confession of love for me, have made them a huge success with the audience. They effortlessly open with a few jokes about fires and feathers and overcooking poultry. But anyone can see that Peeta is preoccupied, so Caesar directs the conversation right into the subject that's on everyone's minds.

"So, Peeta, what was it like when, after all you've been through, you found out about the Quell?" asks Caesar.

"I was in shock. I mean, one minute I'm seeing Katniss looking so beautiful in all these wedding gowns, and the next. . ." Peeta trails off.

"You realized there was never going to be a wedding?" asks Caesar gently.

Peeta pauses for a long moment, as if deciding something. He looks out at the spellbound audience, then at the floor, then finally up at Caesar. "Caesar, do you think all our friends here can keep a secret?"

An uncomfortable laugh emanates from the audience. What can he mean? Keep a secret from who? Our whole world is watching.

"I feel quite certain of it," says Caesar.

"We're already married," says Peeta quietly. The crowd reacts in astonishment, and I have to bury my face in the folds of my skirt so they can't see my confusion. Where on earth is he going with this?

"But . . . how can that be?" asks Caesar.

"Oh, it's not an official marriage. We didn't go to the Justice Building or anything. But we have this marriage ritual in District Twelve. I don't know what it's like in the other districts. But there's this thing we do," says Peeta, and he briefly describes the toasting.

"Were your families there?" asks Caesar.

"No, we didn't tell anyone. Not even Haymitch. And Katniss's mother would never have approved. But you see, we knew if we were married in the Capitol, there wouldn't be a toasting. And neither of us really wanted to wait any longer. So one day, we just did it," Peeta says. "And to us, we're more married than any piece of paper or big party could make us."

"So this was before the Quell?" says Caesar.

"Of course before the Quell. I'm sure we'd never have done it after we knew," says Peeta, starting to get upset. "But who could've seen it coming? No one. We went through the Games, we were victors, everyone seemed so thrilled to see us together, and then out of nowhere – I mean, how could we anticipate a thing like that?"

"You couldn't, Peeta." Caesar puts an arm around his shoulders. "As you say, no one could've. But I have to confess, I'm glad you two had at least a few months of happiness together."

Enormous applause. As if encouraged, I look up from my feathers and let the audience see my tragic smile of thanks. The residual smoke from the feathers has made my eyes teary, which adds a very nice touch.

"I'm not glad," says Peeta. "I wish we had waited until the whole thing was done officially."

This takes even Caesar aback. "Surely even a brief time is better than no time?"

"Maybe I'd think that, too, Caesar," says Peeta bitterly, "if it weren't for the baby."

There. He's done it again. Dropped a bomb that wipes out the efforts of every tribute who came before him. Well, maybe not. Maybe this year he has only lit the fuse on a bomb that the victors themselves have been building. Hoping someone would be able to detonate it. Perhaps thinking it would be me in my bridal gown. Not knowing how much I rely on Cinna's talents, whereas Peeta needs nothing more than his wits.

As the bomb explodes, it sends accusations of injustice and barbarism and cruelty flying out in every direction. Even the most Capitol-loving, Games-hungry, bloodthirsty person out there can't ignore, at least for a moment, how horrific the whole thing is.

I am pregnant.

The audience can't absorb the news right away. It has to strike them and sink in and be confirmed by other voices before they begin to sound like a herd of wounded animals, moaning, shrieking, calling for help. And me? I know my face is projected in a tight close-up on the screen, but I don't make any effort to hide it. Because for a moment, even I am working through what Peeta has said. Isn't it the thing I dreaded most about the wedding, about the future – the loss of my children to the Games? And it could be true now, couldn't it? If I hadn't spent my life building up layers of defences until I recoil at even the suggestion of marriage or a family?

Caesar can't rein in the crowd again, not even when the buzzer sounds. Peeta nods his goodbye and comes back to his seat without any more conversation. I can see Caesar's lips moving, but the place is in total chaos and I can't hear a word. Only the blast of the anthem, cranked up so loud I can feel it vibrating through my bones, lets us know where we stand in the programme. I automatically rise and, as I do, I sense Peeta reaching out for me. Tears run down his face as I take his hand. How real are the tears? Is this an acknowledgement that he has been stalked by the same fears that I have? That every victor has? Every parent in every district in Panem?

I look back to the crowd, but the faces of Rue's mother and father swim before my eyes. Their sorrow. Their loss. I turn spontaneously to Chaff and offer my hand. I feel my fingers close around the stump that now completes his arm and hold fast.

And then it happens. Up and down the row, the victors begin to join hands. Some right away, like the morphlings, or Wiress and Beetee. Others unsure but caught up in the demands of those around them, like Brutus and Enobaria. By the time the anthem plays its final strains, all twenty-four of us stand in one unbroken line in what must be the first public show of unity among the districts since the Dark Days. You can see the realization of this as the screens begin to pop into blackness. It's too late, though. In the confusion they didn't cut us off in time. Everyone has seen.

There's disorder on the stage now, too, as the lights go out and we're left to stumble back into the Training Centre. I've lost hold of Chaff, but Peeta guides me into an elevator. Finnick and Johanna try to join us, but a harried Peacekeeper blocks their way and we shoot upwards alone.

The moment we step out of the elevator, Peeta grips my shoulders. "There isn't much time, so tell me. Is there anything I have to apologize for?"

"Nothing," I say. It was a big leap to take without

my OK, but I'm just as glad I didn't know, didn't have time to second-guess him, to let any guilt over Gale detract from how I really feel about what Peeta did. Which is empowered.

Somewhere, very far off, is a place called District 12, where my mother and sister and friends will have to deal with the fallout from this night. Just a brief hovercraft ride away is an arena where, tomorrow, Peeta and I and the other tributes will face our own form of punishment. But even if all of us meet terrible ends, something happened on that stage tonight that can't be undone. We victors staged our own uprising, and maybe, just maybe, the Capitol won't be able to contain this one.

We wait for the others to return, but when the elevator opens, only Haymitch appears. "It's madness out there. Everyone's been sent home and they've cancelled the recap of the interviews on television."

Peeta and I hurry to the window and try to make sense of the commotion far below us on the streets. "What are they saying?" Peeta asks. "Are they asking the president to stop the Games?"

"I don't think they know themselves what to ask. The whole situation is unprecedented. Even the idea of opposing the Capitol's agenda is a source of confusion for the people here," says Haymitch. "But there's no way Snow would cancel the Games. You know that, right?"

I do. Of course, he could never back down now. The only option left to him is to strike back, and strike back hard. "The others went home?" I ask.

"They were ordered to. I don't know how much luck they're having getting through the mob," says Haymitch.

"Then we'll never see Effie again," says Peeta. We didn't see her on the morning of the Games last year. "You'll give her our thanks."

"More than that. Really make it special. It's Effie, after all," I say. "Tell her how appreciative we are and how she was the best escort ever and tell her . . . tell her we send our love."

For a while we just stand there in silence, delaying the inevitable. Then Haymitch says it. "I guess this is where we say our goodbyes as well."

"Any last words of advice?" Peeta asks.

"Stay alive," Haymitch says gruffly. That's almost an old joke with us now. He gives us each a quick embrace, and I can tell it's all he can stand. "Go to bed. You need your rest."

I know I should say a whole bunch of things to Haymitch, but I can't think of anything he doesn't already know, really, and my throat is so tight I doubt anything would come out, anyway. So, once again, I let Peeta speak for us both.

"You take care, Haymitch," he says.

We cross the room, but in the doorway, Haymitch's voice stops us. "Katniss, when you're in the arena," he begins. Then he pauses. He's scowling in a way that makes me sure I've already disappointed him.

"What?" I ask defensively.

"You just remember who the enemy is," Haymitch tells me. "That's all. Now go on. Get out of here."

We walk down the hallway. Peeta wants to stop by his room to shower off the make-up and meet me in a few minutes, but I won't let him. I'm certain that if a door shuts between us, it will lock and I'll have to spend the night without him. Besides, I have a shower in my room. I refuse to let go of his hand.

Do we sleep? I don't know. We spend the night holding each other, in some halfway land between dreams and waking. Not talking. Both afraid to disturb the other in the hope that we'll be able to store up a few precious minutes of rest.

Cinna and Portia arrive with the dawn, and I know Peeta will have to go. Tributes enter the arena alone. He gives me a light kiss. "See you soon," he says.

"See you soon," I answer.

Cinna, who will help dress me for the Games,

accompanies me to the roof. I'm about to mount the ladder to the hovercraft when I remember. "I didn't say goodbye to Portia."

"I'll tell her," says Cinna.

The electric current freezes me in place on the ladder until the doctor injects the tracker into my left forearm. Now they will always be able to locate me in the arena. The hovercraft takes off, and I look out of the windows until they black out. Cinna keeps pressing me to eat and, when that fails, to drink. I manage to keep sipping water, thinking of the days of dehydration that almost killed me last year. Thinking of how I will need my strength to keep Peeta alive.

When we reach the Launch Room at the arena, I shower. Cinna braids my hair down my back and helps me dress over simple undergarments. This year's tribute outfit is a fitted blue jumpsuit, made of very sheer material, that zippers up the front. A fifteen-centimetre-wide padded belt covered in shiny purple plastic. A pair of nylon shoes with rubber soles.

"What do you think?" I ask, holding the fabric out for Cinna to examine.

He frowns as he rubs the thin stuff between his fingers. "I don't know. It will offer little in the way of protection from cold or water."

"Sun?" I ask, picturing a burning sun over a barren desert.

"Possibly. If it's been treated," he says. "Oh, I almost forgot this." He takes my gold mockingjay pin from his pocket and fixes it to the jumpsuit.

"My dress was fantastic last night," I say. Fantastic and reckless. But Cinna must know that.

"I thought you might like it," he says with a tight smile.

We sit, as we did last year, holding hands until the voice tells me to prepare for the launch. He walks me over to the circular metal plate and zips up the neck of my jumpsuit securely. "Remember, girl on fire," he says, "I'm still betting on you." He kisses my forehead and steps back as the glass cylinder slides down around me.

"Thank you," I say, although he probably can't hear me. I lift my chin, holding my head high the way he always tells me to, and wait for the plate to rise. But it doesn't. And it still doesn't.

I look at Cinna, raising my eyebrows for an explanation. He just gives his head a slight shake, as perplexed as I am. Why are they delaying this?

Suddenly the door behind him bursts open and three Peacekeepers spring into the room. Two pin Cinna's arms behind him and cuff him while the third hits him in the temple with such force he's knocked to his knees. But they keep hitting him with metal-studded gloves, opening gashes on his face and body. I'm screaming my head off, banging on the unyielding glass, trying to reach him. The Peacekeepers ignore me completely as they drag Cinna's limp body from the room. All that's left are the smears of blood on the floor.

Sickened and terrified, I feel the plate begin to rise. I'm still leaning against the glass when the breeze catches my hair and I force myself to straighten up. Just in time, too, because the glass is retreating and I'm standing free in the arena. Something seems to be wrong with my vision. The ground is too bright and shiny and keeps undulating. I squint down at my feet and see that my metal plate is surrounded by blue waves that lap up over my boots. Slowly I raise my eyes and take in the water spreading out in every direction.

I can only form one clear thought.

This is no place for a girl on fire.

PART III

THE ENEMY

19

"Ladies and gentlemen, let the Seventy-fifth Hunger Games begin!" The voice of Claudius Templesmith, the Hunger Games announcer, hammers my ears. I have less than a minute to get my bearings. Then the gong will sound and the tributes will be free to move off their metal plates. But move where?

I can't think straight. The image of Cinna, beaten and bloody, consumes me. Where is he now? What are they doing to him? Torturing him? Killing him? Turning him into an Avox? Obviously his assault was staged to unhinge me, the same way Darius's presence in my quarters was. And it *has* unhinged me. All I want to do is collapse on my metal plate. But I can hardly do that after what I just witnessed. I must be strong. I owe it to Cinna, who risked everything by undermining President Snow and turning my bridal silk into mockingjay plumage. And I owe it to the rebels who, emboldened by Cinna's example, might be fighting to bring down the Capitol at this moment. My refusal to play the Games on the Capitol's terms is to be my last act of rebellion. So I grit my teeth and will myself to be a player.

Where are you? I can still make no sense of my surroundings. *Where are you?!* I demand an answer from myself and slowly the world comes into focus. Blue water. Pink sky. White-hot sun beating down. All right, there's the Cornucopia, the shining gold metal horn, about forty metres away. At first, it appears to be sitting on a circular island. But on closer examination, I see the thin strips of land radiating from the circle like the spokes on a wheel. I think there are ten to twelve, and they seem equidistant from one another. Between the spokes, all is water. Water and a pair of tributes.

That's it, then. There are twelve spokes, each with two tributes balanced on metal plates between them. The other tribute in my watery wedge is old Woof from District 8. He's about as far to my right as the land strip on my left. Beyond the water, wherever you look, a narrow beach and then dense greenery. I scan the circle of tributes, looking for Peeta, but he must be blocked from my view by the Cornucopia.

I catch a handful of water as it washes in and smell it. Then I touch the tip of my wet finger to my tongue. As I suspected, it's salt water. Just like the waves Peeta and I encountered on our brief tour of the beach in District 4. But at least it seems clean.

There are no boats, no ropes, not even a bit of driftwood to cling to. No, there's only one way to get to the Cornucopia. When the gong sounds, I don't even hesitate before I dive to my left. It's a longer distance than I'm used to, and navigating the waves takes a little more skill than swimming across my quiet lake at home, but my body seems oddly light and I cut through the water effortlessly. Maybe it's the salt. I pull myself, dripping, on to the land strip and sprint down the sandy stretch for the Cornucopia. I can see no one else converging from my side, although the gold horn blocks a good portion of my view. I don't let the thought of adversaries slow me down, though. I'm thinking like a Career now, and the first thing I want is to get my hands on a weapon.

Last year, the supplies were spread out quite a distance around the Cornucopia, with the most valuable closest to the horn. But this year, the booty seems to be piled at the seven-metre-high mouth. My eyes instantly home in on a golden bow just in arm's reach and I yank it free.

There's someone behind me. I'm alerted by, I don't know, a soft shift of sand or maybe just a change in the air currents. I pull an arrow from the sheath that's still wedged in the pile and arm my bow as I turn.

Finnick, glistening and gorgeous, stands a few metres away, with a trident poised to attack. A net dangles from his other hand. He's smiling a little, but the muscles in his upper body are rigid in anticipation. "You can swim, too," he says. "Where did you learn that in District Twelve?"

"We have a big bathtub," I answer.

"You must," he says. "You like the arena?"

"Not particularly. But you should. They must have built it especially for you," I say with an edge of bitterness. It seems like it, anyway, with all the water, when I bet only a handful of the victors can swim. And there was no pool in the Training Centre, no chance to learn. Either you came in here a swimmer or you'd better be a really fast learner. Even participation in the initial bloodbath depends on being able to cover twenty metres of water. That gives District 4 an enormous advantage.

For a moment we're frozen, sizing each other up, our weapons, our skill. Then Finnick suddenly grins. "Lucky thing we're allies. Right?"

Sensing a trap, I'm about to let my arrow fly,

hoping it finds his heart before the trident impales me, when he shifts his hand and something on his wrist catches the sunlight. A solid-gold bangle patterned with flames. The same one I remember on Haymitch's wrist the morning I began training. I briefly consider that Finnick could have stolen it to trick me, but somehow I know this isn't the case. Haymitch gave it to him. As a signal to me. An order, really. To trust Finnick.

I can hear other footsteps approaching. I must decide at once. "Right!" I snap, because even though Haymitch is my mentor and trying to keep me alive, this angers me. Why didn't he tell me he'd made this arrangement before? Probably because Peeta and I had ruled out allies. Now Haymitch has chosen one on his own.

"Duck!" Finnick commands in such a powerful voice, so different from his usual seductive purr, that I do. His trident goes whizzing over my head and there's a sickening sound of impact as it finds its target. The man from District 5, the drunk who threw up on the sword-fighting floor, sinks to his knees as Finnick frees the trident from his chest. "Don't trust One and Two," Finnick says.

There's no time to question this. I work the sheath of arrows free. "Each take one side?" I say. He nods, and I dart around the pile. About four spokes apart, Enobaria and Gloss are just reaching land. Either they're slow swimmers or they thought the water might be laced with other dangers, which it might well be. Sometimes it's not good to consider too many scenarios. But now that they're on the sand, they'll be here in a matter of seconds.

"Anything useful?" I hear Finnick shout.

I quickly scan the pile on my side and find maces, swords, bows and arrows, tridents, knives, spears, axes, metallic objects I have no name for . . . and nothing else.

"Weapons!" I call back. "Nothing but weapons!"

"Same here," he confirms. "Grab what you want and let's go!"

I shoot an arrow at Enobaria, who's got in too close for comfort, but she's expecting it and dives back into the water before it can find its mark. Gloss isn't quite as swift, and I sink an arrow into his calf as he plunges into the waves. I sling an extra bow and a second sheath of arrows over my body, slide two long knives and an awl into my belt, and meet up with Finnick at the front of the pile.

"Do something about that, would you?" he says. I see Brutus barrelling towards us. His belt is undone and he has it stretched between his hands as a kind of shield. I shoot at him and he manages to block the arrow with his belt before it can skewer his liver. Where it punctures the belt, a purple liquid spews forth, coating his face. As I reload, Brutus flattens on the ground, rolls a metre to the water, and submerges. There's a clang of metal falling behind me. "Let's clear out," I say to Finnick.

This last altercation has given Enobaria and Gloss time to reach the Cornucopia. Brutus is within shooting distance and somewhere, certainly, Cashmere is nearby, too. These four classic Careers will no doubt have a prior alliance. If I had only my own safety to consider, I might be willing to take them on with Finnick by my side. But it's Peeta I'm thinking about. I spot him now, still stranded on his metal plate. I take off and Finnick follows without question, as if knowing this will be my next move. When I'm as close as I can get, I start removing knives from my belt, preparing to swim out to reach him and somehow bring him in.

Finnick drops a hand on my shoulder. "I'll get him."

Suspicion flickers up inside me. Could this all just be a ruse? For Finnick to win my trust and then swim out and drown Peeta? "I can," I insist.

But Finnick has dropped all his weapons to the ground. "Better not exert yourself. Not in your condition," he says, and reaches down and pats my abdomen.

Oh, right. I'm supposed to be pregnant, I think. While I'm trying to think what that means and how I should act – maybe throw up or something – Finnick has positioned himself at the edge of the water.

"Cover me," he says. He disappears with a flawless dive.

I raise my bow, warding off any attackers from the Cornucopia, but no one seems interested in pursuing us. Sure enough, Gloss, Cashmere, Enobaria and Brutus have gathered, their pack formed already, picking over the weapons. A quick survey of the rest of the arena shows that most of the tributes are still trapped on their plates. Wait, no, there's someone standing on the spoke to my left, the one opposite Peeta. It's Mags. But she neither heads for the Cornucopia nor tries to flee. Instead she splashes into the water and starts paddling towards me, her grey head bobbing above the waves. Well, she's old, but I guess after eighty years of living in District 4 she can keep afloat.

Finnick has reached Peeta now and is towing him back, one arm across his chest while the other propels them through the water with easy strokes. Peeta rides along without resisting. I don't know what Finnick said or did that convinced him to put his life in his hands – showed him the bangle, maybe. Or just the sight of me waiting might have been enough. When they reach the sand, I help haul Peeta up on to dry land.

"Hello, again," he says, and gives me a kiss. "We've got allies."

"Yes. Just as Haymitch intended," I answer.

"Remind me, did we make deals with anyone else?" Peeta asks.

"Only Mags, I think," I say. I nod towards the old woman doggedly making her way towards us.

"Well, I can't leave Mags behind," says Finnick. "She's one of the few people who actually likes me."

"I've got no problem with Mags," I say. "Especially now that I see the arena. Her fishhooks are probably our best chance of getting a meal."

"Katniss wanted her on the first day," says Peeta.

"Katniss has remarkably good judgement," says Finnick. With one hand he reaches into the water and scoops out Mags like she weighs no more than a puppy. She makes some remark that I think includes the word "bob", then pats her belt.

"Look, she's right. Someone figured it out." Finnick points to Beetee. He's flailing around in the waves but managing to keep his head above water.

"What?" I say.

"The belts. They're flotation devices," says Finnick. "I mean, you have to propel yourself, but they'll keep you from drowning."

I almost ask Finnick to wait, to get Beetee and Wiress and take them with us, but Beetee's three spokes over and I can't even see Wiress. For all I know, Finnick would kill them as quickly as he did the tribute from 5, so instead I suggest we move on. I hand Peeta a bow, a sheath of arrows and a knife, keeping the rest for myself. But Mags tugs on my sleeve and babbles on until I've given the awl to her. Pleased, she clamps the handle between her gums and reaches her arms up to Finnick. He tosses his net over his shoulder, hoists Mags on top of it, grips his tridents in his free hand, and we run away from the Cornucopia.

Where the sand ends, woods begin to rise sharply. No, not really woods. At least not the kind I know. *Jungle*. The foreign, almost obsolete word comes to mind. Something I heard from another Hunger Games or learned from my father. Most of the trees are unfamiliar, with smooth trunks and few branches. The earth is very black and spongy underfoot, often obscured by tangles of vines with colourful blossoms. While the sun's hot and bright, the air's warm and heavy with moisture, and I get the feeling I will never really be dry here. The thin blue fabric of my jumpsuit lets the seawater evaporate easily, but it's already begun to cling to me with sweat.

Peeta takes the lead, cutting through the patches of dense vegetation with his long knife. I make Finnick go second because even though he's the most powerful, he's got his hands full with Mags. Besides, while he's a whiz with that trident, it's a weapon less suited to the jungle than my arrows. It doesn't take long, between the steep incline and the heat, to become short of breath. Peeta and I have been training intensely, though, and Finnick's such an amazing physical specimen that even with Mags over his shoulder, we climb rapidly for about two kilometres before he requests a rest. And then I think it's more for Mags's sake than his own.

The foliage has hidden the wheel from sight, so I scale a tree with rubbery limbs to get a better view. And then wish that I hadn't.

Around the Cornucopia, the ground appears to be bleeding; the water has purple stains. Bodies lie on the ground and float in the sea, but at this distance, with everyone dressed exactly the same, I can't tell who lives or dies. All I can tell is that some of the tiny blue figures still battle. Well, what did I think? That the victors' chain of locked hands last night would result in some sort of universal truce in the arena? No, I never believed that. But I guess I had hoped people might show some . . . what? Restraint? Reluctance, at least. Before they jumped right into massacre mode. *And you all knew each other*, I think. *You acted like friends.*

I have only one real friend in here. And he isn't from District 4.

I let the slight, soupy breeze cool my cheeks while I come to a decision. Despite the bangle, I should just get it over with and shoot Finnick. There's really no future in this alliance. And he's too dangerous to let go. Now, when we have this tentative trust, may be my only chance to kill him. I could easily shoot him in the back as we walk. It's despicable, of course, but will it be any more despicable if I wait? Know him better? Owe him more? No, this is the time. I take one last look at the battling figures, the bloody ground, to harden my resolve, and then slide to the ground.

But when I land, I find Finnick's kept pace with my thoughts. As if he knows what I have seen and how it will have affected me. He has one of his tridents raised in a casually defensive position.

"What's going on down there, Katniss? Have they all joined hands? Taken a vow of non-violence? Tossed the weapons in the sea in defiance of the Capitol?" Finnick asks.

"No," I say.

"No," Finnick repeats. "Because whatever happened in the past is in the past. And no one in this arena was a victor by chance." He eyes Peeta for a moment. "Except maybe Peeta."

Finnick knows then what Haymitch and I know. About Peeta. Being truly, deep-down better than the rest of us. Finnick took out that tribute from 5 without blinking an eye. And how long did I take to turn deadly? I shot to kill when I targeted Enobaria and Gloss and Brutus. Peeta would at least have attempted negotiations first. Seen if some wider alliance was possible. But to what end? Finnick's right. I'm right. The people in this arena weren't crowned for their compassion.

I hold his gaze, weighing his speed against my own. The time it will take to send an arrow through his brain versus the time his trident will reach my body. I can see him waiting for me to make the first move. Calculating if he should block first or go directly for an attack. I can feel we've both about worked it out when Peeta steps deliberately between us.

"So how many are dead?" he asks.

Move, you idiot, I think. But he remains planted firmly between us.

"Hard to say," I answer. "At least six, I think. And they're still fighting."

"Let's keep moving. We need water," he says.

So far there's been no sign of a freshwater stream or pond, and the salt water's undrinkable. Again, I think of the last Games, where I nearly died of dehydration.

"Better find some soon," says Finnick. "We need to be undercover when the others come hunting us tonight."

We. Us. Hunting. All right, maybe killing Finnick would be a little premature. He's been helpful so far. He does have Haymitch's stamp of approval. And who knows what the night will hold? If worse comes to worst, I can always kill him in his sleep. So I let the moment pass. And so does Finnick.

The absence of water intensifies my thirst. I keep a sharp eye out as we continue our trek upwards, but with no luck. After about another kilometre, I can see an end to the tree line and assume we're reaching the crest of the hill. "Maybe we'll have better luck on the other side. Find a spring or something."

But there is no other side. I know this before anyone else, even though I am furthest from the top. My eyes catch on a funny, rippling square hanging like a warped pane of glass in the air. At first I think it's the glare from the sun or the heat shimmering up off the ground. But it's fixed in space, not shifting when I move. And that's when I connect the square with Wiress and Beetee in the Training Centre and realize what lies before us. My warning cry is just reaching my lips when Peeta's knife swings out to slash away some vines.

There's a sharp zapping sound. For an instant, the trees are gone and I see open space over a short stretch of bare earth. Then Peeta's flung back from the force field, bringing Finnick and Mags to the ground.

I rush over to where he lies, motionless in a web of vines. "Peeta?" There's a faint smell of singed hair. I call his name again, giving him a little shake, but he's unresponsive. My fingers fumble across his lips, where there's no warm breath although moments ago he was panting. I press my ear against his chest, to the spot where I always rest my head, where I know I will hear the strong and steady beat of his heart.

Instead, I find silence.

20

“Peeta!” I scream. I shake him harder, even resort to slapping his face, but it’s no use. His heart has failed. I am slapping emptiness. “Peeta!”

Finnick props Mags against a tree and pushes me out of the way. “Let me.” His fingers touch points at Peeta’s neck, run over the bones in his ribs and spine. Then he pinches Peeta’s nostrils shut.

“No!” I yell, hurling myself at Finnick, for surely he intends to make certain that Peeta’s dead, to keep any hope of life from returning to him. Finnick’s hand comes up and hits me so hard, so squarely in the chest that I go flying back into a nearby tree trunk. I’m stunned for a moment, by the pain, by trying to regain my wind, as I see Finnick close off Peeta’s nose again. From where I sit, I pull an arrow, whip the notch into place, and am about to let it fly when I’m stopped by the sight of Finnick kissing Peeta. And it's so bizarre, even for Finnick, that I stay my hand. No, he's not kissing him. He's got Peeta's nose blocked off but his mouth tilted open, and he's blowing air into his lungs. I can see this, I can actually see Peeta's chest rising and falling. Then Finnick unzips the top of Peeta's jumpsuit and begins to pump the spot over his heart with the heels of his hands. Now that I've got over my shock, I understand what he's trying to do.

Once in a blue moon, I've seen my mother try something similar, but not often. If your heart fails in District 12, it's unlikely your family could get you to my mother in time, anyway. So her usual patients are burned or wounded or ill. Or starving, of course.

But Finnick's world is different. Whatever he's doing, he's done it before. There's a very set rhythm and method. And I find the arrow tip sinking to the ground as I lean in to watch, desperately, for some sign of success. Agonizing minutes drag past as my hopes diminish. Around the time that I'm deciding it's too late, that Peeta's dead, moved on, unreachable for ever, he gives a small cough and Finnick sits back.

I leave my weapons in the dirt as I fling myself at him. "Peeta?" I say softly. I brush the damp blond strands of hair back from his forehead, find the pulse drumming against my fingers at his neck.

His lashes flutter open and his eyes meet mine. "Careful," he says weakly. "There's a force field up ahead."

I laugh, but there are tears running down my cheeks.

"Must be a lot stronger than the one on the Training Centre roof," he says. "I'm all right, though. Just a little shaken."

"You were dead! Your heart stopped!" I burst out, before really considering if this is a good idea. I clap my hand over my mouth because I'm starting to make those awful choking sounds that happen when I sob.

"Well, it seems to be working now," he says. "It's all right, Katniss." I nod my head but the sounds aren't stopping. "Katniss?" Now Peeta's worried about me, which adds to the insanity of it all.

"It's OK. It's just her hormones," says Finnick. "From the baby." I look up and see him, sitting back on his knees but still panting a bit from the climb and the heat and the effort of bringing Peeta back from the dead.

"No. It's not—" I get out, but I'm cut off by an even more hysterical round of sobbing that seems only to confirm what Finnick said about the baby. He meets my eyes and I glare at him through my tears. It's stupid, I know, that his efforts make me so vexed. All I wanted was to keep Peeta alive, and I couldn't and Finnick could, and I should be nothing but grateful. And I am. But I am also furious because it means that I will never stop owing Finnick Odair. Ever. So how can I kill him in his sleep?

I expect to see a smug or sarcastic expression on his face, but his look is strangely quizzical. He glances between Peeta and me, as if trying to figure something out, then gives his head a slight shake as if to clear it. "How are you?" he asks Peeta. "Do you think you can move on?"

"No, he has to rest," I say. My nose is running like crazy and I don't even have a shred of fabric to use as a handkerchief. Mags rips off a handful of hanging moss from a tree limb and gives it to me. I'm too much of a mess to even question it. I blow my nose loudly and mop the tears off my face. It's nice, the moss. Absorbent and surprisingly soft.

I notice a gleam of gold on Peeta's chest. I reach out and retrieve the disc that hangs from a chain around his neck. My mockingjay has been engraved on it. "Is this your token?" I ask.

"Yes. Do you mind that I used your mockingjay? I wanted us to match," he says.

"No, of course I don't mind." I force a smile. Peeta showing up in the arena wearing a mockingjay is both a blessing and a curse. On the one hand, it should give a boost to the rebels in the district. On the other, it's hard to imagine President Snow will overlook it, and that makes the job of keeping Peeta alive harder.

"So you want to make camp here, then?" Finnick asks.

"I don't think that's an option," Peeta answers. "Staying here. With no water. No protection. I feel all right, really. If we could just go slowly."

"Slowly would be better than not at all." Finnick helps Peeta to his feet while I pull myself together. Since I got up this morning I've watched Cinna beaten to a pulp, landed in another arena, and seen Peeta die. Still, I'm glad Finnick keeps playing the pregnancy card for me, because from a sponsor's point of view, I'm not handling things all that well.

I check over my weapons, which I know are in perfect condition, because it makes me seem more in control. "I'll take the lead," I announce.

Peeta starts to object but Finnick cuts him off. "No, let her do it." He frowns at me. "You knew that force field was there, didn't you? Right at the last second? You started to give a warning." I nod. "How did you know?"

I hesitate. To reveal that I know Beetee and Wiress's trick of recognizing a force field could be dangerous. I don't know if the Gamemakers made note of that moment during training when the two pointed it out to me or not. One way or the other, I have a very valuable piece of information. And if they know I have it, they might do something to alter the force field so I can't see the aberration any more. So I lie. "I don't know. It's almost as if I could hear it. Listen." We all become still. There's the sound of insects, birds, the breeze in the foliage.

"I don't hear anything," says Peeta.

"Yes," I insist, "it's like when the fence around District Twelve is on, only much, much quieter." Everyone listens again intently. I do, too, although there's nothing to hear. "There!" I say. "Can't you hear it? It's coming from right where Peeta got shocked."

"I don't hear it, either," says Finnick. "But if you do, by all means, take the lead."

I decide to play this for all it's worth. "That's weird," I say. I turn my head from side to side as if puzzled. "I can only hear it out of my left ear."

"The one the doctors reconstructed?" asks Peeta.

"Yeah," I say, then give a shrug. "Maybe they did a better job than they thought. You know, sometimes I do hear funny things on that side. Things you wouldn't ordinarily think have a sound. Like insect wings. Or snow hitting the ground." Perfect. Now all the attention will turn to the surgeons who fixed my deaf ear after the Games last year, and they'll have to explain why I can hear like a bat.

"You," says Mags, nudging me forward, so I take the lead. Since we're to be moving slowly, Mags prefers to walk with the aid of a branch Finnick quickly fashions into a cane for her. He makes a staff for Peeta as well, which is good because, despite his protestations, I think all Peeta really wants to do is lie down. Finnick brings up the rear, so at least someone alert has our backs.

I walk with the force field on my left, because that's supposed to be the side with my superhuman ear. But since that's all made up, I cut down a bunch of hard nuts that hang like grapes from a nearby tree and toss them ahead of me as I go. It's good I do, too, because I have a feeling I'm missing the patches that indicate the force field more often than I'm spotting them. Whenever a nut hits the force field, there's a puff of smoke before the nut lands, blackened and with a cracked shell, on the ground at my feet.

After a few minutes I become aware of a smacking sound behind me and turn to see Mags peeling the shell off one of the nuts and popping it in her already-full mouth. "Mags!" I cry. "Spit that out. It could be poisonous."

She mumbles something and ignores me, licking her lips with apparent relish. I look to Finnick for help but he just laughs. "I guess we'll find out," he says.

I go forward, wondering about Finnick, who saved old Mags but will let her eat strange nuts. Who Haymitch has stamped with his seal of approval. Who brought Peeta back from the dead. Why didn't he just let him die? He would have been blameless. I never would have guessed it was in his power to revive him. Why could he possibly have wanted to save Peeta? And why was he so determined to team up with me? Willing to kill me, too, if it comes to that. But leaving the choice of if we fight to me.

I keep walking, tossing my nuts, sometimes catching a glimpse of the force field, trying to press to the left to find a spot where we can break through, get away from the Cornucopia, and hopefully find water. But after another hour or so of this I realize it's futile. We're not making any progress to the left. In fact, the force field seems to be herding us along a curved path. I stop and look back at Mags's limping form, the sheen of sweat on Peeta's face. "Let's take a break," I say. "I need to get another look from above."

The tree I choose seems to jut higher into the air than the others. I make my way up the twisting boughs, staying as close to the trunk as possible. No telling how easily these rubbery branches will snap. Still I climb beyond good sense because there's something I have to see. As I cling to a stretch of trunk no wider than a sapling, swaying back and forth in the humid breeze, my suspicions are confirmed. There's a reason we can't turn to the left, will never be able to. From this precarious vantage point, I can see the shape of the whole arena for the first time. A perfect circle. With a perfect wheel in the middle. The sky above the circumference of the jungle is tinged a uniform pink. And I think I can make out one or two of those wavy squares, chinks in the armour, Wiress and Beetee called them, because they reveal what was meant to be hidden and are therefore a weakness. Just to make absolutely sure, I shoot an arrow into the empty space above the tree line. There's a spurt of light, a flash of real blue sky, and the arrow's thrown back into the jungle. I climb down to give the others the bad news.

"The force field has us trapped in a circle. A dome, really. I don't know how high it goes. There's the Cornucopia, the sea, and then the jungle all around. Very exact. Very symmetrical. And not very large," I say.

"Did you see any water?" asks Finnick.

"Only the salt water where we started the Games," I say.

"There must be some other source," says Peeta, frowning. "Or we'll all be dead in a matter of days."

"Well, the foliage is thick. Maybe there are ponds or springs somewhere," I say doubtfully. I instinctively feel the Capitol might want these unpopular Games over as soon as possible. Plutarch Heavensbee might have already been given orders to knock us off. "At any rate, there's no point in trying to find out what's over the edge of this hill, because the answer is nothing."

"There must be drinkable water between the force field and the wheel," Peeta insists. We all know what this means. Heading back down. Heading back to the Careers and the bloodshed. With Mags hardly able to walk and Peeta too weak to fight.

We decide to move down the slope a few hundred metres and continue circling. See if maybe there's some water at that level. I stay in the lead, occasionally chucking a nut to my left, but we're well out of range of the force field now. The sun beats down on us, turning the air to steam, playing tricks on our eyes. By mid-afternoon, it's clear Peeta and Mags can't go on.

Finnick chooses a campsite about ten metres below the force field, saying we can use it as a weapon by deflecting our enemies into it if attacked. Then he and Mags pull blades of the sharp grass that grows in two-metre-high tufts and begin to weave them together into mats. Since Mags seems to have no ill effects from the nuts, Peeta collects bunches of them and fries them by bouncing them off the force field. He methodically peels off the shells, piling the meats on a leaf. I stand guard, fidgety and hot and raw with the emotions of the day.

Thirsty. I am so thirsty. Finally I can't stand it any more. "Finnick, why don't you stand guard and I'll hunt around some more for water," I say. No one's thrilled with the idea of me going off alone, but the threat of dehydration hangs over us.

"Don't worry, I won't go far," I promise Peeta.

"I'll go, too," he says.

"No, I'm going to do some hunting if I can," I tell him. I don't add, "And you can't come because you're too loud." But it's implied. He would both scare off prey and endanger me with his heavy tread. "I won't be long."

I move stealthily through the trees, happy to find that the ground lends itself to soundless footsteps. I work my way down at a diagonal, but I find nothing except more lush, green plant life.

The sound of the cannon brings me to a halt. The initial bloodbath at the Cornucopia must be over. The death toll of the tributes is now available. I count the shots, each representing one dead victor. Eight. Not as many as last year. But it seems like more since I know most of their names.

Suddenly weak, I lean against a tree to rest, feeling the heat draw the moisture from my body like a sponge. Already, swallowing is difficult and fatigue is creeping up on me. I try rubbing my hand across my belly, hoping some sympathetic pregnant woman will become my sponsor and Haymitch can send in some water. No luck. I sink to the ground.

In my stillness, I begin to notice the animals: strange birds with brilliant plumage, tree lizards with flickering blue tongues, and something that looks like a cross between a rat and a possum clinging on the branches close to the trunk. I shoot one of the latter out of a tree to get a closer look.

It's ugly, all right, a big rodent with a fuzz of mottled grey fur and two wicked-looking gnawing teeth protruding over its lower lip. As I'm gutting and skinning it, I notice something else. Its muzzle is wet. Like an animal that's been drinking from a stream. Excited, I start at its home tree and move slowly out in a spiral. It can't be far, the creature's water source.

Nothing. I find nothing. Not so much as a dewdrop. Eventually, because I know Peeta will be worried about me, I head back to the camp, hotter and more frustrated than ever.

When I arrive, I see the others have transformed the place. Mags and Finnick have created a hut of sorts out of the grass mats, open on one side but with three walls, a floor and a roof. Mags has also plaited several bowls that Peeta has filled with roasted nuts. Their faces turn to me hopefully, but I give my head a shake. "No. No water. It's out there, though. He knew where it was," I say, hoisting the skinned rodent up for all to see. "He'd been drinking recently when I shot him out of a tree, but I couldn't find his source. I swear, I covered every centimetre of ground in a thirty-metre radius."

"Can we eat him?" Peeta asks.

"I don't know for sure. But his meat doesn't look that different from a squirrel's. He ought to be cooked. . ." I hesitate as I think of trying to start a fire out here from complete scratch. Even if I succeed, there's the smoke to think about. We're all so close together in this arena, there's no chance of hiding it.

Peeta has another idea. He takes a cube of rodent meat, skewers it on the tip of a pointed stick, and lets it fall into the force field. There's a sharp sizzle and the stick flies back. The chunk of meat is blackened on the outside but well cooked inside. We give him a round of applause, then quickly stop, remembering where we are.

The white sun sinks in the rosy sky as we gather in the hut. I'm still leery about the nuts, but Finnick says Mags recognized them from another Games. I didn't bother spending time at the edible-plants station in training because it was so effortless for me last year. Now I wish I had. For surely there would have been some of the unfamiliar plants surrounding me. And I might have guessed a bit more about where I was headed. Mags seems fine, though, and she's been eating the nuts for hours. So I pick one up and take a small bite. It has a mild, slightly sweet flavour that reminds me of a chestnut. I decide it's all right. The rodent's strong and gamey but surprisingly juicy. Really, it's not a bad meal for our first night in the arena. If only we had something to wash it down with.

Finnick asks a lot of questions about the rodent, which we decide to call a tree rat. How high was it, how long did I watch it before I shot, and what was it doing? I don't remember it doing much of anything. Snuffling around for insects or something.

I'm dreading the night. At least the tightly woven grass offers some protection from whatever slinks across the jungle floor after hours. But a short time before the sun slips below the horizon, a pale white moon rises, making things just visible enough. Our conversation trails off because we know what's coming.

We position ourselves in a line at the mouth of the hut and Peeta slips his hand into mine.

The sky brightens when the seal of the Capitol appears as if floating in space. As I listen to the strains of the anthem I think, *It will be harder for Finnick and Mags.* But it turns out to be plenty hard for me as well. Seeing the faces of the eight dead victors projected into the sky.

The man from District 5, the one Finnick took out with his trident, is the first to appear. That means that all the tributes in 1 through 4 are alive – the four Careers, Beetee and Wiress, and, of course, Mags and Finnick. The man from District 5 is followed by the male morphling from 6, Cecelia and Woof from 8, both from 9, the woman from 10, and Seeder from 11. The Capitol seal is back with a final bit of music and then the sky goes dark except for the moon.

No one speaks. I can't pretend I knew any of them well. But I'm thinking of those three kids hanging on to Cecelia when they took her away. Seeder's kindness to me at our meeting. Even the thought of the glazed-eyed morphling painting my cheeks with yellow flowers gives me a pang. All dead. All gone.

I don't know how long we might have sat here if it weren't for the arrival of the silver parachute, which glides down through the foliage to land before us. No one reaches for it.

"Whose is it, do you think?" I say finally.

"No telling," says Finnick. "Why don't we let Peeta claim it, since he died today?"

Peeta unties the cord and flattens out the circle of silk. On the parachute sits a small metal object that I can't place. "What is it?" I ask. No one knows. We pass it from hand to hand, taking turns examining it. It's a hollow metal tube, tapered slightly at one end. On the other end a small lip curves downward. It's vaguely familiar. A part that could have fallen off a bicycle, a curtain rod, anything, really.

Peeta blows on one end to see if it makes a sound. It doesn't. Finnick slides his pinkie into it, testing it out as a weapon. Useless.

"Can you fish with it, Mags?" I ask. Mags, who can fish with almost anything, shakes her head and grunts.

I take it and roll it back and forth on my palm. Since we're allies, Haymitch will be working with the District 4 mentors. He had a hand in choosing this gift. That means it's valuable. Life-saving, even. I think back to last year, when I wanted water so badly, but he wouldn't send it because he knew I could find it if I tried. Haymitch's gifts, or lack thereof, carry weighty messages. I can almost hear him growling at me, *Use your brain if you have one. What is it?*

I wipe the sweat from my eyes and hold the gift out in the moonlight. I move it this way and that, viewing it from different angles, covering portions and then revealing them. Trying to make it divulge its purpose to me. Finally, in frustration, I jam one end into the dirt. "I give up. Maybe if we hook up with Beetee or Wiress they can figure it out."

I stretch out, pressing my hot cheek on the grass mat, staring at the thing in aggravation. Peeta rubs a tense spot between my shoulders and I let myself relax a little. I wonder why this place hasn't cooled off at all now that the sun's gone down. I wonder what's going on back home.

Prim. My mother. Gale. Madge. I think of them watching me from home. At least I hope they're at home. Not taken into custody by Thread. Being punished as Cinna is. As Darius is. Punished because of me. Everybody.

I begin to ache for them, for my district, for my woods. Decent woods with sturdy hardwood trees, plentiful food, game that isn't creepy. Rushing streams. Cool breezes. No, cold winds to blow this stifling heat away. I conjure up such a wind in my mind, letting it freeze my cheeks and numb my fingers, and all at once, the piece of metal half buried in the black earth has a name.

"A spile!" I exclaim, sitting bolt upright.

"What?" asks Finnick.

I wrestle the thing from the ground and brush it clean. Cup my hand around the tapered end, concealing it, and look at the lip. Yes, I've seen one of these before. On a cold, windy day long ago, when I was out in the woods with my father. Inserted snugly into a hole drilled in the side of a maple. A pathway for the sap to follow as it flowed into our bucket. Maple syrup could make even our dull bread a treat. After my father died, I didn't know what happened to the handful of spiles he had. Hidden out in the woods somewhere, probably. Never to be found.

"It's a spile. Sort of like a tap. You put it in a tree and sap comes out." I look at the sinewy green trunks around me. "Well, the right sort of tree."

"Sap?" asks Finnick. They don't have the right kind of trees by the sea, either.

"To make syrup," says Peeta. "But there must be something else inside these trees."

We're all on our feet at once. Our thirst. The lack of springs. The tree rat's sharp front teeth and wet muzzle. There can only be one thing worth having inside these trees. Finnick goes to hammer the spile into the green bark of a massive tree with a rock, but I stop him. "Wait. You might damage it. We need to drill a hole first," I say.

There's nothing to drill with, so Mags offers her awl and Peeta drives it straight into the bark, burying the spike five centimetres deep. He and Finnick take turns opening up the hole with the awl and the knives until it can hold the spile. I wedge it in carefully and we all stand back in anticipation. At first nothing happens. Then a drop of water rolls down the lip and lands in Mags's palm. She licks it off and holds out her hand for more.

By wiggling and adjusting the spile, we get a thin stream running out. We take turns holding our mouths under the tap, wetting our parched tongues. Mags brings over a basket, and the grass is so tightly woven it holds water. We fill the basket and pass it around, taking deep gulps and, later, luxuriously, splashing our faces clean. Like everything here, the water's on the warm side, but this is no time to be picky.

Without our thirst to distract us, we're all aware of how exhausted we are and make preparations for the night. Last year, I always tried to have my gear ready in case I had to make a speedy retreat in the night. This year, there's no backpack to prepare. Just my weapons, which won't leave my grasp, anyway. Then I think of the spile and wrest it from the tree trunk. I strip a tough vine of its leaves, thread it through the hollow centre, and tie the spile securely to my belt.

Finnick offers to take the first watch and I let him, knowing it has to be one of the two of us until Peeta's rested up. I lie down beside Peeta on the floor of the hut, telling Finnick to wake me when he's tired. Instead I find myself jarred from sleep a few hours later by what seems to be the tolling of a bell. *Bong! Bong!* It's not exactly like the one they ring in the Justice Building on New Year's Eve but close enough for me to recognize it. Peeta and Mags sleep through it, but Finnick has the same look of attentiveness I feel. The tolling stops.

"I counted twelve," he says.

I nod. Twelve. What does that signify? One ring for each district? Maybe. But why? "Mean anything, do you think?"

"No idea," he says.

We wait for further instructions, maybe a message from Claudius Templesmith. An invitation to a feast. The only thing of note appears in the distance. A dazzling bolt of electricity strikes a towering tree and then a lightning storm begins. I guess it's an indication of rain, of a water source for those who don't have mentors as smart as Haymitch.

"Go to sleep, Finnick. It's my turn to watch, anyway," I say.

Finnick hesitates, but no one can stay awake for ever. He settles down at the mouth of the hut, one hand gripped around a trident, and drifts into a restless sleep.

I sit with my bow loaded, watching the jungle, which is ghostly pale and green in the moonlight. After an hour or so, the lightning stops. I can hear the rain coming in, though, pattering on the leaves a few hundred metres away. I keep waiting for it to reach us but it never does.

The sound of the cannon startles me, although it makes little impression on my sleeping companions. There's no point in awakening them for this. Another victor dead. I don't even allow myself to wonder who it is.

The elusive rain shuts off suddenly, like the storm did last year in the arena.

Moments after it stops, I see the fog sliding softly in from the direction of the recent downpour. *Just a reaction. Cool rain on the steaming ground*, I think. It continues to approach at a steady pace. Tendrils reach forward and then curl like fingers, as if they are pulling the rest behind them. As I watch, I feel the hairs on my neck begin to rise. Something's wrong with this fog.

The progression of the front line is too uniform to be natural. And if it's not natural. . .

A sickeningly sweet odour begins to invade my nostrils and I reach for the others, shouting for them to wake up.

In the few seconds it takes to rouse them, I begin to blister.

21

Tiny, searing stabs. Wherever the droplets of mist touch my skin.

"Run!" I scream at the others. "Run!"

Finnick snaps awake instantly, rising to counter an enemy. But when he sees the wall of fog, he tosses a still-sleeping Mags on to his back and takes off. Peeta is on his feet but not as alert. I grab his arm and begin to propel him through the jungle after Finnick.

"What is it? What is it?" he says in bewilderment.

"Some kind of fog. Poisonous gas. Hurry, Peeta!" I urge. I can tell that however much he denied it during the day, the aftereffects of hitting the force field have been significant. He's slow, much slower than usual. And the tangle of vines and undergrowth, which unbalance me occasionally, trip him at every step.

I look back at the wall of fog extending in a

straight line as far as I can see in either direction. A terrible impulse to flee, to abandon Peeta and save myself, shoots through me. It would be so simple, to run full out, perhaps to even climb a tree above the fog line, which seems to top out at about twelve metres. I remember how I did just this when the muttations appeared in the last Games. Took off and only thought of Peeta when I'd reached the Cornucopia. But this time, I trap my terror, push it down, and stay by his side. This time my survival isn't the goal. Peeta's is. I think of the eyes glued to the television screens in the districts, seeing if I will run, as the Capitol wishes, or hold my ground.

I lock my fingers tightly into his and say, "Watch my feet. Just try to step where I step." It helps. We seem to move a little faster, but never enough to afford a rest, and the mist continues to lap at our heels. Droplets spring free of the body of vapour. They burn, but not like fire. Less a sense of heat and more of intense pain as the chemicals find our flesh, cling to it, and burrow down through the layers of skin. Our jumpsuits are no help at all. We may as well be dressed in tissue paper, for all the protection they give.

Finnick, who bounded off initially, stops when he realizes we're having problems. But this is not a thing you can fight, only evade. He shouts encouragement, trying to move us along, and the sound of his voice acts as a guide, though little more.

Peeta's artificial leg catches in a knot of creepers and he sprawls forward before I can catch him. As I help him up, I become aware of something scarier than the blisters, more debilitating than the burns. The left side of his face has sagged, as if every muscle in it has died. The lid droops, almost concealing his eye. His mouth twists in an odd angle towards the ground. "Peeta—" I begin. And that's when I feel the spasms run up my arm.

Whatever chemical laces the fog does more than burn – it targets our nerves. A whole new kind of fear shoots through me and I yank Peeta forward, which only causes him to stumble again. By the time I get him to his feet, both of my arms are twitching uncontrollably. The fog has moved in on us, the body of it less than a metre away. Something is wrong with Peeta's legs; he's trying to walk but they move in a spastic, puppetlike fashion.

I feel him lurch forward and realize Finnick has come back for us and is hauling Peeta along. I wedge my shoulder, which still seems under my control, under Peeta's arm and do my best to keep up with Finnick's rapid pace. We put about ten metres between us and the fog when Finnick stops.

"It's no good. I'll have to carry him. Can you take Mags?" he asks me.

"Yes," I say stoutly, although my heart sinks. It's true that Mags can't weigh more than about thirty-five kilos, but I'm not very big myself. Still, I'm sure I've carried heavier loads. If only my arms would stop jumping around. I squat down and she positions herself over my shoulder, the way she rides on Finnick. I slowly straighten my legs and, with my knees locked, I can manage her. Finnick has Peeta slung across his back now and we move forward, Finnick leading, me following in the trail he breaks through the vines.

On the fog comes, silent and steady and flat, except for the grasping tendrils. Although my instinct is to run directly away from it, I realize Finnick is moving at a diagonal down the hill. He's trying to keep a distance from the gas while steering us towards the water that surrounds the Cornucopia. *Yes, water,* I think as the acid droplets bore deeper into me. Now I'm so thankful I didn't kill Finnick, because how would I have got Peeta out of here alive? So thankful to have someone else on my side, even if it's only temporarily.

It's not Mags's fault when I begin falling. She's doing everything she can to be an easy passenger, but the fact is, there is only so much weight I can handle.

Especially now that my right leg seems to be going stiff. The first two times I crash to the ground, I manage to make it back on my feet, but the third time, I cannot get my leg to cooperate. As I struggle to get up, it gives out and Mags rolls off on to the ground before me. I flail around, trying to use vines and trunks to right myself.

Finnick's back by my side, Peeta hanging over him. "It's no use," I say. "Can you take them both? Go on ahead, I'll catch up." A somewhat doubtful proposal, but I say it with as much surety as I can muster.

I can see Finnick's eyes, green in the moonlight. I can see them as clear as day. Almost like a cat's, with a strange reflective quality. Maybe because they are shiny with tears. "No," he says. "I can't carry them both. My arms aren't working." It's true. His arms jerk uncontrollably at his sides. His hands are empty. Of his three tridents, only one remains, and it's in Peeta's hands. "I'm sorry, Mags. I can't do it."

What happens next is so fast, so senseless, I can't even move to stop it. Mags hauls herself up, plants a kiss on Finnick's lips, and then hobbles straight into the fog. Immediately, her body is seized by wild contortions and she falls to the ground in a horrible dance.

I want to scream, but my throat is on fire. I take one futile step in her direction when I hear the cannon blast, know her heart has stopped, that she is dead. "Finnick?" I call out hoarsely, but he has already turned from the scene, already continued his retreat from the fog. Dragging my useless leg behind me, I stagger after him, having no idea what else to do.

Time and space lose meaning as the fog seems to invade my brain, muddling my thoughts, making everything unreal. Some deep-rooted animal desire for survival keeps me stumbling after Finnick and Peeta, continuing to move, although I'm probably dead already. Parts of me are dead, or clearly dying. And Mags is dead. This is something I know, or maybe just think I know, because it makes no sense at all.

Moonlight glinting on Finnick's bronze hair, beads of searing pain peppering me, a leg turned to wood. I follow Finnick until he collapses on the ground, Peeta still on top of him. I seem to have no ability to stop my own forward motion and simply propel myself onwards until I trip over their prone bodies, just one more on the heap. *This is where and how and when we all die*, I think. But the thought is abstract and far less alarming than the current agonies of my body. I hear Finnick groan and manage to drag myself off the others. Now I can see the wall of fog, which has taken on a pearly white quality. Maybe it's my eyes playing tricks, or the moonlight, but the fog seems to be transforming. Yes, it's becoming thicker, as if it has pressed up against a glass window and is being forced to condense. I squint harder and realize the fingers no longer protrude from it. In fact, it has stopped moving forward entirely. Like other horrors I have witnessed in the arena, it has reached the end of its territory. Either that or the Gamemakers have decided not to kill us just yet.

"It's stopped," I try to say, but only an awful croaking sound comes from my swollen mouth. "It's stopped," I say again, and this time I must be clearer, because both Peeta and Finnick turn their heads to the fog. It begins to rise upwards now, as if being slowly vacuumed into the sky. We watch until it has all been sucked away and not the slightest wisp remains.

Peeta rolls off Finnick, who turns over on to his back. We lie there gasping, twitching, our minds and bodies invaded by the poison. After a few minutes pass, Peeta vaguely gestures upwards. "Mon-hees." I look up and spot a pair of what I guess are monkeys. I have never seen a live monkey – there's nothing like that in our woods at home. But I must have seen a picture, or one in the Games, because when I see the creatures, the same word comes to my mind. I think these have orange fur, although it's hard to tell, and are about half the size of a full-grown human. I take the monkeys for a good sign. Surely they would not hang around if the air was deadly. For a while, we quietly observe one another, humans and monkeys. Then Peeta struggles to his knees and crawls down the slope. We all crawl, since walking now seems as remarkable a feat as flying; we crawl until the vines turn to a narrow strip of sandy beach and the warm water that surrounds the Cornucopia laps our faces. I jerk back as if I've touched an open flame.

Rubbing salt in a wound. For the first time I truly appreciate the expression, because the salt in the water makes the pain of my wounds so blinding I nearly black out. But there's another sensation, of drawing out. I experiment by gingerly placing only my hand in the water. Torturous, yes, but then less so. And through the blue layer of water, I see a milky substance leaching out of the wounds on my skin. As the whiteness diminishes, so does the pain. I unbuckle my belt and strip off my jumpsuit, which is little more than a perforated rag. My shoes and undergarments are inexplicably unaffected. Little by little, one small portion of a limb at a time, I soak the poison out of my wounds. Peeta seems to be doing the same. But Finnick backed away from the water at first touch and lies face down on the sand, either unwilling or unable to purge himself.

Finally, when I have survived the worst, opening

my eyes underwater, sniffing water into my sinuses and snorting it out, and even gargling repeatedly to wash out my throat, I'm functional enough to help Finnick. Some feeling has returned to my leg, but my arms are still riddled with spasms. I can't drag Finnick into the water, and possibly the pain would kill him, anyway. So I scoop up shaky handfuls and empty them on his fists. Since he's not underwater, the poison comes out of his wounds just as it went in, in wisps of fog that I take great care to steer clear of. Peeta recovers enough to help me. He cuts away Finnick's jumpsuit. Somewhere he finds two shells that work much better than our hands do. We concentrate on soaking Finnick's arms first, since they have been so badly damaged, and even though a lot of white stuff pours out of them, he doesn't notice. He just lies there, eyes shut, giving an occasional moan.

I look around with growing awareness of how dangerous a position we're in. It's night, yes, but this moon gives off too much light for concealment. We're lucky no one's attacked us yet. We could see them coming from the Cornucopia, but if all four Careers attacked, they'd overpower us. If they didn't spot us at first, Finnick's moans would give us away soon.

"We've got to get more of him into the water," I whisper. But we can't put him in face-first, not while he's in this condition. Peeta nods to Finnick's feet. We each take one, pull him one hundred and eighty degrees around, and start to drag him into the salt water. Just a few centimetres at a time. His ankles. Wait a few minutes. Up to his mid-calf. Wait. His knees. Clouds of white swirl out from his flesh and he groans. We continue to detoxify him, bit by bit. What I find is that the longer I sit in the water, the better I feel. Not just my skin, but my brain and muscle control continue to improve. I can see Peeta's face beginning to return to normal, his eyelid opening, the grimace leaving his mouth.

Finnick slowly begins to revive. His eyes open, focus on us, and register awareness that he's being helped. I rest his head on my lap and we let him soak about ten minutes with everything immersed from the neck down. Peeta and I exchange a smile as Finnick lifts his arms above the seawater.

"There's just your head left, Finnick. That's the worst part, but you'll feel much better after, if you can bear it," Peeta says. We help him to sit up and let him grip our hands as he purges his eyes and nose and mouth. His throat is still too raw to speak.

"I'm going to try to tap a tree," I say. My fingers fumble at my belt and find the spile still hanging from its vine.

"Let me make the hole first," says Peeta. "You stay with him. You're the healer."

That's a joke, I think. But I don't say it out loud, since Finnick has enough to deal with. He got the worst of the fog, although I'm not sure why. Maybe because he's the biggest or maybe because he had to exert himself the most. And then, of course, there's Mags. I still don't understand what happened there. Why he essentially abandoned her to carry Peeta. Why she not only didn't question it, but ran straight to her death without a moment's hesitation. Was it because she was so old that her days were numbered, anyway? Did they think that Finnick would stand a better chance of winning if he had Peeta and me as allies? The haggard look on Finnick's face tells me that now is not the moment to ask.

Instead I try to put myself back together. I rescue my mockingjay pin from my ruined jumpsuit and pin it to the strap of my undershirt. The flotation belt must be acid resistant, since it looks as good as new. I can swim, so the flotation belt's not really necessary, but Brutus blocked my arrow with his, so I buckle it back on, thinking it might offer some protection. I undo my hair and comb it with my fingers, thinning it out considerably since the fog droplets damaged it. Then I braid back what's left of it.

Peeta has found a good tree about ten metres from the narrow strip of beach. We can hardly see him, but the sound of his knife against the wooden trunk is crystal clear. I wonder what happened to the awl. Mags must've either dropped it or taken it into the fog with her. Anyway, it's gone.

I have moved out a bit further into the shallows, floating alternately on my belly and back. If the seawater healed Peeta and me, it seems to be transforming Finnick altogether. He begins to move slowly, just testing his limbs, and gradually begins to swim. But it's not like me swimming, the rhythmic strokes, the even pace. It's like watching some strange sea animal coming back to life. He dives and surfaces, spraying water out of his mouth, rolls over and over in some bizarre corkscrew motion that makes me dizzy even to watch. And then, when he's been underwater so long I feel certain he's drowned, his head pops up right next to me and I start.

"Don't do that," I say.

"What? Come up or stay under?" he says.

"Either. Neither. Whatever. Just soak in the water and behave," I say. "Or if you feel this good, let's go help Peeta."

In just the short time it takes to cross to the edge of the jungle, I become aware of the change. Put it down to years of hunting, or maybe my reconstructed ear does work a little better than anyone intended. But I sense the mass of warm bodies poised above us. They don't need to chatter or scream. The mere breathing of so many is enough.

I touch Finnick's arm and he follows my gaze upwards. I don't know how they arrived so silently. Perhaps they didn't. We've all been absorbed in restoring our bodies. During that time they've assembled. Not five or ten but scores of monkeys weigh down the limbs of the jungle trees. The pair we spotted when we first escaped the fog felt like a welcoming committee. This crew feels ominous.

I arm my bow with two arrows and Finnick adjusts the trident in his hand. "Peeta," I say as calmly as possible. "I need your help with something."

"OK, just a minute. I think I've just about got it," he says, still occupied with the tree. "Yes, there. Have you got the spile?"

"I do. But we've found something you'd better take a look at," I continue in a measured voice. "Only move towards us quietly, so you don't startle it." For some reason, I don't want him to notice the monkeys, or even glance their way. There are creatures that interpret mere eye contact as aggression.

Peeta turns to us, panting from his work on the

tree. The tone of my request is so odd that it's alerted him to some irregularity. "OK," he says casually. He begins to move through the jungle, and although I know he's trying hard to be quiet, this has never been his strong suit, even when he had two sound legs. But it's all right, he's moving, the monkeys are holding their positions. He's just five metres from the beach when he senses them. His eyes only dart up for a second, but it's as if he's triggered a bomb. The monkeys explode into a shrieking mass of orange fur and converge on him.

I've never seen any animal move so fast. They slide down the vines as if the things were greased. Leap impossible distances from tree to tree. Fangs bared, hackles raised, claws shooting out like switchblades. I may be unfamiliar with monkeys, but animals in nature don't act like this. "*Mutts!*" I spit out as Finnick and I crash into the greenery.

I know every arrow must count, and they do. In the eerie light, I bring down monkey after monkey, targeting eyes and hearts and throats, so that each hit means a death. But still it wouldn't be enough without Finnick spearing the beasts like fish and flinging them aside, Peeta slashing away with his knife. I feel claws on my leg, down my back, before someone takes out the attacker. The air grows heavy with trampled plants, the scent of blood, and the musty stink of the monkeys. Peeta and Finnick and I position ourselves in a triangle, a few metres apart, our backs to one another. My heart sinks as my fingers draw back my last arrow. Then I remember Peeta has a sheath, too. And he's not shooting, he's hacking away with that knife. My own knife is out now, but the monkeys are quicker, can spring in and out so fast you can barely react.

"Peeta!" I shout. "Your arrows!"

Peeta turns to see my predicament and is sliding off his sheath when it happens. A monkey lunges out of a tree for his chest. I have no arrow, no way to shoot. I can hear the thud of Finnick's trident finding another mark and know his weapon is occupied. Peeta's knife arm is disabled as he tries to remove the sheath. I throw my knife at the oncoming mutt but the creature somersaults, evading the blade, and stays on its trajectory.

Weaponless, defenceless, I do the only thing I can think of. I run for Peeta, to knock him to the ground, to protect his body with mine, even though I know I won't make it in time.

She does, though. Materializing, it seems, from thin air. One moment nowhere, the next reeling in front of Peeta. Already bloody, mouth open in a high-pitched scream, pupils enlarged so her eyes seem like black holes.

The insane morphling from District 6 throws up her skeletal arms as if to embrace the monkey, and it sinks its fangs into her chest.

22

Peeta drops the sheath and buries his knife into the monkey's back, stabbing it again and again until it releases its jaw. He kicks the mutt away, bracing for more. I have his arrows now, a loaded bow, and Finnick at my back, breathing hard but not actively engaged.

"Come on, then! Come on!" shouts Peeta, panting with rage. But something has happened to the monkeys. They are withdrawing, backing up trees, fading into the jungle, as if some unheard voice calls them away. A Gamemaker's voice, telling them this is enough.

"Get her," I say to Peeta. "We'll cover you."

Peeta gently lifts up the morphling and carries her the last few metres to the beach while Finnick and I keep our weapons at the ready. But except for the orange carcasses on the ground, the monkeys are gone. Peeta lays the morphling on the sand. I cut away the material over her chest, revealing the four deep puncture wounds. Blood slowly trickles from them, making them look far less deadly than they are. The real damage is inside. By the position of the openings, I feel certain the beast ruptured something vital, a lung, maybe even her heart.

She lies on the sand, gasping like a fish out of water. Sagging skin, sickly green, her ribs as prominent as a child's dead of starvation. Surely she could afford food, but turned to the morphling just as Haymitch turned to drink, I guess. Everything about her speaks of waste – her body, her life, the vacant look in her eyes. I hold one of her twitching hands, unclear whether it moves from the poison that affected our nerves, the shock of the attack, or withdrawal from the drug that was her sustenance. There is nothing we can do. Nothing but stay with her while she dies.

"I'll watch the trees," Finnick says before walking away. I'd like to walk away, too, but she grips my hand so tightly I would have to prise off her fingers, and I don't have the strength for that kind of cruelty. I think of Rue, how maybe I could sing a song or something. But I don't even know the morphling's name, let alone if she likes songs. I just know she's dying.

Peeta crouches down on the other side of her and strokes her hair. When he begins to speak in a soft voice, it seems almost nonsensical, but the words aren't for me. "With my paint box at home, I can make every colour imaginable. Pink. As pale as a baby's skin. Or as deep as rhubarb. Green like spring grass. Blue that shimmers like ice on water."

The morphling stares into Peeta's eyes, hanging on to his words.

"One time, I spent three days mixing paint until I found the right shade for sunlight on white fur. You see, I kept thinking it was yellow, but it was much more than that. Layers of all sorts of colour. One by one," says Peeta.

The morphling's breathing is slowing into shallow catch-breaths. Her free hand dabbles in the blood on her chest, making the tiny swirling motions she so loved to paint with.

"I haven't figured out a rainbow yet. They come so quickly and leave so soon. I never have enough time to capture them. Just a bit of blue here or purple there. And then they fade away again. Back into the air," says Peeta.

The morphling seems mesmerized by Peeta's words. Entranced. She lifts up a trembling hand and paints what I think might be a flower on Peeta's cheek.

"Thank you," he whispers. "That looks beautiful."

For a moment, the morphling's face lights up in a grin and she makes a small squeaking sound. Then her blood-dappled hand falls back on to her chest, she gives one last huff of air, and the cannon fires. The grip on my hand releases.

Peeta carries her out into the water. He returns and sits beside me. The morphling floats out towards the Cornucopia for a while, then the hovercraft appears and a four-pronged claw drops, encases her, carries her into the night sky, and she's gone.

Finnick rejoins us, his fist full of my arrows still wet with monkey blood. He drops them beside me on the sand. "Thought you might want these."

"Thanks," I say. I wade into the water and wash off the gore, from my weapons, my wounds. By the time I return to the jungle to gather some moss to dry them, all the monkeys' bodies have vanished.

"Where did they go?" I ask.

"We don't know exactly. The vines shifted and they were gone," says Finnick.

We stare at the jungle, numb and exhausted. In the quiet, I notice that the spots where the fog droplets touched my skin have scabbed over. They've stopped hurting and begun to itch. Intensely. I try to think of this as a good sign. That they are healing. I glance over at Peeta, at Finnick, and see they're both scratching at their damaged faces. Yes, even Finnick's beauty has been marred by this night.

"Don't scratch," I say, wanting badly to scratch myself. But I know it's the advice my mother would give. "You'll only bring infection. Think it's safe to try for the water again?"

We make our way back to the tree Peeta was tapping. Finnick and I stand with our weapons poised while he works the spile in, but no threat appears. Peeta's found a good vein and the water begins to gush from the spile. We slake our thirst, let the warm water pour over our itching bodies. We fill a handful of shells with drinking water and go back to the beach.

It's still night, though dawn can't be too many hours away. Unless the Gamemakers want it to be. "Why don't you two get some rest?" I say. "I'll watch for a while."

"No, Katniss, I'd rather," says Finnick. I look in his eyes, at his face, and realize he's barely holding back tears. Mags. The least I can do is give him the privacy to mourn her.

"All right, Finnick, thanks," I say. I lie down on the sand with Peeta, who drifts off at once. I stare into the night, thinking of what a difference a day makes. How yesterday morning, Finnick was on my kill list, and now I'm willing to sleep with him as my guard. He saved Peeta and let Mags die and I don't know why. Only that I can never settle the balance owed between us. All I can do at the moment is go to sleep and let him grieve in peace. And so I do.

It's mid-morning when I open my eyes again. Peeta's still out beside me. Above us, a mat of grass suspended on branches shields our faces from the sunlight. I sit up and see that Finnick's hands have not been idle. Two woven bowls are filled with fresh water. A third holds a mess of shellfish.

Finnick sits on the sand, cracking them open with a stone. "They're better fresh," he says, ripping a chunk of flesh from a shell and popping it into his mouth. His eyes are still puffy but I pretend not to notice.

My stomach begins to growl at the smell of food and I reach for one. The sight of my fingernails, caked with blood, stops me. I've been scratching my skin raw in my sleep.

"You know, if you scratch you'll bring on infection," says Finnick.

"That's what I've heard," I say. I go into the salt water and wash off the blood, trying to decide which I hate more, pain or itching. Fed up, I stomp back on to the beach, turn my face upwards, and snap, "Hey, Haymitch, if you're not too drunk, we could use a little something for our skin."

It's almost funny how quickly the parachute appears above me. I reach up and the tube lands squarely in my open hand. "About time," I say, but I can't keep the scowl on my face. Haymitch. What I wouldn't give for five minutes of conversation with him.

I plunk down on the sand next to Finnick and screw the lid off the tube. Inside is a thick, dark ointment with a pungent smell, a combination of tar and pine needles. I wrinkle my nose as I squeeze a glob of the medicine on to my palm and begin to massage it into my leg. A sound of pleasure slips out of my mouth as the stuff eradicates my itching. It also stains my scabby skin a ghastly grey-green. As I start on the second leg I toss the tube to Finnick, who eyes me doubtfully.

"It's like you're decomposing," says Finnick. But I guess the itching wins out, because after a minute Finnick begins to treat his own skin, too. Really, the combination of the scabs and the ointment looks hideous. I can't help enjoying his distress.

"Poor Finnick. Is this the first time in your life you haven't looked pretty?" I say.

"It must be. The sensation's completely new. How have you managed it all these years?" he asks.

"Just avoid mirrors. You'll forget about it," I say.

"Not if I keep looking at you," he says.

We slather ourselves down, even taking turns rubbing the ointment into each other's backs where the undershirts don't protect our skin. "I'm going to wake Peeta," I say.

"No, wait," says Finnick. "Let's do it together. Put our faces right in front of his."

Well, there's so little opportunity for fun left in my life, I agree. We position ourselves on either side of Peeta, lean over until our faces are centimetres from his nose, and give him a shake. "Peeta. Peeta, wake up," I say in a soft, singsong voice.

His eyelids flutter open and then he jumps like we've stabbed him. "Aa!"

Finnick and I fall back in the sand, laughing our heads off. Every time we try to stop, we look at Peeta's attempt to maintain a disdainful expression and it sets us off again. By the time we pull ourselves together, I'm thinking that maybe Finnick Odair is all right. At least not as vain or self-important as I'd thought. Not so bad at all, really. And just as I've come to this conclusion, a parachute lands next to us with a fresh loaf of bread. Remembering from last year how Haymitch's gifts are often timed to send a message, I make a note to myself. *Be friends with Finnick. You'll get food.*

Finnick turns the bread over in his hands, examining the crust. A bit too possessively. It's not necessary. It's got that green tint from seaweed that the bread from District 4 always has. We all know it's his. Maybe he's just realized how precious it is, and that he may never see another loaf again. Maybe some memory of Mags is associated with the crust. But all he says is, "This will go well with the shellfish."

While I help Peeta coat his skin with the ointment, Finnick deftly cleans the meat from the shellfish. We gather round and eat the delicious sweet flesh with the salty bread from District 4.

We all look monstrous – the ointment seems to be causing some of the scabs to peel – but I'm glad for the medicine. Not just because it gives relief from the itching, but also because it acts as protection from that blazing white sun in the pink sky. By its position, I estimate it must be going on ten o'clock, that we've been in the arena for about a day. Eleven of us are dead. Thirteen alive. Somewhere in the jungle, ten are concealed. Three or four are the Careers. I don't really feel like trying to remember who the others are.

For me, the jungle has quickly evolved from a place of protection to a sinister trap. I know at some point we'll be forced to re-enter its depths, either to hunt or be hunted, but for right now I'm planning to stick to our little beach. And I don't hear Peeta or Finnick suggesting we do otherwise. For a while the jungle seems almost static, humming, shimmering, but not flaunting its dangers. Then, in the distance, comes screaming. Across from us, a wedge of the jungle begins to vibrate. An enormous wave crests high on the hill, topping the trees and roaring down the slope. It hits the existing seawater with such force that, even though we're as far as we can get from it, the surf bubbles up around our knees, setting our few possessions afloat. Among the three of us, we manage to collect everything before it's carried off, except for our chemical-riddled jumpsuits, which are so eaten away no one cares if we lose them.

A cannon fires. We see the hovercraft appear over the area where the wave began and pluck a body from the trees. *Twelve*, I think.

The circle of water slowly calms down, having absorbed the giant wave. We rearrange our things back on the wet sand and are about to settle down when I see them. Three figures, about two spokes away, stumbling on to the beach. "There," I say quietly, nodding in the newcomers' direction. Peeta and Finnick follow my gaze. As if by previous agreement, we all fade back into the shadows of the jungle.

The trio's in bad shape – you can see that right off. One is being practically dragged out by a second, and the third wanders in loopy circles, as if deranged. They're a solid brick-red colour, as if they've been dipped in paint and left out to dry.

"Who is that?" asks Peeta. "Or what? Muttations?"

I draw back an arrow, readying for an attack. But all that happens is that the one who was being dragged collapses on the beach. The dragger stamps the ground in frustration and, in an apparent fit of temper, turns and shoves the circling, deranged one over.

Finnick's face lights up. "Johanna!" he calls, and runs for the red things.

"Finnick!" I hear Johanna's voice reply.

I exchange a look with Peeta. "What now?" I ask.

"We can't really leave Finnick," he says.

"Guess not. Come on, then," I say grouchily, because even if I'd had a list of allies, Johanna Mason would definitely not have been on it. The two of us tromp down the beach to where Finnick and Johanna are just meeting up. As we move in closer, I see her companions, and confusion sets in. That's Beetee on the ground on his back and Wiress who's regained her feet to continue making loops. "She's got Wiress and Beetee."

"Nuts and Volts?" says Peeta, equally puzzled. "I've

got to hear how this happened."

When we reach them, Johanna's gesturing towards the jungle and talking very fast to Finnick. "We thought it was rain, you know, because of the lightning, and we were all so thirsty. But when it started coming down, it turned out to be blood. Thick, hot blood. You couldn't see, you couldn't speak without getting a mouthful. We just staggered around, trying to get out of it. That's when Blight hit the force field."

"I'm sorry, Johanna," says Finnick. It takes a moment to place Blight. I think he was Johanna's male counterpart from District 7, but I hardly remember seeing him. Come to think of it, I don't even think he showed up for training.

"Yeah, well, he wasn't much, but he was from home," she says. "And he left me alone with these two." She nudges Beetee, who's barely conscious, with her shoe. "He got a knife in the back at the Cornucopia. And her—"

We all look over at Wiress, who's circling around, coated in dried blood, and murmuring, "Tick, tock. Tick, tock."

"Yeah, we know. Tick, tock. Nuts is in shock," says Johanna. This seems to draw Wiress in her direction and she careens into Johanna, who harshly shoves her to the beach. "Just stay down, will you?"

"Lay off her," I snap.

Johanna narrows her brown eyes at me in hatred. "Lay off her?" she hisses. She steps forward before I can react and slaps me so hard I see stars. "Who do you think got them out of that bleeding jungle for you? You—" Finnick tosses her writhing body over his shoulder and carries her out into the water and repeatedly dunks her while she screams a lot of really insulting things at me. But I don't shoot. Because she's with Finnick and because of what she said, about getting them for me.

"What did she mean? She got them for me?" I ask Peeta.

"I don't know. You did want them originally," he reminds me.

"Yeah, I did. Originally." But that answers nothing. I look down at Beetee's inert body. "But I won't have them long unless we do something."

Peeta lifts Beetee up in his arms and I take Wiress by the hand and we go back to our little beach camp. I sit Wiress in the shallows so she can get washed up a bit, but she just clutches her hands together and occasionally mumbles, "Tick, tock." I unhook Beetee's belt and find a heavy metal cylinder attached to the side with a rope of vines. I can't tell what it is, but if he thought it was worth saving, I'm not going to be the one who loses it. I toss it up on the sand. Beetee's clothes are glued to him with blood, so Peeta holds him in the water while I loosen them. It takes some time to get the jumpsuit off, and then we find his undergarments are saturated with blood as well. There's no choice but to strip him naked to get him clean, but I have to say this doesn't make much of an impression on me any more. Our kitchen table's been full of so many naked men this year. You kind of get used to it after a while.

We put down Finnick's mat and lay Beetee on his stomach so we can examine his back. There's a gash about eighteen centimetres long running from his shoulder blade to below his ribs. Fortunately it's not too deep. He's lost a lot of blood, though – you can tell by the pallor of his skin – and it's still oozing out of the wound.

I sit back on my heels, trying to think. What do I have to work with? Seawater? I feel like my mother when her first line of defence for treating everything was snow. I look over at the jungle. I bet there's a whole pharmacy in there if I knew how to use it. But these aren't my plants. Then I think about the moss Mags gave me to blow my nose. "Be right back," I tell

Peeta. Fortunately the stuff seems to be pretty common in the jungle. I rip an armful from the nearby trees and carry it back to the beach. I make a thick pad out of the moss, place it on Beetee's cut, and secure it by tying vines around his body. We get some water into him and then pull him into the shade at the edge of the jungle.

"I think that's all we can do," I say.

"It's good. You're good with this healing stuff," he says. "It's in your blood."

"No," I say, shaking my head. "I got my father's blood." The kind that quickens during a hunt, not an epidemic. "I'm going to see about Wiress."

I take a handful of the moss to use as a rag and join Wiress in the shallows. She doesn't resist as I work off her clothing, scrub the blood from her skin. But her eyes are dilated with fear, and when I speak, she doesn't respond except to say with ever-increasing urgency, "Tick, tock." She does seem to be trying to tell me something, but with no Beetee to explain her thoughts, I'm at a loss.

"Yes, tick, tock. Tick, tock," I say. This seems to calm her down a little. I wash out her jumpsuit until there's hardly a trace of blood, and help her back into it. It's not damaged like ours were. Her belt's fine, so I fasten that on, too. Then I pin her undergarments, along with Beetee's, under some rocks and let them soak.

By the time I've rinsed out Beetee's jumpsuit, a shiny clean Johanna and peeling Finnick have joined us. For a while, Johanna gulps water and stuffs herself with shellfish while I try to coax something into Wiress. Finnick tells them about the fog and the monkeys in a detached, almost clinical voice, avoiding the most important detail of the story.

Everybody offers to guard while the others rest, but in the end, it's Johanna and I who stay up. Me because I'm really rested, she because she simply refuses to lie down. The two of us sit in silence on the beach until the others have gone to sleep.

Johanna glances over at Finnick, to be sure, then turns to me. "How'd you lose Mags?"

"In the fog. Finnick had Peeta. I had Mags for a while. Then I couldn't lift her. Finnick said he couldn't take them both. She kissed him and walked right into the poison," I say.

"She was Finnick's mentor, you know," Johanna says accusingly.

"No, I didn't," I say.

"She was half his family," she says a few moments later, but there's less venom behind it.

We watch the water lap up over the undergarments.

"So what were you doing with Nuts and Volts?" I ask.

"I told you – I got them for you. Haymitch said if we were to be allies I had to bring them to you," says Johanna. "That's what you told him, right?"

No, I think. But I nod my head in assent. "Thanks. I appreciate it."

"I hope so." She gives me a look filled with loathing, like I'm the biggest drag possible on her life. I wonder if this is what it's like to have an older sister who really hates you.

"Tick, tock," I hear behind me. I turn and see Wiress has crawled over. Her eyes are focused on the jungle.

"Oh, goody, she's back. OK, I'm going to sleep. You and Nuts can guard together," Johanna says. She goes over and flings herself down beside Finnick.

"Tick, tock," whispers Wiress. I guide her in front of me and get her to lie down, stroking her arm to soothe her. She drifts off, stirring restlessly, occasionally sighing out her phrase. "Tick, tock."

"Tick, tock," I agree softly. "It's time for bed. Tick, tock. Go to sleep."

The sun rises in the sky until it's directly over us. *It must be noon*, I think absently. Not that it matters. Across the water, off to the right, I see the enormous flash as the lightning bolt hits the tree and the electrical storm begins again. Right in the same area it did last night. Someone must have moved into its range, triggered the attack. I sit for a while watching the lightning, keeping Wiress calm, lulled into a sort of peacefulness by the lapping of the water. I think of last night, how the lightning began just after the bell tolled. Twelve bongs.

"Tick, tock," Wiress says, surfacing to consciousness for a moment and then going back under.

Twelve bongs last night. Like it was midnight. Then lightning. The sun overhead now. Like it's noon. And lightning.

Slowly I rise up and survey the arena. The lightning there. In the next pie wedge over came the blood rain, where Johanna, Wiress and Beetee were caught. We would have been in the third section, right next to that, when the fog appeared. And as soon as it was sucked away, the monkeys began to gather in the fourth. Tick, tock. My head snaps to the other side. A couple of hours ago, at around ten, that wave came out of the second section to the left of where the lightning strikes now. At noon. At midnight. At noon.

"Tick, tock," Wiress says in her sleep. As the lightning ceases and the blood rain begins just to the right of it, her words suddenly make sense.

"Oh," I say under my breath. "Tick, tock." My eyes sweep around the full circle of the arena and I know she's right. "Tick, tock. This is a clock."

23

A clock. I can almost see the hands ticking around the twelve-sectioned face of the arena. Each hour begins a new horror, a new Gamemaker weapon, and ends the previous. Lightning, blood rain, fog, monkeys – those are the first four hours on the clock. And at ten, the wave. I don't know what happens in the other seven, but I know Wiress is right.

At present, the blood rain's falling and we're on the beach below the monkey segment, far too close to the fog for my liking. Do the various attacks stay within the confines of the jungle? Not necessarily. The wave didn't. If that fog leaches out of the jungle, or the monkeys return. . .

"Get up," I order, shaking Peeta and Finnick and Johanna awake. "Get up – we have to move." There's enough time, though, to explain the clock theory to them. About Wiress's tick-tocking and how the movements of the invisible hands trigger a deadly force in each section.

I think I've convinced everyone who's conscious except Johanna, who's naturally opposed to liking anything I suggest. But even she agrees it's better to be safe than sorry.

While the others collect our few possessions and get Beetee back into his jumpsuit, I rouse Wiress. She awakes with a panicked "tick, tock!"

"Yes, tick, tock, the arena's a clock. It's a clock, Wiress, you were right," I say. "You were right."

Relief floods her face – I guess because somebody has finally understood what she's known probably from the first tolling of the bells. "Midnight."

"It starts at midnight," I confirm.

A memory struggles to surface in my brain. I see a clock. No, it's a watch, resting in Plutarch Heavensbee's palm. "*It starts at midnight*," Plutarch said. And then my mockingjay lit up briefly and vanished. In retrospect, it's like he was giving me a clue about the arena. But why would he? At the time, I was no more a tribute in these Games than he was. Maybe he thought it would help me as a mentor. Or maybe this had been the plan all along.

Wiress nods at the blood rain. "One-thirty," she says.

"Exactly. One-thirty. And at two, a terrible poisonous fog begins there," I say, pointing at the nearby jungle. "So we have to move somewhere safe now." She smiles and stands up obediently. "Are you thirsty?" I hand her the woven bowl and she gulps down about a litre. Finnick gives her the last bit of bread and she gnaws on it. With the inability to communicate overcome, she's functioning again.

I check my weapons. Tie up the spile and the tube of medicine in the parachute and fix it to my belt with vine.

Beetee's still pretty out of it, but when Peeta tries to lift him, he objects. "Wire," he says.

"She's right here," Peeta tells him. "Wiress is fine. She's coming, too."

But still Beetee struggles. "Wire," he insists.

"Oh, I know what he wants," says Johanna impatiently. She crosses the beach and picks up the cylinder we took from his belt when we were bathing him. It's coated in a thick layer of congealed blood. "This worthless thing. It's some kind of wire or something. That's how he got cut. Running up to the Cornucopia to get this. I don't know what kind of weapon it's supposed to be. I guess you could pull off a piece and use it as a garrotte or something. But really, can you imagine Beetee garrotting somebody?"

"He won his Games with wire. Setting up that electrical trap," says Peeta. "It's the best weapon he could have."

There's something odd about Johanna not putting this together. Something that doesn't quite ring true. Suspicious. "Seems like you'd have figured that out," I say. "Since you nicknamed him Volts and all."

Johanna's eyes narrow at me dangerously. "Yeah, that was really stupid of me, wasn't it?" she says. "I guess I must have been distracted by keeping your little friends alive. While you were . . . what, again? Getting Mags killed off?"

My fingers tighten on the knife handle at my belt.

"Go ahead. Try it. I don't care if you are knocked up, I'll rip your throat out," says Johanna.

I know I can't kill her right now. But it's just a matter of time with Johanna and me. Before one of us offs the other.

"Maybe we all had better be careful where we step," says Finnick, shooting me a look. He takes the coil and sets it on Beetee's chest. "There's your wire, Volts. Watch where you plug it."

Peeta picks up the now-unresisting Beetee. "Where to?"

"I'd like to go to the Cornucopia and watch. Just to make sure we're right about the clock," says Finnick. It seems as good a plan as any. Besides, I wouldn't mind the chance of going over the weapons again. And there are six of us now. Even if you count Beetee and Wiress out, we've got four good fighters. It's so different from where I was last year at this point, doing everything on my own. Yes, it's great to have allies as long as you can ignore the thought that you'll have to kill them.

Beetee and Wiress will probably find some way to die on their own. If we have to run from something, how far would they get? Johanna, frankly, I could easily kill if it came down to protecting Peeta. Or maybe even just to shut her up. What I really need is for someone to take out Finnick for me, since I don't think I can do it personally. Not after all he's done for Peeta. I think about manoeuvring him into some kind of encounter with the Careers. It's cold, I know. But what are my options? Now that we know about the clock, he probably won't die in the jungle, so someone's going to have to kill him in battle.

Because this is so repellent to think about, my mind frantically tries to change topics. But the only thing that distracts me from my current situation is fantasizing about killing President Snow. Not very pretty daydreams for a seventeen-year-old girl, I guess, but very satisfying.

We walk down the nearest sand strip, approaching

the Cornucopia with care, just in case the Careers are concealed there. I doubt they are, because we've been on the beach for hours and there's been no sign of life. The area's abandoned, as I expected. Only the big golden horn and the picked-over pile of weapons remain.

When Peeta lays Beetee in the bit of shade the Cornucopia provides, he calls out to Wiress. She crouches beside him and he puts the coil of wire in her hands. "Clean it, will you?" he asks.

Wiress nods and scampers over to the water's edge, where she dunks the coil in the water. She starts quietly singing some funny little song, about a mouse running up a clock. It must be for children, but it seems to make her happy.

"Oh, not the song again," says Johanna, rolling her eyes. "That went on for hours before she started tick-tocking."

Suddenly Wiress stands up very straight and points to the jungle. "Two," she says.

I follow her finger to where the wall of fog has just begun to seep out on to the beach. "Yes, look, Wiress is right. It's two o'clock and the fog has started."

"Like clockwork," says Peeta. "You were very smart to figure that out, Wiress."

Wiress smiles and goes back to singing and dunking

her coil. "Oh, she's more than smart," says Beetee. "She's intuitive." We all turn to look at Beetee, who seems to be coming back to life. "She can sense things before anyone else. Like a canary in one of your coal mines."

"What's that?" Finnick asks me.

"It's a bird that we take down into the mines to warn us if there's bad air," I say.

"What's it do, die?" asks Johanna.

"It stops singing first. That's when you should get out. But if the air's too bad, it dies, yes. And so do you." I don't want to talk about dying songbirds. They bring up thoughts of my father's death and Rue's death and Maysilee Donner's death and my mother inheriting her songbird. Oh, great, and now I'm thinking of Gale, deep down in that horrible mine, with President Snow's threat hanging over his head. So easy to make it look like an accident down there. A silent canary, a spark, and nothing more.

I go back to imagining killing the president.

Despite her annoyance at Wiress, Johanna's as happy as I've seen her in the arena. While I'm adding to my stock of arrows, she pokes around until she comes up with a pair of lethal-looking axes. It seems an odd choice until I see her throw one with such force it sticks in the sun-softened gold of the Cornucopia. Of course. Johanna Mason. District 7. Lumber. I bet she's been tossing around axes since she could toddle. It's like Finnick with his trident. Or Beetee with his wire. Rue with her knowledge of plants. I realize it's just another disadvantage the District 12 tributes have faced over the years. We don't go down in the mines until we're eighteen. It looks like most of the other tributes learn something about their trades early on. There are things you do in a mine that could come in handy in the Games. Wielding a pick. Blowing things up. Give you an edge. The way my hunting did. But we learn them too late.

While I've been messing with the weapons, Peeta's been squatting on the ground, drawing something with the tip of his knife on a large, smooth leaf he brought from the jungle. I look over his shoulder and see he's creating a map of the arena. In the centre is the Cornucopia on its circle of sand with the twelve strips branching out from it. It looks like a pie sliced into twelve equal wedges. There's another circle representing the waterline and a slightly larger one indicating the edge of the jungle. "Look how the Cornucopia's positioned," he says to me.

I examine the Cornucopia and see what he means. "The tail points towards twelve o'clock," I say.

"Right, so this is the top of our clock," he says, and

quickly scratches the numbers one through twelve around the clock face. "Twelve to one is the lightning zone." He writes *lightning* in tiny print in the corresponding wedge, then works clockwise adding *blood*, *fog* and *monkeys* in the following sections.

"And ten to eleven is the wave," I say. He adds it. Finnick and Johanna join us at this point, armed to the teeth with tridents, axes and knives.

"Did you notice anything unusual in the others?" I ask Johanna and Beetee, since they might have seen something we didn't. But all they've seen is a lot of blood. "I guess they could hold anything."

"I'm going to mark the ones where we know the Gamemakers' weapon follows us out past the jungle, so we'll stay clear of those," says Peeta, drawing diagonal lines on the fog and wave beaches. Then he sits back. "Well, it's a lot more than we knew this morning, anyway."

We all nod in agreement, and that's when I notice it. The silence. Our canary has stopped singing.

I don't wait. I load an arrow as I twist and get a glimpse of a dripping-wet Gloss letting Wiress slide to the ground, her throat slit open in a bright red smile. The point of my arrow disappears into his right temple, and in the instant it takes to reload, Johanna has buried an axe blade in Cashmere's chest. Finnick knocks away a spear Brutus throws at Peeta and takes Enobaria's knife in his thigh. If there wasn't a Cornucopia to duck behind, they'd be dead, both of the tributes from District 2. I spring forward in pursuit. *Boom! Boom! Boom!* The cannon confirms there's no way to help Wiress, no need to finish off Gloss or Cashmere. My allies and I are rounding the horn, starting to give chase to Brutus and Enobaria, who are sprinting down a sand strip towards the jungle.

Suddenly the ground jerks beneath my feet and I'm flung on my side in the sand. The circle of land that holds the Cornucopia starts spinning fast, really fast, and I can see the jungle going by in a blur. I feel the centrifugal force pulling me towards the water and dig my hands and feet into the sand, trying to get some purchase on the unstable ground. Between the flying sand and the dizziness, I have to squeeze my eyes shut. There is literally nothing I can do but hold on until, with no deceleration, we slam to a stop.

Coughing and queasy, I sit up slowly to find my companions in the same condition. Finnick, Johanna and Peeta have hung on. The three dead bodies have been tossed out into the seawater.

The whole thing, from missing Wiress's song to now, can't have taken more than a minute or two. We sit there panting, scraping the sand out of our mouths.

"Where's Volts?" says Johanna. We're on our feet. One wobbly circle of the Cornucopia confirms he's gone. Finnick spots him about twenty metres out in the water, barely keeping afloat, and swims out to haul him in.

That's when I remember the wire and how important it was to him. I look frantically around. Where is it? Where is it? And then I see it, still clutched in Wiress's hands, far out in the water. My stomach contracts at the thought of what I must do next. "Cover me," I say to the others. I toss aside my weapons and race down the strip closest to her body. Without slowing down, I dive into the water and start for her. Out of the corner of my eye, I can see the hovercraft appearing over us, the claw starting to descend to take her away. But I don't stop. I just keep swimming as hard as I can and end up slamming into her body. I come up gasping, trying to avoid swallowing the bloodstained water that spreads out from the open wound in her neck. She's floating on her back, borne up by her belt and death, staring into that relentless sun. As I tread water, I have to wrench the coil of wire from her fingers, because her final grip on it is so tight. There's nothing I can do then but close her eyelids, whisper goodbye, and swim away. By the time I swing the coil up on to the sand and pull myself from the water, her body's gone. But I can still taste her blood mingled with the sea salt.

I walk back to the Cornucopia. Finnick's got Beetee back alive, although a little waterlogged, sitting up and snorting out water. He had the good sense to hang on to his glasses, so at least he can see. I place the reel of wire on his lap. It's sparkling clean, no blood left at all. He unravels a piece of the wire and runs it through his fingers. For the first time I see it, and it's unlike any wire I know. A pale golden colour and as fine as a piece of hair. I wonder how long it is. There must be miles of the stuff to fill the large spool. But I don't ask, because I know he's thinking of Wiress.

I look at the others' sober faces. Now Finnick, Johanna and Beetee have all lost their district partners. I cross to Peeta and wrap my arms around him, and for a while we all stay silent.

"Let's get off this stinking island," Johanna says finally. There's only the matter of our weapons now, which we've largely retained. Fortunately the vines here are strong and the spile and tube of medicine wrapped in the parachute are still secured to my belt. Finnick strips off his undershirt and ties it around the wound Enobaria's knife made in his thigh; it's not deep. Beetee thinks he can walk now, if we go slowly, so I help him up. We decide to head to the beach at twelve o'clock. That should provide hours of calm and keep us clear of any poisonous residue. And then Peeta, Johanna and Finnick head off in three different directions.

"Twelve o'clock, right?" says Peeta. "The tail points to twelve."

"Before they spun us," says Finnick. "I was judging by the sun."

"The sun only tells you it's going on four, Finnick," I say.

"I think Katniss's point is, knowing the time doesn't mean you necessarily know where four is on the clock. You might have a general idea of the direction. Unless you consider that they may have shifted the outer ring of jungle as well," says Beetee.

No, Katniss's point was a lot more basic than that. Beetee's articulated a theory far beyond my comment on the sun. But I just nod my head like I've been on the same page all along. "Yes, so any one of these paths could lead to twelve o'clock," I say.

We circle around the Cornucopia, scrutinizing the jungle. It has a baffling uniformity. I remember the tall tree that took the first lightning strike at twelve o'clock, but every sector has a similar tree. Johanna thinks to follow Enobaria's and Brutus's tracks, but they have been blown or washed away. There's no way to tell where anything is. "I should have never mentioned the clock," I say bitterly. "Now they've taken that advantage away as well."

"Only temporarily," says Beetee. "At ten, we'll see the wave again and be back on track."

"Yes, they can't redesign the whole arena," says Peeta.

"It doesn't matter," says Johanna impatiently. "You had to tell us or we never would have moved our camp in the first place, brainless." Ironically, her logical, if demeaning, reply is the only one that comforts me. Yes, I had to tell them to get them to move. "Come on, I need water. Anyone have a good gut feeling?"

We randomly choose a path and take it, having no idea what number we're headed for. When we reach the jungle, we peer into it, trying to decipher what may be waiting inside.

"Well, it must be monkey hour. And I don't see any of them in there," says Peeta. "I'm going to try to tap a tree."

"No, it's my turn," says Finnick.

"I'll at least watch your back," Peeta says.

"Katniss can do that," says Johanna. "We need you to make another map. The other washed away." She yanks a large leaf off a tree and hands it to him.

For a moment, I'm suspicious they're trying to

divide and kill us. But it doesn't make sense. I'll have the advantage on Finnick if he's dealing with the tree and Peeta's much bigger than Johanna. So I follow Finnick about fifteen metres into the jungle, where he finds a good tree and starts stabbing to make a hole with his knife.

As I stand there, weapons ready, I can't lose the uneasy feeling that something is going on and that it has to do with Peeta. I retrace our steps, starting from the moment the gong rang out, searching for the source of my discomfort. Finnick towing Peeta in off his metal plate. Finnick reviving Peeta after the force field stopped his heart. Mags running into the fog so that Finnick could carry Peeta. The morphling hurling herself in front of him to block the monkey's attack. The fight with the Careers was so quick, but didn't Finnick block Brutus's spear from hitting Peeta even though it meant taking Enobaria's knife in his leg? And even now Johanna has him drawing a map on a leaf rather than risking the jungle. . .

There is no question about it. For reasons completely unfathomable to me, some of the other victors are trying to keep him alive, even if it means sacrificing themselves.

I'm dumbfounded. For one thing, that's my job. For another, it doesn't make sense. Only one of us can get out. So why have they chosen Peeta to protect? What has Haymitch possibly said to them, what has he bargained with to make them put Peeta's life above their own?

I know my own reasons for keeping Peeta alive. He's my friend, and this is my way to defy the Capitol, to subvert its terrible Games. But if I had no real ties to him, what would make me want to save him, to choose him over myself? Certainly he is brave, but we have all been brave enough to survive a Games. There is that quality of goodness that's hard to overlook, but still . . . and then I think of it, what Peeta can do so much better than the rest of us. He can use words. He obliterated the rest of the field at both interviews. And maybe it's because of that underlying goodness that he can move a crowd – no, a country – to his side with the turn of a simple sentence.

I remember thinking that was the gift the leader of our revolution should have. Has Haymitch convinced the others of this? That Peeta's tongue would have far greater power against the Capitol than any physical strength the rest of us could claim? I don't know. It still seems like a really long leap for some of the tributes. I mean, we're talking about Johanna Mason here. But what other explanation can there be for their decided efforts to keep him alive?

"Katniss, got that spile?" Finnick asks, snapping me back to reality. I cut the vine that ties the spile to my belt and hold the metal tube out to him.

That's when I hear the scream. So full of fear and pain it ices my blood. And so familiar. I drop the spile, forget where I am or what lies ahead, only know I must reach her, protect her. I run wildly in the direction of the voice, heedless of danger, ripping through vines and branches, through anything that keeps me from reaching her.

From reaching my little sister.

24

Where is she? What are they doing to her? "Prim!" I cry out. "Prim!" Only another agonized scream answers me. *How did she get here? Why is she part of the Games?* "Prim!"

Vines cut into my face and arms, creepers grab my feet. But I am getting closer to her. Closer. Very close now. Sweat pours down my face, stinging the healing acid wounds. I pant, trying to get some use out of the warm, moist air that seems empty of oxygen. Prim makes a sound – such a lost, irretrievable sound – that I can't even imagine what they have done to evoke it.

"Prim!" I rip through a wall of green into a small clearing and the sound repeats directly above me. Above me? My head whips back. Do they have her up in the trees? I desperately search the branches but see nothing. "Prim?" I say pleadingly. I hear her but can't see her. Her next wail rings out, clear as a bell, and there's no mistaking the source. It's coming from the mouth of a small, crested black bird perched on a branch about three metres over my head. And then I understand.

It's a jabberjay.

I've never seen one before – I thought they no longer existed – and for a moment, as I lean against the trunk of the tree, clutching the stitch in my side, I examine it. The muttation, the forerunner, the father. I pull up a mental image of a mockingbird, fuse it with the jabberjay, and yes, I can see how they mated to make my mockingjay. There is nothing about the bird that suggests it's a mutt. Nothing except the horribly lifelike sounds of Prim's voice streaming from its mouth. I silence it with an arrow in its throat. The bird falls to the ground. I remove my arrow and wring its neck for good measure. Then I hurl the revolting thing into the jungle. No degree of hunger would ever tempt me to eat it.

It wasn't real, I tell myself. *The same way the muttation wolves last year weren't really the dead tributes. It's just a sadistic trick of the Gamemakers.*

Finnick crashes into the clearing to find me wiping my arrow clean with some moss. "Katniss?"

"It's OK. I'm OK," I say, although I don't feel OK

at all. "I thought I heard my sister but—" The piercing shriek cuts me off. It's another voice, not Prim's, maybe a young woman's. I don't recognize it. But the effect on Finnick is instantaneous. The colour vanishes from his face and I can actually see his pupils dilate in fear. "Finnick, wait!" I say, reaching out to reassure him, but he's bolted away. Gone off in pursuit of the victim, as mindlessly as I pursued Prim. "Finnick!" I call, but I know he won't turn back and wait for me to give a rational explanation. So all I can do is follow him.

It's no effort to track him, even though he's moving so fast, since he leaves a clear, trampled path in his wake. But the bird is at least half a kilometre away, most of it uphill, and by the time I reach him, I'm winded. He's circling around a giant tree. The trunk must be over a metre in diameter and the limbs don't even begin until six metres up. The woman's shrieks emanate from somewhere in the foliage, but the jabberjay's concealed. Finnick's screaming as well, over and over. "Annie! Annie!" He's in a state of panic and completely unreachable, so I do what I would do anyway. I scale an adjacent tree, locate the jabberjay, and take it out with an arrow. It falls straight down, landing right at Finnick's feet. He picks it up, slowly making the connection, but when I slide down to join him, he looks more despairing than ever.

"It's all right, Finnick. It's just a jabberjay. They're playing a trick on us," I say. "It's not real. It's not your . . . Annie."

"No, it's not Annie. But the voice was hers. Jabberjays mimic what they hear. Where did they get those screams, Katniss?" he says.

I can feel my own cheeks grow pale as I understand his meaning. "Oh, Finnick, you don't think they. . ."

"Yes. I do. That's exactly what I think," he says.

I have an image of Prim in a white room, strapped to a table, while masked, robed figures elicit those sounds from her. Somewhere they are torturing her, or did torture her, to get those sounds. My knees turn to water and I sink to the ground. Finnick is trying to tell me something, but I can't hear him. What I do finally hear is another bird starting up somewhere off to my left. And this time, the voice is Gale's.

Finnick catches my arm before I can run. "No. It's not him." He starts pulling me downhill, towards the beach. "We're getting out of here!" But Gale's voice is so full of pain I can't help struggling to reach it. "It's not him, Katniss! It's a mutt!" Finnick shouts at me. "Come on!" He moves me along, half dragging, half carrying me, until I can process what he said. He's right, it's just another jabberjay. I can't help Gale by chasing it down. But that doesn't change the fact that it is Gale's voice, and somewhere, sometime, someone has made him sound like this.

I stop fighting Finnick, though, and like the night in the fog, I flee what I can't fight. What can only do me harm. Only this time it's my heart and not my body that's disintegrating. This must be another weapon of the clock. Four o'clock, I guess. When the hands tick-tock on to the four, the monkeys go home and the jabberjays come out to play. Finnick is right – getting out of here is the only thing to do. Although there will be nothing Haymitch can send in a parachute that will help either Finnick or me recover from the wounds the birds have inflicted.

I catch sight of Peeta and Johanna standing at the tree line and I'm filled with a mixture of relief and anger. Why didn't Peeta come to help me? Why did no one come after us? Even now he hangs back, his hands raised, palms towards us, lips moving but no words reaching us. Why?

The wall is so transparent, Finnick and I run smack into it and bounce back on to the jungle floor. I'm lucky. My shoulder took the worst of the impact, whereas Finnick hit face-first and now his nose is gushing blood. This is why Peeta and Johanna and even Beetee, who I see sadly shaking his head behind them, have not come to our aid. An invisible barrier blocks the area in front of us. It's not a force field. You can touch the hard, smooth surface all you like. But Peeta's knife and Johanna's axe can't make a dent in it. I know, without checking more than a metre to one side, that it encloses the entire four-to-five-o'clock wedge. That we will be trapped like rats until the hour passes.

Peeta presses his hand against the surface and I put my own up to meet it, as if I can feel him through the wall. I see his lips moving but I can't hear him, can't hear anything outside our wedge. I try to make out what he's saying, but I can't focus, so I just stare at his face, doing my best to hang on to my sanity.

Then the birds begin to arrive. One by one. Perching in the surrounding branches. And a carefully orchestrated chorus of horror begins to spill out of their mouths. Finnick gives up at once, hunching on the ground, clenching his hands over his ears as if he's trying to crush his skull. I try to fight for a while. Emptying my quiver of arrows into the hated birds. But every time one drops dead, another quickly takes its place. And finally I give up and curl up beside Finnick, trying to block out the excruciating sounds of Prim, Gale, my mother, Madge, Rory, Vick, even Posy, helpless little Posy. . .

I know it's stopped when I feel Peeta's hands on me,

feel myself lifted from the ground and out of the jungle. But I stay eyes squeezed shut, hands over my ears, muscles too rigid to release. Peeta holds me on his lap, speaking soothing words, rocking me gently. It takes a long time before I begin to relax the iron grip on my body. And when I do, the trembling begins.

"It's all right, Katniss," he whispers.

"You didn't hear them," I answer.

"I heard Prim. Right in the beginning. But it wasn't her," he says. "It was a jabberjay."

"It was her. Somewhere. The jabberjay just recorded it," I say.

"No, that's what they want you to think. The same way I wondered if Glimmer's eyes were in that mutt last year. But those weren't Glimmer's eyes. And that wasn't Prim's voice. Or if it was, they took it from an interview or something and distorted the sound. Made it say whatever she was saying," he says.

"No, they were torturing her," I answer. "She's probably dead."

"Katniss, Prim isn't dead. How could they kill Prim? We're almost down to the final eight of us. And what happens then?" Peeta says.

"Seven more of us die," I say hopelessly.

"No, back home. What happens when they reach the final eight tributes in the Games?" He lifts my chin so I have to look at him. Forces me to make eye contact. "What happens? At the final eight?"

I know he's trying to help me, so I make myself think. "At the final eight?" I repeat. "They interview your family and friends back home."

"That's right," says Peeta. "They interview your family and friends. And can they do that if they've killed them all?"

"No?" I ask, still unsure.

"No. That's how we know Prim's alive. She'll be the first one they interview, won't she?" he asks.

I want to believe him. Badly. It's just . . . those voices. . .

"First Prim. Then your mother. Your cousin, Gale. Madge," he continues. "It was a trick, Katniss. A horrible one. But we're the only ones who can be hurt by it. We're the ones in the Games. Not them."

"You really believe that?" I say.

"I really do," says Peeta. I waver, thinking of how Peeta can make anyone believe anything. I look over at Finnick for confirmation, see he's fixated on Peeta, his words.

"Do you believe it, Finnick?" I ask.

"It could be true. I don't know," he says. "Could they do that, Beetee? Take someone's regular voice and make it. . ."

"Oh, yes. It's not even that difficult, Finnick. Our children learn a similar technique in school," says Beetee.

"Of course Peeta's right. The whole country adores Katniss's little sister. If they really killed her like this, they'd probably have an uprising on their hands," says Johanna flatly. "Don't want that, do they?" She throws back her head and shouts, "Whole country in rebellion? Wouldn't want anything like that!"

My mouth drops open in shock. No one, ever, says anything like this in the Games. Absolutely, they've cut away from Johanna, are editing her out. But I have heard her and can never think about her again in the same way. She'll never win any awards for kindness, but she certainly is gutsy. Or crazy. She picks up some shells and heads towards the jungle. "I'm getting water," she says.

I can't help catching her hand as she passes me. "Don't go in there. The birds—" I remember the birds must be gone, but I still don't want anyone in there. Not even her.

"They can't hurt me. I'm not like the rest of you. There's no one left I love," Johanna says, and frees her hand with an impatient shake. When she brings me back a shell of water, I take it with a silent nod of thanks, knowing how much she would despise the pity in my voice.

While Johanna collects water and my arrows, Beetee fiddles with his wire, and Finnick takes to the water. I need to clean up, too, but I stay in Peeta's arms, still too shaken to move.

"Who did they use against Finnick?" he asks.

"Somebody named Annie," I say.

"Must be Annie Cresta," he says.

"Who?" I ask.

"Annie Cresta. She was the girl Mags volunteered for. She won about five years ago," says Peeta.

That would have been the summer after my father died, when I first began feeding my family, when my whole being was occupied with battling starvation. "I don't remember those Games much," I say. "Was that the earthquake year?"

"Yeah. Annie's the one who went mad when her district partner got beheaded. Ran off by herself and hid. But an earthquake broke a dam and most of the arena got flooded. She won because she was the best swimmer," says Peeta.

"Did she get better after?" I ask. "I mean, her mind?"

"I don't know. I don't remember ever seeing her at the Games again. But she didn't look too stable during the reaping this year," says Peeta.

So that's who Finnick loves, I think. *Not his string of fancy lovers in the Capitol. But a poor, mad girl back home.*

A cannon blast brings us all together on the beach. A hovercraft appears in what we estimate to be the six-to-seven-o'clock zone. We watch as the claw dips down five different times to retrieve the pieces of one body, torn apart. It's impossible to tell who it was. Whatever happens at six o'clock, I never want to know.

Peeta draws a new map on a leaf, adding a *JJ* for jabberjays in the four-to-five-o'clock section and simply writing *beast* in the one where we saw the tribute collected in pieces. We now have a good idea of what seven of the hours will bring. And if there's any positive to the jabberjay attack, it's that it let us know where we are on the clock face again.

Finnick weaves yet another water basket and a net for fishing. I take a quick swim and put more ointment on my skin. Then I sit at the edge of the water, cleaning the fish Finnick catches and watching the sun drop below the horizon. The bright moon is already on the rise, filling the arena with that strange twilight. We're about to settle down to our meal of raw fish when the anthem begins. And then the faces. . .

Cashmere. Gloss. Wiress. Mags. The woman from District 5. The morphling who gave her life for Peeta. Blight. The man from 10.

Eight dead. Plus eight from the first night. Two-thirds of us gone in a day and a half. That must be some kind of record.

"They're really burning through us," says Johanna.

"Who's left? Besides us five and District Two?" asks Finnick.

"Chaff," says Peeta, without needing to think about it. Perhaps he's been keeping an eye out for him because of Haymitch.

A parachute comes down with a pile of bite-sized square-shaped rolls. "These are from your district, right, Beetee?" Peeta asks.

"Yes, from District Three," he says. "How many are there?"

Finnick counts them, turning each one over in his hands before he sets it in a neat configuration. I don't know what it is with Finnick and bread, but he seems obsessed with handling it. "Twenty-four," he says.

"An even two dozen, then?" says Beetee.

"Twenty-four on the nose," says Finnick. "How should we divide them?"

"Let's each have three, and whoever is still alive at

breakfast can take a vote on the rest," says Johanna. I don't know why this makes me laugh a little. I guess because it's true. When I do, Johanna gives me a look that's almost approving. No, not approving. But maybe slightly pleased.

We wait until the giant wave has flooded out of the ten-to-eleven-o'clock section, wait for the water to recede, and then go to that beach to make camp. Theoretically, we should have a full twelve hours of safety from the jungle. There's an unpleasant chorus of clicking, probably from some evil type of insect, coming from the eleven-to-twelve-o'clock wedge. But whatever is making the sound stays within the confines of the jungle and we keep off that part of the beach in case they're just waiting for a carelessly placed footfall to swarm out.

I don't know how Johanna's still on her feet. She's only had about an hour of sleep since the Games started. Peeta and I volunteer for the first watch because we're better rested, and because we want some time alone. The others go out immediately, although Finnick's sleep is restless. Every now and then I hear him murmuring Annie's name.

Peeta and I sit on the damp sand, facing away from each other, my right shoulder and hip pressed against his. I watch the water as he watches the jungle, which is better for me. I'm still haunted by the voices of the jabberjays, which unfortunately the insects can't drown out. After a while I rest my head against his shoulder. Feel his hand caress my hair.

"Katniss," he says softly, "it's no use pretending we don't know what the other one is trying to do." No, I guess there isn't, but it's no fun discussing it, either. Well, not for us, anyway. The Capitol viewers will be glued to their sets so they don't miss one wretched word.

"I don't know what kind of deal you think you've made with Haymitch, but you should know he made me promises as well." Of course, I know this, too. He told Peeta they could keep me alive so that he wouldn't be suspicious. "So I think we can assume he was lying to one of us."

This gets my attention. A double deal. A double promise. With only Haymitch knowing which one is real. I raise my head, meet Peeta's eyes. "Why are you saying this now?"

"Because I don't want you forgetting how different our circumstances are. If you die, and I live, there's no life for me at all back in District Twelve. You're my whole life," he says. "I would never be happy again." I start to object but he puts a finger to my lips. "It's different for you. I'm not saying it wouldn't be hard.

But there are other people who'd make your life worth living."

Peeta pulls the chain with the gold disc from around his neck. He holds it in the moonlight so I can clearly see the mockingjay. Then his thumb slides along a catch I didn't notice before and the disc pops open. It's not solid, as I had thought, but a locket. And within the locket are photos. On the right side, my mother and Prim, laughing. And on the left, Gale. Actually smiling.

There is nothing in the world that could break me faster at this moment than these three faces. After what I heard this afternoon . . . it is the perfect weapon.

"Your family needs you, Katniss," Peeta says.

My family. My mother. My sister. And my pretend cousin Gale. But Peeta's intention is clear. That Gale really is my family, or will be one day, if I live. That I'll marry him. So Peeta's giving me his life and Gale at the same time. To let me know I shouldn't ever have doubts about it. Everything. That's what Peeta wants me to take from him.

I wait for him to mention the baby, to play to the cameras, but he doesn't. And that's how I know that none of this is part of the Games. That he is telling me the truth about what he feels.

"No one really needs me," he says, and there's no

self-pity in his voice. It's true his family doesn't need him. They will mourn him, as will a handful of friends. But they will get on. Even Haymitch, with the help of a lot of white liquor, will get on. I realize only one person will be damaged beyond repair if Peeta dies. Me.

"I do," I say. "I need you." He looks upset, takes a deep breath as if to begin a long argument, and that's no good, no good at all, because he'll start going on about Prim and my mother and everything and I'll just get confused. So before he can talk, I stop his lips with a kiss.

I feel that thing again. The thing I only felt once before. In the cave last year, when I was trying to get Haymitch to send us food. I kissed Peeta about a thousand times during those Games and after. But there was only one kiss that made me feel something stir deep inside. Only one that made me want more. But my head wound started bleeding and he made me lie down.

This time, there is nothing but us to interrupt us. And after a few attempts, Peeta gives up on talking. The sensation inside me grows warmer and spreads out from my chest, down through my body, out along my arms and legs, to the tips of my being. Instead of satisfying me, the kisses have the opposite effect, of making my need greater. I thought I was something of an expert on hunger, but this is an entirely new kind.

It's the first crack of the lightning storm – the bolt hitting the tree at midnight – that brings us to our senses. It rouses Finnick as well. He sits up with a sharp cry. I see his fingers digging into the sand as he reassures himself that whatever nightmare he inhabited wasn't real.

"I can't sleep any more," he says. "One of you should rest." Only then does he seem to notice our expressions, the way we're wrapped around each other. "Or both of you. I can watch alone."

Peeta won't let him, though. "It's too dangerous," he says. "I'm not tired. You lie down, Katniss." I don't object because I do need to sleep if I'm to be of any use keeping him alive. I let him lead me over to where the others are. He puts the chain with the locket around my neck, then rests his hand over the spot where our baby would be. "You're going to make a great mother, you know," he says. He kisses me one last time and goes back to Finnick.

His reference to the baby signals that our time-out from the Games is over. That he knows the audience will be wondering why he hasn't used the most persuasive argument in his arsenal. That sponsors must be manipulated.

But as I stretch out on the sand I wonder, could it be more? Like a reminder to me that I could still one day have kids with Gale? Well, if that was it, it was a mistake. Because for one thing, that's never been part of my plan. And for another, if only one of us can be a parent, anyone can see it should be Peeta.

As I drift off, I try to imagine that world, somewhere in the future, with no Games, no Capitol. A place like the meadow in the song I sang to Rue as she died. Where Peeta's child could be safe.

25

When I wake, I have a brief, delicious feeling of happiness that is somehow connected with Peeta. Happiness, of course, is a complete absurdity at this point, since at the rate things are going, I'll be dead in a day. And that's the best-case scenario, if I'm able to eliminate the rest of the field, including myself, and get Peeta crowned as the winner of the Quarter Quell. Still, the sensation's so unexpected and sweet I cling to it, if only for a few moments. Before the gritty sand, the hot sun and my itching skin demand a return to reality.

Everyone's already up and watching the descent of a parachute to the beach. I join them for another delivery of bread. It's identical to the one we received the night before. Twenty-four rolls from District 3. That gives us thirty-three in all. We each take five, leaving eight in reserve. No one says it, but eight will divide up perfectly after the next death. Somehow, in the light of day, joking about who will be around to eat the rolls has lost its humour.

How long can we keep this alliance? I don't think anyone expected the number of tributes to drop so quickly. What if I am wrong about the others protecting Peeta? If things were simply coincidental, or it's all been a strategy to win our trust to make us easy prey, or I don't understand what's actually going on? Wait, there's no ifs about that. I *don't* understand what's going on. And if I don't, it's time for Peeta and me to clear out of here.

I sit next to Peeta on the sand to eat my rolls. For some reason, it's difficult to look at him. Maybe it was all that kissing last night, although the two of us kissing isn't anything new. It might not even have felt any different for him. Maybe it's knowing the brief amount of time we have left. And how we're working at such cross-purposes when it comes to who should survive these Games.

After we eat, I take his hand and tug him towards the water. "Come on. I'll teach you how to swim." I need to get him away from the others where we can discuss breaking away. It will be tricky, because once they realize we're severing the alliance, we'll be instant targets.

If I was really teaching him to swim, I'd make him take off the belt since it keeps him afloat, but what does it matter now? So I just show him the basic stroke and let him practise going back and forth in waist-high water. At first, I notice Johanna keeping a careful eye on us, but eventually she loses interest and goes to take a nap. Finnick's weaving a new net out of vines and Beetee plays with his wire. I know the time has come.

While Peeta has been swimming, I've discovered something. My remaining scabs are starting to peel off. By gently rubbing a handful of sand up and down my arm, I clean off the rest of the scales, revealing fresh new skin underneath. I stop Peeta's practice, on the pretext of showing him how to rid himself of the itchy scabs, and as we scrub ourselves, I bring up our escape.

"Look, the pool is down to eight. I think it's time we took off," I say under my breath, although I doubt any of the tributes can hear me.

Peeta nods, and I can see him considering my proposition. Weighing whether the odds will be in our favour. "Tell you what," he says. "Let's stick around until Brutus and Enobaria are dead. I think Beetee's trying to put together some kind of trap for them now. Then, I promise, we'll go."

I'm not entirely convinced. But if we leave now, we'll have two sets of adversaries after us. Maybe three, because who knows what Chaff's up to? Plus the clock to contend with. And then there's Beetee to think of. Johanna only brought him for me, and if we leave she'll surely kill him. Then I remember. I can't protect Beetee, too. There can only be one victor and it has to be Peeta. I must accept this. I must make decisions based on his survival only.

"All right," I say. "We'll stay until the Careers are dead. But that's the end of it." I turn and wave to Finnick. "Hey, Finnick, come on in! We figured out how to make you pretty again!"

The three of us scour all the scabs from our bodies, helping with the others' backs, and come out the same pink as the sky. We apply another round of medicine because the skin seems too delicate for the sunlight, but it doesn't look half as bad on smooth skin and will be good camouflage in the jungle.

Beetee calls us over, and it turns out that during all those hours of fiddling with wire, he has indeed come up with a plan. "I think we'll all agree our next job is to kill Brutus and Enobaria," he says mildly. "I doubt they'll attack us openly again, now that they're so outnumbered. We could track them down, I suppose, but it's dangerous, exhausting work."

"Do you think they've figured out about the clock?" I ask.

"If they haven't, they'll figure it out soon enough. Perhaps not as specifically as we have. But they must know that at least some of the zones are wired for attacks and that they're reoccurring in a circular fashion. Also, the fact that our last fight was cut off by Gamemaker intervention will not have gone unnoticed by them. We know it was an attempt to disorient us, but they must be asking themselves why it was done, and this, too, may lead them to the realization that the arena's a clock," says Beetee. "So I think our best bet will be setting our own trap."

"Wait, let me get Johanna up," says Finnick. "She'll be rabid if she thinks she missed something this important."

"Or not," I mutter, since she's always pretty much rabid, but I don't stop him, because I'd be angry myself if I was excluded from a plan at this point.

When she's joined us, Beetee shoos us all back a bit so he can have room to work in the sand. He swiftly draws a circle and divides it into twelve wedges. It's the arena, not rendered in Peeta's precise strokes but in the rough lines of a man whose mind is occupied by other, far more complex things. "If you were Brutus and Enobaria, knowing what you do now about the jungle, where would you feel safest?" Beetee asks. There's nothing patronizing in his voice, and yet I can't help thinking he reminds me of a schoolteacher about to ease children into a lesson. Perhaps it's the age difference, or simply that Beetee is probably about a million times smarter than the rest of us.

"Where we are now. On the beach," says Peeta. "It's the safest place."

"So why aren't they on the beach?" says Beetee.

"Because we're here," says Johanna impatiently.

"Exactly. We're here, claiming the beach. Now where would you go?" says Beetee.

I think about the deadly jungle, the occupied beach. "I'd hide just at the edge of the jungle. So I could escape if an attack came. And so I could spy on us."

"Also to eat," Finnick says. "The jungle's full of strange creatures and plants. But by watching us, I'd know the seafood's safe."

Beetee smiles at us as if we've exceeded his expectations. "Yes, good. You do see. Now here's what I propose: a twelve o'clock strike. What happens exactly at noon and at midnight?"

"The lightning bolt hits the tree," I say.

"Yes. So what I'm suggesting is that after the bolt hits at noon, but before it hits at midnight, we run my wire from that tree all the way down into the salt water, which is, of course, highly conductive. When the bolt strikes, the electricity will travel down the wire and into not only the water but also the surrounding beach, which will still be damp from the ten o'clock wave. Anyone in contact with those surfaces at that moment will be electrocuted," says Beetee.

There's a long pause while we all digest Beetee's plan. It seems a bit fantastical to me, impossible even. But why? I've set thousands of snares. Isn't this just a larger snare with a more scientific component? Could it work? How can we even question it, we tributes trained to gather fish and lumber and coal? What do we know about harnessing power from the sky?

Peeta takes a stab at it. "Will that wire really be able to conduct that much power, Beetee? It looks so fragile, like it would just burn up."

"Oh, it will. But not until the current has passed through it. It will act something like a fuse, in fact. Except the electricity will travel along it," says Beetee.

"How do you know?" asks Johanna, clearly not convinced.

"Because I invented it," says Beetee, as if slightly surprised. "It's not actually wire in the usual sense. Nor is the lightning natural lightning, nor the tree a real tree. You know trees better than any of us, Johanna. It would be destroyed by now, wouldn't it?"

"Yes," she says glumly.

"Don't worry about the wire – it will do just what I say," Beetee assures us.

"And where will we be when this happens?" asks Finnick.

"Far enough up in the jungle to be safe," Beetee replies.

"The Careers will be safe, too, then, unless they're in the vicinity of the water," I point out.

"That's right," says Beetee.

"But all the seafood will be cooked," says Peeta.

"Probably more than cooked," says Beetee. "We will most likely be eliminating that as a food source for good. But you found other edible things in the jungle, right, Katniss?"

"Yes. Nuts and rats," I say. "And we have sponsors."

"Well, then. I don't see that as a problem," says Beetee. "But as we are allies and this will require all our efforts, the decision of whether or not to attempt it is up to you four."

We *are* like schoolchildren. Completely unable to dispute his theory with anything but the most elementary concerns. Most of which don't even have anything to do with his actual plan. I look at the others' disconcerted faces. "Why not?" I say. "If it fails, there's no harm done. If it works, there's a decent chance we'll kill them. And even if we don't and just kill the seafood, Brutus and Enobaria lose it as a food source, too."

"I say we try it," says Peeta. "Katniss is right."

Finnick looks at Johanna and raises his eyebrows. He will not go forward without her. "All right," she says finally. "It's better than hunting them down in the jungle, anyway. And I doubt they'll figure out our plan, since we can barely understand it ourselves."

Beetee wants to inspect the lightning tree before he has to rig it. Judging by the sun, it's about nine in the morning. We have to leave our beach soon, anyway. So we break camp, walk over to the beach that borders the lightning section, and head into the jungle. Beetee's still too weak to hike up the slope on his own, so Finnick and Peeta take turns carrying him. I let Johanna lead because it's a pretty straight shot up to the tree, and I figure she can't get us too lost. Besides, I can do a lot more damage with a sheath of arrows than she can with two axes, so I'm the best one to bring up the rear.

The dense, muggy air weighs on me. There's been no break from it since the Games began. I wish Haymitch would stop sending us that District 3 bread and get us some more of that District 4 stuff, because I've sweated out buckets in the last two days, and even though I've had the fish, I'm craving salt. A piece of ice would be another good idea. Or a cold drink of water. I'm grateful for the fluid from the trees, but it's the same temperature as the seawater and the air and the other tributes and me. We're all just one big, warm stew.

As we near the tree, Finnick suggests I take the lead. "Katniss can hear the force field," he explains to Beetee and Johanna.

"Hear it?" asks Beetee.

"Only with the ear the Capitol reconstructed," I say. Guess who I'm not fooling with that story? Beetee. Because surely he remembers that he showed me how to spot a force field, and probably it's impossible to hear force fields, anyway. But, for whatever reason, he doesn't question my claim.

"Then by all means, let Katniss go first," he says, pausing a moment to wipe the steam off his glasses. "Force fields are nothing to play around with."

The lightning tree's unmistakable as it towers so high above the others. I find a bunch of nuts and make everybody wait while I move slowly up the slope, tossing the nuts ahead of me. But I see the force field almost immediately, even before a nut hits it, because it's only about fifteen metres away. My eyes, which are sweeping the greenery before me, catch sight of the rippled square high up and to my right. I throw a nut directly in front of me and hear it sizzle in confirmation.

"Just stay below the lightning tree," I tell the others.

We divide up duties. Finnick guards Beetee while he examines the tree, Johanna taps for water, Peeta gathers nuts, and I hunt nearby. The tree rats don't seem to have any fear of humans, so I take down three easily. The sound of the ten o'clock wave reminds me I should get back, and I return to the others and clean my kill. Then I draw a line in the dirt a metre from the force field as a reminder to keep back, and Peeta and I settle down to roast nuts and sear cubes of rat.

Beetee is still messing around the tree, doing I don't know what, taking measurements and such. At one point he snaps off a sliver of bark, joins us, and throws it against the force field. It bounces back and lands on the ground, glowing. In a few moments it returns to its original colour. "Well, that explains a lot," says Beetee. I look at Peeta and can't help biting my lip to keep from laughing, since it explains absolutely nothing to anyone but Beetee.

About this time we hear the sound of clicks rising from the sector adjacent to us. That means it's eleven o'clock. It's far louder in the jungle than it was on the beach last night. We all listen intently.

"It's not mechanical," Beetee says decidedly.

"I'd guess insects," I say. "Maybe beetles."

"Something with pincers," adds Finnick.

The sound swells, as if alerted by our quiet words to the proximity of live flesh. Whatever is making that clicking, I bet it could strip us to the bone in seconds.

"We should get out of here, anyway," says Johanna. "There's less than an hour before the lightning starts."

We don't go that far, though. Only to the identical tree in the blood-rain section. We have a picnic of sorts, squatting on the ground, eating our jungle food, waiting for the bolt that signals noon. At Beetee's request, I climb up into the canopy as the clicking begins to fade out. When the lightning strikes, it's dazzling, even from here, even in this bright sunlight. It completely encompasses the distant tree, making it glow a hot blue-white and causing the surrounding air to crackle with electricity. I swing down and report my findings to Beetee, who seems satisfied, even if I'm not terribly scientific.

We take a circuitous route back to the ten o'clock beach. The sand is smooth and damp, swept clean by the recent wave. Beetee essentially gives us the afternoon off while he works with the wire. Since it's his weapon and the rest of us have to defer to his knowledge so entirely, there's the odd feeling of being let out of school early. At first we take turns having naps in the shadowy edge of the jungle, but by late afternoon everyone is awake and restless. We decide, since this might be our last chance for seafood, to make a sort of feast of it. Under Finnick's guidance we spear fish and gather shellfish, even dive for oysters. I like this last part best, not because I have any great appetite for oysters. I only ever tasted them once, in the Capitol, and I couldn't get around the sliminess. But it's lovely, deep down under the water, like being in a different world. The water's very clear, and schools of bright-hued fish and strange sea flowers decorate the sand floor.

Johanna keeps watch while Finnick, Peeta and I clean and lay out the seafood. Peeta's just prised open an oyster when I hear him give a laugh. "Hey, look at this!" He holds up a glistening, perfect pearl about the size of a pea. "You know, if you put enough pressure on coal it turns to pearls," he says earnestly to Finnick.

"No, it doesn't," says Finnick dismissively. But I crack up, remembering that's how a clueless Effie Trinket presented us to the people of the Capitol last year, before anyone knew us. As coal pressured into pearls by our weighty existence. Beauty that arose out of pain.

Peeta rinses the pearl off in the water and hands it to me. "For you." I hold it out on my palm and examine its iridescent surface in the sunlight. Yes, I will keep it. For the few remaining hours of my life I will keep it close. This last gift from Peeta. The only one I can really accept. Perhaps it will give me strength in the final moments.

"Thanks," I say, closing my fist around it. I look coolly into the blue eyes of the person who is now my greatest opponent, the person who would keep me alive at his own expense. And I promise myself I will defeat his plan.

The laughter drains from those eyes, and they are staring so intensely into mine, it's like they can read my thoughts. "The locket didn't work, did it?" Peeta says, even though Finnick is right there. Even though everyone can hear him. "Katniss?"

"It worked," I say.

"But not the way I wanted it to," he says, averting his glance. After that he will look at nothing but oysters.

Just as we're about to eat, a parachute appears bearing two supplements to our meal. A small pot of spicy red sauce and yet another round of rolls from District 3. Finnick, of course, immediately counts them. "Twenty-four again," he says.

Thirty-two rolls, then. So we each take five, leaving seven, which will never divide equally. It's bread for only one.

The salty fish flesh, the succulent shellfish. Even the oysters seem tasty, vastly improved by the sauce. We gorge ourselves until no one can hold another bite, and even then there are leftovers. They won't keep, though, so we toss all the remaining food back into the water so the Careers won't get it when we leave. No one bothers about the shells. The wave should clear those away.

There's nothing to do now but wait. Peeta and I sit at the edge of the water, hand in hand, wordless. He gave his speech last night but it didn't change my mind, and nothing I can say will change his. The time for persuasive gifts is over.

I have the pearl, though, secured in a parachute

with the spile and the medicine at my waist. I hope it makes it back to District 12.

Surely my mother and Prim will know to return it to Peeta before they bury my body.

26

The anthem begins, but there are no faces in the sky tonight. The audience will be restless, thirsting for blood. Beetee's trap holds enough promise, though, that the Gamemakers haven't sent in other attacks. Perhaps they are simply curious to see if it will work.

At what Finnick and I judge to be about nine, we leave our shell-strewn camp, cross to the twelve o'clock beach, and begin to quietly hike up to the lightning tree in the light of the moon. Our full stomachs make us more uncomfortable and breathless than we were on the morning's climb. I begin to regret those last dozen oysters.

Beetee asks Finnick to assist him, and the rest of us stand guard. Before he even attaches any wire to the tree, Beetee unrolls metres and metres of the stuff. He has Finnick secure it tightly around a broken branch and lay it on the ground. Then they stand on either side of the tree, passing the spool back and forth as they wrap the wire around and around the trunk. At first it seems arbitrary, then I see a pattern, like an intricate maze, appearing in the moonlight on Beetee's side. I wonder if it makes any difference how the wire's placed, or if this is merely to add to the speculation of the audience. I bet most of them know as much about electricity as I do.

The work on the trunk's completed just as we hear the wave begin. I've never really worked out at what point in the ten o'clock hour it erupts. There must be some build-up, then the wave itself, then the aftermath of the flooding. But the sky tells me ten-thirty.

This is when Beetee reveals the rest of the plan. Since we move most swiftly through the trees, he wants Johanna and me to take the coil down through the jungle, unwinding the wire as we go. We are to lay it across the twelve o'clock beach and drop the metal spool, with whatever is left, deep into the water, making sure it sinks. Then run for the jungle. If we go now, right now, we should make it to safety.

"I want to go with them as a guard," Peeta says immediately. After the moment with the pearl, I know he's less willing than ever to let me out of his sight.

"You're too slow. Besides, I'll need you on this end.

Katniss will guard," says Beetee. "There's no time to debate this. I'm sorry. If the girls are to get out of there alive, they need to move now." He hands the coil to Johanna.

I don't like the plan any more than Peeta does. How can I protect him at a distance? But Beetee's right. With his leg, Peeta is too slow to make it down the slope in time. Johanna and I are the fastest and most sure-footed on the jungle floor. I can't think of any alternative. And if I trust anyone here besides Peeta, it's Beetee.

"It's OK," I tell Peeta. "We'll just drop the coil and come straight back up."

"Not into the lightning zone," Beetee reminds me. "Head for the tree in the one-to-two-o'clock sector. If you find you're running out of time, move over one more. Don't even think about going back on the beach, though, until I can assess the damage."

I take Peeta's face in my hands. "Don't worry. I'll see you at midnight." I give him a kiss and, before he can object any further, I let go and turn to Johanna. "Ready?"

"Why not?" says Johanna with a shrug. She's clearly no happier about being teamed up than I am. But we're all caught up in Beetee's trap. "You guard, I'll unwind. We can trade off later."

Without further discussion, we head down the slope. In fact there's very little discussion between us at all. We move at a pretty good clip, one manning the coil, the other keeping watch. About halfway down, we hear the clicking beginning to rise, indicating it's after eleven.

"Better hurry," Johanna says. "I want to put a lot of distance between me and that water before the lightning hits. Just in case Volts miscalculated something."

"I'll take the coil for a while," I say. It's harder work laying out the wire than guarding, and she's had a long turn.

"Here," Johanna says, passing me the coil.

Both of our hands are still on the metal cylinder when there's a slight vibration. Suddenly the thin golden wire from above springs down at us, bunching in tangled loops and curls around our wrists. Then the severed end snakes up to our feet.

It only takes a second to register this rapid turn of events. Johanna and I look at each other, but neither of us has to say it. Someone not far above us has cut the wire. And they will be on us at any moment.

My hand frees itself from the wire and has just closed on the feathers of an arrow when the metal cylinder smashes into the side of my head. The next thing I know, I'm lying on my back in the vines, a terrible pain in my left temple. Something's wrong with my eyes. My vision blurs in and out of focus as I strain to make the two moons floating up in the sky into one. It's hard to breathe, and I realize Johanna's sitting on my chest, pinning me at the shoulders with her knees.

There's a stab in my left forearm. I try to jerk away but I'm still too incapacitated. Johanna's digging something, I guess the point of her knife, into my flesh, twisting it around. There's an excruciating ripping sensation and warmth runs down my wrist, filling my palm. She swipes down my arm and coats half my face with my blood.

"Stay down!" she hisses. Her weight leaves my body and I'm alone.

Stay down? I think. *What? What is happening?* My eyes shut, blocking out the inconsistent world, as I try to make sense of my situation.

All I can think of is Johanna shoving Wiress to the beach. "*Just stay down, will you?*" But she didn't attack Wiress. Not like this. I'm not Wiress, anyway. I'm not Nuts. "*Just stay down, will you?*" echoes around inside my brain.

Footsteps coming. Two pairs. Heavy, not trying to conceal their whereabouts.

Brutus's voice. "She's as good as dead! Come on, Enobaria!" Feet moving into the night.

Am I? I drift in and out of consciousness looking for an answer. Am I as good as dead? I'm in no position to make an argument to the contrary. In fact, rational thinking is a struggle. This much I know. Johanna attacked me. Smashed that cylinder into my head. Cut my arm, probably doing irreparable damage to veins and arteries, and then Brutus and Enobaria showed up before she had time to finish me off.

The alliance is over. Finnick and Johanna must have had an agreement to turn on us tonight. I knew we should have left this morning. I don't know where Beetee stands. But I'm fair game, and so is Peeta.

Peeta! My eyes fly open in panic. Peeta is waiting up by the tree, unsuspecting and off guard. Maybe Finnick has even killed him already. "No," I whisper. That wire was cut from a short distance away by the Careers. Finnick and Beetee and Peeta – they can't know what's going on down here. They can only be wondering what has happened, why the wire has gone slack or maybe even sprung back to the tree. This, in itself, can't be a signal to kill, can it? Surely this was just Johanna deciding the time had come to break with us. Kill me. Escape from the Careers. Then bring Finnick into the fight as soon as possible.

I don't know. I don't know. I only know that I must get back to Peeta and keep him alive. It takes every ounce of will I have to push up into a sitting position and drag myself up the side of a tree to my feet. It's lucky I have something to hold on to because the jungle's tilting back and forth. Without any warning, I lean forward and vomit up the seafood feast, heaving until there can't possibly be an oyster left in my body. Trembling and slick with sweat, I assess my physical condition.

As I lift up my damaged arm, blood sprays me in the face and the world makes another alarming shift. I squeeze my eyes shut and cling to the tree until things steady a little. Then I take a few careful steps to a neighbouring tree, pull off some moss, and without examining the wound further, tightly bandage my arm. Better. Definitely better not to see it. Then I allow my hand to tentatively touch my head wound. There's a huge lump but not too much blood. Obviously I've got some internal damage, but I don't seem in danger of bleeding to death. At least not through my head.

I dry my hands on moss and get a shaky grip on my bow with my damaged left arm. Secure the notch of an arrow to the string. Make my feet move up the slope.

Peeta. My dying wish. My promise. To keep him alive. My heart lifts a bit when I realize he must be alive because no cannon has fired. Maybe Johanna was acting alone, knowing Finnick would side with her once her intentions were clear. Although it's hard to guess what goes on between those two. I think of how he looked to her for confirmation before he'd agree to help set Beetee's trap. There's a much deeper alliance based on years of friendship and who knows what else. Therefore, if Johanna has turned on me, I should no longer trust Finnick.

I reach this conclusion only seconds before I hear someone running down the slope towards me. Neither Peeta nor Beetee could move at this pace. I duck behind a curtain of vines, concealing myself just in time. Finnick flies by me, his skin shadowy with medicine, leaping through the undergrowth like a deer. He soon reaches the sight of my attack, must see the blood. "Johanna! Katniss!" he calls. I stay put until he goes in the direction Johanna and the Careers took.

I move as quickly as I can without sending the world into a whirl. My head throbs with the rapid beat of my heart. The insects, possibly excited by the smell of blood, have increased their clicking until it's a continuous roar in my ears. No, wait. Maybe my ears are actually ringing from the hit. Until the insects shut up, it will be impossible to tell. But when the insects go silent, the lightning will start. I have to move faster. I have to get to Peeta.

The boom of a cannon pulls me up short. Someone has died. I know that with everyone running around armed and scared right now, it could be anybody. But whoever it is, I believe the death will trigger a kind of free-for-all out here in the night. People will kill first and wonder about their motives later. I force my legs into a run.

Something snags my feet and I sprawl out on the ground. I feel it wrapping around me, entwining me in sharp fibres. A net! This must be one of Finnick's fancy nets, positioned to trap me, and he must be nearby, trident in hand. I flail around for a moment, only working the web more tightly around me, and then I catch a glimpse of it in the moonlight. Confused, I lift my arm and see it's entangled in shimmering golden threads. It's not one of Finnick's nets at all, but Beetee's wire. I carefully rise to my feet and find I'm in a patch of the stuff that caught on a trunk on its way back to the lightning tree. Slowly I disengage myself from the wire, step out of its reach, and continue uphill.

On the good side, I'm on the right path and have not been so disoriented by the head injury as to lose my sense of direction. On the bad side, the wire has reminded me of the oncoming lightning storm. I can still hear the insects, but are they starting to fade?

I keep the loops of wire a metre to my left as a guide as I run but take great care not to touch them. If those insects are fading and the first bolt is about to strike the tree, then all its power will come surging down that wire and anyone in contact with it will die.

The tree swims into view, its trunk festooned with gold. I slow down, try to move with some stealth, but I'm really just lucky to be upright. I look for a sign of the others. No one. No one is there. "Peeta?" I call softly. "Peeta?"

A soft moan answers me and I whip around to find a figure lying higher up on the ground. "Beetee!" I exclaim. I hurry and kneel beside him. The moan must have been involuntary. He's not conscious, although I can see no wound except a gash below the crook of his elbow. I grab a nearby handful of moss and clumsily wrap it while I try to rouse him. "Beetee! Beetee, what's going on! Who cut you? Beetee!" I shake him in the way you should never shake an injured person, but I don't know what else to do. He moans again and briefly raises a hand to ward me off.

This is when I notice he's holding a knife, one

Peeta was carrying earlier, I think, which is wrapped loosely in wire. Perplexed, I stand and lift the wire, confirming it's attached back at the tree. It takes me a moment to remember the second, much shorter strand that Beetee wound around a branch and left on the ground before he even began his design on the tree. I'd thought it had some electrical significance, had been set aside to be used later. But it never was, because there's probably a good twenty, twenty-five metres here.

I squint hard up the hill and realize we're only a few paces from the force field. There's the telltale square, high up and to my right, just as it was this morning. What did Beetee do? Did he actually try to drive the knife into the force field the way Peeta did by accident? And what's the deal with the wire? Was this his back-up plan? If electrifying the water failed, did he mean to send the lightning bolt's energy into the force field? What would that do, anyway? Nothing? A great deal? Fry us all? The force field must mostly be energy, too, I guess. The one in the Training Centre was invisible. This one seems to somehow mirror the jungle. But I've seen it falter when Peeta's knife struck it and when my arrows hit. The real world lies right behind it.

My ears are not ringing. It was the insects after all.

I know that now because they are dying out quickly and I hear nothing but the jungle sounds. Beetee is useless. I can't rouse him. I can't save him. I don't know what he was trying to do with the knife and the wire and he's incapable of explaining. The moss bandage on my arm is soaked and there's no use fooling myself. I'm so light-headed I'll black out in a matter of minutes. I've got to get away from this tree and—

"Katniss!" I hear his voice though he's a far distance away. But what is he doing? Peeta must have figured out that everyone is hunting us by now. "Katniss!"

I can't protect him. I can't move fast or far and my shooting abilities are questionable at best. I do the one thing I can to draw the attackers away from him and over to me. "Peeta!" I scream out. "Peeta! I'm here! Peeta!" Yes, I will draw them in, any in my vicinity, away from Peeta and over to me and the lightning tree that will soon be a weapon in and of itself. "I'm here! I'm here!" He won't make it. Not with that leg in the night. He will never make it in time. "Peeta!"

It's working. I can hear them coming. Two of them. Crashing through the jungle. My knees start to give out and I sink down next to Beetee, resting my weight on my heels. My bow and arrow lift into position. If I can take them out, will Peeta survive the rest?

Enobaria and Finnick reach the lightning tree. They can't see me, sitting above them on the slope, my skin camouflaged in ointment. I home in on Enobaria's neck. With any luck, when I kill her, Finnick will duck behind the tree for cover just as the lightning bolt strikes. And it will be any second. There's only a faint insect click here and there. I can kill them now. I can kill them both.

Another cannon.

"Katniss!" Peeta's voice howls for me. But this time I don't answer. Beetee still breathes faintly beside me. He and I will soon die. Finnick and Enobaria will die. Peeta is alive. Two cannons have sounded. Brutus, Johanna, Chaff. Two of them are already dead. That will leave Peeta with only one tribute to kill. And that is the very best I can do. One enemy.

Enemy. Enemy. The word is tugging at a recent memory. Pulling it into the present. The look on Haymitch's face. "*Katniss, when you're in the arena. . .*" The scowl, the misgiving. "*What?*" I hear my own voice tighten as I bristle at some unspoken accusation. "*You just remember who the enemy is,*" Haymitch says. "*That's all.*"

Haymitch's last words of advice to me. Why would I need reminding? I have always known who the enemy is. Who starves and tortures and kills us in the arena. Who will soon kill everyone I love.

My bow drops as his meaning registers. Yes, I know who the enemy is. And it's not Enobaria.

I finally see Beetee's knife with clear eyes. My shaking hands slide the wire from the hilt, wind it around the arrow just above the feathers, and secure it with a knot picked up in training.

I rise, turning to the force field, fully revealing myself but no longer caring. Only caring about where I should direct my tip, where Beetee would have driven the knife if he'd been able to choose. My bow tilts up at the wavering square, the flaw, the . . . what did he call it that day? The chink in the armour. I let the arrow fly, see it hit its mark and vanish, pulling the thread of gold behind it.

My hair stands on end and the lightning strikes the tree.

A flash of white runs up the wire, and for just a moment, the dome bursts into a dazzling blue light. I'm thrown backwards to the ground, body useless, paralysed, eyes frozen wide, as feathery bits of matter rain down on me. I can't reach Peeta. I can't even reach my pearl. My eyes strain to capture one last image of beauty to take with me.

Right before the explosions begin, I find a star.

27

Everything seems to erupt at once. The earth explodes into showers of dirt and plant matter. Trees burst into flames. Even the sky fills with brightly coloured blossoms of light. I can't think why the sky's being bombed until I realize the Gamemakers are shooting off fireworks up there, while the real destruction occurs on the ground. Just in case it's not enough fun watching the obliteration of the arena and the remaining tributes. Or perhaps to illuminate our gory ends.

Will they let anyone survive? Will there be a victor of the Seventy-fifth Hunger Games? Maybe not. After all, what is this Quarter Quell but . . . what was it President Snow read from the card?

"*. . .a reminder to the rebels that even the strongest among them cannot overcome the power of the Capitol. . .*"

Not even the strongest of the strong will triumph. Perhaps they never intended to have a victor in these Games at all. Or perhaps my final act of rebellion forced their hand.

I'm sorry, Peeta, I think. *I'm sorry I couldn't save you.* Save him? More likely I stole his last chance at life, condemned him, by destroying the force field. Maybe, if we had all played by the rules, they might have let him live.

The hovercraft materializes above me without warning. If it was quiet, and a mockingjay perched close at hand, I would have heard the jungle go silent and then the bird's call that precedes the appearance of the Capitol's aircraft. But my ears could never make out anything so delicate in this bombardment.

The claw drops from the underside until it's directly overhead. The metal talons slide under me. I want to scream, run, smash my way out of it but I'm frozen, helpless to do anything but fervently hope I'll die before I reach the shadowy figures awaiting me above. They have not spared my life to crown me victor but to make my death as slow and public as possible.

My worst fears are confirmed when the face that greets me inside the hovercraft belongs to Plutarch Heavensbee, Head Gamemaker. What a mess I have made of his beautiful Games with the clever ticking clock and the field of victors. He will suffer for his failure, probably lose his life, but not before he sees me punished. His hand reaches for me, I think to strike me, but he does something worse. With his thumb and his forefinger, he slides my eyelids shut, sentencing me to the vulnerability of darkness. They can do anything to me now and I will not even see it coming.

My heart pounds so hard the blood begins to stream from beneath my soaked moss bandage. My thoughts grow foggy. Possibly I can bleed to death before they can revive me after all. In my mind, I whisper a thank-you to Johanna Mason for the excellent wound she inflicted as I black out.

When I swim back into semi-consciousness, I can feel I'm lying on a padded table. There's the pinching sensation of tubes in my left arm. They are trying to keep me alive because, if I slide quietly, privately into death, it will be a victory. I'm still largely unable to move, open my eyelids, raise my head. But my right arm has regained a little motion. It flops across my body, feeling like a flipper; no, something less animated, like a club. I have no real motor coordination, no proof that I even still have fingers. Yet I manage to swing my arm around until I rip the tubes out. A beeping goes off but I can't stay awake to find out who it will summon.

The next time I surface, my hands are tied down to the table, the tubes back in my arm. I can open my eyes and lift my head slightly, though. I'm in a large room with low ceilings and a silvery light. There are two rows of beds facing each other. I can hear the breathing of what I assume are my fellow victors. Directly across from me I see Beetee with about ten different machines hooked up to him. *Just let us die!* I scream in my mind. I slam my head back hard on the table and go out again.

When I finally, truly wake up, the restraints are gone. I raise my hand and find I have fingers that can move at my command again. I push myself to a sitting position and hold on to the padded table until the room settles into focus. My left arm is bandaged but the tubes dangle off stands by the bed.

I'm alone except for Beetee, who still lies in front of me, being sustained by his army of machines. Where are the others, then? Peeta, Finnick, Enobaria and . . . and . . . one more, right? Either Johanna or Chaff or Brutus was still alive when the bombs began. I'm sure they'll want to make an example of us all. But where have they taken them? Moved them from hospital to prison?

"Peeta. . ." I whisper. I so wanted to protect him. Am still resolved to. Since I have failed to keep him safe in life, I must find him, kill him now before the Capitol gets to choose the agonizing means of his death. I slide my legs off the table and look around for a weapon. There are a few syringes sealed in sterile plastic on a table near Beetee's bed. Perfect. All I'll need is air and a clear shot at one of his veins.

I pause for a moment, consider killing Beetee. But if I do, the monitors will start beeping and I'll be caught before I get to Peeta. I make a silent promise to return and finish him off if I can.

I'm naked except for a thin nightgown, so I slip the syringe under the bandage that covers the wound on my arm. There are no guards at the door. No doubt I'm miles beneath the Training Centre or in some Capitol stronghold, and the possibility of my escape is non-existent. It doesn't matter. I'm not escaping, just finishing a job.

I creep down a narrow hallway to a metal door that stands slightly ajar. Someone is behind it. I take out the syringe and grip it in my hand. Flattening myself against the wall, I listen to the voices inside.

"Communications are down in Seven, Ten and Twelve. But Eleven has control of transportation now, so there's at least a hope of them getting some food out."

Plutarch Heavensbee. I think. Although I've only

really spoken with him once. A hoarse voice asks a question.

"No, I'm sorry. There's no way I can get you to Four. But I've given special orders for her retrieval if possible. It's the best I can do, Finnick."

Finnick. My mind struggles to make sense of the conversation, of the fact that it's taking place between Plutarch Heavensbee and Finnick. Is he so near and dear to the Capitol that he'll be excused his crimes? Or did he really have no idea what Beetee intended? He croaks out something else. Something heavy with despair.

"Don't be stupid. That's the worst thing you could do. Get her killed for sure. As long as *you're* alive, they'll keep *her* alive for bait," says Haymitch.

Says Haymitch! I bang through the door and stumble into the room. Haymitch, Plutarch and a very beat-up Finnick sit around a table laid with a meal no one is eating. Daylight streams in the curved windows, and in the distance I see the top of a forest of trees. We are flying.

"Done knocking yourself out, sweetheart?" says Haymitch, the annoyance clear in his voice. But as I careen forward he steps up and catches my wrists, steadying me. He looks at my hand. "So it's you and a syringe against the Capitol? See, this is why no one lets you make the plans." I stare at him uncomprehendingly. "Drop it." I feel the pressure increase on my right wrist until my hand is forced to open and I release the syringe. He settles me in a chair next to Finnick.

Plutarch puts a bowl of broth in front of me. A roll. Slips a spoon into my hand. "Eat," he says in a much kinder voice than Haymitch used.

Haymitch sits directly in front of me. "Katniss, I'm going to explain what happened. I don't want you to ask any questions until I'm through. Do you understand?"

I nod numbly. And this is what he tells me.

There was a plan to break us out of the arena from the moment the Quell was announced. The victor tributes from 3, 4, 6, 7, 8 and 11 had varying degrees of knowledge about it. Plutarch Heavensbee has been, for several years, part of an undercover group aiming to overthrow the Capitol. He made sure the wire was among the weapons. Beetee was in charge of blowing a hole in the force field. The bread we received in the arena was code for the time of the rescue. The district where the bread originated indicated the day. Three. The number of rolls the hour. Twenty-four. The hovercraft belongs to District 13. Bonnie and Twill, the women I met in the woods from 8, were right about its existence and its defence capabilities. We are currently on a very roundabout journey to District 13. Meanwhile, most of the districts in Panem are in full-scale rebellion.

Haymitch stops to see if I am following. Or maybe he is done for the moment.

It's an awful lot to take in, this elaborate plan in which I was a piece, just as I was meant to be a piece in the Hunger Games. Used without consent, without knowledge. At least in the Hunger Games, I knew I was being played with.

My supposed friends have been a lot more secretive.

"You didn't tell me." My voice is as ragged as Finnick's.

"Neither you nor Peeta were told. We couldn't risk it," says Plutarch. "I was even worried you might mention my indiscretion with the watch during the Games." He pulls out his pocket watch and runs his thumb across the crystal, lighting up the mockingjay. "Of course, when I showed you this, I was merely tipping you off about the arena. As a mentor. I thought it might be a first step towards gaining your trust. I never dreamed you'd be a tribute again."

"I still don't understand why Peeta and I weren't let in on the plan," I say.

"Because once the force field blew, you'd be the

first ones they'd try to capture, and the less you knew, the better," says Haymitch.

"The first ones? Why?" I say, trying to hang on to the train of thought.

"For the same reason the rest of us agreed to die to keep you alive," says Finnick.

"No, Johanna tried to kill me," I say.

"Johanna knocked you out to cut the tracker from your arm and lead Brutus and Enobaria away from you," says Haymitch.

"What?" My head aches so and I want them to stop talking in circles. "I don't know what you're—"

"We had to save you because you're the mockingjay, Katniss," says Plutarch. "While you live, the revolution lives."

The bird, the pin, the song, the berries, the watch, the cracker, the dress that burst into flames. I am the mockingjay. The one that survived despite the Capitol's plans. The symbol of the rebellion.

It's what I suspected in the woods when I found Bonnie and Twill escaping. Though I never really understood the magnitude. But then, I wasn't meant to understand. I think of Haymitch's sneering at my plans to flee District 12, start my own uprising, even the very notion that District 13 could exist. Subterfuges and deceptions. And if he could do that, behind his mask of sarcasm and drunkenness, so convincingly and for so long, what else has he lied about? I know what else.

"Peeta," I whisper, my heart sinking.

"The others kept Peeta alive because if he died, we knew there'd be no keeping you in an alliance," says Haymitch. "And we couldn't risk leaving you unprotected." His words are matter-of-fact, his expression unchanged, but he can't hide the tinge of grey that colours his face.

"Where is Peeta?" I hiss at him.

"He was picked up by the Capitol along with Johanna and Enobaria," says Haymitch. And finally he has the decency to drop his gaze.

Technically, I am unarmed. But no one should ever underestimate the harm that fingernails can do, especially if the target is unprepared. I lunge across the table and rake mine down Haymitch's face, causing blood to flow and damage to one eye. Then we are both screaming terrible, terrible things at each other, and Finnick is trying to drag me out, and I know it's all Haymitch can do not to rip me apart, but I'm the mockingjay. I'm the mockingjay and it's too hard keeping me alive as it is.

Other hands help Finnick and I'm back on my table, my body restrained, my wrists tied down, so I slam my head in fury again and again against the table. A needle pokes my arm and my head hurts so badly I stop fighting and simply wail in a horrible, dying-animal way, until my voice gives out.

The drug causes sedation, not sleep, so I am trapped in fuzzy, dully aching misery for what seems like always. They reinsert their tubes and talk to me in soothing voices that never reach me. All I can think of is Peeta, lying on a similar table somewhere, while they try to break him for information he doesn't even have.

"Katniss. Katniss, I'm sorry." Finnick's voice comes from the bed next to me and slips into my consciousness. Perhaps because we're in the same kind of pain. "I wanted to go back for him and Johanna, but I couldn't move."

I don't answer. Finnick Odair's good intentions mean less than nothing.

"It's better for him than Johanna. They'll figure out he doesn't know anything pretty fast. And they won't kill him if they think they can use him against you," says Finnick.

"Like bait?" I say to the ceiling. "Like how they'll use Annie for bait, Finnick?"

I can hear him weeping but I don't care. They probably won't even bother to question her, she's so far gone. Gone right off the deep end years ago in her Games. There's a good chance I'm headed in the same direction. Maybe I'm already going crazy and no one has the heart to tell me. I feel crazy enough.

"I wish she was dead," he says. "I wish they were all dead and we were, too. It would be best."

Well, there's no good response to that. I can hardly dispute it since I was walking around with a syringe to kill Peeta when I found them. Do I really want him dead? What I want . . . what I want is to have him back. But I'll never get him back now. Even if the rebel forces could somehow overthrow the Capitol, you can be sure President Snow's last act would be to cut Peeta's throat. No. I will never get him back. So then dead is best.

But will Peeta know that or will he keep fighting? He's so strong and such a good liar. Does he think he has a chance of surviving? Does he even care if he does? He wasn't planning on it, anyway. He had already signed off on life. Maybe, if he knows I was rescued, he's even happy. Feels he fulfilled his mission to keep me alive.

I think I hate him even more than I do Haymitch.

I give up. Stop speaking, responding, refuse food and water. They can pump whatever they want into my arm, but it takes more than that to keep a person going once she's lost the will to live. I even have a funny notion that if I do die, maybe Peeta will be allowed to live. Not as a free person but as an Avox or something, waiting on the future tributes of District 12. Then maybe he could find some way to escape. My death could, in fact, still save him.

If it can't, no matter. It's enough to die of spite. To punish Haymitch, who, of all the people in this rotting world, has turned Peeta and me into pieces in his Games. I trusted him. I put what was precious in Haymitch's hands. And he has betrayed me.

"*See, this is why no one lets you make the plans,*" he said.

That's true. No one in their right mind would let me make the plans. Because I obviously can't tell a friend from an enemy.

A lot of people come by to talk to me, but I make all their words sound like the clicking of the insects in the jungle. Meaningless and distant. Dangerous, but only if approached. Whenever the words start to become distinct, I moan until they give me more painkiller and that fixes things right up.

Until one time, I open my eyes and find someone I cannot block out looking down at me. Someone who will not plead, or explain, or think he can alter my design with entreaties, because he alone really knows how I operate.

"Gale," I whisper.

"Hey, Catnip." He reaches down and pushes a strand of hair out of my eyes. One side of his face has been burned fairly recently. His arm is in a sling, and I can see bandages under his miner's shirt. What has happened to him? How is he even here? Something very bad has happened back home.

It is not so much a question of forgetting Peeta as remembering the others. All it takes is one look at Gale and they come surging into the present, demanding to be acknowledged.

"Prim?" I gasp.

"She's alive. So is your mother. I got them out in time," he says.

"They're not in District Twelve?" I ask.

"After the Games, they sent in planes. Dropped firebombs." He hesitates. "Well, you know what happened to the Hob."

I do know. I saw it go up. That old warehouse embedded with coal dust. The whole district's covered with the stuff. A new kind of horror begins to rise up inside me as I imagine firebombs hitting the Seam.

"They're not in District Twelve?" I repeat. As if saying it will somehow fend off the truth.

"Katniss," Gale says softly.

I recognize that voice. It's the same one he uses to approach wounded animals before he delivers a death blow. I instinctively raise my hand to block his words but he catches it and holds on tightly.

"Don't," I whisper.

But Gale is not one to keep secrets from me. "Katniss, there is no District Twelve."

END OF BOOK TWO

LET THE GAMES CONTINUE. . .

www. thehungergames.co.uk